quiet chaos

sandro veronesi

translated by michael f. moore

An Imprint of HarperCollins*Publishers*

quiet chaos

a novel

Image on title page and part openers reproduced based on "Simulated chaotic oscillation from solitons" by Nan Sun, Kyoungho Woo, and Donhee Ham / Harvard University. Copyright © 2007 by *IEEE*. First published by David S. Ricketts, Xiaofeng Li, Nan Sun, Kyoungho Woo, and Donhee Ham, "On the Self-Generation of Electrical Soliton Pulses," *IEEE Journal of Solid-State Circuits* 42, no. 8 (August 2007): 1666, fig. 18(c).

HarperCollins books may be purchased for educational, business, or sales promotional use. For information please write: Special Markets Department, HarperCollins Publishers, 10 East 53rd Street, New York, NY 10022.

Originally published as *Caos Calmo* in Italy © 2005 Bompiani/RCS Libri S.p.A.

First U.S. edition published by Ecco in 2011.

Designed by Suet Yee Chong

Library of Congress Cataloging-in-Publication Data has been applied for.

ISBN 978-0-06-157294-4

11 12 13 14 15   OV/RRD   10 9 8 7 6 5 4 3 2 1

To my children

I can't go on. I'll go on.
— Samuel Beckett

part one

chapter one

— Over there! — I say.

We've just finished surfing, Carlo and I. *Surfing,* like we did twenty years ago. We borrowed the boards from a couple of kids and dove into the high long waves, so unusual in the Tyrrhenian Sea that has bathed us our whole lives. Carlo, more aggressive and daring, howling, tattooed, over the hill, with long, windblown hair and an earring that glitters in the sun; me more prudent and *stilista,* more diligent and controlled, better camouflaged, as always. His Beat Generation shabby chic and my traditional understatement, on two surfboards racing in the sun, and our two worlds dueling again like in the formidable quarrels of our youth — rebellion versus subversion — when the shit hit the fan, no joke. Not that we put on much of a show, since it was all we could do to keep from falling off the boards. It's more like we were making a spectacle of ourselves, two no-longer-young guys who for a short period had actually believed certain forces would prevail and during that period learned to do all sorts of things that later turned out to be supremely useless, like playing the congas, or rolling a coin between our fingers like David Hemmings in *Blow-Up,* or slowing down our heartbeats to simulate bradycardia and thus be exempted from military service, or dancing the ska, or rolling a joint with one hand, or shooting with a bow and arrow, or doing transcendental meditation, or, in this case, surfing. The two surfer kids would never understand. Lara and Claudia had already gone home. Nina 2004 left early this morning (Carlo changes girlfriends every year, so Lara and I have taken to counting them by the thousands): we had no audience; it was just a little show that he and I put on for each other, one of those

games that make sense only between brothers, because a brother
is witness to an invulnerability that no one else sees in you after a
certain point.

— Over there! — I say all of a sudden.

We had lain down on the sand to dry, dumb with exhaustion,
our eyes closed and the breeze dancing over our chests, and we
sank into silence, to relax. But it suddenly struck me that to enjoy
this feeling we were ignoring a noise that had been making itself
heard with growing urgency: shouts. I sat up, followed immediately by Carlo.

— Over there! — I say all of a sudden, pointing to a cluster of
extremely agitated people a few hundred yards upwind.

We leap up, our muscles still warm from the long ride on the
waves, and we dash toward the small crowd. We leave behind our
cell phones, sunglasses, money, everything: suddenly the only
thing that exists is this small cluster of people and those shouts.
Some things you do without thinking.

The minutes that follow take place in a kind of high-voltage
trance in which my only sensation is of unity with my brother:
the questions about what happened, the lifeless old man on the
beach, the blond man trying to resuscitate him, the desperation of two children crying "Mamma!," the dismayed faces of
people pointing their fingers at the sea, two little heads bobbing between the waves, and no one taking action. Standing out
from the frenzied stasis is Carlo's gaze: blue, intense, filled with a
boundless kinetic energy. His gaze says that, for some inarguable
reason, it's up to us to rescue those two poor souls and that, in
reality, it's as if we already had, yes, as if the whole business were
already over and we brothers were already heroes to that rabble
of strangers, because we're extraordinary aquatic creatures, we
are, we're the sons of Poseidon, and to save human lives we can
tame the waves now just as easily as we tamed them earlier on

the surfboards. Not to mention that nobody else seems capable of doing a thing.

We race into the water and make it to where the first waves break. There we run into a strange man, lanky and redheaded, intent on awkwardly casting a short rope toward the open sea, although the people floundering in the waves are at least thirty yards away. We rush past him, and he looks at us with eyes I will never forget — the eyes of someone who would let people die — and in a wimpy voice worthy of those eyes, he tries to dissuade us: "Don't go," he sputters, "you'll risk getting sucked in yourselves." "Fuck you, asshole!" Carlo replies, a moment before diving under a wave and starting to swim. I follow suit, and while I'm swimming, against the light I can see the black silhouettes of mullets gliding against the green wall formed every time a wave rises and then crashes over me: the fish are surfing, having fun, like we were only a few minutes ago.

From the shore the two heads had looked close, but they are actually pretty far apart, so far that at a certain point Carlo and I have to separate: I signal to him to head toward the one on the right while I go after the one on the left. He looks at me again, smiling, nods, and again I feel invincible. We both set out energetically.

When I'm close enough, I realize it's a woman. I remember the two desperate children on the shore: "Mamma!" The head disappears beneath the water and bobs back up through an unfathomable combination of forces to which the woman seems completely alien. I shout at her to hang in there and I stroke harder, while an even stronger current tries to pull me in the opposite direction. She's right in the middle of a whirlpool. When I get within two yards of her, I can distinguish her strong features, a slightly flat nose, like Julie Christie's, but especially the veil of pure terror that has fallen over her eyes: her strength is failing, she can't even shout. All she can do is sob. I switch to a breaststroke and reach her. From the depths of her body a kind of sinister gurgling arises, like a clogged sink.

— Calm down, lady, — I tell her, — now I'm going to take yo—

In a split second, as if she'd been planning it, she grabs ahold of my collarbone and with all her strength pulls me underwater. Caught in mid-sentence, I swallow, then I struggle to resurface, coughing.

— Calm down, — I say, — don't dro—

Again she drags me underwater before I can finish my sentence, and again I find myself swallowing and struggling to resurface and catch my breath. Immediately she tries to drag me back down, and I have to break away to escape her grip. Her nails are dug deep into my skin, and they scratch my chest till I bleed. It hurts like hell. Gasping for breath and bleeding from my wounds, I take a couple of backstrokes. And all my energy, that amazing feeling of invincibility I had when I rushed in from the shore, has disappeared.

— Don't leave me! — gurgles the woman. — Don't leave me!

— Lady, — I say, keeping my distance. — We're not getting anywhere this way! Now, calm down!

Her only answer is to disappear beneath the water and not resurface. Shit! I dive back down and manage to grab ahold of her hair while she's sinking like a stone, then I take her by her armpits and bring her up, fighting the undertow that's pulling us down. She's heavy as hell. When I reemerge, my lungs are ready to explode, but at least the woman gives me enough time to take a couple of breaths before she tries to pull me back down.

— Don't leave me! — same story all over again.

I dodge another attempt to pull me under, warding her off with a kick to the loins. She's not going to catch me off guard anymore, and I'm not going to swallow any more water, but it's taking everything I've got to keep her from killing me, and things are looking pretty bad.

— Don't leave me!

— I won't leave you! — I shout, — but knock it off! Otherwise we're both going to dr—

Nothing doing. At this point it's obvious the woman doesn't want to be saved. She only wants someone to die with her. But I don't want to die, I'm thinking. I love life. I have a woman and a daughter waiting for me at home. I'm supposed to get married in five days. I'm forty-three years old. I have a job, dammit, I *can't* die . . .

I think of swimming away, of letting this woman's rapacious fingernails make a few last scratches so I can wriggle out of her fatal embrace, leaving her to drown all alone. But her watery green eyes, which must be really beautiful under normal conditions, look so defeated and so terrified and so blank that they practically force me to try to save her. I think about those children again. About that idiot who told me not to go. About my brother; wondering what shape he's in right now.

— Don't leave me!

No, I don't leave her. I don't swim away, and I actually come up with a solution. Disentangling myself from her grip, I manage to swim behind her, a position from which I'm able to lock her arms inside my elbows. With her two flailing tentacles immobilized, she can't kill me, and this is already a huge improvement. Except that now my arms are just as useless as her immobilized limbs, and bringing her to shore is proving complicated. I have to find a way to transmit to her limp body the small amount of energy left in mine, and in the middle of a sea so choppy we were able to go surfing, in the dead center of a whirlpool that keeps sucking us down, and deprived of the use of my arms. What a mess. I wrack my brain, and I see no possibility other than to use my legs and my pelvis. So, with a big kick of my legs, I bang my pelvis into hers: we inch along toward the shore. I repeat the operation. All the while her suicidal subconscious makes her thrash around and fight to make things more difficult: another kick of the legs and thrust of the pelvis and we make a little more progress toward the shore. Another kick, another inch: patiently, calmly, and meting out my efforts in small doses, I realize that this way we can do it, and I feel more calm. I'm saying "pelvis," because it's more polite, but the truth is we're in an obscene position, and her pelvis is really her ass, the soft, fat ass of an abbess, while my pelvis is my cock, to put it bluntly. I'm slamming my cock against her ass again and again, that's what I'm doing, with all my strength, keeping her arms twisted behind her, pushing madly with my legs, in a pose that's so absurd and shameless and savage that all of a sudden something absurd and shameless and savage happens: I get a hard-on. I notice it while it's happening, when this feverish sense of potency comes out of nowhere (*where was it* a second ago?) to bear down on a single point and from there expand my muscles, and, if possible, *bend them,* immediately after which it reluctantly spreads to the rest of my body in warm waves, filling me up, giving my whole body a hard-on in a few seconds, as if my position with this woman had landed me not in the middle of a stormy sea with both our lives in jeopardy but rather in the act of savagely sodomizing her on a big, unknown bed in a make-believe Moorish chamber. I notice it while it's happening, and I'm embarrassed, but all the embarrassment in the world won't stop my cock from swelling and getting harder in my bathing suit, like an autonomous entity, independent of me, an indomitable hormonal minority that refuses to accept the idea of death, or maybe has accepted it and thus decided to let loose its last ridiculous battle cry to the universe.

So this is who I am. Look at me, in danger, jabbing my hard cock against the ass of this unknown woman who's gone mad with death, and I'm telling myself I'm doing it for her sake, but at this point I'm also doing it for my sake, for Lara's sake, for Claudia, for my brother, and for all the people who in five minutes could absorb the news of an unknown woman drowning in the sea before my eyes but who would suffer, weep, and never be the same again if together with her, here and now, I, too, were to drown. Yes, I am doing this to save someone, to save myself, but this incongruity scares me even more than death, because I have never been so close to it, and to realize here and now that staring death in the face has this effect on me, and to discover in the end — after so much thinking and refusing to think about it, after so much bereavement in the tremendous year of 1999, when first Lara's father and then her mother and then mine, too, were taken away from us in the space of only ten months, and then after so much talking about it, accepting it, taming it, domesticating it until it had become a kind of fuzzy drawing room lioness — that death turns me on like a second-rate sexual fantasy I never remember having, *all this* is what frightens me, goddamn it, not death.

Yet besides frightening me it also calms me. Strange but true. Despite the objective uncertainty into which my survival has suddenly plunged, I again feel the protective wing of invincibility over me, which the blue and never before so plural gaze of my brother had promised to me while I was diving into the sea ("We will save them, we will not die") and vanished upon my first contact with this woman. This guardian spirit bearing youth and invulnerability has suddenly returned to visit me, but this time in the singular ("*I* will save her, *I* will not die"), and now I sense something functional about my self-damnation that wasn't there until a few moments ago, as if I were only truly beginning to save this woman now. The hard-on fills me with a new equilibrium, my breathing becomes synchronized with my movements, and I pump, push, and progress, blindly resisting the temptation to stop and catch my breath or to shift my position ever so slightly in order to see over her shoulders how far we are from the shore — because no matter how far we have to go, I still have to reach it, and knowing how far we are won't change a thing. I simply press onward, convulsively, compulsively, with this load of flesh that's shuddering and sobbing and still struggling to oppose my heroic action — because there can be no doubt that besides being involuntary and uncouth and increasingly obscene, on account of my hardon and the grunts I'm emitting to focus my efforts, like Serena Williams when she whacks the ball, no, there can be no doubt that the action I'm performing is heroic. And there is something awesome in this naked repetition, a kind of Zen I have sought all my life — through the most varied practices, at the most varied ages, to flee the most varied threats — and never gotten close to, which seems to have arrived now, thanks to this simple combination of primary elements — Eros, Thanatos, Psyche — finally in harmony through a single apelike act . . .

But all this is gone in an instant. A huge thwack shoves me back down in the water, and everything suddenly changes: there is no woman, no light, no air. Everything is water. I feel a kind of harpoon jab me in the leg and another one in the hip, and I splash about more from pain than from any effort to resurface. I thrash about and I swim wildly like a bass struck by a spear, even though by doing so — a complete accident, I have to admit — I manage to come to the surface.

I breathe, I start to see again, but the light almost blinds me, and now the woman is holding me firmly by the pelvis, and the harpoons are her nails digging into my hips. For an endless moment I see her swollen face, her imploring gaze, and I have the impression that those eyes drenched in terror are begging my forgiveness, yes, and promising me that they will not drown me anymore, that she will allow herself to be rescued like she should have from the start.

Except that now I'm out of breath, and I can't seem to breathe properly and my heart is bursting inside my chest and my erection is gone and I feel cramps squeezing me tighter and tighter and I realize we're at the very point where the waves break and I have the sudden, absolute certainty that with the sliver of strength I have left I can still manage to make it to the shore alone, but there's no longer any sense in bringing her along with me, too. And I don't know how, but I also realize that there's no more time left, that I have to get rid of her as soon as possible, immediately, if I seriously don't want to end up dying as wretchedly as I had seemed destined just a moment ago. Suddenly I hate this woman. Who do you think you are, you fucking bitch, coming here to drown before my eyes in the place where I've spent all my summers, ever since I was little, the place where I learned to swim and to dive and to surf and to sail and to water-ski and to dive fifteen yards down without an oxygen tank, holding my breath, and thus feel immune, do you get it, *immune* from death by drowning, and when I answer your call and I do what you want me to do, namely, I come running to your rescue despite the fact that I don't even know you, and in five days I'm supposed to get married, and I've got a ton of things to lose, probably much more than that redheaded fuckface who told me to let you die, when I come to you, you try to kill me? And then you repent? Go fuck yourself.

A punch in the face. I decide to throw her a punch in the face, and to leave her here to die alone, and to let myself be tossed toward the shore by this gigantic wave, mother of God, this truly gigantic wave coming toward us, and I'm about to do it, and I really have already started to, since I'm leaning back to get myself within punching range, since she's holding on to my hips with her fingernails, and my target — her semisubmerged face desperately turned toward the sky — is swashing around at the level of my knee, when the gigantic wave crashes over us and everything is darkness and water and claws digging even deeper into my flesh — into my thighs now — and there's no up and no down, it's all an indistinct whorl of water and foam and sand and water bubbles, until in my posture of defeat — the languid, relentless spinning of the drowned — my face hits bottom. Thump. The impact gives me back life and a sense of direction, and if where I am is down then the opposite is up, and I try to pull my legs toward me to help work my way back up, and they cooperate, yes, but with immense difficulty, as if they were being gripped not by one but by a dozen dying women, and somehow I manage to place one foot on the bottom and give myself a push, which immediately proves to be so crooked and disappointing, so feeble, considering the super-human effort I thought I had put into it, and then I feel that all is lost, because I have missed my last opportunity to come up and I really am dying, yes, that's what it is, now I'm dying, in this precise moment I'm dying, so it's happened, I died, a second ago, I died by drowning, like an ashole; and suddenly my head finds itself above water again.

Yes, goddamn it, my head is *above water*.

While I feel like I'm breathing for the first time in my life, I see a kind of big white beak hanging over me and I hear a voice shouting, "Grab ahold of it! Grab ahold of the surfboard!" and I do so immediately, automatically, I dig my nails into the board like the woman digging her nails into my thighs, and the board pulls us toward the shore, the short distance it takes to find ourselves, me and my human anchor, past the spot where the waves break. I stretch my legs downward and my feet touch the bottom — never, I swear, never has contact been more amazing — the water is up to my chest, the waves hitting me now are depleted, threads of dead foam. In a flash, I see a long human chain reaching toward me from the shore, like a conga line at a party, at the head of which is one of the two kids astride the surfboard telling me

something, I don't understand what. I let go of the surfboard, my
legs hold me up, I try to get my bearings, to *understand*. In the meantime, the human chain is broken and I immediately start to yearn
for it: I saw it for only an instant, and it was one of those unforgettable visions that gives meaning to an entire lifetime — *other people
holding each other's hands trying to reach you* — and obviously it
did not last long enough. But even for that one second, the vision
pierced me with its immense beauty, because it made me feel suddenly *saved*, goddamn it, me who was doing the saving, and I don't
like the sound of that. So I immediately resume my mission, I grab
the woman under her armpits, pull her up, because she seems
determined to drown even here, where you can touch bottom,
but already many people are around me and they slip her out of
my hands, and they try to carry me, too, the shitheads, to lift me
up, to comfort me, and I have to ward them off, I have to tell them
that I'm okay, that everything's okay, that I don't need anything
but that I don't have the strength to fight, to defend my prey and
carry it in my arms to the shore, like I wanted to, to her children,
safe, thanks to me. No, I don't have the strength, and the woman
is gone, sliding softly away, flowing into the arms of the redheaded
man, no less, or maybe not, it's not him carrying her, it's someone
else, and he's standing off to the side but then he is there at the
decisive moment, he's coming out of the sea together with her
and the giant carrying her and all the others who are taking credit
for saving her, and even the surf kid, who is the last one to make
sure that I'm okay, that I don't want to grab ahold of his surfboard,
for Christ's sake, to be hauled in to shore, and I repeat to him or
rather I snarl that I'm okay, that I don't need anything, thanks
anyway, and even he goes back toward the crowd on the beach,
and I find myself alone. It's over. It's over. I'm not at all okay, obviously: my body is shaking, my breathing is still choked, I'm cold,
but I wanted everyone to believe I was okay, and they did. They

believed me and they left me alone. Breathe. Breathe. Breathe.

All of a sudden, as if to awaken me from a phenomenal night-
mare, the priorities of my life rush back to me. Lara. Claudia.
Carlo. *Carlo.* How long ago did I stop thinking about him? Where
is he? I look around desperately, like when you think you've lost
your daughter at the supermarket because you were distracted for
a minute, and instead there she is, close by; and Carlo is there,
too, a few yards upwind, still in the water like me, talking to the
other kid with a surfboard, like I was a moment ago, surrounded
by what looks like the remains of the human chain that was
formed to reach him and then splintered forever and is now flock-
ing toward the beach with its saved human life. He sees me, Carlo
does, and waves to me. I wave back. He comes toward me. I go
toward him, and the already obvious symmetry of our conditions
becomes perfect when his surfer leaves him alone, too, and goes
on about his business. We meet halfway — as we always do, he and
I, whenever we meet.

We even hug. We tell each other how it went, and it went more
or less the same for both of us. We show each other our scratches,
the bloody streaks that our two dying women left all over our
bodies (his was a woman, too). But Carlo is less troubled than I
am, or else it must have had less of an effect on him, and I'm a
little embarrassed by this. In the meantime, we proceed slowly toward the shore, the water comes up to our waists, and through
the frenzied movements of the rescue workers we can also hear
the audio — a feverish clamor of voices synchronized with the
chaos of movements around the spot where the two women have
been laid down. Smiling, Carlo looks at me.

— Do you know what's about to happen? — he says.

— What?

— We're coming out of the water, right? The water is up to our
thighs, we're almost there.

— Yes, — I say.

— Well, correct me if I'm wrong, — says Carlo, — but in my opinion, if we make it to the beach without anyone thanking us, it'll be as if we had done nothing.

— So where the fuck are we?

We continue to advance, the water is up to our knees. Everyone is caught up in the rescue operation. No one notices us. Carlo keeps smiling; I keep shivering and feeling cold. The water is up to our calves. No one sees us. To our ankles. No one pays us any mind.

— Three more steps, — says Carlo, — and we'll be just two more shitheads that came by to see what happened.

— No way, — I answer, but I'm starting to get the same feeling.

We've made it. We're out of the water. No one bothers to give us a look. Many people are on their cell phones. There seems to be a problem with the ambulances. Others — the majority — are crowding around the two women laid out on the sand. Carlo goes near one of the two clusters, makes his way through, and I follow him. It's my woman: stretched out, as pale as death and wrapped in towels, she is drinking water from a paper cup. Everyone is around her: the hunk who brought her ashore, the redheaded man, two other guys, some distraught-looking old folks, the surfing kid. They see me, but it's as if I were someone else. They don't recognize me. But the woman doesn't even see me: her blank gaze, her pained expression, she's caressing her children, who are huddled close to her in what looks like an unbearably intimate scene. Carlo takes a few steps back, and I do the same. A wall of flesh immediately closes the woman off from sight. Carlo stares at a woman with flabby skin and devastating cellulite on her thighs.

— What happened? — he asks her.

— Two women almost drowned, — she replies, toying with

her cell phone, — today was no day to go swimming. They should put in lifeguards, red flags. First a man and then those two poor women.

— Go figure, — says Carlo, then he looks at me and sniggers.
— But are they all right? I mean, are they safe?

— Yes, — the woman says, — but they can't find an ambulance. There's only one in town, and it's busy.

— Go figure, — Carlo repeats.

Now I can hardly stand looking at him. He's feeling so self-righteous: we rescued two bitches, surrounded by a bunch of bitches who didn't even notice, since they're nothing but bitches themselves. And the fact that Carlo realized this before me is the final humiliation.

We walk away. As far as anyone can tell, all we did was poke our noses into someone else's drama for a minute and then continued on our way. We get to our towels, gather up the stuff we had left behind, and leave the beach in silence. On my cell phone there are four calls from home, and, in fact, it's really late. Two thirty has come and gone, and Lara and Claudia will be worried. I decide not to call back, because I'll be home in five minutes anyway and I'll explain everything. Except that I don't know how to make it through these five minutes. My head is so crowded with things I can't speak. I'm mad at the world, and I have the vague feeling that if Carlo doesn't say something in the next five minutes, either, it'll dig a deep rift between us. A really deep rift. That's how bad it is.

— What a bunch of fat, ugly bitches! — Carlo exclaims while we descend the path through the dunes. It's a real pleasure to hear him say this, since now I can, too, we can speak together, and by speaking we can affirm that in the end we don't give a flying fuck about those people, that what matters is we're alive, we're broth-ers, we did something together that no one else could do, just like that, out of the goodness of our hearts, and we're about to tell it

to the people who are waiting for us and care about us. All it takes
is a few sentences to give us the right distance from what just happened, the right cynicism, the right irony, and we find ourselves
flip-flopping toward home laughing and swearing at the world —
the two of us, grown men — like the kids we used to be, who were
together, even inseparable for a time, like Laurel and Hardy.

When we get closer to home, I start to prepare my sanitized
version to tell Lara and Claudia — minus the hard-on, minus
the danger of dying — centered on the no longer frightening but
for now simply cynical and even joyous realization that you can
do great things in life, like saving a drowning person, and no one
will say thank you; and I automatically wonder whether it might
be too much for a ten-year-old girl like Claudia, and whether
it wouldn't be better to shield her from this, too, by telling her
what happened in an even more sanitized version or even lying
("at one point we formed two human chains with all the people
that were on the beach, *right, Carlo*? And we pushed the two boys
with the surfboards toward them, so they could grab onto the
surfboards, and . . ."), and at that moment I see the flashing blue
light. I look at Carlo, and he, too, is speechless, quickens his step,
and at the end of the road, parked next to our cars, I see the ambulance with its back doors open. I start running home, and in
those ten yards I see, in this order, the Bernocchis, our neighbors
to the right; the Valianis, our neighbors to the left; Maria Grazia, the cleaning lady; Mac, who's Claudia's nanny; and Claudia
with her arms wrapped around her. For an endless moment I see
nothing, and what I do see is already enough to give me lethal
anxiety. But what I don't see in the midst of all these sobbing,
overwrought people is that Lara is not there. And I don't even see
that Lara actually is there, in a big way, and that she's right in the
center of the scene, surrounded by a doctor and EMS workers,
lying on the ground next to a useless aluminum stretcher, circled

by shards of a shattered white vase and red and yellow splotches (prosciutto and melon) on the pavement all around her, beautiful, tanned, and immobile in a twisted and unnatural pose. For an interminable moment, I don't see any of this, but then I do; all of a sudden, I see everything, because there's no avoiding it: in the middle of this scene, at my house, in front of my daughter, two employees, two neighboring couples, and my brother, with a flashing ambulance parked off to the side next to my car, *all of this is there.*

chapter two

My name is Pietro Paladini. I'm forty-three years old and I'm a widower. Legally speaking, this second statement is incorrect, because Lara and I were never married, but we'd been together for twelve years and lived together for eleven, and had a daughter who is now ten, and as if this isn't enough we'd just decided to get married ("finally," as many people said), and had already started receiving gifts, and suddenly Lara is dead, and the day of our wedding became the day of her funeral instead. But our legal status is not the best observation point if you want the full picture. I'm pretty well off, too. I own a nice apartment in downtown Milan; a fox terrier mix called Dylan; a nice house by the sea in Maremma, which I share with my brother, Carlo; and a black Audi A6 3000 complete with expensive accessories, which at the moment I'm driving through the Milan traffic to take my daughter, Claudia, to school. Today, in fact, is the first day of school, and Claudia is starting fifth grade.

I'm in a daze, numb. The past two weeks have been a roller coaster of visits, hugs, tears, reassurances, phone calls, advice, morbid details, coincidences, telegrams, obituaries, religious rites, practical problems, wedding gifts that are still coming, coffees, words, and understanding — so much understanding. But despite everything, I'm still not really grieving. And Claudia seems to be following my example: in a daze, numb, but still distant from true grief. We were both in that whirlwind together, never apart, and we also did many ordinary things, like finishing up her vacation assignments, buying new school supplies, taking Dylan to the vet for an eye inflammation. Every moment felt like the *last*, like a strange appendix to our former life that had outlasted the event which ended it forever, and every moment I expected that lurking behind the long-division exercises, the Simpsons' notebook, or the eye drops for the dog the real blow was waiting, for both of us, the big one that had not yet arrived. But every time, to my great surprise, we emerged unscathed. So now I'm wondering whether today isn't the dreaded day; whether the time bomb isn't actually scheduled to go off on the first day of school, the first day that she and I will truly be apart and normality will prevail over the soft, promiscuous emergency that has enveloped us for the past two weeks. At this point, everyone's gone back to their regular lives, although they've all told me to call anytime: my sister-in-law, who has two children and already has enough on her hands; my brother, who lives in Rome; my colleagues, who are stressed by the merger, and their wives, who are suffering from secondhand stress; even my father, who's ailing and is living in Switzerland with his nurse/lover, Chantal, cut off from the world, completely absorbed by his studies of Napoleon, with whom he identifies like the crazy guy in the cartoon . . . Everyone says to call anytime, yes, everyone is ready to lend us a hand, but there's nothing they can do against the blow that's going to smack us in the face — because it will come, it has to come, and this sunny morning is the perfect moment for it to arrive.

We're early. In front of the school we even find a parking space, easy, without having to maneuver. Claudia has her hair tied in a single braid, and she keeps playing with it, quietly and peacefully, in the backseat. "Come, sweetheart, it's time to go," I tell her, since she's hesitating even after I've switched the engine off. Is she going to be hit with it *now*, perhaps? It's time for us to separate, sweetheart, to give each other a kiss and for each of us to return to our daily chores, because life goes on with even more love than before, as the priest said at the funeral, and Mamma is watching over us and protecting us from heaven above where the true Father has summoned her (nice father); and since you're ten years old, it would be understandable if you were to raise your head slowly right now and stare at me with bloodshot eyes, like in *The Exorcist*, and rather than slipping on your new backpack and getting out of the car, you were to vomit all over my jacket the toast you just ate in the kitchen of the apartment where your mother will never have breakfast with you again, or if you were to melt into unholy sobs and convulsions, maybe blaming me, openly and in a cavernous voice, or even worse, silently, mentally, for having let your mother die before your eyes without granting you the pleasure of my company, since I was too busy at the moment, as some psychology genius has told you (I still haven't figured out who: definitely not Carlo, he swears it wasn't him), rescuing from the grip of death another woman, another wife, another mother, who I didn't even know. Is this what's about to happen, sweetheart? Is this what's about to happen?

But I don't know what's happening: Claudia gets out of the car, docile, peaceful, and tags along behind me through the big door to the school, to the lobby where there are already a couple of parents swapping stories about their summer vacations, where they went, how much they spent, while their children sniff each other out like dogs. It's a nice school, this one: big, bright, nineteenth century, the kind you remember longingly years after graduation.

It's named after Enrico Cernuschi, "Milanese patriot," and something vaguely reminiscent of the Italian Risorgimento really does hover in the air, a sense of hope quite appropriate to those facing the open future. While I observe Claudia looking around to find some of her old friends, I am pleased, yes, I am very pleased that my daughter attends this school.

The first person to come toward us is one of her teachers, Gloria, a lovely and always smiling woman with salt-and-pepper hair. Naturally, she *knows*. Condolence is written all over her face, and from the caution with which she conveys her words I catch a glimpse of the treatment others will be reserving for me from now on and for a long time to come: now that we're done with the orgy of relatives and close friends, who have gone back out into the big world, the manifestations of grief have given way to expressions of sympathy. It's normal. The other teacher, Paolina, arrives, too, and then the mother of Benedetta, Claudia's best friend, whom I had already met at the funeral, and slowly but surely all the other mothers that I know, and even several fathers, since today is the first day of school. Once again everyone offers their help for everything in the world, to take Claudia to school or to take her back home if I'm busy with work, to let her stay with them if I have to travel, and it's odd but there's something almost threatening about these promises: as if everyone here is assuming I can't take care of my own daughter, as if they want to take her away from me. Of course there's affection in these offers; and as I was saying, there's all the sympathy I'm going to have to get used to being aimed in my direction, a sympathy reserved for those who have suffered a misfortune; but there's also the colossal quirk of people trying to imagine a condition they could never have conceived before, and they have to improvise. More often than not this quirk keeps people from understanding how deeply someone is suffering, how lost he feels and how hopeless, and it prompts them to offer advice that is almost always ridiculous; but in some cases this same quirk can lead to the exact opposite error and decree the sheer unbearability of someone else's grief, although the grief is not or has not yet become unbearable. Yes, because no matter what these people think, I can still see that the blow still hasn't arrived, not even today, not even for Claudia, who's joking with her friends and showing off her new school supplies . . .

— I'll wait for you here, — I tell her when the bell rings, — until four thirty, when you come out, I won't budge from here.

Claudia is speechless for a moment, then she figures I'm joking and she smiles. I squat down to be at her level.

— I mean it, sweetheart, — I whisper. — I might move around a little bit, since the day is so nice, and smoke a cigarette in the park, grab a cup of coffee at the café, just remember that I'll be here waiting for you when you come out. Even if you don't see me, understand? I'll be here.

She smiles again, my daughter, and she *understands,* again. It's so great to realize you really do have an understanding with your children. I give her a kiss on the forehead, she gives me a peck on the cheek, then she starts down the corridor with all the other children looking back and waving good-bye. And when she's far away, she, too, turns around and waves; smiling, I signal to her that I'll be here waiting for her until four thirty. Then she disappears up the stairs, and I stand where I am for a little while, giving the other parents time to swarm away without me, without inviting me to have a cup of coffee, without continuing to convey their sympathy. I've had enough for this morning.

By the time I move, the other parents have already left. No one dared to disturb me. The custodian, Maria, who had been watching me stare at the empty corridor, smiles at me maternally. Sympathy, understanding. I wave to her, go out to the street, and light a cigarette. I had decided to quit the day I got married, and

I would have, but the day never came and now I'm back, smoking more than ever. I turn on my cell phone, and the display tells me it's 8:39. I look at the school, the checkerboard windowpanes marking the classrooms, and I wonder which classroom is Claudia's. Last year it was the first one on the second floor. There's an intense, even summery sun bathing the surrounding buildings in a golden light. There's a very non-Milanese breeze rustling the leaves of the trees in the nearby park. We're about ten yards above the street, and the noises of the city come to us dully, inoffensively. It's a nice place, this, no question about it. You can even hear the birds chirping.

From a distance I press the remote to my car. The signal lights go on and the car goes *beep*. A woman walks by the car, holding a Down syndrome child by the hand, and something strange happens: the child turns toward the car — slowly, but in what, for him, is a flash, since he has Down — and stares at it intensely, as if the beep and the flickering of lights were a personal greeting. It's as clear as day, but I'm the only one who notices, since his mother seems to be in a hurry and keeps dragging him behind her by the hand, staring ahead, and now he's walking behind her reluctantly, turning around to look at my car, waiting for another signal. Which comes, because I press the remote again, and I do it just for him. Then he smiles, pleased, and turns toward his mother to tell her that the car greeted him twice, with a beep and with the signal lights. But he's slow and his mother's in a hurry. She doesn't listen to him. She drags him along. They cross the street and slip through the entrance of a white, fairly elegant, modern building. Before going in, the child turns around to see my car once again when I press the remote a third time.

All set. 8:44. I get in the car and start it up. Now I'll go to the office, I think, and be back at my job after this strange vacation. I'll be back with my colleagues, my friends, my enemies, and the sword of Damocles, the merger, hanging over us. Special treatment will be reserved for me, out of sympathy and understanding. Jean-Claude will summon me to his executive office and repeat that I don't have to worry about anything, that I should stay close to my daughter, take my time. Then he'll invite me to lunch. And it might be right there and then, at the restaurant, over carpaccio, a carpaccio made with branzino, mind you, at around a quarter to two on this beautiful day. It might be right there and then that it hits me . . .

A guy in a Renault is waiting to take my spot. He's begging me, through gestures and words — below his breath, of course, as you do with someone who can't hear. I glance at him. He already looks exhausted at nine in the morning. Who knows how long he's been driving around looking for a parking spot. With his signal light blinking, he indicates to those behind him that the spot is his and he's ready to punch out anyone who dares to claim otherwise.

— No, — I tell him through the lowered window, — I'm not leaving. Sorry.

He takes it badly. He was convinced I was leaving. He insists, convinced that he misunderstood, he asks again, and this time my answer is unequivocal. I get out of the car and lock it with the remote. *Beep.*

— I just got here, I'm sorry, — I tell him, exploiting my huge advantage in being outside, calm, on my feet, free to speak at will without tying up traffic. He, on the other hand, is locked inside a car, nervous, disappointed, and behind him a small, malodorous line has already formed. He looks at me. He hates me. He shifts gears and takes off, peeling out with his blinker still on. The line is freed up in an instant. The air is immediately crisper. I fish my cell phone out of my pocket and call Annalisa, my secretary. She, too, came to the funeral, and she cried. I tell her that I won't be coming in to the office today and to transfer calls to my cell phone.

She reminds me that I have an appointment at eleven and another one at twelve thirty. I tell her to reschedule both. I tell her
to forward faxes to the device in my car, so it'll finally be useful
for something. I'll check my e-mail on my cell phone, even if the
wi-fi system sucks since you can't open attachments. Annalisa says
nothing, writes it down, and doesn't ask me anything, of course,
but I can tell that she's bristling with curiosity to know what's
going on with me. And all at once it sounds nice. Yes, it would be
nice to tell her.

— You know, — I tell her, — I promised my daughter that
today I would wait in front of the school until she gets out at four
thirty.

— Oh, — she says.

— It's nice out here, — I add, — it's a nice day, and I can work
from my car.

Annalisa says nothing, flustered. I'm well acquainted with the
face she is making. I can almost see her! She's a good girl —efficient,
loyal — but she always seems to be grappling with things bigger
than herself, and her face, which is normally quite pretty, has taken
on an almost permanent look of bewilderment, which doesn't become her at all. Like a person who's always thinking: "It wasn't me.
I only do what I'm told and do my best to fit into an incomprehensible world." I think her facial expression has to do with the fact
that she doesn't have a boyfriend. It's either the cause or the effect.

— The president asked for you, — she mumbles, — if he asks
me again, what should I tell him?

— Tell him I'm sitting in front of my daughter's school.

— Oh, — she repeats, and puts on that bewildered look again.

— Bye, Annalisa, — I tell her. — See you tomorrow.

— See you tomorrow, sir.

I turn the phone off and feel like I've done the right thing. Telling Claudia I would stay here all day was sweet, but doing so is

another matter entirely. Every now and then you have to treat the
things you say to children very literally. If I said it, there must be a
reason, right? If she smiled, there must also be a reason. Well, the
reason is simple: it would be too risky to be separated today — for
her, and maybe for me, too. I did the right thing, yes.

The sky is clear, blue, sparkling. An airplane that has just taken
off glitters in the sun and slowly begins its turn while it continues
to climb. It shouldn't, according to safety regulations, but in reality that's how things work at Linate Airport: the planes take off
and turn immediately, before they've reached the proper altitude.
Supposedly it's a favor they did for Berlusconi when he was still a
businessman, to prevent planes from flying over the Milano 2 resi-
dential district. With my eyes I follow the plane while it continues
to climb, even after it turns and heads south. Toward Rome, because nowadays the only place you can fly to from Linate is Rome.
In all probability, the airplane is carrying, inside a briefcase with a
combination lock (the date of birth of the owner, usually, or of his
wife, lover, or child), documents related to the merger that, with
the rumble of its approach, is paralyzing my company. Nowadays
almost every airplane departing from Milan is carrying something
related to the merger.

A quarter past nine.

I feel like a coffee.

chapter three

List of the airlines I've flown on:

*Alitalia, Air France, British Airways, Aeroflot, Iberia, Air Dolomiti, Air
One, Sudan Air, Lufthansa, Aerolineas Argentinas, Egyptair, Cathay Pacific,
American Airlines, United Airlines, Continental Airlines, Delta, Alaska Air-
lines, VARIG, KLM, TWA, Pan Am, Meridiana, Jat.*

This is what I wrote down in my notebook. Because of a strange idea I had while drinking coffee, drawing up this list was important to me. A kind of exercise, I think: not to test my memory so much as to keep it at bay, dominate and even *bend it* to a purpose as specific as it is abstract and fundamentally useless. What good did this list do me? What did it add to my life? Nothing. Yet I'm proud to have drawn it up: first, because it wasn't easy and I had to really rack my brains out to retrieve, for example, Alaska Airlines, which I took once by chance in a rush for the Calgary-Seattle leg of a bumpy trip from Vancouver to Miami; second, because I managed to do it by venturing into an area that frightens me in the here and now. I'm afraid of remembering, yes. I'm afraid of every single memory I have. And I am comforted to discover that I can wander around in my memories chasing butterflies for an hour, remembering trips that were exciting or simply nice and pleasant — many of which I took with Lara or while we were together — without feeling bad. So I can go so far as to say that this list is important, now that it's on a page of my notebook with the objectivity that only completed tasks have earned. I look at it again and again. It's a distillation of my memory, a concentration of information about my life, and it doesn't make me suffer. It's important.

The cell phone rang several times while I was drawing up my list. Short business calls preceded by long prologues of condolence, embarrassed voices of men and women who, while assuring me of their availability, seemed in reality to be testing me: the purpose of the phone calls was always vague, never work-related, as if it were a pretext to check whether I'm still a reliable interlocutor now that I'm back. A mix of solidarity and cynicism. On the other hand, the situation at the company is confusing enough to justify this kind of check-up call. The merger bearing down on us is enormous, and literally no one at the office is impervious to its effects. Everyone more or less is looking around with their ears pricked, as frightened as monkeys in the savannah. At least that's the way it was until two weeks ago, before I broke away from the herd because of my personal situation. And there's no reason to think anything has changed in the meantime. So I understand these personal check-ups, especially of me. What's the sense of criticizing them? I'd do the same thing in their place. It's a wild world.

A wild world.

For example, who told Claudia that while her mother was dying I was saving another woman? Carlo swore it wasn't him, and I believe him; but when I asked him whether he had told any-one else, he candidly answered yes: my sister-in-law, our cousins in Bologna, even Aunt Jenny . . . The result: everyone in the fam-ily knows the life-saving story, and Claudia knows better than anyone, since she spoke to me about it a few nights ago, making my blood run cold; she asked me bluntly whether I had heard any news about the woman I'd saved, and I answered no, but I didn't have the heart to ask her who had told her the story. I was very worried about the fact that she knew, yes. God only knows what she must have thought. Who knows what might be gener-ated over time, knowing that while your mother was dying before your eyes, your father was saving an unknown woman.

But it's also true that children can be surprising: sometimes they seem to know everything already. That same night, for ex-ample, after asking me for news about "that woman," when she was already in her pajamas and in bed and I was about to read to her a chapter from a book she adores (*The Adventures of Pizzano Pizza*), Claudia nailed me with a perfect question: "Do you know," she asked, "what used to upset me more than anything else in life?" Those were her exact words, I swear. And before I could start worrying even more, realizing how implicitly she had grasped that the life-saving story had something to do with the verb "to upset," and how her ruthless conjugation of it as *used to upset* could imply "until Mom died" — but, even more subtly, "until I learned what you were doing while Mom was dying" — before I could plunge into all this, immediately after she formulated the question, she also gave me the answer: "It was when I discovered that *my* grandmother was also *your* mother," she told me, smiling self-indulgently. And so, that night, while I was feeling a mounting and insidious anguish, since this, too, could be the prelude to the real blow, Claudia was the one who reminded me that children reason very differently from adults and are not necessarily upset by the things that adults think upset them, while at the same time they can be upset by things that adults don't even see. Which is why, at this point, there may be no need to worry so much about the fact that she knows about the rescue or about who told her, but only to acknowledge that now she knows, and that's that . . .

Another plane that has just taken off veers over my head, and I am reminded of two other airlines to add to the list: Aero Mexico and Mexicana Airlines, on which I flew from Mérida to Cuba and then back to Mérida twenty years ago, over the course of a long, meandering trip through Latin America. Who knows why I didn't remember it when I was drawing up my list earlier. And then there was Air Lingus: the trip to Dublin right after graduating from high school. And Swissair, when I went to New York from Zurich with an abscessed tooth. And Itavia, the airline that failed after one of its planes crashed at Ustica, killing everyone on board; I flew with it once, as well. And Alisarda, too, when it used to be around. And that Hungarian airline, what was its name? Malev . . .

I add these names to the list, which is becoming quite respectable. I count them: thirty. I've traveled with thirty different airlines. Leaning against my car, with my jacket off because it's hot, I take a look around: a traffic cop, a couple of elderly gentlemen on a park bench, a pretty girl in a tank top walking a golden retriever, three construction workers redoing the façade of a building, an elderly Pakistani man cleaning windshields at the intersection, a limping woman dragging a child's bicycle behind her. None of them has traveled as much as I have, that much I can bet on. And for people who never travel, or who travel very little, a life filled with travel is, of course, a great life. But this is not always the case: I know some poor souls who have to take six airplanes a week for business and on the weekends travel again, maybe by car, with their families, to go to the seaside or the mountains, or take yet another airplane, using frequent-flier miles, with their girlfriends or lovers to Sardinia, Morocco, or London, to throw away money, and every time they do they say they can't take it anymore, but they carry on all the same till they're wiped out. But not me. The life I've lived so far has really been a great life, and the long list of airlines I've used really proves it.

I look at the school's big windows, and I wonder again which one belongs to Claudia's classroom. I wish she would take a peek outside the window and see me. I mean, I wish I would notice. A wave of her hand, the smile of surprise you can imagine on her face, just enough to make sense of the fact that I'm here. Not that it doesn't make sense. On the contrary: I'm definitely better off here than in the office, and the big blow hasn't struck. But it would be nice if at some point in this strange day my daughter would realize that I really am waiting in front of the school all day, as I told her I would when she thought I was joking. And it would be even nicer if I was looking at her when she realized it . . .

The door of the school opens, and out comes her teacher, Miss Gloria. I'm right in front of her, leaning against my car, on the other side of the street, but she doesn't see me: the sun is shining in her face, and she has to use her hand as a visor to cover her eyes; then she has to fumble around in her purse in that jaunty

pose women never lose, not even when they're older, with one leg
raised and the bag resting on top of it like when they were young
and their boyfriends accompanied them home late at night, and
they started to worry that they'd lost their keys and in that same
identical pose they started looking for them in the chaos of their
bags, and their boyfriends waited, in the car, with the engine running, wondering how they should behave if the keys didn't turn
up and they really did have to ring the bell at that hour: leave the
girl there by herself or accompany her as far as the doorway and
bear the brunt of a probable fit of paternal ire? The uncertainty
lasted awhile, and with it the pose: then the keys were found —
always: never once were they truly lost — they were allowed to
glitter between her fingers in the glow of the headlights, and everyone went their ways off to sleep with a sigh of relief. And so
Miss Gloria, after rummaging through her purse a few times, extracts a pair of sunglasses and puts them on, and at that point she
sees me. I smile at her, but I don't walk toward her. I wait for her
to come to me, if she wants. To kill a little time, I decide what I'm
going to tell her. But the time is up, and Miss Gloria has already
crossed the street and is standing in front of me.

— How's Claudia doing? — I ask, as if it were the most normal
thing in the world.

— Fine, — she replies. — She's calm, paying attention.

I can't see her eyes, which are hidden by her dark lenses, and
I can't understand *just how* surprised she might be to see me here.

— She has a really strong character, — Miss Gloria adds, —
but you have to be close to her, because in cases like this any little
thing and . . .

And this generic, throwaway, *overly* judicious sentence that everyone can and does utter so effortlessly dies in her throat. Obviously: she's finished her three hours of teaching and gone out
thinking about the grocery shopping she has to race through at

the minimarket or about her application for a transfer that she has to take to the school superintendent's office by one o'clock, and the first thing that she sees is me, here, leaning against my car in front of the school. Why in the world did she finish that sentence?

— Of course, — I say, and my phone rings. I make a gesture of apology to her and answer: it's Annalisa, calling about some documents that have been sitting in the office for more than ten days now and that I should sign as soon as possible. She says she's tried to send them to my car fax but it's not working. All this, obviously, Miss Gloria doesn't hear. The only words she hears are mine.

— I've never used it, Annalisa, — I reply. — Come to think of it, maybe it's out of paper. Couldn't this wait until tomorrow? One day more, one day less, what difference does it make?

Annalisa pauses, then says that it basically doesn't make any difference. She only wanted to inform me that the car fax is not working.

— Unless, — I add, — you wouldn't mind bringing them to me. I won't move from here until four thirty.

How strange to know the exact expression of a person you can't see, on the other end of the phone, and not to know the expression of a person right in front of you, because of a pair of sunglasses. Annalisa is shocked, she's definitely sinking into her bewildered look: the problem for her right now is to figure out whether I just gave an instruction or made a proposal she can question.

— But wait, forget about it, — I tell her. — I'll sign them to-morrow. In fact, while we're at it, why don't you take the after-noon off?

Annalisa thanks me and tells me that she'll stay in the office.

She probably wouldn't know how to behave outside: she's alone.
You can see it in her eyes.

Miss Gloria, on the other hand, is motionless and impenetrable
behind her glasses. I put the cell phone back in my pocket and
smile.

— Sorry about that, — I say.

A strange silence comes over us. I think I know what Miss Gloria wants to say, and I could help her, I could make the first move.
But I don't. I'm used to speaking a lot, sometimes too much, and
now it seems important not to. Without my help, she can't say
anything, and this silence, I'm not sure why, is very precious.

A clamor of car horns echoes from the side road, and Miss Gloria shakes herself, as if she were being summoned.

— Well, good-bye, — she tells me.

— See you tomorrow, — I say.

While she turns around and starts to walk toward the park, I
am struck by myriad details about her life, all at once, as if they
had tumbled out of her pockets with that one movement: a faded
passion for dancing, loving care of plants on her balcony, dirty
Band-Aids on her heels, a weekly meeting with a culture circle
in the Navigli neighborhood, a parquet floor that needs to be
refinished in the living room, nights spent studying manuals to
refresh her teaching methods, hopeless diets to prevent weight
gain, Caetano Veloso CDs that her husband doesn't like, unassum-
ing white underwear, risottos prepared for dinners with friends,
checkups every six months at the Tumor Prevention Center, a bad
picture on her ID card, and a good picture framed and sitting on a
shelf in the living room, in which she looks almost pretty, almost
happy, with one son in her arms and another hugging her leg,
twelve years ago, in Sardinia, against the backdrop of a peaceful
and inimitably green sea . . .

— Excuse me! — I shout after her. She stops and turns around suddenly, almost as if she was expecting to be called.

— Can you tell me which one of the windows is to your classroom this year? — I ask, and again the sunglasses conceal her eyes, not to mention the six or seven steps now separating us, and prevent me from understanding the impact of my question. Miss Gloria looks up at the school and stares at the façade for a few seconds, as if she is thinking about it: "Hmmm, the window of our classroom . . ." This question had plainly not yet occurred to her. Then she raises her hand and points to a spot.

— The third one! — she answers, — the third one from the left on the third floor!

— Thank you!

Miss Gloria stares at me one last time, trying perhaps to muster the courage to go back and ask me what the hell I'm doing out here. But even if that's the case, she doesn't find the strength and limits herself to nodding and going on her way. And in that same manner of letting the minutiae of her life tumble out behind her, visible and sad: the desire to spend a weekend at an overpriced thermal spa, the passion for books by Daniel Pennac, the nuisance of a tiny unauthorized alteration of her parents' home, the profuse sweating . . .

Looking at the window to my daughter's classroom, I feel a sudden boundless tenderness. On the other side of the window, she is sitting at her desk, with her new things with their new smell, surrounded by unwitting classmates, struggling. Maybe she doesn't even realize that she's struggling with all her might, struggling to be herself, to be a little girl, to save herself. And she has to do all this by herself. Oh, I think, if only something would inspire her to look out the window: a little bird alighting on the windowsill, a sudden noise, or even the mute animal call of my uplifted gaze, the cry of the blood I feel pulsing violently in my chest, in my throat, in my temples, as if I were about to faint: "Come, my little one, stop paying attention, let your mind wander, stand up, go to the window, look outside, look down . . ."

The phone rings. I let it keep ringing.

chapter four

The first parents arrive at five to four. Two fathers. I don't know them. I don't remember ever seeing them. They arrive together, nice and tan, wearing ties, jackets over their shoulders, conversing energetically about God knows what, and they station themselves in front of the school door, which is still closed. You get the impression it's not a coincidence. You get the impression it's a habit. It's fairly clear when a person is doing something he does all the time: he doesn't look around, doesn't look at other people, is apparently at ease, at home. That's how these two are. They arrive early, the first ones there, and converse, laughing, gesticulating like the best of friends, even if the herd of other parents hasn't arrived yet to shield them and make them less visible. They look like two child-hood friends, and maybe they are: two childhood friends who went to elementary and maybe middle school together, parted ways in high school, and then met up later, maybe because they married two girlfriends, yes, and all at once discovered that they were much more similar and compatible than they had thought, and the fact that they had known each other since they were little reassured them and made them become true friends. It's clear from observing them that when one has a problem, he calls the other. It's so obvious. They watch the sports roundup on TV to-gether, cover up each other's marital infidelities, take their vaca-tions together with their families, and their wives are reassured, in turn, by their own long ties to each other, and their same-age children are forced to participate in this joint intimacy, even in the event they can't stand each other. They have arrived together to pick up their children from school, and they've decided that this year they'll do it as often as they can, yes, they'll get off work early, with an *eros* that would be missing had they been leaving early to see their wives, and this pause will be a big help in making their life workable, in making it acceptable, to them both . . .

The other parents arrive en masse, all together, as if they had been released from a holding pen: some by moped, others by car, others on foot, chatting on their cell phones, each creating problems that the traffic cop can't solve. There's a new cop: it's not the same guy as this morning. Some people want to double-park right in front of the main door. Some want to carry on conversations in the middle of the road, blocking the traffic. He's got his hands full trying to maintain a modicum of order. But he can't manage, he's being attacked on all sides, and at four twenty-five, there's the usual pandemonium, just as I remember from the times I used to come to pick up Claudia. The chaos. But a joyous chaos, drama-free, because the children, even if they haven't exited the school yet, have already started emitting the substance that enables them to survive among adults, the natural antihistamine that helps parents relax and regress, making them not only compatible but also complicit with the chaos to which the children feel entitled: the chaos of their little rooms before they're ordered to straighten them out, the chaos of their backpacks when they get home from school, the folders, the pencil boxes, the notebooks; the simple and fundamentally quiet chaos in which they would live all the time, if they were allowed, without completely understanding most of the things that happen but, for this reason precisely, able to live very intensely. This is exactly what happens — now I understand — at around this time outside elementary schools throughout the Western Hemisphere: for a very short time, parents forget the civility to which they are glued all day long and act like children, chaotically, at the risk of being run over, losing the dog, scratching the car in the attempt to squeeze it into a narrow slot, and the traffic cop who's supposed to call them to order can't do a thing about it. But then all it takes is the actual exiting of the children from the school, bubbling over beyond reach with that chaos — with their torn collars, unlaced shoes, pee-stained trousers, holes in the knees, flute forgotten in the music room, the shoving and shouting — to startle them and shepherd them back toward the order from which they have come, which will be fully restored once they arrive home, with the family schedule that dictates the when and what of the things that have to get done before dinner, no questions asked.

It's strange, but when I used to pick up Claudia in past years, I didn't realize I was part of such an absurd phenomenon: I was in a hurry, too, and I, too, tried to outsmart the traffic cop by double-parking my car. I, too, used to stop to talk in the middle of the road. I, too, would achieve physical contact with my daughter after transgressing for ten minutes almost all the rules that I had obeyed the rest of the day, and in those ten minutes I, too, felt better. Although I didn't come very often to pick up Claudia, for me it was normal to always find complete chaos here at four thirty. Now, instead, after seeing it generated by the fluttering wings of two childhood friends deep in conversation, this chaos looks much more complex and structured; a phenomenon that is too obvious, too common, and too absurd to be somehow necessary: necessary, yes, so that parents could retake responsibility for their children in the least abrupt way possible — meeting them halfway, so to speak, and allowing themselves to be infected by the same quiet chaos that inspires their children.

The main door of the school is opened, and from inside you can hear the timeless ringing of the bell. Maria, the custodian,

asks the parents not to cluster by the door, to arrange themselves
in a semicircle around it, and her instruction produces a modicum of geometry in the fractal complexity of the mob. Although
today is a special day, it is clear that Maria the custodian has to
repeat this operation day in and day out, because otherwise the
parents/regressees would crowd around the door. Benedetta's
mother breaks away from a clutch of other mothers and comes
toward me, from the other side of the street, to where I have been
standing still, leaning against my car, excluding myself from the
competition to win a spot in the front row. She's a beautiful forty-
year-old with Egyptian eyes, short blond hair, and a strong jaw.
She's wearing a short tank top, like a young girl, that reveals a nice
strip of flat, tight stomach above and below her belly button. She
must do a lot of aerobics to be in such good shape. But the skin of
her face is worn out, almost withered, from all the sunlamps she's
used to maintain a permanent tan. She has even white teeth that
are gleaming at me now.

— How did it go? — she asks, as if this were a sensible question.
If she knew I had been outside here all day, it might have been, but
she doesn't, and her question is senseless.

— Fine.

— Would you like me to take Claudia home with Benedetta
and then bring her back to you at dinnertime?

The children start piling up at the door, led by their teachers
and looking around. But they're the littlest ones, first and second
graders. From the parental semicircle hands start to go up.

— I don't know, — I reply, — why don't we ask them?

— I was saying it for your sake, in case you're busy.

— Oh, well, thanks anyway. I don't have anything better to do.

I don't know what it is, maybe the expression on my face while
I'm saying these ordinary things or the simple fact that it's true,
and the fact of the matter is that a shadow of compassion slowly

travels across her face. I'll have to be careful of what I say from now on, and of how I say it, if I don't want people to feel sorry for me.

— Well, — she says, — I suppose it'll be better for her to stay with you, then. — She takes a breath. — Anyway, the offer's still good, and if you can't pick her up some afternoon or you're busy, just give me a call. Anything I can do, I mean it. Benedetta and Claudia get along so well . . .

Above the parents' heads, meanwhile, I can see the sorting of the older kids, third and fourth grades. The teachers look around, holding the children back by force if necessary (since they would obviously plunge into the crowd of parents and only later wonder how they would find their own), until they spot the mother, father, or authorized babysitter raising their hand and waving: only then do they loosen their grip on the child and point to where he or she should go, but the child almost always knows it already.

— Thank you, — I repeat, and all of a sudden, wanting to add something to my thanks, I realize that I don't remember her name (is it Barbara or Beatrice?). So my "thank you" remains suspended in the air, and I have to improvise another closer. — You're very kind.

— Don't be a stranger, promise? — she insists.

Often the children spot their parents before the teacher does, and they point them out while the teacher is busy looking for someone else's. So they upset the order by which their teachers had hoped to carry out the last task of the day, the parental assignments overlap, and the chaos spreads from outside to in.

— You know something? — I say. — It's like an auction.

— What?

— This way of giving children back to their parents. It's like an auction.

Benedetta's mother turns toward the main door and looks.

— It's like the children are being auctioned off one by one and the parents are competing for them, raising their hands and making a bid. The teacher awards them to the highest bidder, who in the end is always the real parent.

Now come the older children. The fifth-graders. Benedetta's mother stands still, her gaze fixed on the little girl she can't see from down here. She's not very tall, and a wall of people is still in front of her. I suddenly feel a strange lump rising in my throat.

— On the other hand, — I add, but I'd rather be quiet, — how else could they do it?

And here comes Miss Paolina. Next to her I recognize Francesco, Nilowfer, and Alex, plus a little girl I don't remember ever seeing. Behind them, in the shadow of the lobby, all the others pile up, including, I imagine, our own two daughters, whom we still can't see.

— It's our turn, — says Benedetta's mother, flashing her pearly white smile at me again. We cross the street, which is blocked by the loitering and talking and planning of parents who already have their kids, including the two childhood friends, holding their two little boys by the hands and chatting with a pretty young mother. The traffic is paralyzed, and the line of cars is held back by the traffic cop, as if without his intervention the cars might plunge into the crowd and cause a bloodbath. There's only so much you can do: as soon as we reach the mob, we squeeze into the nonexistent space between one person and the next so we can take the front row, like excited children, which we would never do for a line at the post office or supermarket. "Excuse me. Excuse me . . ." No one complains.

When we look at the door again, Claudia and Benedetta are standing there, next to Miss Paolina. Claudia spots me immediately, smiles, and the lump in my throat gets bigger; then she elbows her friend, who was staring in another direction, to point out her mother to her. At this point the only thing left is for Miss

Paolina to see us, too, and it's done. I raise my hand. I, too, make my little bid: Miss Paolina sees me, nods, and with her head indicates to Claudia that she can come to me. Sold to the highest bidder.

— How did it go, sweetheart? — I ask after giving her a kiss.

— Okay, — she replies, and it really does seem true. She's smiling, relaxed, serene. The lump starts to melt.

— What did you do today?

— Bye-bye, Pietro, — Benedetta's mother interrupts. She seems to be in a hurry.

— See you tomorrow, — I say. Then I stroke my daughter's hair.

— You're so tan, Benedetta. So pretty.

The little girl smiles, casts a knowing glance at Claudia, before leaving with her mother. Who, after one step, stops and turns around to face me again.

— Like I said, — she repeats, — don't be a stranger.

— Of course, — I reply.

Then everything is a succession of quick hellos and good-byes exchanged with the parents of Claudia's other classmates, and it takes me a few minutes to free myself.

Claudia stays close to me, like a good little girl, and her serenity helps to keep me from getting agitated, because the only thing I can think of is being alone with her. She didn't notice that I waited outside all day, I'm almost sure of it, but the look she traded with Benedetta brought the lump back to my throat, because it could mean that she had noticed, in fact, and that she told her friend, and that together they came up with a strategy for fun . . .

Then, when Miss Paolina says good-bye to me, too, we can finally slip into the car.

— So, — I say, before turning the key. — What did you do today?

My cell phone starts ringing, and I don't answer. I look at the display to see who's calling. Claudia is speechless for a second, toying with her braid. Then she takes a breath, as if to speak, but says ·nothing.

Did I guess right? She saw me but doesn't know how to tell me?

— What's wrong, sweetheart? — I ask, smiling.

— *I topi non avevano nipoti,* — she says, and stares at me. I turn the key, for the sake of doing something. Her look nails me, and a mischievous gleam dances in her eyes. My cell starts ringing, and I turn it off. *I topi non avevano nipoti.*

— I don't get it, — I admit.

Claudia looks pleased with herself and nods imperceptibly, lowering her eyes. When she's twenty and makes the same gesture, she's going to be gorgeous.

— We did palindromes, — she says. — You know, the phrases that read the same way backwards as forwards?

In the meantime, I exit the parking lot and advance slowly through the remainders of the parental mob, which is breaking up.

— *I topi non avevano nipoti,* the mice had no nephews, reads the same way backwards, — she adds. — Try it . . .

And I try; with a stupid smile on my face, I recite this fanciful sentence backward: itopin onaveva non ipot i.

— It's true, — I say.

I remember an English palindrome I learned at Harvard when I was a student there: Able I was ere saw I Elba. Napoleon. I was struck by the sentence, because in addition to being a palindrome it had a meaning. But "the mice had no nephews" is much better precisely because it's nonsense but, unlike the Napoleonic code, it sounds perfectly natural.

— Nice, — I say, — and why were you doing palindromes?

— Miss Gloria was explaining reversibility to us.

— Reversibility. I'm impressed. And how did she explain it to you?

— She explained that in math there are some operations that are reversible and others that are irreversible. And then she explained that the same thing happens in life. And that it's a lot better to do reversible things, if you have the choice.

— You're right. And did she give you some example of reversible things in life?

— No.

— But you thought of some, didn't you?

Claudia nodded.

— Uh-huh!

— For example? Tell me a reversible thing that you do in life.

— Get married.

— What?

— There's divorce, right? Miss Gloria told us that everything you can go back on is reversible.

And she smiles. Incredible. Her mother and I were supposed to get married ten days ago. We had decided that since Lara's parents were no longer with us, she would be accompanied to city hall by Claudia. We had bought Claudia a beautiful dress, and she couldn't wait to wear it, but her mother died before her eyes and she won't wear that dress anymore . . . This little girl is hanging by a thread, and not only can she deal with subjects of this kind, but she can even smile while she's doing it. So what can I say to her now?

— Of course.

There's traffic. We advance slowly through the river of cars with our windows down, voiding the labors of the climate control unit. The wind ruffles Claudia's hair, highlighting its beauty and shine. Only her braid stays still, to the side, next to her temples. What can I say? How can I change the subject before the conversation turns to things that are *irreversible,* instead?

— Do you know something, sweetheart? — I say. — I forgot the name of Benedetta's mamma. Is it Barbara or Beatrice?

— Barbara, — she replies. But then she adds, combatively:

— Why doesn't she want you to be a stranger?

— A stranger? Oh . . . Oh, no, sweetheart. It's just an expression. It's something we were talking about before. . .

That's what it was. About the things that upset children and the things that don't.

chapter five

Another day of summer. Another early arrival . . .

To kill time, Claudia and I played "Unfortunately" with the GPS: as our destination, we set the address of the school, then we systematically disobeyed the orders of the female voice — cold, peremptory, and quite unpleasant — that was giving us the shortest route. "Turn right NOW!" the voice said, but I answered, "*Unfortunately* I don't feel like it," and drove straight. The navigator got confused, started recalculating the route for our destination, and Claudia laughed. Then, after it was reset, the female voice started up again: "Turn left in three hundred feet." I answered, "*Unfortunately* that might be difficult." The voice insisted. "Turn left NOW!" and this time it was Claudia, while I was turning right instead, who told the navigator, "*Unfortunately* we have turned right." Once again the navigator was confounded and recalculated the route from the top, and we laughed. Because there was something so comical about the contrast between the decisiveness of those orders and the sheepish submissiveness with which, after the orders had been disobeyed, the computer started recalculating the route without protest: a kind of obtuse digital patience that automati-

cally ridicules the intransigent voice that's firing off commands;
the desperate hilarity of machines, with their blind repetition, always and everywhere, of the same things, without alternatives and
without any possible redemption besides transgression. A hilarity
that children know well, which is why they enjoy breaking things:
because they have a natural talent for finding the weak points of
any device and downright ferocity when it comes to machines.
Claudia could have kept on tormenting the GPS system tirelessly,
and her quicksilver laughter was a powerful antidote to the mal-
aise that the traffic jam was trying to insinuate into my day. So
even though disobeying the navigator made the trip — and therefore our time in traffic — last longer, we arrived at school in good
spirits; and since, on the pretext that we would have breakfast at
the café (but, in reality, because we were both ready to leave home
at a quarter past seven), we left very early, we also arrived early.
Once again, like yesterday, we found a good place to park the car,
and once again, like yesterday, we saw everyone else arriving at the
school entrance, one by one. While Claudia was chatting with her
classmates, I was exposed to new salvos of goodwill from parents
who had kept their distance yesterday because we either weren't
on close terms or were almost complete strangers — especially
the mothers, since by the second day of school the fathers have
disappeared almost completely. All good people, whose sharing
of my grief was sincere, of course, and whose names were added to
the long list of people I shouldn't hesitate to contact for anything
I needed — even if it's hard for me to imagine myself asking for
help from them, of all people. Anyway, they know perfectly well
I will never call them; but they still made the gesture and I appreciate it. Except that all this business has made time fly and the
bell rang a moment ago, catching me off guard. Claudia gave me
a kiss, walked down the corridor with Benedetta, and right away

the lump came back to my throat. And now the things I'm supposed to do (smile and watch her disappear with her classmates)
feel shamefully inadequate.

— Claudia! — I shout, and she stops. I signal for her to come
back and she does. Her friend Benedetta stops, too, but doesn't follow her, while her mother, Barbara, stares at me, and I smile back
at her. And here she is, Claudia, with the inquisitive air of someone who doesn't know what to expect. Why did I call her back? I
bend down and kiss her on the forehead, but it's obvious that this
isn't enough to justify my impulse. Why did I call her back?

— Yesterday I really did wait outside here all day, sweetheart,
— I hear myself whisper.

Her eyes open wide.

Of course. But it's not enough. The lump is still there.

— And do you know something? — I add. — I'm going to stay
here today, too. All day. Until school is out. I'll be right out here.

Now it's enough. Claudia takes in my news elegantly, without
losing her composure, but the expression on her face is amazed,
pleasantly amazed. She turns toward her friend, who is waiting
for her halfway down the corridor. Then she turns to look at me.

Amazed.

— And so, — I continue, still under my breath, — take a peek
outside the window during recess. I'll be down here.

I give her another kiss on the forehead and straighten up. I
read somewhere that European parents, unlike Americans, never
make the smart move of squatting down when they speak with
their children: I don't know if it's true, but I've always done it,
I've always bent down to speak with my daughter. It always came
to me spontaneously. Claudia looks up and doesn't say a word,
but she strokes my hand in such a delicate, languid, and perfect
way that her caress is worth all the words she doesn't say. Then
she turns around and leaves, reaching Benedetta, and the two of

them are swallowed up by the dark womb of the large and almost empty corridor.

So it's done. This is what woke me up so early this morning. This is what I had in mind. To spend the day in front of the school again today. The lump in my throat is gone.

Barbara and Nilowfer's mother (she's Egyptian, I don't remember her name) invite me to join them for a coffee at the café, and I accept. We talk about our children as if it were nothing. This is completely different from hearing promises of understanding and availability: Nilowfer had a bad case of otitis that ruined her vacation. Benedetta wrote in her new diary, "I want to be tough, sexy, and mean," something along those lines. I talk about Claudia's little cousin, Giovanni, who this summer, while he was staying with us at the seaside with his mother and little brother, uttered the most beautiful threat I've ever heard, one that should be set in stone. I explain that he's smaller and more delicate than Claudia, although they're the same age, and that he always gets picked on because Claudia is (or maybe I should say was; who knows what she's going to be like from now on) a little bit of a bully with him. I tell the story of how one morning he appeared on the beach with a brand-new scuba mask that his mother had just bought for him; he knew perfectly that Claudia would take it away from him immediately so she could use it first, the way she did with almost all his toys, but this time he decided to confront her resolutely, and he was ready, and he advanced courageously, smeared with sunblock, skinny, delicate, *inferior,* and holding on tight to the mask; and when he was right in front of my daughter, and she already had her eyes on the mask and was about to grab it without so much as asking, because that's how things usually went with them, she prevailed and he submitted, and he had accepted this state of things for so long that it had become natural by now — at that very moment, in all probability the last moment in which the mask would still be in his hands, he burst out with the first threat in his whole life: "You'd better watch out 'cause *I'm a good boy!*" That's what he said. To Claudia it didn't make any difference, it only caused a slight hesitation before the inevitable act, which happened anyway — predictable, ferocious, innocent — and the mask changed hands all the same; but to me, to his mother, to Lara, and now also to these other two mothers who, I realize, look thunderstruck, in other words, to all these adults, this little boy suddenly became a romantic hero and his sentence a kind of loser's manifesto.

We return to the front of the school, and while saying goodbye to them, I see the Down child from yesterday, holding his mother's hand as he passes by my car. I immediately press my remote key — *beep* — and he smiles contentedly, because he expected it, and once again the mother doesn't notice and drags him behind her without listening to him. Barbara and Nilowfer's mother don't notice, either. They see my gesture but take it for what it appears to be: I'm getting ready to go to the office and I unlock the car; and the funny thing is that today the child doesn't notice me, either, and so, in fact, it's become an exclusive, emotional, and secret matter between him and a black car. Dragged along by his mother, he reluctantly enters the same lobby as yesterday, and the first thing that I do, as soon as I'm alone, is to walk over there to figure out where they might be going every morning at this hour. On the panel, there are twelve buzzers, plus three elegant nameplates, in brass, of law offices, and one in Plexiglas, more common, indicating a physical therapy office on the ground floor. So that's where he goes . . .

I go back to the car and call Annalisa in the office. Annalisa, I'm going to wait in front of the school today, too. Pause. Cancel all my appointments, forward all calls to my cell phone, come here to bring me the documents that have to be signed, since it's such a nice day. Pause. I give her the address. See you in a little while. Stop. Go ahead and be shocked; go ahead and tell Emanuela, Piquet's secretary, whose desk is next door, behind the partition, in that lousy open-space layout that the Australians wanted when they bought the business several years ago and that the French, last year, when they took over, decided to dismantle but still haven't; go ahead and tell her, in a whisper, "Paladini is going to wait in front of his daughter's school all day today, too"; go ahead and release your expressions of dismay: what do I care. I can do what I want. I'm an executive; I don't have to punch in. Until they fire me I'll be the one to decide where I do my job, and if they fire me it'll be because of the merger, not because I've spent a couple of days over here.

I go back to looking up again at the big window on the third floor, third from the left. Five past nine. I wonder whether Claudia has already looked outside and didn't see me because I was at the café. But if she didn't see me, she must have seen the car, and as soon as she can she'll take another look. Of this much I'm sure: Claudia trusts me. This time I told her seriously, and she believed me. Leaning against the car, I take a look around: the traffic cop, the Pakistani cleaning windshields, the birds chirping, not many cars, not many passersby, two teenagers kissing on a park bench. Like yesterday, the surprising, bucolic tranquillity of this corner of the world comforts me, even if inside I still feel turmoil, or better the rumbling of turmoil: a kind of distant but not too distant agitation, the way the rumbling of traffic is distant but not too distant, down there, that sounds muffled and soft up here but still makes it up here anyway. Quiet chaos, I think: like the spirit that inhabited the parents gathered at the school exit yesterday afternoon, like every moment in the spirits of all the children in the world. Except that now I'm thinking about me, about this pause that continues to save me from the grief that everyone, yes, every-

one, imagines I'm feeling and that's not how it is yet. A quiet chaos
is what I feel inside. A quiet chaos.

The two teenagers on the bench are still kissing, blissfully.
What time do you think recess will start?

chapter six

List of the girls I've kissed:

*Lara, Caterina, Patrizia, Silvia, Michela, the French camper, the German
camper, Giuditta, Laura, Lucia, Gabriella, Cristina, Marina, Luisa, Betty, Antonella, Monica, Nicoletta, Amelia, the girl from Cagliari, Paola, Beatrice,
Daria, Leopoldina, Sonia, the pranotherapist friend of Sonia, Barbara, Eva, Silvia
2, Antonella 2, Eleonora, Isabelle, the German girl in Paris, Alessandra, Mar-
cella, Daniela, Isabella, Carmen, Laura 2, Annalisa, Marta, Angelica, Betta,
Maria Grazia, Mia, Claudia, Phil, Patty, Sandra, Chiara, Patricia, Valentina.*

Fifty-two. I've kissed fifty-two girls. Girls, not women, because
almost all of them came before Lara, when I was young. Almost
all of them. No, I wasn't completely faithful to Lara. It would have
been nice to be able to say that I never cheated on her, that I never
even kissed another woman when I was with her, but I can't. I
cheated on her. How many times doesn't matter — not very
many, at any rate — and the fact that I cheated on her doesn't
even matter anymore. What matters, again, is that a list I drew up
by plunging into my memories doesn't bother me. It didn't bother
me while I was compiling it, and it doesn't bother me now, when
I'm rereading it and counting the names a second time. Fifty-two.
How many girls do you think the traffic cop has kissed? And the
Pakistani windshield cleaner?

Yet despite my reluctance to dredge them up from my past —
and the risk that, in doing so, it would finally hit me — those
kisses, like Lara, are no longer here. Those kisses are no longer

kisses. They're nothing. Most of them don't even evince the memory of a kiss. They happened, and maybe even if I don't feel like remembering it now, while I was kissing each one of those girls I was
brimming with emotion, and my heart was beating hard, and I felt
good: yet nothing has remained, nothing except the authority of
this number grouping them all together and, in the brief space
of these two syllables, reawakening each of them, every last one,
conjuring up the impression of a life filled with love and passion.
So I hold on tight to the number, even if in the end it's nothing, either. But it is still a big number, an honor. It's still something you
can boast about, seated at a bar in Lorenteggio at two o'clock in
the morning, drunk as a skunk, trying to detain the last customer
before he pays his tab. "You want to know something, buddy? I've
kissed fifty-two girls." "Fantastic. Can I go now?"

— Pietro!

Jean-Claude. I recognize him even before turning around to
see him — and more than anything I'm surprised that he's come
here, and at this hour of the morning, he who never arrives in the
office before eleven. I recognize him by his French r and his raspy,
unmistakable voice. Then I turn around right away and see him.
Jean-Claude.

He comes toward me with a smile, walking slowly, in his shirt-
sleeves. Behind him is his gray Alfa Romeo, one of the perks of
being CEO, idling near the park, with Lino, the driver, at the
wheel. It's a very strange image: one of the most powerful men I
know — and among them the most brilliant, ingenious, and independent by far — coming toward me with a smile in front of my
daughter's school. What's he doing here? He's my boss, after all.
He can order me to return to the office. He can fire me. I close the
notebook with the list of kissed girls and toss it in the car, furtively,
with a sudden fear of being reprimanded.

We shake hands. How's it going, splendid day, summer's lasting longer this year, we should be at the seaside . . . He's already expressed his condolences on several occasions. He came to the funeral, sent a beautiful wreath. He was the one who told me to take as much time as I needed and to come back to the office only when I'd gotten past the acute phase.

— It's nice out here, — he says, looking around. Then he contemplates the austere school building. — Is this it?

— Yes, — I say. — Claudia's classroom is up there, the third window from the left, — and I point it out to him.

Jean-Claude looks up and stares at the window. No, he hasn't come to bring me back to the office. I stare at him, with his wild gray beard, as unruly and long as bin Laden's. It's a clamorously incongruous feature of his appearance, a kind of challenge to the conventions of the world in which he excels. A blatant affront to the West, you could say, that initially baffles people, generating an instinctive distrust, and immediately after forces you, for the sake of your peace of mind, to scan his person for all the good qualities that accompany the beard: the chiseled beauty of his features, the blue steadiness of his overpowering gaze, the cosmopolitan grace of his gestures, the refinement of his bespoke suits, the sophisticated details, like the tantric wedding ring — he's married to an Indian woman — or the vintage watch he wears on his wrist. One by one, you find yourself separating these qualities from his Taliban beard, and while you're at it you find yourself thinking of how conformist and prejudiced you are if all it takes is an unusual beard to put you on your guard when, in fact, you're facing a rare and noble creature; and someone who forces you to do all this has already conquered you.

— Is that your daughter? — he asks. I look up and see a little head popping out past the windowsill, between the suddenly opened windowpanes. *Boom boom,* my heart's in my throat: it's Claudia, yes, even if you can barely recognize her, so high up, in the shade, with such a little head amid the archaic mass of the window.

— Yes.

It's Claudia, and she waves to me. *Boom boom.* I wave to her, too. She must be smiling, even if you can't see from here, and this smile I can't even see still moves me. I must be weak, still, extremely weak, to be moved by so little: no, Jean-Claude, the acute phase is not over. He waves to her, too. This summer, when he came to visit us at the seaside with his wife, he gave her a fantastic T-shirt.

— My father was a fighter pilot, — he says, — and maybe a secret agent. He was always away. He never came to pick me up at school, not once.

His French accent softens considerably the roughness of his Marseillean voice, making it sound gentle. This is another good quality. Claudia is still at the window, and next to her is another little girl, whom I don't recognize. I look at the time: ten thirty-five. So recess must be at ten thirty. We wave to each other again.

— How's she doing? — Jean-Claude asks me.

— Fine, — I reply. — I don't understand how she gets by, but she's fine.

— Oh, Annalisa gave me some documents for you to sign, — he says. — I've got them in my car.

I feel like laughing, because life really is a mystery. You think you know someone, and then things happen that, as far as you know, are simply impossible. How did this happen? Where did Annalisa find the gumption to give the CEO the small amount of paperwork I was supposed to sign, since he was coming here?

— They took away my *aero*, my airplane, — says Jean-Claude, pronouncing it *aero*. The only defect in his Italian is that he can't pronounce the word for *airplane*. But maybe this, too, is a charming flourish.

I look at him: he smiles, but it's obvious that he's announced something terrible. The absurd breeze continues to blow, as if we weren't in Milan but rather in Izmir, Rhodes, or Tangiers, ruffling his sideburns and the tips of his beard.

— What do you mean, took away?

— Took away. A decision from Paris. I can no longer use the company jet.

Claudia waves to me one last time from upstairs, then she vanishes and the window is closed. There's no one in the park. The kissing teenagers have disappeared, the benches are empty.

— Shall we sit down over there? — I propose, and Jean-Claude nods. We walk by his car, where Lino is reading *La Gazetta dello Sport*. He looks up from his newspaper, waves to me, and goes back to reading. He's a great driver. And a Juventus fan.

On the park bench Jean-Claude lights a Gitane, then leans back and inhales deeply. I light a cigarette, too. From somewhere in the distance, the wind carries strains of music that sound like, yes, *"Cuccuruccucú Paloma."*

— Why did they take it away? — I ask.

Jean-Claude bursts out laughing.

— Budget cuts . . .

Ahiahiahiahiahi, cantava . . .

— Do you know what that means? — he adds.

— I don't think so.

— It means I'm history, Pietro.

De pasión mortal, moría . . .

— What do you mean, history? Come on, now, you're exaggerating.

I say these words for the sake of saying them, without realizing how absurd they sound. People like Jean-Claude are so far ahead of the pack, have been sitting in the lap of a most comfortable, bourgeois luxury for so long, that of course they are sincerely, atrociously pained by the thought that now, years later, they, too, have to wait in line at the airport to check in. However obscene it might sound by comparison to the suffering of other people, right now Jean-Claude is suffering like a dog: he's suffering because the meaning of the decision is clear, and so tomorrow he might receive another decision, instructing him to shave his beard before the next board meeting; but mainly, he's suffering because by now he's gotten used to traveling with his own private *aero* and was having fun inviting other people along, and piloting it also, for stretches at a time, with the captain sitting next to him saying *bravo* — he did it both times when he took me along — and now that he's told me his father was a pilot, it naturally takes on a much deeper significance, but even if that weren't the case, there is always a father lurking behind the satisfactions men seek in life — even if the jet was just a giant toy for top managers, like I thought, taking it away from him all at once, *zap,* when he was convinced that the jet was his, must have given him the same maddening and unbearable pain that my nephew Giovanni felt when Claudia tore his scuba mask out of his hands. With the difference that a high roller like Jean-Claude can't even fax a reply to Paris saying, *"Prenez garde de moi, car je suis sage!"*

Cuccuruccucú, paloma . . .

— It's true, it's just a jet. And do you know who signed the decision?

— Thierry?

— *Oui.*

Cuccuruccucú, no llores . . .

— Well, he had to sign it, didn't he?

— No. He could have had Boesson sign it. He could have pretended he didn't even know about it . . . — he takes a deep puff on his Gitane, then he slowly exhales the smoke and adds: — He betrayed me.

— But weren't you already on the outs, you and Thierry? — I ask. — Weren't you expecting it, in the end?

Rather than reply, Jean-Claude smiles, stares for a while at the cigarette butt, as if deciding whether to take another puff, then he tosses it aside.

Silence . . .

De pasión mortal, moría . . .

Tiziana. Of course. She was older than me. One night we were kissing on her bed when she got a phone call and had to run. Her daughter wasn't feeling well. Tiziana. Fifty-three.

— He betrayed me, — Jean-Claude repeats.

chapter seven

We had made a pact, Pietro. A secret pact. Because Thierry, like me, was opposed to the merger, right from the start, from the moment Boesson started to talk about it. Thierry also realized immediately what was at stake: our past, our passion, our freedom, everything. It was one year ago, believe it or not. We went out to dinner together, to da Toni, in Venice, on the island of Le Vignole — I was there for the film festival. We went to dinner, he and I, secretly, without saying a word to anybody. It was my wedding anniversary, and Elegance was with me, and she and I were supposed to go out to dinner to celebrate; but Thierry phoned from Paris and said in two hours I'm going to be at da Toni, come by yourself, don't tell anyone, we have to talk, it's important . . . And I realized that something major had happened, because that day the board had met in Paris, although I hadn't been there. I told Ely that we'd have to postpone our dinner until the next day and I left, without telling her about Thierry. Because that's how things were between us: he always came first for me, and I always came first for him.

And while I was waiting for him at the table at da Toni, beneath the trees, and I was drinking that sparkling white wine they serve and looking at the Venice skyline standing out against the reddest sunset I have ever seen anywhere, I swear, including Africa, I was overcome with emotion, Pietro: overcome and happy. I thought of all the things that we'd done together, Thierry and I, of all the impossible victories we had won, against all odds, against all logic, since the days when they derided us as *les outsiders;* and I thought of how nice my life must be if my best friend was about to come to talk to me about something very important. Don't get me wrong, very important not only for the two of us, but truly very important, for the national economy, for the stock market, for politics; something that would end up on the front page of newspapers. What was that special thing, I wondered, that made my life so nice? The world is full of top executives that go out to dinner together to decide on important things. What was so unique about my case? It was friendship, Pietro. None of those executives is *friends* with the person sitting in front of him. In fact, he often hates him. And so he doesn't drink during dinner, doesn't look at the panorama, doesn't even eat, only pretends. He listens, questions, calculates, speaks. He's a machine. He can't trust anyone, can't let down his guard, can't feel anything: he can only fight, even there, all the time. And this makes his life ugly. But I was about to have dinner with my friend, and I could enjoy the evening breeze and look at the panorama and drink the wine while I was waiting for him and his big news, and my life was beautiful.

Then he arrived and he was a wreck, and he was high, I think, because every now and then he still snorted, and, in short, he immediately, you see, immediately said that we had to stop the merger. He said this even before telling me that Boesson had spoken about a merger with the Americans that afternoon; he said, *"Jean-Claude, la fusion jamais,"* and I had to ask him, "What merger?"

because till that day no one had ever imagined that Boesson could be such a megalomaniac. He was sincere that night, Thierry; he was high, hotheaded, and sincere . . .

He had no problem convincing me: I hate Boesson, I hate all the énarques, and I also hate the Americans to boot. And we made a pact. Either we would stop it, or *both of us* would have to chop wood in front of our houses in Aspen. Either of us could have blocked it, for that matter: he had Paris, I had the International and Italy, we were the number one and the number two. With the merger, the only companies in the group that Boesson was fucking over were ours. Not the others, because the others had no soul, like almost every company in the world: simple machines to make money, to put the squeeze on the investors, to generate value. But our corporations had soul, and it was our soul, which of course couldn't be merged with something else. Boesson might compensate us, of course he would, and after the merger he might give us, say, the presidency of some cosmetics or alcohol multinational, or he might send us to Hollywood, what a laugh, to teach cinema to the Americans . . . But our soul would be fucked for all time. And so we made a pact. No to the merger, we said, and since both of us were a little buzzed, me on the wine and him on his Colombian cocaíne, we made a blood pact. Think about it: two French baby boomers sitting at a table at da Toni, who cut their palms with Toni's knife and then mix their blood together by shaking hands and toasting each other with Toni's wine. No to the merger! But it wasn't prudent for the two of us to fight it right away, and we decided that we would play good cop, bad cop: he would be the good cop — with Boesson, I mean — and I would be the bad cop. So I was supposed to say no to the merger from the beginning, and I did, I told everyone to their face, every time I could, in interviews, at board meetings, everywhere, while he, instead, was supposed to be more positive and play the part

of the peacemaker. From that night on we started arguing with
each other in front of Boesson, and even publicly: never a quarrel but contradicting each other, dissenting, arguing. To give that
piece of shit the impression that we were divided, that *les temps des
outsiders c'étaient finis.* But it was an act, don't you see, Pietro? It was
all fake. In reality we were both working to fuck over Boesson.
We knew, Pietro, that a merger of such proportions creates a very
weak god, namely Boesson, and an army of frustrated, humiliated, repressed, transferred, and fired men; we knew that it creates value in the stock market when it's announced, but then it
depreciates and cancels out the quality of the work produced by
the companies involved, and that in the long term it turns into a
failure for everyone. We knew it because we had seen it happen
before, and we had also often taken advantage of it.

So we pretended to be at odds with each other — locking
horns in a quarrel that was supposed to always create the impression it could be mended — and in the meanwhile we continued
to meet secretly, in Milan, in London, and especially in Venice,
to brief each other on the situation. And things were going well,
because, as predicted, after the euphoria and the big stock market
gains following the announcement, when the Americans started
laying down tough conditions in the negotiation, the problems
began for Boesson. He had Steiner in his sights, you see? A real
shark, an *owner* in the sense that Boesson doesn't own any of the
things he controls, while Steiner does, he controls and owns. And
however much Boesson might have had the impression that he
was getting favorable conditions — to *win* the merger, as he says,
and become God — the fact remained that *he* could be thrown
out from one moment to the next while the shark couldn't. At
those secret dinners, when everyone thought we had parted
ways and were no longer the united force that we had been for
twenty years, Thierry and I had victory right there, seated at the

table beside us: our victory was not wanting to become any bigger, not wanting to become any richer, not wanting to go any higher, wanting to stay the way we were, friends, powerful, and still relatively small. We were on the side of right, Pietro, I don't know if you get my drift. Which never happens in this world: you fight, you win or you lose, but you never feel like you're on the side of right, in the sense that there's almost never right or wrong, there's only someone who wins and someone who loses. But Thierry and I, this time, were in the right. And we laughed at the thought of Boesson, who, one fine day, when things would turn out badly for him and a simple political snag or an antitrust suit would kill the merger, would feel surrounded, surrounded and defeated. We laughed, Pietro, thinking of the day when the board of directors would take away Boesson's *aero* with a decision signed by Thierry, and he would realize . . .

It went on like this until last spring. Then Thierry and I started seeing less of each other. Once he couldn't make it, another time it was me. Our secret dinners came to an end. It didn't seem serious, even though now I feel like an idiot for not realizing right away what was happening. Unlike me, living here in Milan, peacefully, and saying what I really thought, Thierry was in touch every day with Boesson, whose megalomania must have infected him. Having spent so much time with a man who thought he was God, Thierry ended up thinking he was God, too: well, not exactly God, perhaps, but *a* god; someone who turns everything they do into right. And he betrayed me. And he let me know it only when he was sure there was no turning back; and he didn't tell me to my face, in private or at a board meeting: he took away my *aero*.

Now the merger is definitely going through. I'm out, since I was always opposed to the merger. A paranoid, Shakespearean time is about to begin for everyone. Heads will fly all over the place, others will explode by themselves, everyone will have their chance to betray, and those who don't betray will be betrayed. After having torn him away from me, Boesson will get rid of Thierry pretty easily, and when Boesson's the only one left, Steiner will eat him alive, the way he's always treated those who dared to swim too close to him. And so the Americans will land in Europe thanks to the Frenchman who wanted to land in America and the former outsider who sold his soul. That's how it'll go, according to script. It'll take months, maybe even years; how long depends on many unknown factors, but it will happen. It's like when you take a cup of boiling-hot coffee and leave it on the kitchen table: you can't say how long it will take, but you do know that the moment will definitely come when the temperature of the coffee becomes the same as the temperature of the cup, the table, and the whole kitchen . . .

From now on, I won't do anything anymore, because in reality anything I do will make things easier for them. I'll stay still, I'll wait, I'll show my face, but I'll be like those stars that are dead but continue to emit light because they are so far away. My style of working, from now on, will be to not work. My way of communicating will be to not communicate. Do the same thing, Pietro. Stay here. Stay for as long as you can.

chapter eight

And I have. I've stayed here. After all, Jean-Claude is still my boss: even if they took away his *aero,* even if he's slated to be history soon, he's still my boss. So we can put it this way: until the day his bearded head rolls on the business pages of newspapers, I'll

do whatever Jean-Claude tells me. He told me, "Stay here," and I
have. I've stayed in front of this school.

Now it's been ten days that I've been staying here from eight to
four thirty, and it doesn't even seem like that big a deal. It comes
to me naturally. Quite simply, I have the impression that I'm better off here than I would be anywhere else. Claudia is happy: a
little dismayed, perhaps, but happy; she doesn't stop paying attention in class to look out the window. She limits herself to peeking out the window when she can and waving to me. Then, when
she leaves the building, we go home and don't even talk about it.
I told her once, and it was enough: sweetheart, I told her, I've decided to remain in front of your school for a while; it's something
I'm doing for myself, and Jean-Claude agrees. She thought about
it, leaning her head to one side, and then said, "What about if it
rains?" If it rains, I replied, I'll stay inside the car. I have everything
I need to work from there. She smiled. End of story. That was six
days ago.

For two days now, it's been raining. The summer ended all at
once, the temperature dropped, and the pleasantness of this corner
of the world seems to have dissolved. But not for me. I had thermal paper inserted in the car fax, put on warmer clothes, bought
a nice new umbrella, and waited in front of the school in the rain.
I observed the changes that the beginning of fall had brought to
the neighborhood, all of them for the worse, but I continued to
feel good. I worked, doing the little you can in a company that's
paralyzed: I received people in my car, or at the café opposite the
school, and I signed the contracts I was supposed to sign. I repeat:
although it might sound like a big deal, it really wasn't. It's something between me and myself, mostly, besides being between me
and my daughter; a wish that I have and that I fulfill every day.
Rarely have I felt so focused on a single wish that is so satisfying and
— let me come right out and say it — so *exciting* to fulfill: to leave

the house every morning with the curiosity you should always
have, but never really do, to discover variations on the theme that
you've decided to give the day: it's a very pleasant feeling that in
and of itself would be enough to make me stay here. If I, then, compare it to what I expected to feel, given the situation, I feel blessed.
I'm supposed to be grieving: all of a sudden, a finger pointed at me
and a voice thundered, "You, Pietro Paladini! Grieve!" But I'm not
grieving, you see, and I can spend all my time with my daughter,
which is what I want, and retreat from the daily bedlam that is
wearing out all my colleagues; and I can remember, compile my
lists, look at people on the street, and go home to watch TV and
eat and sleep like before; and if this isn't a miracle, it's pretty damn
close. And it doesn't make me feel guilty. My wife is dead, and I'm
not grieving. I don't know how long it will last, but for now that's
how it is: I'm not grieving, and I don't feel guilty.

How are other people reacting? Not that it matters, but that's
the most surprising thing about this business. Everyone knows by
now, also because I don't hide it — nor could I: how can you hide
the fact that you spend the whole day in front of a school? Everyone around here knows by now: the teachers, the custodians, the
other parents, the guys at the café, the men at the newsstand, the
traffic cop — the one in the morning even saves a parking spot
for me — and their reaction is a mix of respect and sympathy,
although, given our lack of familiarity, no one dares to comment
on or even talk about it. I stay here from eight to four thirty, and
for these people that's fine. Maybe, I told myself, it's because I'm
considered a *big shot:* I suddenly realized that being an executive at
a cable TV channel to which everyone either subscribes or wishes
they subscribed is a prestigious position; and if, after your wife dies,
you do such an unusual but clearly inoffensive thing as spending
every day in front of your daughter's school, that prestige counts
in the eyes of others. It's not right, of course, and there was a time

when, like many others, I, too, fought against this trend: but that's still the way of the world. If a relatively well-to-do and powerful man like me does it, then it's accepted and respected; if, let's say, a day laborer does it, then it's suspect. Maybe I'm wrong — which would be nice, meaning that we didn't fight in vain — but in my opinion that's the way things are. I see it, I feel it: the simpler they are, the more people feel honored that I'm here. Strangers are no problem.

A little different, but even more surprising in the end, is the reaction of friends and family. Since they're close to me, they use their intimacy; they feel authorized to ask, to object, to try to dissuade me. But it's an effort that lasts only a few minutes. Whether they drop by in person or simply phone me, they, too, after a while, accept that I am here in front of the school all day. It's odd how simple things can be, after all: quite simply, they accept it. I realize that everyone starts out with the suspicion that I might have gone a little crazy, and their first approach is mainly to check up on me: have I by any chance lost my mind? But I haven't lost my mind, and by answering their questions, telling them the truth, I show them. There's nothing wrong with my being here: I'm not neglecting my work or my person, I'm not shirking any of my duties, and I even have a kind of unlimited authorization from my boss — whose cruel fate is not yet known to anyone. They're forced to accept it. Over the past few days, I've repeated the same lines to a bunch of people, who are, in order: my secretary; my brother; my sister-in-law, Marta; my aunt Jenny; my two colleagues Enoch and Piquet — and even my father, who called, from Switzerland, to ask me what was going on. But I always had to tell them only once, never twice, because evidently my explanations must have been reassuring. And not only: I even got the impression that, after I reassured them, just about all of them envied me. I got this impression because I know them well, and I know that none of them is happy, although I'm maybe not completely up to date on the actual issues complicating their existence. Starting with the certainty that I'm grieving — but here there's a misunderstanding, because I'm not grieving — and imagining me stranded in front of my daughter's school like a vagabond, and seeing instead that I'm enjoying an entirely unexpected peace of mind and rationality, they must have thought of their own suffering and of how standing still in one specific corner of the world was a happy move that might extend some peace to them, too, if only they had the courage to do it; something along the lines of "I'm stopping here. Go on ahead without me," which is not what I did but rather what they would like to do — but they can't. Envied in this sense, is what I'm saying.

But maybe I'm exaggerating, and the biggest mistake I'm making is to generalize: my brother, for example, still seems somewhat perplexed and is maybe only postponing his objections until he comes to Milan — he lives in Rome — well aware of the fact, having experienced it more than anyone else, that no matter how hard it is to do in person, it's absolutely impossible to get me to change my mind over the telephone.

If I'm exaggerating, on the other hand, it's because things have happened that deserve consideration. I've received two rather strange visits, each one quite terrible in its own way. One yesterday and one this morning. One from my colleague Piquet and one from my sister-in-law, Marta. They had both been here already some days ago, like everyone else, to inspect my mental state, and one afternoon Marta came back with her children to wait for Claudia at the exit from the school; but they were very normal visits: Piquet and I spoke about the situation at the company while with Marta I spoke about family matters, vacation plans, and issues related to Lara's estate. Normal visits. But the ones yesterday and this morning were not, they were not normal visits, and not because of what Piquet and Marta had purportedly come here to do: shoot the breeze, keep me company, or put to rest any lingering doubts they had over my mental condition. They came here to suffer: both of them, like Jean-Claude. They came to me to unload all their pain on me, blindly, relentlessly, in front of this school.

Piquet arrived yesterday afternoon at around two thirty, in a taxi, in the pouring rain. He got into my car, sat down next to me, and looked at me for a while, forcing himself to smile but saying nothing. His gaze, which is already paranoid on a normal basis, blinking and shifting side to side, was like a flock of birds after a gunshot, darting off in every direction in a fatal frenzy: the gaze of a person in grave danger. His ugliness, which was usually compensated for by a rather assertive elegance and harsh and insistent facial expressions, seemed to be naked in its complete helplessness: his acne-scarred complexion, his no-lipped mouth, his abnormal protruding forehead — like a cassowary, Claudia had remarked; and Lara and I, who had never heard of cassowaries, confirmed her simile when we looked it up in a science book. Although Piquet looked at me, he was really demanding to be looked at, because of his obvious state of shock, and finally he asked me whether he couldn't talk to me about a personal matter. I said yes, but in reality it wasn't so natural, because Piquet and I had never spoken about personal matters; indeed the only personal thing between us in the past had been his alleged aversion for me, motivated by my appointment to an executive position that everyone coveted, which had led him to circulate lugubrious predictions of my future at the company that were totally unjustified but descriptive enough for some people to start calling me "dead man walking." Then, over time, our relationship smoothed out, he even apologized, and I have to admit that he turned out to be a loyal colleague, but we never did establish the intimacy that would have made it natural to talk to each other about our respective personal affairs. But I said yes anyway — what was I supposed to do? So he lit a cigarette and remained in silence for a little while longer, as if to assess his last chance of not speaking at all and of leaving as he had come, without saying a word. Then he started, sparing me no details: he summarized a series of things that I already knew, namely that two years ago he had left his wife and son to take up with a young and beautiful designer, Francesca; that his wife hadn't taken it at all well and had dragged him through a huge legal battle; that his son had taken it even worse and started to manifest strange psychosomatic disturbances (actually, I didn't know this); and that nevertheless he was happier with the designer than he had ever been. Everyone knew these things; at the office it was common knowledge and fodder for gossip — obviously, in his absence. More stuff about his wild life with this Francesca, the wild sex they had every night, the profound interior rebirth he had consequently achieved, and at that point you didn't have to be a genius to know the lengths to which he would go to shield his personal affairs. But I never could have predicted what Piquet was getting ready to tell me. He continued to expatiate for a while longer, accurately describing the transition from the blind passion phase to a more conscious bonding, the important step of moving in together — something else that I was well acquainted with, since it's always the same, always the same when a man leaves his wife for a younger woman, as I had been told many times. All without neglecting the viciousness he'd suffered at the hands of his ex-wife, the pain of seeing his son overcome by twitching and stuttering, and finally the growing sense of frustration in the office caused by the rumblings of the imminent Great Merger.

At this point it had stopped raining, and I proposed that he continue his story outside. He had smoked one cigarette after the other, polluting the car — in which I, on account of Claudia, carefully avoid smoking. We got out, although he, in his Replay jacket, was dressed too lightly not to feel the cold. We walked as far as the park, which we couldn't enter on account of the rain, and we stopped at a random point on the sidewalk, like two drug dealers. It wasn't a good place to talk, but Piquet kept smoking like a fiend and I didn't want him in the car anymore. But for him this place was fine; he was just impatient to continue his story.

— And so, — he began, — one evening, last June, I invited Tardioli over for dinner. On the spur of the moment; we had been working on the budget for the Venice Festival and as usual there wasn't enough money, and as usual your friend Jean-Claude told us it was our problem, and we worked late, till around nine. When I'm getting ready to knock off I see Tardioli, all by his lonesome; I know that his girlfriend broke up with him, I know that at home there's no one waiting for him, and I tell him to come over to dinner at my place. He gets all shy, says he doesn't want to be a bother, you know how he is, and I tell him to knock it off, if there isn't enough to eat at home we'll go to a restaurant. And he comes. I think of informing Francesca, but then I change my mind and don't telephone, we'll be home in ten minutes anyway. We get home, go in, and Francesca's in the kitchen ironing. She works like a dog, but then she gets her mind set on ironing; I must have told her a thousand times, why are you ironing, we've got Lou, that's what she's paid to do, let her do the ironing, relax. But she ignores me, says that the maid doesn't know how to iron, that she ruins the clothes, and that basically ironing is a way of relaxing for her, even if I don't think so. At any rate, Francesca is in the kitchen ironing. Hi sweetheart, hello honey, from the hall. I tell her that we have Tardioli over for dinner, and if she prefers we can go out for dinner. And she calls out, still from the kitchen, that she doesn't feel like going out, she'd be happy to cook some pasta, and apologizes to Tardioli for not coming out to say hello, but she's finishing ironing a shirt. I tell her that I can cook the pasta, she says not to bother, that she'll take care of it. Nice, peaceful; normal, in other words. I was going slow, because for a little while now, I don't know, we'd been starting to read each other wrong: misunderstandings, mix-ups like "Wasn't I the one that was supposed to come?" "No, we had agreed that I was supposed to come," and such. Silly things, apparently, but I didn't underestimate them, because two people who live together should understand each other, no? It's no good if they don't understand each other. This is why I insisted on the idea of going to a restaurant: because she's in there ironing after working all day, and I'm bringing her an unexpected guest, and the idea of having to start cooking might piss her off — right? But she repeats that she's fine with staying home and that as soon as she finishes ironing she'll come and have a gin and tonic with us. All this via the corridor, you remember my house? Tardioli and I in the living room, Francesca in the kitchen, and all this shouted from either end of the corridor. I get busy making the gin and tonics, Tardioli sits down on the sofa, and after five minutes she appears, holding a big pile of pressed clothes in her hands. Smiling, pretty, relaxed. She hands the pile of clothes over to me and says: "Could you throw them out the window, please?" I'm dumbfounded. "What did you say?" I ask, and she, with the exact same expression, Pietro, the same smile, the same tone of voice, and the same cadence as before, says: "Could you place them on the armchair, please?" I took the pressed clothes, but I was speechless, because the first time she said to throw them out the window, I was absolutely sure of it. Francesca goes to Tardioli, apologizes again, gives him a peck on the cheek as if it were nothing . . . And so I do something, instinctively, yes, I say stop everything and I ask Tardioli, who was there and must have heard, I ask him to repeat what Francesca said the first time. Francesca doesn't understand, Tardioli is embarrassed, but I persist, I ask him to repeat what Francesca said the first time. *The first time,* I insist, and not the second. And Tardioli, you know how shy he is, turns all red, lowers his eyes, and says, in a tiny voice, "She said: Could you throw them out the window, please." Jesus. Thank God he was there, otherwise who knows how long that story of our not understanding each other would have lasted. Francesca bursts out laughing: "What did I supposedly say?" and starts to think we're teasing her, like we'd gotten together to play a joke on her. She doesn't want to believe us. I tell her again: I'm serious, Francesca, we're not joking, you asked me to throw the clothes out the window, he heard it, too; she keeps going with the idea that it's a joke, laughs, says to cut it out, but I insist, it's become important, dammit, you can't just leave something like this alone; Francesca, I tell her, you asked me to throw these clothes out the window, and at that point she gets pissed off. All of a sudden she's really pissed off and says that she knows perfectly well what she said, says that both of us are deaf and need professional help; we're either stoneheads or shitheads, to keep the joke going, and at that point I drop it. I drop it, Pietro, because I realize she's *sincere,* do you get it? I know her inside out, I know when she's pretending and when she's sincere, and that night she was sincere. She was really convinced that she hadn't said anything. I drop it, and Tardioli drops it, too, go figure, we tell her that the two of us must have misheard her, that she had the pile of clothes in front of her mouth, that it can happen, of course, sometimes you're sure you heard something and instead something else is said, and in fact it was too absurd, the clothes from the window, ha ha, in other words the crisis is over. Francesca calms down right away, prepares a nice dinner, we eat out on the balcony, drink, talk, laugh, joke, the swallows, the jasmine, and when Tardioli leaves, Francesca and I make love on the sofa, clothes on, and then again in bed, clothes off, and we fall asleep tired and happy. But she said it, Pietro, that's what she said. She asked me to throw the clothes out the window, I swear . . .

Only then did Piquet pause, and only because it had started raining again. He spoke for, I don't know, ten minutes straight almost without stopping to catch his breath, his deer-caught-in-the-headlights eyes, the crushed, defeated look on his face. A sudden downpour came, and we ran to the car again, and right at that moment Claudia showed her face at the window and waved to me. I waved back while getting into the car with Piquet, and Claudia immediately disappeared: she must have thought I was working, that the cassowary had come on some business matter — I've been out here for ten days and it already seems normal to her that I work from my car. But there was nothing normal about that moment: Piquet was beside himself, and I didn't know what to say, so in the car I said nothing, I put on a CD — always the same one, the one I've been listening to ever since I've been here, a CD by Radiohead that I didn't even know I had, because it must be Lara's, she must have left it here — and I even lit a cigarette, *me*. The rain beat against the windshield and we got as wet as drowned rats. Piquet's hair was standing straight up in the middle of his head. He no longer looked like a cassowary: he *was* a cassowary. Who knows what he was thinking; maybe he was ashamed, maybe he realized the absurdity of what he was doing. Why was he telling this to me, of all people? And in the end he, too, was quiet, and his silence was taut, the silence of a rope about to break. I realized that he needed me to ask him a question, to give him the illusion he was satisfying my curiosity, so he could start talking again.

— And then what happened? — I asked him, but I had no desire to know. Whatever it was, it had to be ugly.

— What happened? — he said, starting to laugh. — All hell broke loose, that's what happened. She did the same thing again two more times over the summer. Francesca would say something awful or absurd, I would ask her: "What did you say?" and she would say something else that was completely normal, in the exact same tone, and I would forget about it. Once, at dinner, I asked her to pass me the salt, but like that, nicely, I didn't tell her that her fucking salad had no taste, I simply asked her to please pass me the salt, and passing me the salt, she, smiling, told me: "I'll pass the salt up your ass" — I swear to God. And me: "What did you say, Francesca?" And she: "You're right, it needs more salt." And then in August, in a boat, while we were docking in Porto Vecchio, in front of a couple of friends who had gone on a cruise with us, she comes near me, holding some boat fenders, and says: "This is the last time, you fucking asshole." Our friends turned around to look at me, appalled. I said: "Huh?" and she, all innocent, raises her voice so I can hear her better and says: "I said that I'll put in the fenders!" This really happened!

He stopped speaking for a moment, laughing like a maniac, then he stopped laughing and asked me what CD I was listening to. I told him Radiohead, and he sat in silence for a while to listen; it was the point when the song goes, "We are accidents waiting to happen." He commented on this line, saying he liked it. But you could see he wasn't done yet. In fact, a little while later:

— But last night she went too far. Last night she really went too far. I couldn't keep on acting like nothing was happening, Pietro, and last night I told her. Francesca, I told her, there's something wrong with you. You say these awful things without even realizing it, I can't keep pretending. Calmly and placidly, but I told her. Tonight, I told her, at dinner with Fiorenza and company, you really put your foot in it and everyone heard, don't you realize? They heard. And so we start the whole story over again. She goes, "What did I supposedly say?" I repeat it, to the letter, because I'll never forget it, and she immediately gets pissed off, BAM, like that night with Tardioli, and you know I never said anything to her about it since then. She got pissed off, denied everything, but since I insisted, I tried to stay calm and considerate but I insisted, she told me that I was the crazy one, do you get it, *me,* she actually told me that I'm not normal and that I frighten her, and she went to spend the night at her sister's. That's exactly what happened!

Piquet's story was starting to irritate me more and more. I was really embarrassed. The bad part was that, the way he told it, so wild-eyed, made me think that he really was the crazy one — and he had been next door to me in the office, for years, and at that moment he was also in my car: it's not a very pleasant sensation. But at the same time, there was something plausible in it that led me to believe him and to imagine that his Francesca was possessed by a ruthless syndrome that, every now and then, and unbeknown to her, would make her suspend for one moment her daily struggle to paper over with banality the evil harbored within her — since she was sick to death of the cassowary man with whom she had rashly linked herself, though she still could not admit it. So in the end, rather than force me to choose who was crazier, him or her, Piquet's story made me think they both were, in that desperate way, innocuous to the rest of the world, that people who think they love each other sometimes realize they don't and go crazy, and realize it was only a serotonin surge at a critical moment in their lives, and they end up hating and mortally wounding each other until the day they leave each other for good. That's why I didn't like this story and it made me so uncomfortable. And then I was curious, morbidly curious, I would say, against my better judgment, to know what Francesca had said the night before, but I didn't know whether Piquet had consciously neglected to tell me or whether, as I thought, he was so upset that he didn't even realize he hadn't said it. This, too, was unpleasant. He stopped talking again, but he wasn't done, you could see it, and all I could do was stare at the clock in the dashboard. Three fifty: in the worst of cases this situation would last another half hour, then Claudia would leave school and it would all be over.

— I went to Tardioli this morning, — Piquet told me after a long silence. — He's the only witness I have. He knows I'm not crazy.

— And what did he tell you?

— Because it might even be true, you know. I can't take it anymore: my wife is persecuting me, my son is sick, that damn merger is wearing us all out . . . It might even be true that Francesca never said those things, that I was only hearing them because I'm going nuts. If Tardioli hadn't been at my house that night, you know, I think that I'd go see a psychiatrist. It would be easier, after all: Doctor, I've been hearing things, I'm sick, please cure me, give me some pills. End of story. It would be easier. But Tardioli was there, he heard, he saw. And the first thing I did this morning was go to him. With the hope, I swear, that he didn't remember anything. No clothes from the window, nothing whatsoever. With the hope that he'd look at me like I was crazy . . .

— And instead?

— And instead he wasn't in. He's in Paris, can you guess why? For the merger.

At that point Piquet laughed, then he dug his cell phone out of his pocket, turned it on, and called a taxi. It was still raining, but not so hard. He didn't remember the name of the street, he asked me, I told him. He waited for them to give him the taxi's number, then he hung up and turned the cell off.

— Well, Pietro, I'm off, — he said. — Sorry for going on like that, I really mean it. You must think I'm an egotist: here you are with your own cross to bear, and I come telling you all about my little problems. But I couldn't keep this frog inside anymore, not after last night.

— Don't worry about it, — I mumbled, — you did good to get
it off your chest.

— In the office you can't talk with anyone, you know. I don't
have any true friends. You're the only person I trust. Maybe because, — he sniggered, — I was unfair to you some time ago . . .

— Water under the bridge.

— Yeah . . .

He embraced me, kissed my cheeks, told me "hang in there,"
and got out of the car — absurdly, seeing as it was still raining,
he didn't have an umbrella, and the taxi still hadn't arrived. He
circled around me and came close to my window, signaling me to
lower it. I did.

— Please don't say anything about this to anyone. We're already vulnerable enough at the company: if people found out
something like this, I'd be dead.

— No need to worry, — I told him.

— Plus, I'm ashamed, Pietro. Above all, don't tell anyone what
Francesca said last night. I beg you . . .

So I had understood correctly: *he didn't realize* that he hadn't
told me.

— No problem, — I answered. — I won't tell a soul.

Leaning against the window in the rain, wet, imploring, his
eyes bloodshot with suffering, yet completely focused on trying
to smile, he reminded me of Harvey Keitel in *Bad Lieutenant,* when
he molests the two little girls.

— Thanks, Pietro.

But much uglier than Harvey Keitel. Much more ridiculous:
with his Pleistocene forehead and teenager's jacket to make him
look thin. I hate to say it, and maybe I have no right, having heard
myself called "dead man walking" because of his envy, and so it
might sound like some kind of a vendetta: but he was ridiculous.
There was nothing glamorous about him: there could have been

— a man trapped in the jaws of a big city, stressed out, threat-
ened by danger from all sides and alone in his sorrow, waiting for
a taxi in the rain at four o'clock in the afternoon to go back to the
hellhole that awaited him wherever he went; maybe there actually was *supposed* to be something glamorous about him; but there
wasn't: he was merely ridiculous.

chapter nine

And this morning, Marta.

   Marta is my sister-in-law, but I have a very hard time calling her
sister-in-law. She's always been gorgeous, and one morning thirteen years ago, when she was nineteen, rather than go to school
she went downtown to do some window-shopping with a friend.
All of a sudden something happened, or rather, two things happened, and her good looks went public: at the Krizia boutique on
Via della Spiga, a drug addict committed armed robbery, ran out of
the store, and fired a gunshot into the air; at that very moment, a
Japanese tourist (who was later discovered to be a spy sent to Italy
to copy designs) was taking a picture of the window. All hell breaks
loose: shouts, the addict gets away, the terrified salesgirls leave, the
police arrive, Marta and her friend slip away and don't want to be
seen. The next day the newspapers print the photo taken by the
Japanese guy, thanks to which the drug addict is identified and
arrested, and this is what it shows: Marta, in the foreground, to
the right, a dead ringer for Natalie Wood in *Splendor in the Grass,* in
perfect focus even if she was turning around quickly, with a lock
of hair flying up from the movement, and in her eyes there's an
expression of irrepressible joy (a joy that she was obviously not
feeling, since it was a case of surprise, rather, or maybe shock, because of the gunshot that had just gone off), and the robber in

the background, with his weapon in one hand and the bag with the loot in the other, recognizable but completely insignificant in comparison to her. The girlfriend is gone: she was cut out by the photo editor. A fantastic shot, filled with beauty and movement. Seen by millions of people, including me; it was the first time I saw Marta. Like all of those people, when I saw the photo I didn't think of the robbery, or the chance taking of the photo at that moment, or the rotten luck of that poor devil who'd end up paying for much more than the wrongs he had committed: I only thought of how beautiful that girl was. I had just moved to Milan, I had a contract as a writer for a show on Canale 5. I fixated on convincing the other writers to track her down so she could work on our show. It took us a couple of days, but we did. She came for an audition and got the job. I took her to dinner the next evening, and on that same night, to my great surprise, I ended up in bed with her. After me, three other guys who worked on the same program went to bed with her, including the host, who was famous, and all this before the program even began. In September Marta had her debut on the show, but she was already well known: the photo of the robbery had been purchased by a company that made hair-care products, and it appeared in newspapers all over Italy, on posters along the highways, on the buses. The show was a hit, and Marta became a TV star.

It was then that I met Lara, her older sister: every now and then she would accompany Marta to the tapings, and she wasn't as pretty, as young, or nearly as dangerous as Marta. We fell in love, as they say, and started going out. The next year, in a bit of a surprise, Lara got pregnant: we decided to keep the baby and moved in together. During the same period, in an even bigger surprise, Marta got pregnant, too, by a choreographer, but when she also decided to keep the baby, the choreographer dumped her. She lost her job, had the baby, struggled to make ends meet, started working for television again, but by then the winds had shifted, and it wasn't easy. Then, when the baby was four, the winds shifted again, and Marta was hired to host an important program on fashion. The show was a hit, but she got pregnant, by the producer this time, and the whole story started all over again: she wanted to keep the baby, the producer dumped her, she couldn't host the second season of the show because she had to give birth, and she hit bottom. A really ugly period followed. Marta lost all interest in work, in her looks, in the future, and even in her children, and devoted herself to relentless self-destruction; but when she seemed on the verge of completing it, her parents suddenly died, first one, then the other, in the space of six months, and she stopped. She was twenty-seven and she was still gorgeous, but she had two little children and nothing was going her way. She decided to forget about television, bought a house with her inheritance money, got herself out of trouble, and started hanging out with Lara and me more regularly. She devoted a lot of time to her children and started taking acting classes. She had an affair with a married architect; it lasted a year and a half, but when he left his family to be with her, she dumped him. From that moment on she got into the esoteric, macrobiotics, ayurvedic medicine, and yoga. She started working in the theater, small stuff, with a lot of enthusiasm and not much satisfaction. Then this summer she came and stayed with us at the seaside and was content because in December she's doing Beckett's *Happy Days,* as the lead and with a good company. She had even started acting like a sister-in-law: she helped Lara with the wedding preparations, took care of the children on evenings that Lara and I went out to eat, made the picnic table outside a riot of flowered tablecloths, and even cooked — Mexican food, no less, and once even sushi. Then she went back to Milan, we stayed at the seaside for another week, and at the end of that week Lara died. So at the age of thirty-two Marta is still very beautiful, still looks like

Natalie Wood, and is practically alone in the world. I really can't call her sister-in-law.

This morning, three hours ago, she called to say that we had to talk. I told her to come by whenever she wanted, and she said she'd come right away. She arrived fifteen minutes later, in her battered old Renault Twingo, and she passed close to me, indicating that she was looking for a parking spot. I stayed in the car, since it was raining, and my eyes followed her through the windshield. I saw her stopping about sixty feet ahead, where there was a guy talking on his cell phone by the open window of a Smart car. Through gestures, she asked him whether he was leaving and he nodded yes but kept talking on the phone while Marta waited in the middle of the street. A short line started to form behind her while the guy kept talking on the phone as if it were nothing. An elderly man at the wheel of a Peugeot, right behind her, lost his patience and started honking his horn; other cars farther back did the same, and Marta had to stick her head out the window to explain, still using gestures, that she was waiting to take the Smart car's place. The guy finished his phone call, closed his umbrella, jumped in his car very calmly, spent a little time rummaging through God knows what, and finally took off, leaving the spot free. Marta shifted into gear but immediately took the wrong angle, cutting too close, and wasn't able to center it. She went into reverse, but when she tried again she made exactly the same mistake and got stuck again. The old man started honking his horn again, and so immediately did the other people behind him. Marta shifted into reverse to try again, but in the meantime she'd gone even farther off track, and at that point the maneuver she needed to enter the spot had gotten too complicated. The old man in the Peugeot literally glued himself to the horn, getting all the others going as well — and the line had gotten long: an infernal racket. I got out of my car to help her, waved my hand to tell her to wait for me, but she went forward, driven savagely by the horns of the line of cars, trying again to park in the free space at the usual wrong angle, and ended up getting trapped with her side stuck in the bumper of the car parked next to her, a brand-new Citroën C3. It sounded like every horn in Milan was honking at her, and I saw her turn around, overwhelmed by the noise, with the side of her Twingo stuck in the other car, unable to move either forward or backward; I was at a distance, but in her eyes I could still distinguish a flash of true desperation, during a long moment when she must have tried one last time to tackle the situation, after which her head turned around and her arms started whirling about her. The old man was starting to climb out of his Peugeot, and I scared him back in. When I got to the Twingo, Marta was emptying her purse onto the seat: cosmetics, keys, change purse, diary, mints, Kleenex, receipts, scraps of paper, scattered all over the seat, while the blaring horns echoed like the trumpets of Armageddon. I dove in, by which time Marta had also emptied her pockets: more keys, more scraps of paper, candies, change. "Marta," I said, "move over," but she was beside herself: a look of defeat, a blissed-out smile on her lips, she was starting to get undressed: off with her jacket, off with her sweater, her boots. She was doing it with an urgency but also a strange, tempered serenity, as if she were freeing herself from all this stuff before plunging into the sea, knowing she would be swallowed by a whale that would keep her safe forever in its belly. In the meantime the old man had gotten out of the Peugeot and was shouting at her rear window. I slipped into the driver's seat, crushing the half-naked Marta against the door on the passenger's side so I could reach the pedals with my feet, grabbed ahold of the steering wheel, and shifted into first. For two infinitely long seconds, the noise from the metal on the side of the car against the bumper of the C3 covered the noise of the horns and sounded truly catastrophic — the sound of an irreparable event — but then it all came to an end: the Twingo was no longer in the middle of the street, the line disappeared, and silence returned. I relaxed, moved over to the side, trying not to ruin Marta's things scattered all over the seat; as soon as I'd stopped crushing her against the door, she smiled at me, finished unbuttoning her blouse, and sat there in her brassiere. Only then did I realize her stereo was playing the same song by Radiohead that Piquet had noticed — the one that says, "We are accidents waiting to happen."

A half hour later, we were sitting at a table at the café in front of the school. Marta was crying, but she had calmed down because I kept repeating to her that everything was taken care of — and it was true, everything was taken care of. Sobbing, she told me she needed to get out, in the open, and we did. It had stopped raining. We passed by the school, crossed the path of the Down syndrome boy and his mother, I played the usual game with the car alarm, and I told her about the secret between me and the child. She stopped crying, she smiled. We sat down on a park bench and, smiling, Marta told me what she had to say.

— I'm pregnant, — she told me.

— Jesus Christ! Who's the father?

— The set designer. A boy younger than me.

— How much younger?

— Six years.

— Does he know?

— No. We've stopped seeing each other.

— What do you mean, you've stopped seeing each other? What about the play?

— We see each other at rehearsals sometimes. But we're not together anymore.

— How many months along are you?

— Four.

She started crying again, maybe because she guessed what I was thinking: if it's four months, that means that in August, at the seaside, she already knew but she kept it hidden from us — most of all she kept it hidden from Lara. And now Lara is gone.

It was very hard to tell her anything. I'm not her father, I'm not her brother, I'm not even the father of one of her children, but suddenly I'm all Marta has in the world, and in fact I am the one she has come to: it was up to me to tell her something. Except that it was hard, and I didn't tell her anything. I hugged her, that's what I did. I hugged her close, and she kept crying in my arms, sniffing that she was unlucky, that now she was going to lose the part in the play and would end up with her ass on the ground, like always, like always . . .

I couldn't say how long our hug lasted — for a while, anyway — and the situation was embarrassing me, among other reasons, because almost all the eyes that could see us — the custodians, the teachers, the newspaper man — belonged to people who had only recently adjusted to considering me the widowed father of one of the schoolgirls and none of them knew that Marta was my sister-in-law. But no one probably saw us: it was completely deserted out there at that hour. Someone who definitely did see us was the girl who always takes her golden retriever to the park — she's very pretty, too — who doesn't know a thing about me and, although we see each other every day, we never say hello: but to her face, on the contrary, to the brazen look she gave me in the midst of that hug, I actually felt proud that I could be mistaken for the lover of someone like Marta — because it meant that I could have been hers, too. It was a wicked thought, I have to admit, of a narcissism, an egotism, and a superficiality that amazed me, given the situation; but I had it, and hiding it wouldn't do anything to make me a better person. Nor was it a particularly noble moment for Marta, who had just lost her sister but was suffering for com-

pletely different reasons, and I truly hope that Lara is not spending
all her time "looking down upon us from heaven," as so many
people told Claudia, to console her, or at least that Lara was momentarily distracted: Marta and I were the persons closest to her,
and rather than hugging and crying over the immense void left
by her death, here we were reacting to something completely different. Marta was thinking of the evaporation of her part in *Happy
Days* and I of what a beautiful, unknown woman thought of seeing
me in Marta's arms. Reprehensible. Yet while we were hugging
I did not feel any of the moral abasement I feel now in remembering it, of being either truly ashamed or genuinely proud to be
seen in her arms, by the same token as she — I sensed it clearly
— was truly desperate over the new mess in which she'd gotten
herself; and quite simply, Lara had nothing to do with any of this.
For the duration of our embrace it was as if our bodies, glued to
each other so tenderly, conspiratorially, and sensually, deflected
each other's sense of guilt over excising Lara from our thoughts,
and even completely short-circuited it. I'm saying this now, some
three hours later, to explain what happened next, when the embrace was over. Because although I had said nothing, had asked no
questions, and had been careful not to remark that there is such
a thing as the Pill in the world, goddamn it, and condoms, especially if you go to bed with teenagers whom you break up with one
month later, and especially if you already have two children by
two different men and you've decided to set your life in order; as
I was saying, although I kept my mouth shut, Marta stopped crying, pulled away from me all of a sudden, and gave me a spiteful
look. Why? And why did she say to me the things she then started
saying? Thinking back, I'm convinced that it had something to do
with the sense of guilt that her body glued to mine was able to
stifle, which couldn't be contained when we were apart.

    What Marta said to me from that point on was . . .

— Have you already started? — she said, and began to cry again.

— To do what?

— To stop smiling?

— Who?

— You, people, everybody.

There was spite in her eyes. Spite.

— Like the last time, the same, — she insisted. — What is it you don't like? Why is it that when children turn four you stop smiling at them?

I kept my mouth shut. It was absurd to defend myself from such an accusation, which I couldn't understand; but to her it didn't matter. She started in on me as if I did.

— You don't realize it, do you? — she continued. — Yet you do it, everyone does, as if you were obeying some fucking law. Well, could you tell me, please, where it's written that when a child turns four people should stop smiling at it? So why not stop smiling at it earlier? Why bother smiling at it when it's in a baby carriage, for Christ's sake? You bust your ass, keep your eye on your child day in and day out, make sacrifices, care for it, and it's not as if you're asking for something in return, you do it and that's all there is to it. Then you go out, take it to the doctor, to nursery school, go there to pick it up, drag it along with you to the supermarket, and everyone that you meet, everyone, even those fucking tourists, when they run into you with your child, they smile at you. They smile at the child, because of the child, but they also smile at you, smile at what the two of you are together. It's nice, you know, and it's also right, yes, it's right to smile at a mother taking a walk with her child. Everyone does the right thing, in other words, and you get used to it, am I making sense? Those smiles are energy being made available to you, and you get used to having it available, you start to think that, no matter how messed up your life is, there are still big smiles for you out there,

there's energy, and this calms you down. People smile at you, at least there's that. But then, all of a sudden, from one day to the next, it stops: it happened with Giovanni, when he turned four, and I felt horrible. I went into the shops, walked down the streets, *came to visit you,* and no one smiled at me anymore. What is it, I wanted to ask, is he too big? At the age of four? What, you don't like him anymore? What's wrong? Why the fuck aren't you smiling anymore? Then Giacomo was born, and you started smiling again, everyone did. There was not a single time I left the house with Giacomo that you all didn't smile at me whenever you ran into me. You, too, don't fool yourself, don't go making that face, I noticed it, you all behaved the same way. In the baby carriage, in the baby sling, and then when he started walking and I pranced along next to him holding him by the hand: it was a flash, a goddamn instant, but when our eyes would cross, you all smiled again, all of you, and I went back to feeling the energy of those smiles, and to helping myself to them. But now that Giacomo has turned four, too, you've stopped again, and I can't stand it. I'd understand if you stopped when he turned eight or nine, it would still be hard to accept, but I'd understand; but at the age of four it's too soon. It's too soon . . .

While she was saying this, Marta was looking at me with spite, I repeat, as if she considered me personally responsible for all of this stuff about the smiles, *the leader* of all those who had stopped smiling. I continued to keep my mouth shut because I thought that half an hour earlier she had suffered a kind of nervous breakdown and her ranting was probably the tail end of it; everyone has the right to be aggressive, I told myself, and she was taking it out on me because I was all she had. But in her aggressiveness I sensed something a little too personal, something that her explanations failed to explain. After all, I had just gotten her out of a small hell, calmed her down, and not uttered a word about her umpteenth demonstration of spite: why didn't she notice? The answer to this question might be irrelevant or have nothing whatsoever to do with me, except for the fact that in our embrace I had felt for the first time a profound bond between her and me, something accidental but also radical that united our fates in a tight knot, like suddenly discovering that you're hanging from the same hook. So tight that, after a pause, another short tear jag, and a quick movement of Kleenex from purse to nose, Marta switched to a direct attack, much more lucid and brash: not that she apologized, not that she asked for my understanding of the difficult moment she was going through: she attacked me head-on.

— I don't want to end up like Lara, — she said. — I want to be loved.

This had absolutely nothing to do with anything she had said so far, but it had the air of being the real reason she had come to see me. To tell me that. Once again I kept my mouth shut, and once again it was useless, because Marta kept on as if I had objected to something.

— Apart from Claudia we were all she had, Pietro, and we didn't love her. It's awful. Maybe Claudia, too, who as fate would have it resembles us more than she does her, maybe Claudia didn't love her, either. I don't want to end up like that.

At this point, since keeping my mouth shut hadn't worked, I answered her.

— Marta, what are you talking about? — I said, and I realize that as replies go it was no bombshell. But it's the best I could come up with. Marta smiled at me, the spite in her eyes disappeared, and it gave way to a conspiratorial, familiar expression: she had done it, she had managed to get a rise out of me.

— You said it yourself, that Claudia is calm, — she said, — that she never cries, that at night she sleeps as if nothing had happened, and that she doesn't even seem to be sad. Well, Claudia doesn't seem sad, you don't seem sad, maybe this is because *you aren't* sad? Lara dies, and the two of you aren't sad: nice story. I'm sad, I am, I even get panic attacks, but for completely different reasons: I'm not suffering because of her death, either. I didn't love her, either.

Once again — and even more awkwardly than before, because I was literally dragged into the discussion — I reacted, and I shouldn't have.

— What in the world are you talking about, Marta? We loved Lara.

Now she looked very pleased with herself, and she smiled.

— Bullshit, Pietro. I know what the poor woman was going through. I was the one that took her to yoga classes, to the Chinese wise man, to the witch doctor. She knew perfectly well that you didn't love her, she knew about your *escapades,* as she used to call them, but she didn't even tell you, because you would always throw it back in her face with all the bullshit about your harmony, about the spirit of your family, and she would end up believing it. She couldn't face reality, you see, but she knew everything, she really did, and it made her sick.

— Lara wasn't sick. You're the one that was sick. She's the one that accompanied you to the witch doctors.

— What do you know! — Her temper flared. — Lara was very sick! And she was right to be sick, because her husband was cheating on her all over town and no one loved her, not even her daughter.

— Knock it off, Marta. Stop exaggerating.

— Unless . . . — She smiled. — Unless . . . — And for a moment she wore the same mythical expression immortalized in the photo in front of Krizia's thirteen years ago. — Unless you didn't realize, either. Look me in the eyes, Pietro; answer me. Did you really not know that Lara was sick?

— Lara wasn't sick. You were sick, you have always been sick, and you continue to be sick, apparently. Not her.

She looked me straight in the eyes, incredulous, and suddenly she burst out laughing.

— Fantastic! Unbelievable! *You're sincere!* You didn't know your wife was sick! She was so sick that her heart was literally breaking and you didn't even —

— That's enough, knock it off. Lara was fine, and I loved her. And I didn't have any affairs.

— You didn't? — She raised her voice. — So how do you explain Gabriella Parigi? Lara took me with her, you know, when she followed you once, and I saw you with my own eyes going into that house on Corso Lodi when you were supposed to be in London! What were you going there for, a business meeting?

— What's that got to do with anything, Marta, it was ten years ago.

— So, if it was ten years ago it doesn't matter? May I remind you that your daughter was three months old at the time, three months old, and Lara was suffering from postpartum depression. Or you didn't know about that, either?

— Marta, please . . .

— And that other woman, the TV presenter? That was, like, *five* years ago? Yes, it was five years ago, because I was pregnant with Giacomo; is five years also too long ago? Does that not matter, either? The night of the Oscars in Los Angeles, do you remember? Do you remember the girl you shared the Imperial Bedroom with at the Beverly Hills Hotel? Oh, you want to know how I know certain things? Well, it just so happens that —

— Listen, I don't know why you're digging up all these things, and I especially don't see how it's any of your business, but the only thing I can tell you is that I loved Lara, and she knew it, that's all. I may have cheated on her those two times, and if you really must know I cheated on her a couple of other times, that's right, four times altogether, and all at the beginning, in the early years, when, if you don't mind, I had a right to do some stupid things myself; but I loved her, I respected her, and she was not at all sick.

Here she got really mad, and it served me right, I realize now, since I should have kept my big mouth shut.

— Hey, don't go feeding me your bullshit! — she screamed. — Don't try it with me, do you understand? I won't put up with it, I'm not her! I'm even worse than you, don't you realize it? The truth is I'm *just like* you! You always did whatever the fuck you wanted and didn't give a shit how Lara felt, that's how much you respected her! You even went to bed with me!

— Give me a break! I hadn't even met her then!

— So what!

— What do you mean, so what? Have you gone crazy, Marta? Maybe you shouldn't be here. Maybe you should go to a —

And finally, halfway through that useless sentence, after all the other useless sentences that I had unfortunately already said, a lightbulb went on and I did the right thing: I got up and walked away. I left her there and I went back to my car, because I was getting angry, indeed I was already angry, I was beside myself, and beside myself the situation grew more confused and grotesque, while inside myself it remained calm. I left her there, sitting on the park bench, and she, out of pride, who knows, or because she didn't know what to do, stayed on the bench for a long while — for one hour, at least. Recess came, Claudia stuck her little head out the window, and we waved to each other; Miss Paolina came out of the entrance, and we waved at each other, too; I made a couple of business calls, had a cigarette, ate a sandwich, and slowly but surely tried to calm myself down, because at that moment calming myself down was an absolute priority. And I succeeded; I was calm again when Marta stood up from the bench and walked toward me. I hoped that she would ignore me, that she would walk straight to the half-crushed Twingo that *I* had parked while she was tearing her clothes off — after which I had put *my* business card under the windshield wipers of the C3 that *she* had dented, giving *my* phone number to pay out of *my* pocket for the damages that *she* had caused — but instead she came to my window and leaned over to speak with me, just as Piquet had done yesterday. And just like yesterday, a light drizzle began to fall, and it was odd to see such a perfect repeat but with such completely reversed aesthetic parameters: the day before, one of the ugliest men I know; the day after, one of the prettiest girls I know; both in the same absurd position in the rain to tell me one last thing through the window after having poured out an anguish they had concealed for who knows how long.

— Do you know the last thing we did together, Lara and I?

— No.

— We went to a fortune-teller, in Gavorrano, the day you took the children to the Water Park. Didn't Lara tell you?

— No.

— And do you know what the fortune-teller told us? She read our cards, and she told us a few things. First she did mine, and she told me that I'd be successful, very successful, in my work and in my love life, and that many, many men would fall madly in love with me, but that unfortunately I'd die young. Then she did Lara's, but after turning them over she didn't want to speak. But Lara insisted, and so the fortune-teller told her not only that she, too, would die young, but that she wouldn't be successful at anything, that she would end up alone, without a man, just as she had always been. Then Lara started laughing and told the fortune-teller that she was wrong because she did have a man. The woman looked at the cards again and, unmoved, repeated that she didn't. Lara insisted, amused, and she said your name, she said that she had been with you for eleven years, she told her that you had a daughter and that you were going to get married in early September, and so the cards had to be wrong. The fortune-teller heard her out, looked at me, looked at the cards again, looked at Lara again, and with the sweet tone of voice people use when they give you bad news, she told her, "I'm sorry, my dear, but *you do not have that man . . .*"

And she left; her hair wet, her face wet, her clothes wet, Marta went back to the Twingo with her lovely gait. She started it up and easily pulled out of the parking spot that she had been unable to enter two hours earlier. I didn't care how she felt or what she might do: she also seemed to have calmed down, and, I don't know why, but I have the impression she went to her children's school and stayed there in her car, like me, waiting for them to come out.

chapter ten

Now I'm here, in the bleachers of this old gym, and I can't take my mind off it. Claudia leaps, flexes, and twists four yards below me, and training with her are other girls and boys, and older boys and girls, all together in a triumph of the purest spirits — they hope to successfully complete the exercise, to successfully eliminate the flaw, to successfully get on the team for the next championship — and I have to focus to avoid thinking about Marta. It's upsetting. Usually these two hours are my form of yoga, but today Marta upset me and I'm afraid that something's changed. And not only Marta: mostly her, but also Piquet yesterday and Jean-Claude the other day. They came to me, all three, *to suffer*, to unload their pain on me, then they left. It must mean something. To be honest, however, I've only recently learned to enjoy this place: taking

Claudia to the gym used to be Lara's job; I've only started taking
her since Lara's been gone, now that classes have started again, and
it's been a real discovery. It's nice here, I really mean it. An old gym
that offers four courses in artistic gymnastics at the same time,
from beginner's to competition, is a spectacle I could never have
imagined; meditative, pure, but also energetic, cheerful, harmoni-
ous: it's perfect for people like me, who want to be close to their
daughters, but with lightness, without thinking about it too much.
And it is a temple of lightness: here the force of gravity seems old-
fashioned, obsolete; you look down from the bleachers and see
handstands, vaults, arches, splits, tumbles, flips, as if the gymnasts
were truly weightless — and for me, with the detour my life has
taken, it's a precious gift to be here two hours straight three times
a week. And to think it was right here, within reach, for more than
five years, and I didn't even realize it; Lara didn't, either, and she
was the one who used to accompany Claudia, it's true, but she
didn't stay in the gym to watch her, using those two hours to go to
the supermarket, see the hairdresser, or do other errands: what
kind of a life were we living? *She was sick* — the sense of guilt Marta
tried to slip between my ribs like a knife. It's not true: Lara wasn't
sick, so why is Marta saying she was? Why is she saying that I and
even Claudia didn't love Lara? I loved my wife, and Claudia loved
her mother: what Marta said is untrue, so far. And what about
Marta? Did she love her sister? Did she not love her? Did she maybe
hate her and is simply looking for someone to share her guilt with?
That must be why Lara disappeared from my thoughts during our
embrace and why I could be so selfish that the only person I cared
about was Claudia, down there in the gym: I have to focus on her.
The freestyle exercises: along the diagonal of the springboard, second in line after Gemma, Claudia is standing there being scolded
by Gaia, the instructor, because of a bad habit she has of moving
her pelvis. An error I can't even see, barely perceptible, which nev-

ertheless seems to be her weak point. Watch: Gemma goes first
again, immediately followed by Claudia; there she goes, doing a
brave series of handsprings, one, two, three, and to me her pelvis
seems to be in the right position, this time I'd say she did nothing
wrong, but no, here comes the instructor, stops the whole class,
goes up to Claudia, and, in front of everyone, Jesus, without the
minimum tact, tells her that she moved her pelvis again. She
shows her by doing a handspring herself, but grossly exaggerating
the error so that even I can see it, while before, when I was watching Claudia, I swear you couldn't — and that's not right, oh, no,
my dear Gaia: Claudia was not moving her pelvis like that at all;
there's no way she can know, but her classmates do and they'll tell
her, Gemma will tell her, she'll tell her, Look, Claudia — or rather
Claudina (because that's what she calls her, *Claudina,* from the
heights of her thirteen and a half years, which make her the oldest
girl in the group as well as the captain of the team, already a junior
champion, always running around winning medals and thus a
kind of idol, especially for Claudia, who is always following her
around trying to imitate her, immoderately, not only in the exercises but also in her attitudes and poses outside the gym, at home,
and at school, with obviously grotesque results, because in her still
nymphlike but already statuesque beauty Gemma is already physically formed, and some stridently feminine poses might look natural on her, but they definitely do not on Claudia, who to all intents
and purposes is still a little girl) — look, Claudina, she'll tell her,
you barely move your pelvis, she's exaggerating, don't take it to
heart; and I myself would like to bring in a camcorder to the next
class and film the whole thing so Claudia can see with her own two
eyes the difference between the error she really made and what
Gaia is showing her. An error that ultimately boils down to the
fact that, at the age of ten and a half, she's not perfect. What the
fuck. It's what impresses me most about this place, the attitude

toward perfection. Because what matters here is not your age, or the difficulty of what you're learning, or the almost mathematical certainty that you're never going to find yourself losing an Olympic medal by bare thousandths of a point; what you have to focus on here is perfection, pure and simple — which rules me out, since I've never felt this kind of pressure in my life and I have no idea what it means: I've always tried to do the best I could, of course, and in some cases I was obliged to do things well, at the risk of loss of esteem, money, even affection, but I have never dreamed of achieving perfection — the absolute good, a *ten*. My daughter's a different story: ever since she was diagnosed with a talent for gymnastics, she's had people breathing down her neck about perfection, and I have no idea what it means. Maybe Lara did: for years she studied classical ballet, in which everything is also difficult and everything also has to be done perfectly; Lara may have known what Claudia is feeling, but I don't. Marta was the one who was good at ballet, the perfect one: the prettiest, the youngest, the best, the most rebellious, the most everything, and also the luckiest, until she started in earnest to build her misfortune with her own two hands — so successfully, in fact, that she became *the unluckiest*, too. So, if anything, Lara should have been the one who didn't love Marta, who hated her, which wasn't the case, I can testify to it: Lara cared deeply about her sister. Maybe the opposite was true? Absurdly, like something out of Dostoyevsky? *Why do you hate this son of yours, Fyodor Pavlovitch? What wrongs has he done to you? He to me, none, but I have done many to him* . . . And I really don't understand how Claudia was able to handle the pressure without exploding. But she did, she does. So they wanted perfection? She simply began to strive for it, a little at a time — and apparently even achieved it sometimes. I was shocked the day I came by the gym to register Claudia for the new year when Gaia, while praising my decision to have Claudia continue (someone must have told her what had happened, scaring her into thinking she wouldn't be coming back), she listed the points where Claudia was already perfect: her split, the arch of her foot . . . "In what sense perfect?" I asked, thinking she would say, "Well, we are talking about a ten-year-old girl, after all, so I mean perfect in the sense of satisfactory," but she replied with a Nietzschean purity: "Perfect in an absolute sense." Her perfect points are utterly useless in and of themselves, of course, amounting to little more than the perfection, let's say, of lacing your sneakers before a tennis match. But the fact of the matter is that she has achieved them, which justifies belief that she still has more to achieve, and this world that is so alien to me has become naturalized in my daughter's life. Not to mention the most difficult things, in which Claudia is still far from perfection — like everyone else, for that matter — but she still *does them,* and to me this is already miraculous, since we're talking about handstands, splits, pirouettes, walkovers, and front and back flips — and by a ten-year-old girl. The way things operate in here, however, what matters is not so much doing the exercises as doing them perfectly. Even Gemma misses more than she nails, so despite the amazement you feel when you see what these little children can do, to the instructor's eyes it's one mistake after the other. Here's an example of adult-child relations in which the child doesn't get a single break, except for permission to stop smiling. It's true that I'm not grieving, yes, and that Claudia doesn't seem to be, either: but — it's ridiculous to even think it! — this doesn't mean we didn't love Lara. We — and I include Marta, because she loved Lara, too, until I hear proof to the contrary — we're not grieving *yet;* we're dealing with it as best we can, for now, I'd even say we haven't yet absorbed it, we're still circling it, acting as if nothing happened, as if Lara were on a trip, perhaps, and we're waiting for the pain to arrive and flood our lives, and meanwhile we limit ourselves to attracting the pain of others, in my case, or to having a meltdown in the middle of traf-

fic, in Marta's — and it would be interesting to understand why
her version of going nuts, of all the ways she could have done it,
was to take her clothes off. Now they're getting into a circle, sitting
down, legs wide apart, and bending their upper bodies forward
until they are stretched literally down to the ground, assuming an
impossible position. And they start playing like that, spread out on
the floor: you can't tell what game they're playing, but Gemma is
clearly the ringleader. They're supposed to take turns saying something, and now it's Claudia's turn, she says God knows what, and
the others laugh. Gemma laughs, too, and Claudia is proud. Good
girl, you made your idol laugh. Lara wasn't sick. She went to the
fortune-teller to accompany Marta, like she always did. Over the
years Marta took her to a variety of healers, pranotherapists, yogis,
wise men, shamans, witch doctors, ayurvedics, maharishis, acupuncturists, needleless acupuncturists, those who lay stones on
your chakra — whatever the fuck they're called; podologists, who
read your feet; tricomants, who read your hair; Tibetan monks,
who cleanse your aura with a sword; samurais, who cleanse you
with the katana; last year they even went to see a vampire, I swear,
on Corso Magenta, a Romanian from Transylvania named Vlad, of
course, who for €150 extracts twenty-five centiliters of blood using
a sterile syringe, *drinks it,* and then tells you what's ailing you and
how to restore your balance. But it was Marta who was taking Lara
with her, not the other way around, and Lara accompanied her
sister so she wouldn't have to go alone. Marta's version simply reversed their roles — like Dostoyevsky, again — and now the girls
have moved to the balance beam, one leg on the mat, the other
behind them, practicing their splits. On this apparatus Claudia is
perfect, like Gemma. So good that, from their superior heights,
they start to chat, ignoring the others, and Gaia scolds them. You
can see the satisfaction in Claudia's expression, not because she's
doing something miraculous with her body — having to plant her

feet on the mat means the split is even wider than 180 degrees —
and she's actually doing it "perfectly," but because the scolding
likens her to her idol, with whom she starts chatting again as if
nothing had happened, and who knows what they're saying right
now, who knows what Claudia is saying and what Gemma is answering, while they stretch the tendons and muscles in their legs,
and their bodies — Claudia's simple, tiny, and provisory body and
Gemma's important, feminine, and fully formed one — earn a few
angstroms in their endless journey toward perfection. Marta obviously wants me to suffer, she wants me to feel guilty. She wants me
to think about what the fortune-teller told Lara shortly before she
died: "You'll die young"; "I'm sorry, you do not have that man."
But when those words were uttered Lara was alive and well, and if
she weren't dead she'd be laughing herself, I'm sure of it, she'd be
telling me about the fortune-teller the same way she told me
about the samurai or the vampire and we would laugh about it
together, because they didn't merit a second thought. Look at how
things ended up instead. She's dead, and hindsight is the only thing
that makes these words sound ominous. Any word, even the most
ridiculous, pronounced shortly before a person's death wavers on
the dark border of prophecy, but we should never forget that time
runs in only one direction and what we see when we look backward is misleading. Time is not a palindrome: starting at the end
and moving all the way back to the beginning always seems to ac-
cumulate a variety of disturbing meanings, and we should not let
ourselves be influenced by these things. I remember the notorious
trial of Judas Priest, the heavy metal group accused of causing the
suicide of two boys through subliminal messages that could be
heard by listening to their songs backward — sentences like "Do
it!" as in "Try suicide" or "Suicide is nice!" Halfway through the
trial the group's singer appeared in court with a bunch of tapes and
made the court listen to them being played backward. On one

there was a song by Diana Ross, and at a certain point, if you listened to it in reverse, the lyrics said distinctly, "Death to all. He is
the only one. Satan is love." On the others there were songs by his
own group, and while the official text said things like "To build a
line, strategic force / They will not take a man," listening to it in
reverse yielded "It's so unlikely / It's what I deserve" or "Oh,
Momma, look, this chair is broken!" No, the fact that the fortune-
teller predicted she would die young doesn't mean a thing. The
fact that she so tenaciously denied my presence by her side doesn't
mean a thing. The fact that Lara actually did die a few days after all
that bullshit doesn't mean a thing. The boys are practicing on the
other side of the gym, doing handstands on the parallel bars. The
instructor spurs them on. But only four of them, the oldest ones,
are on the apparatus: the others are sitting down, attentive, watching them. There is no relationship between the boys and the girls
in here, neither words nor glances, nothing, not even between the
older kids, who on the outside have already started checking each
other out, teasing each other; the majority here are children, who
impose on everyone the chaotic calm of their senses, leaving no
room for heterosexual attraction. It's as if there were a wall between the boys and the girls — and thanks to this wall, ultimately,
everyone is able to focus on their exercises much better. It's extraordinary how a group dominated by children almost always
ends up being more productive than a group dominated by adults.
True, but *how many* days later did she die? Marta said they went to
the fortune-teller when I took the children to the Water Park, so it
was already the second half of August, around August 20, I'd say, in
fact it was the same day as the Luigi Berlusconi Trophy game here
in Milan, I remember it clearly because Jean-Claude phoned to ask
me to join him on the grandstand and I was at the Water Park and
I told him I couldn't, so it was around the 19th or 20th of August.
Lara died on August 30, ten days later. And now, at this late date,

Marta wants me to wonder why, for ten long days, Lara never told me a thing about the fortune-teller; and why for ten long days she deprived herself of the pleasure of laughing with me at her absurd prophecies. Marta wants me to believe that Lara had secrets, that she knew her better than I did, in fact, that I didn't know her at all; she wants me to start tearing my hair out and to start doing things I've scrupulously avoided so far, like rummaging through her things or checking out her computer, which I refuse to do. Marta wants to be loved, but by whom? A body that's still perfect, breasts that are still gorgeous, another son, Fyodor Pavlovitch . . . Down goes the upper body, her legs still in a split, her forehead resting on her knee (incredible that my daughter *is doing this*); and who knows where Jean-Claude is right now, who knows what Gabriella Parigi is doing, who knows what the girl with the golden retriever is doing, I have a sudden urge to meet her, an urge to meet Piquet's girlfriend and hear her drop one of her bombshells; I have an urge to find out whether at the moment Lara was dying someone else was thinking of her — there must be some way — since I was too busy saving our lady of the fat ass. Claudia has been in a split for more than a quarter of an hour now, Lara wasn't sick, she didn't have secrets, I'll never go through her e-mail, and that song is right to say we are only accidents waiting to happen, and today Marta is what happened to me.

chapter eleven

> From: "Josie" <Europa@thelightoflife.com>
> To: "Lara Siciliano" <larasic@libero.it>
> Subject: Howard Y. Lee Workshop
> Date: Monday, August 30, 2004 1:38 P.M.

> Dear Friends,
> I wish to inform individuals registered for the seminar,
> FREE OF FEAR AND ANGER, on November 15 in Bologna,
> that the location of the seminar has been changed, for
> reasons beyond the control of the organization. The new
> address is:
>
> FORTITUDO PALESTRA FURLA
> Via Ugo Lenzi 10 Bologna (downtown)
>
> 200 yds from Paladozza, the original location for the seminar.
> A person from the organization will be in front of the
> Paladozza to assist anyone unaware of the change in venue.
>
> further information is available @ http://www.
> thelightoflife.com
>
> ************************
> Healing Light & Longevity Center Bologna, Italy
> Tel: (+39) 051 588.3808   Fax: (+39) 051 588.3753
> Email: europa@thelightoflife.com

chapter twelve

> From: "Gianni Orzan" <qwertyuiop@flashnet.it>
> To: "Lara" <larasic@libero.it>
> Subject: paranoia
> Date: Monday, August 30, 2004 5:28 P.M.
>
> Lara, I'm writing to you in a sudden fit of paranoia.
> I don't know how, but right now I'm here at home at two

> in the afternoon, high as a kite, with an enormous black
> dog that wants to claw me to death. E-nor-mous, Lara.
> Enormous. How did this happen? How the fuck did this
> happen? The dog sniffs at me, circles me. How did this
> happen? Well: Belinda arrived. You don't know her, Lara,
> I've only just met her myself. Her name is Belinda Berardi
> and she's an actress. We'd been speaking on the phone and
> we were supposed to see each other face-to-face about a
> job, a reading for children we're supposed to do together,
> and this morning, to get to the point, this morning she
> phoned and asked if I was free, and I told her yes, come on
> over, and she — here goes — she tells me yes, but there's a
> problem. I've got the dog, she says; and I tell her no
> problem, bring the dog with you, and she says okay, I'll be
> there in a little while, and she comes. And she's a real
> basket case, this girl, a fantastic, fluorescent basket case, she
> forgets her house keys knocks over the mineral water gets
> pastry cream on her clothes absurd coincidences happen to
> her she's always a little drugged out she always seems half-
> dead and yet she's a breath of fresh air that comes into the
> house and clears it. Right away I can feel certain things,
> you know, I feel them inside. For me she's the real thing.
> She looks like the real thing, Lara. With all the
> implications. Like I was saying, we were supposed to
> prepare a reading, she and I, but we didn't. I can't
> remember just what happened but she pulled out some
> weed and we started smoking. Instead of doing what we
> were supposed to be doing, I mean, we smoked this fat
> joint. And well there was the dog, but less enormous than
> he is now, and the weed started to have a major effect on
> me, and I found myself talking to her about the number 4
> and the Neutral Mind, you see it, and she goes, yeah, yeah,

> I've always been real neutral — duh: you were born in '76,
> $7 + 6 = 13, 3 + 1 = 4$, i.e., Neutral Mind as Divine Gift,
> you're neutral, yeah. I get up and give some water to the
> dog, I remember, things like that. Then she starts talking,
> and she makes me laugh, she has a problem but you can't
> tell what. Acting class. Some teacher with verbal diarrhea.
> She dropped out. I can't understand a thing, but I can tell
> she's got it. Awesome, I think. The Real Thing. Just look at
> how she fucking keeps beating herself up over this problem
> and you can't even tell what it is. But she's funny, she
> laughs, too, and despite her problem you can see she's
> relaxed, cool: a girl who's smoking pot and has the whole
> afternoon ahead of her. And I relax, too, because I've got
> the whole afternoon ahead of me, too, and we talk about
> the Neutral Mind, we laugh, etc., until *drrinnn,* the cell
> phone rings. She answers and — listen to this — she
> blanches. What do you mean, today? I thought it was the
> thirty-first, not the thirtieth, I was convinced, I swear, I
> don't know what to say, sorry sorry sorry, and now what
> do we do? Really? Yes, I'll hurry, I'll be there in fifteen
> minutes. She had a dubbing gig, the moron. Completely
> slipped her mind. Everyone there waiting for her. So she
> jumps to her feet, and fuck this and fuck that, why do I
> have to be this way, it always happens to me, it always
> happens to me, and now what am I supposed to do, and
> where am I going to put the dog, and me — here it comes
> — I say leave it here, Belinda, I'll watch it for you. Here?
> With you? No, I couldn't, I don't want to bother you —
> of course, but where would I leave it then? You would
> really look after it? So take him. And she left. Do you get it?
> She LEFT. High as a kite, dizzy, gaga, in a ridiculous rush,
> she ran off to her dubbing gig. Belinda, I tell her, what's the

> rush? Slow down. Think. Protect yourself. You're getting
> ready to drive your car through the maze of Roman traffic,
> high as a kite, to reach a dubbing studio where you're going
> to make an absolute idiot out of yourself. What's the rush?
> What the fuck are you going to say when you get there?
> That you were sitting around smoking weed and talking
> about the Neutral Mind? What the fuck are you going to
> say, eh Beli'? Use your head. Use your head, please, slow
> down, and be careful: it's a jungle out there. And while
> you're at it, I add, could you by any chance tell me when
> your dubbing gig is supposed to be over? Not for nothing
> — I'm getting there — I need to know what to do about
> this dog. You know, if I have to take him outside to pee,
> etc., or not. I have parquet floors, if you get my drift. At five
> thirty, she tells me. She'll be done at five thirty. And she
> goes. And she leaves her dog here with me. Except that at
> first he wasn't so enormous. Goddamn but he's enormous.
> He's hanging all over me, sniffing at me. Now he's going to
> get all pissed off, knowing that his master's dumped him,
> I'll bet on it. He sees me, and with his little pea-brain he
> associates his master's absence with me and he takes it out
> on me. And he lunges for my throat, to tear it out. I swear.
> And what am I supposed to do? How am I supposed to
> defend myself? I can try to strangle him. Of course. I've
> heard of dogs strangled by men. It's actually supposed to be
> the most common way for men to kill dogs. They strangle
> them. Sure, it's possible. But I have to prepare carefully. I
> have to be ready to fight for survival. With this enormous
> and way too symbolic black dog. And I start to prepare
> myself. I get myself ready mentally to grab his throat when
> he lunges at me, and right away to squeeze tight — this is
> fundamental — decisively, terminally. No, I'm an idiot.

> Why give him the advantage of choosing when? No, I won't
> wait for him to attack me, I'll beat him to it. I'll attack him.
> Yeah: be the first to strike. I'll grab him by the neck and
> strangle him. He'll put up a fight, of course, but what the
> fuck do I care, fight all you want, I've got you by the throat
> so you can't bite me, heavy pressure for twenty, thirty,
> forty seconds, all concentrated in that gesture, all there,
> like Carmelo Bene's *Lorenzaccio* when he plunges his sword
> into the tyrant's chest, I'll attack this fucking dog first —
> you get it? — BEFORE he attacks me. And I'll strangle him.
> End of story. And when she comes back to pick him up
> she'll find a corpse. Yeah. She'll feel bad, it's unavoidable,
> but I'll tell her that's how it goes in the world, baby, only
> the strong survive. That dog made a big mistake, my pretty.
> He underestimated me, he attacked me. Do you see what
> he did? He wanted to dig his teeth into my throat, he tried
> to tear me to pieces. That's why he's dead. I defended
> myself, sweetheart, I had no choice. It was either him or
> me. No, there's no use putting your arms around him,
> trying to revive him, he's dead as a doornail. I guarantee. I
> checked. She'll keep crying and I'll comfort her, that's life,
> baby, and she'll accept, because that's the way Real Things
> are, Lara, they know how to accept evil, they even know
> how to love it . . . That's how it should go, and it all
> depends on me. I have to strangle it. I have to focus,
> prepare myself. That's it. He's sniffing at me, the fucker. It's
> his old tactic, sniff around a few times until the prey is used
> to being sniffed at, accepts the contact fearlessly, and then
> when he sniffs at you one more time, bam, he sinks his
> teeth into your neck. You take me for a fool? You think I
> don't know what's going on? He sniffs at me, or rather
> pretends to sniff at me, because in reality my smell disgusts

> him, because it's the smell of He Who Wishes To Replace
> His Queen, and that's why He hates me. He wants to kill
> me. A black dog, for crying out loud. It doesn't get more
> symbolic than that. He's not even the symbol of the demon
> anymore. He *is* the demon. The Beast personified. Dog with
> a capital *D*. I've got the demon in my house, for Christ's
> sake, and I have to strangle him before He Gets Me. But I'm
> still not strong enough, I feel ready but I'm not. I have to
> fortify myself. I have to pull myself together so I don't
> succumb. And what is my strong point? Writing. Of course,
> writing: that's where I'm strong. That's it, Lara, that's it:
> now I remember. I decided to make myself stronger by
> writing. I told myself to gather my strength, to write. I'll
> write to Lara and then I'll strangle the Dog. That's my
> strategy. And I came here, I went online, and I started
> writing. To fight the Demon, Lara, to triumph over Evil.
> Ah, and then there's another paranoia: what if my
> sometime roommate arrives — Simona, who doesn't know
> shit about this dog and is maybe terrified of dogs, especially
> Enormous Black ones, I really don't know her that well,
> maybe she's afraid of dogs, maybe just seeing one will give
> her a heart attack, just to hear the word DOG, what the
> fuck do I know? Maybe. Let's say she comes in. That she
> comes in now. What'll happen? She screams, she faints, and
> I'd be very vulnerable, well yeah, because out of nobility of
> spirit I'd rush to help her, I'd kneel by her side, and at that
> moment the Dog could lunge for my neck, from behind
> my back, of course, and while I'm trying to save a human
> life, you see, we're talking about Him, people, not about
> some nobody, about Ipso in person, the biggest son of a
> bitch ever, he'd do it, he really would, and he'd enjoy it,
> and I would succumb, and he would kill me. He, me. No. I

> can't let that happen. I have to prevent it. I have to think of
> something. I have to put a sign outside the door. Writing a
> sign is still a form of writing. I'll write it and I'll put it up
> outside the door. SIMONA I CAN'T EXPLAIN THERE'S A BIG DOG
> AT HOME TAKE A WALK AND I'LL CALL YOU WHEN HE'S GONE.
> Something along those lines. Well written. Clear. Outside
> the door. But I have to do it now. Otherwise she'll come in,
> she could come in from one moment to the ne— Help.
> He's barking. He's howling. Help. The Dog's barking. He's
> stopped. He's started again. He's stopped again. I lock
> myself inside. Here in the study. If Simona arrives, that's
> her fucking problem. I lock myself in the den, there, I'm
> locked in, and now maybe I'll phone Simona, of course.
> And I'll tell her on the phone, because the sign is a fucking
> stupid idea. I'll phone her, of course. On her cell. It's easy,
> this is the dawning of the Age of the Mobile Phone. There,
> I'm calling her. It's ringing. Come on, pick up, Simona,
> pick up. Nothing, no answer. Fuck, she doesn't hear it. Her
> phone rings to save her life and she doesn't hear it, the
> moron. But wait, what about text messages? I text her.
> Much more efficient than a sign. Done: "Don't go home
> UFN (which means until further notice, the way kids
> abbreviate it). CFY (Calling for you — I don't think she'll
> understand, I don't like this abbreviating, and Simona's
> young but not that young) — CMB (Call me back). I press
> send. She'll understand. Good ol' Simo will understand,
> and she'll keep her distance from the house, where I'll
> resist Evil all by myself. I'll resist. No fucking way will I
> open this door. It's even better than strangling him. I'll stay
> locked inside here. That way he can't have me. But — oh
> no: I suddenly remember the interview I'm supposed to do
> with Canada, any moment now. With Canada. In English.

> What can I tell them? *The Adventures of Pizzano Pizza,* or rather
> Pizano Piza, as they pronounce it, but who cares about
> Pizano Piza? "I'm Here Fighting Against The Dark And
> Thou Darest Ask Me About Pizano Piza?" The interview,
> yeah. Fuck. Now the phone rings and it's Canada for the
> interview; and like an idiot I do the interview and who
> knows what the fuck I say I'm so high, I talk about Demons
> and Black Dogs and phosphorescent Real Things, and I
> fuck up my chances with the Canadian market for good.
> Canada: a country where it's so damn cold people read a
> lot. They read children's books to their kids at night, sitting
> on the side of their beds, reassuring, patient, civil, and one
> of those books might be mine. Canada. Ooops, and with
> one move I fuck it up, I fuck up my chances with one of
> the eight most industrialized countries in the world.
> Because I think Canada belongs to the G8. I really think it
> does. It doesn't count for shit, but it's there. Like Italy, for
> that matter. No, it's not right. It took me years to get an
> interview with the Canadians. An entire lifetime. And now
> that they go for it I fuck it all up because of this bullshit.
> Oh, Belinda, come back, come back quickly. Hurry. You
> who are always hurrying, hurry to me. Save me. This dog is
> yours, after all. This Black Demon is yours. Please, tell the
> people at the dubbing studio, all of them, to go fuck
> themselves. I've already ended up looking like an asshole.
> Show some balls, don't let them humiliate you, tell them
> to go fuck themselves and then come back to me right
> away. To Him. Not that I'm scared of him, you know, in a
> way I like him, and it's the very fact that I like him that
> scares me. That's why I'm asking you to come back. Come.
> It's even less absurd than death, at least we'll be together
> when your demon attacks me and tears me to pieces.

> Because he will, he really will. Because I know that I'll
> never strangle him. Me strangle a dog: where did I get such
> an idea? He'll Get Me, he will definitely Get Me, but at least
> you can be here with me, Belinda, when He Gets Me. What
> the fuck. At least be by me at the hour of my death. Please,
> come back. The sooner the better. I'm here, helpless
> against Evil, against Your Evil, more alone than I've ever
> been. This weed is ass-kicking, look how long it's fucking
> lasting. Come back, Belinda. Now I'm going to count to
> three and the doorbell will ring and it will be you. One.
> Two. Three. Come back, I'm begging you, come back.
> Come back. One two three: come on. Now, right now, your
> finger is about to press the doorbell. One two three, come
> back . . . Come come come, and you still don't come. And I
> have to manage on my own. Now It's whimpering behind
> the door. Scratching. Whining. It wants to overwhelm me
> with emotion, the son of a bitch. Tactic number 2: play the
> victim. Anyone who falls for it is fucked. But I don't fall for
> it. Whine as long as you fucking want, Big Black Dog, I'm
> not going to console you. I'm not the cause of this
> situation. Don't go blaming me. Even if, by some absurd
> chance, you were not The Dog, but an ordinary black dog,
> sweet and innocent, abandoned by its master, and therefore
> sad and in need of petting, even then I would still have the
> right to let you suffer. To avoid any risk, you understand?
> So whine all you want, I'm not going to feel guilty on
> account of you. And I'm not going to feel any sympathy.
> And even if I did I would never admit it, so go ahead and
> die of a broken heart, I will not open this door — but don't
> forget that the same woman who dumped you dumped
> me. Well, Dog, she dumped the two of us, so we can
> become friends and get drunk together and talk about all

> the other women who did us wrong. There were lots,
> weren't there. So there must be something a little off about
> us, don't you think? If they all end up dumping us there
> must be a reason. They dump us for another guy, for a
> dubbing gig, even for nothing, Jesus Christ, we could even
> get dumped for nothing. You don't think so, little brother?
> We can't even get the better of nothing. Like Luciano
> Rispoli, whose reruns of *Flying Carpet* got an even lower
> market share than the blank screen that RAI-2 broadcasts
> when there are technical difficulties. We're less than zero.
> Let's become friends, you and I! Now I'm going to open the
> door for you. Here you are. Nice dog. Nice dog, come on.
> You only wanted to curl up here, right buddy? Yes, that's it.
> Between my feet, like my old dog Roy before Anna took
> him, too, took everything, including the dog, but at least I
> came out on top that time and after two and a half years I'll
> have Franceschino and the dog back, goddamn it, and
> whatever happens will happen but I'll always know that I
> saved the two of them, don't ask me from what I don't
> know but I do know that it was tough and had something
> to do with that terrifying deep black well that starts inside
> of her and reaches all the way down to the bowels of hell.
> Apropos of Real Things. The well I liked so much. Namely
> you, Big Black Dog, whose name I don't even know, curled
> up here like old Roy used to do, like he'll do again starting
> next month. Come here, buddy, come over here. Our
> mistress has dumped us, yeah. She's left us all alone, yes.
> You're nice, you know that? So soft. See how you like it.
> Aw, he likes to play, look at him. *Driiin.* THE CANADIANS!
> My home phone! No one has that number! I gave it to the
> Canadians this morning! Help . . . Hello? Who? Marcella?
> From Viareggio? What does she want? I haven't heard from

> her for years! I'm not exaggerating. Years. How did she get
> my number? Did something serious happen? Nah, she just
> wants to know how to rent an apartment in Rome. Rent in
> the sense of find a tenant. So after all these years, this
> Marcella phones me to ask me how to advertise a rental
> apartment in Rome. She explains the whole story about
> how it's empty, belongs to her old aunt, her uncle on his
> deathbed, her grandfather in a wheelchair. Go to an
> agency, I tell her. Oh, she says, an agency? Yeah, I say. An
> agency. Why didn't you think of that, Marcella? I can't
> believe you never thought of a damn agency, tell me the
> truth. Sure, I thought of it, but I thought it was dangerous.
> Dangerous? In the sense that maybe they try to rip you off,
> so I wanted to ask your advi— Dangerous, Marcella? Since
> when is going to a real estate agency dangerous? Do you
> want to know what dangerous is, Marcella? You want to
> know? Dangerous is staying home with a Big Black Dog
> between your legs after smoking God knows what together
> with a fantastic girl related to all the fantastic girls who
> ever tore your heart out. THAT is dangerous! Christ. An
> agency is dangerous? Thanks anyway, she says, how're you
> doing, everything all right, how's your son, is he okay, do
> you ever come to Viareggio, I've been coming every other
> weekend for two and a half fucking years, Marcella, and
> you can't not know that even if we haven't spoken for
> years, indeed I know for a fact that you do know, what the
> fuck kind of questions are you asking me, and to make a
> long story short she says is everything fine, and I go yes,
> fine, give me a call when you're around, sure, why not, bye,
> bye. Absolute bullshit. An agency's dangerous. Well at least
> this time it wasn't those Canadian bastards, which is
> already an improvement. And the black dog is curled up

> between my legs, nice and quiet, look at him, rather than
> Biting Me and Eating Me. And this is even better. And
> there's a nice breeze, and I'm fine, the pot isn't affecting me
> as much (but it's really kicking) and I could even say that
> now I'm feeling great, I'd say, and I can't complain about a
> thing, it's peaceful, wiping out any unhappiness, I'm here
> and I'm fine. At any rate, shit happens, end of story. What
> the fuck am I doing here cooking up trouble for myself? If
> Simona still hasn't come home to face down this big black
> dog it's because that's not the way it was supposed to go.
> You think it's just luck? No way. She still hasn't arrived
> because she wasn't supposed to arrive. End of story. It
> wasn't preordained by the karmic order, it has nothing to
> do with luck. Besides, she could still arrive any time, so it
> would be better to talk about this Simona stuff later. But I
> even texted her. I warned her. I did my fucking duty. And
> who knows whether or not she's afraid of dogs. Maybe she
> actually adores them. Beats me. Maybe she'll save me and is
> better at dealing with dogs than I am. And to tell the truth,
> who is there to save? And from what? From this mutt
> curled up between my legs, so meek — look at him —
> grateful, submissive? I'm forgetting the most important
> thing of all, the Symbolic Fury he was sent here to unleash
> upon me. Or rather, *Left* here, and by Her, by this sudden
> New Real Thing related to all the Real Things who tore
> hearts out — and yet, to be honest, who also made them
> incomparably happy for remarkable fleeting instants
> overripe with beauty that I will never forget, with their
> Black Dogs curled up inside, soft and sleek, and the beach,
> the moon, the lights of the fishing boats, even the fucking
> fireworks somewhere, and the best sex in the world, Lara,
> on the beach. *Will you marry me? Yes.* Hah. What time did you

> say this dubbing gig was over? Five thirty? And what time is
> it now? 5:06. Twenty-four minutes. Big deal. I can make it.
> I'm fine. The dog with a small *d* is huddled at my feet. Time
> is passing and playing into my hands. 5:07. The effect of the
> pot is finally lifting. Quite a kick, though — who gave you
> this pot, hey, Beli'? Come back whenever you want, take
> your sweet time, don't worry about me. I'm here with your
> dog. With your big black sin that I like so much. And don't
> get hurt, drive carefully, and think, always think calmly
> before acting. *Drinnn.* My cell phone — and the Canadians
> only have my landline. It's her. I know even before
> answering because I associate her with the much sexier
> ring of the cell phone, that electrifying sound. *Drindrindrin.*
> Hi, Beli'. She wants to know how it's going. Fine, I tell her,
> everything's smooth. How did Cruise behave? Good, Cruise
> was good. So his name is Cruise. He didn't scratch the
> door? He didn't whine? No, I tell her, not even a little. You
> abandoned us, I tell her, and we got along just fine. We're
> good friends now, me and old Cruise. Look at him. He's
> here at my feet. Cruise! Lie! Over there! Strange, she says,
> usually he makes a big fuss when I leave him. It must mean
> that he found positive energy in your house, she says.
> Fantastic, I think. Of course the dog was good. I emanate
> positive energy: truth is, everyone's trying to glom on to
> me, I swear, men, women, dogs; my aura must be fucking
> incandescent lately; my body superradiant. Charisma.
> Energy. Authority. I'm on my way back, she tells me, do
> you want me to bring you anything? Maybe a couple of
> beers, Beli', I'm all out. And she says yes, a couple of beers,
> I'll be right there. Fantastic. She's fantastic. Who knows
> what will happen later. With her you never know. I barely
> know her, yet I also know her too well. Lara, I know all too

> well what makes her so awesome in the eyes of a poor guy
> who's sick in the head like me. And if I think about it, if I
> have the courage to think about it, I know all too well
> what happened to her when she was a little girl. Only
> abused girls for me. Only them. Are you looking to find a
> girl who was abused when she was a child? Simple: just
> pretend my dick is an arrow, follow my erection, and you'll
> run right into her. By now I know. That's the way it works,
> Lara. Belinda is so fantastic because inside her there's
> something savage, and there's something savage inside her
> because someone put it there when she was a child.
> Savagely. By now I know. And so who can say what will
> happen when she comes back here? With the beers and that
> demo — now I remember — that she wants me to listen
> to, of her singing with that tired-ass group of hers. Maybe
> she's really good, you know. They're full of talent, these
> Real Things. Then they waste it all, but they've always got
> tons of it. But I'm out of the danger zone now, I can stop
> writing. I'm not entirely sure I was really fighting in the
> past three hours, but if I was then I won. It's all over,
> everything's fine. Life is good and I'm strong. I emanate.
> And I bless you, Lara. I bless you for being near me in my
> moment of need, like you always are. Let's talk on the
> phone tomorrow. I can't come to the wedding, you know,
> I've got Franceschino for the weekend, not to mention how
> much it pisses me off that you're marrying that fucking
> yuppie, but basically it's as if you already were married,
> you've been together for a long time, it's obvious that you
> like it like that, there's no accounting for tastes, if you're
> happy we're all happy, Sean Connery is better-looking in
> his old age than he was when he was young — let's talk
> tomorrow, on the phone. As if nothing happened, because

> in the end it really was nothing. Like the astronauts said a
> few weeks ago, I don't know if you followed it, those two
> dickheads that have been in the orbiting space station for
> months, the Russian and the American, well one morning
> they heard a *noise,* you see, like a wrench banging against
> the stern of the space station, *TA-DAA,* and they didn't
> understand what caused it and they asked the control
> center, "Houston, do you read me, what the fuck was that
> thump?" And at headquarters they started to do all the
> housekeeping, all the checks with the computers and the
> tests, very scrupulously, and at the end of all that fuss one
> of them replied, "Nothing, guys. It was nothing." . . . It was
> nothing. It's always nothing. Who knows if a message this
> long will make it through the Internet. I'll give it a try.
> Big kiss.
> Gianni.

chapter thirteen

I did it, yes. I stuck my big nose in her e-mails. Theoretically I
should not have been able to, since Lara didn't connect automatically and I didn't know her password. But I nailed it on my second
try: TOANSE. It's because I remember perfectly what happened
when she took that intelligence test, the one they say NASA gives
in order to select astronauts. If you are given a sequence of letters
O T T F F S S E N T E T T F F S S E N T T T . . . what letter would
come next? Forty seconds to answer, but anyone who can't do it
in twenty will never be an astronaut. Go. I couldn't solve it when
they asked me. None of the people I asked could, and I asked a lot
of people. But Lara, after twenty seconds she said *T.* What did you
say? I said *T:* the next letter in the sequence would be *T.* That's im-

possible: you were just guessing, tell the truth. No, I didn't guess: *T* as in twenty-three. They're all numbers: one, two, three, four, five, six, etc. And they stop at twenty-two, so . . . So you already knew, someone gave you the test: come on, tell the truth. Not out of any lack of respect, but I can't believe that of all the people I know you're the only one who could become an astronaut: you already knew the answer, admit it, no harm done. No, I didn't know, I swear. It's that I used the same system for my passwords: I take important dates, the ones I could never forget, and rather than expressing them in numbers, which would be too easy to guess, I use the initials of these numbers. Do you see? For me it's normal when I see the letter *O* to think immediately of one, or when I see *T* to think of two, or twenty, it's the first thing that comes to mind. I'm no more intelligent than you, don't worry . . .

ATNSE. April Twentieth Nineteen Sixty-Eight. Her date of birth. I got it on the second try, because the first time I tried ATNNF, April Thirteenth Nineteen Ninety-Four, Claudia's date of birth. In other words I did it, I went into her e-mail: I never spied on her when she was alive, but I have done it now that she's dead.

I didn't feel at all good when I started. Opening Outlook I felt as if Lara's computer was scolding me, and I sat for more than half an hour with the downloaded mail in front of my eyes without clicking on it. Resist, I told myself, she's not here anymore, what you want to do doesn't make any sense — delete everything instead. And the funny thing is the more I said this to myself the stronger I felt, far from the doubts that had driven me to this point, more and more determined to give the computer the only commands that made any sense — SELECT ALL, DELETE — after which I could go to bed with my mind at peace. The list of messages Lara received after her death was right there in front of my eyes, but I managed to not read a word, as if they were written in Arabic, and I enjoyed sitting there perched on the edge of an abyss that had opened up beneath

my feet, it gave me an inebriating sense of inviolability, the same way
you feel playing sports sometimes, in those rare moments of grace
in which you feel that everything, absolutely everything, depends
on you, and you feel sure that — surfing, let's say — the surfboard
will go exactly where you want it, because you don't have the least
doubt that your feet are exerting just the right amount of pressure
to make it cut into the wave at the angle that will connect you to
it for as long as you want. Or else, since it's the same thing, the feeling of immunity I had twice in the space of a few minutes on the
day that Lara died — probably right while she was dying — first
together with Carlo when we dove in to rescue the two women
who were struggling, or to tell the truth when we looked into each
other's eyes before diving in and it really seemed that it was already
all over, and then by myself, a little later, when I was struggling
with the drowning woman who was trying to pull me under, when
I grabbed her from behind and pushed her toward the shore with
thrusts of my cock and got maybe the most memorable erection of
my life. Just as I was sitting here in front of Lara's inbox and I cher-
ished this wise sense not to go through it and was more and more
certain that, effortlessly, indeed with a feeling that all of Creation
was inclined like the plane of a pinball flipper toward that imminent
gesture, I was about to hit DELETE.

Because of that pleasure, I think, because of my naïve, greedy
desire to prolong it indefinitely, I made the mistake of not deleting
it right away. For one fatal second my eyes stopped scanning and
came to a stop on an arid piece of alphanumeric information in
two messages bearing the fatal date, *Monday 8/30/2004* — one prior
to and one following the time of her death, established by the ambulance medic at 1:55 P.M. It was a matter of one or two seconds,
then my eyes started scanning down the list without focusing on
anything in particular, but those two seconds were long enough to
break the spell and suck me into a series of truly stupid actions that

I carried out almost unconsciously, as if I were on automatic pilot. I opened the first of the two messages, yes I did; and I read it; and then I opened the second one; and I read it, too, even though it was long, in one sitting; and then I stopped again, but this time with immense exhaustion, and I started to think again about deleting everything, only to realize that now such a gesture was impossible, ruled out by the ideas that were crowding my head with remarkable urgency, to search for and read all the previous messages from that sender to Lara, for example, and to go dipping into her sent mail to find all the ones she had written to him for the sake of this unknown but evidently long and very intimate friendship, and to do the same with the New Age association that Lara had never mentioned to me, or to go looking through her archives and read all the correspondence between her and Marta, or better yet — to read everything, yes, start from the beginning and move forward a little bit every night, methodically, immediately after putting my daughter to bed, read every e-mail sent and received by Lara in the past . . . — when did Lara buy that computer? It was 2000, I think, yes, the summer of 2000, Italy had lost the final of the European soccer cup against France, and to console herself she decided to buy a computer — . . . in the past four years. So once again I was frozen before Lara's e-mail, once again I was repeating to myself to resist, to delete everything, etc., but unlike before I felt dirty and irremediably weak, certain I would never overcome the urge. Because yes, those moments of grace are spectacular, they're beautiful, but experience should have taught me that things last as long as they're going to last, after which they're always followed by a very powerful opposing force: the surfboard that rears up and then swooshes down, the fatigue that takes the place of inviolability, *the list of messages that destroys you.*

I don't know how, from the logjam of thoughts that were paralyzing me, a modest, gray, bureaucratic act emerged: why not print the two messages I had just read — I say "I don't know how" because I really am ignoring what dictated this urgency, why I considered it so necessary. Except that at the very moment I hit the PRINT command, the only thing that could have possibly torn me away happened: Claudia called out to me. I ran to her room, and she was sitting on the bed drinking a bottle of water. What's wrong, sweetheart? Did you have a bad dream? Claudia shook her head and kept drinking, but her eyes were frightened, her breathing labored, she had just called to me in the middle of the night — *she'd had a bad dream*. She finished drinking, put the top back on the bottle, and lay down again, silently, closing her eyes. I sat there in silence and began to pat her, waiting for her to fall back asleep so I could go back to the transgression I had interrupted; and I'm still here: quiet, caressing my daughter, waiting for her to fall back asleep, so I can go back to rummaging through the e-mails of her dead mother.

But you never know how long children are going to take to fall back asleep, you always risk leaving the room too soon: I can't tell you how many times over the years I've miscalculated, fooled by her somewhat heavier breathing or by my haste to get back to a movie or to chat or sometimes even to fuck Lara (but before today, *never* to spy on her), I've moved with wasted caution before Claudia was actually asleep; I've had a lot of experience with these slow leave-takings filled with creaking tendons, followed by three or four mine-sweeping steps toward the door, after the completion of which, just when you're about to relax because she *hasn't* called you back — a sign that she really was asleep, despite the vague, extrasensory perception that she wasn't and the consequent fear that you had left too soon — she calls you back, and you have to go back there and start all over again. That's why I'm staying here so long, to pat her. Only for this. Tonight it's not a loving gesture, it's not a tender gesture: it's a calculated gesture.

This is the worst moment since Lara died — and it comes at the end of the worst day. I'm stroking my little girl mechanically, hypocritically, my thoughts elsewhere. The gnawing doubt that Marta planted is contaminating everything, even my time with my daughter, because my mind is fixated on only one thing: going back to the computer. On only one true desire: to continue reading Lara's e-mail. On only one true hope: to find something fishy, murky, rotten — hidden objective reasons, in other words — to feel bad about. My most fervent hope is to discover an affair, obviously, maybe with the maniac who called me a fucking yuppie, whose book I keep reading to Claudia at bedtime, one chapter a night, but it appeared in our home before the summer, on Lara's initiative; a secret liaison, yes, stark and inadmissible, hidden from Marta, too, and protracted beyond all limits of prudence, that became practically unbearable but also, because of its ambiguous nature, closer and more unbreakable, so much so that it generated the pain her sister described and involved recourse to Eastern practices in the hope of soothing it, as well as visits to shamans, to vampires, seminars on overcoming fear and rage, without ever obtaining results, of course, which only increased her pain, as if it were further aggravated by the need to hide it from me, given its cause, and to pretend to live the normal and serene life I thought she was living, the way things used to be, and the way they would definitely have continued to be if at the hour of truth she had done the right rather than the wrong thing — and rejected that first invitation to dinner rather than accept it, closed her lips and turned her face to the side rather than return that first kiss, tell herself, "I'm a married woman, I have a daughter, I can't do this," rather than "Fuck it, let's see." . . . Yes, a suffocating sense of guilt that, combined with the aortic aneurysm that condemned her to a premature death in any case, as turned up in the autopsy ordered by the judicial authorities of Grosseto (it's procedure, they told me, since we're dealing with, ahem, a *suspicious* death, not that the adjective was meant to insinuate anything untoward about the circumstances, nor further add to — they realized — the already unbearable grief of her family; *suspicious* in the sense of without obvious cause, in a subject who was apparently healthy and still young; it's the term used in the scientific literature, of course: *suspicious* in the sense of *unusual* — and I told them yes, but then why doesn't the literature use the word *unusual*?); a suffocating sense of guilt that, as I was saying, combined with the deformity that Lara had unknowingly been suffering from since birth, may have contributed to generating, yes, at that precise moment, yes, the fatal rupture — apropos of which, contrary to what Marta thinks, my personal responsibilities, not to say my faults, should be considered equal to . . .

— Papà . . .

. . . zero.

— Here I am.

Claudia sits up. She turns on the blue star lamp that IKEA sells for €9.90, the same one that millions of other children in the West have screwed to the wall by their beds, and looks at me. I was right to stay: she didn't sleep a wink.

— Where were you going?

— When?

— Just now.

— When you called?

— Yes, where were you going?

What an angel . . .

— Nowhere, sweetheart.

I pat her head, smiling.

— It was just a bad dream, — I say. — Settle down now. Go to sleep.

Claudia settles down, docile. *Where was I going . . .*

— But it didn't seem like a dream, — she whispers.

And in fact it wasn't, sweetheart. I really was going someplace I shouldn't. A place full of evil, guilt, far from you. But
you saved me . . .

— Bad dreams never seem like dreams, — I say. — But then
you wake up, and they disappear forever.

I continue to pat her, and everything already feels different:
she's tired, and in a little while she'll fall asleep. She's completed
her mission.

— I'm not going anywhere, you know that . . .

She saved me, yes, and now I'm strong again, and the world
is tilted toward the right hole again. I'll delete that message, I'll
delete everything, and I won't repeat my earlier mistake, I won't
mess around with this simple intention when I'm feeling weak, I'll
do it right away . . .

— Did you hear me? Now I have to go to the other room to
finish something important, sweetheart: go to sleep, quietly, I'll
be right back to turn out the light. Okay?

— Okay.

Four giant steps, and I'm there. It's easy. EDIT, SELECT ALL. 4332
MESSAGES SELECTED. DELETE. Zap, deleted, without even passing
through the recycle bin. Lara's e-mails are gone. They never existed. That writer is now a perfect stranger again, and as far as I
know he's living with his wife, his son, Francesco, and his dog,
Roy — according to the blurb on the inside jacket of his book.
But that's not enough; screwdriver and hammer in the third
drawer; who would have figured that Piquet's paranoid advice
would prove useful: "Destroy the hard disc." Every time there
was a change of owners at the company — and it had already
happened three times — Piquet destroyed the hard disc of his
computer and blamed it on a virus. The last time I saw him do
it: *bam, bam,* with blows of the hammer. But do you really have

such important things to hide? I asked him. You never know, he replied. *Bam, bam.* Exactly like I'm doing now: here goes, *bam, bam,* the hard disk disappears, Lara never had a computer, she died without ever owning one; three and a half years ago she wanted to buy one, but during the finals of the European soccer cup she made a vow: with five minutes to go, when Italy was trailing France by one goal, she said: "If we win I won't buy a computer," and then the game went the way it went, everyone knows, tie at the last minute by Delvecchio and the golden goal by Del Piero, fantastic, in an overhead kick, *bam, bam,* Italy's the European champion and Lara gets no computer. A Lara who is *serene,* who is healthy — whose only concern, perhaps, was the low spirits of her beautiful, crazy sister. *Bam.*

Done. How long did it take me? Two minutes. What time is it? I don't have my watch. I look for my cell phone to see the time. It's in the kitchen, who knows why. Twelve forty-four. A new text message. Quarter of an hour ago. From Marta. "Sorry for today. I'm ashamed of what I said. You're the best part of me."

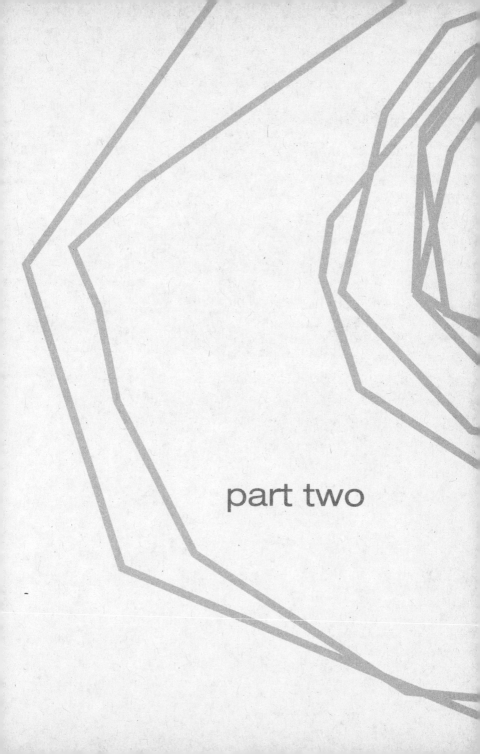

part two

chapter fourteen

The owner of the C3 still hasn't called. Strange. His car was smashed up almost twenty-four hours ago, and he still doesn't know. This morning, after Claudia entered the school, I realized that the rain had turned the business card with my phone number into pulp, and I replaced it with a new one, this time inside a cellophane slip case from Claudia's Magic cards, for protection. I even changed its position: not under the front windshield wiper but under the rear window wiper, so the driver would notice it more easily if it fell or got ruined again. On the card I added my cell phone number, while I was at it, and also a — completely useless, I admit it — "Sorry." The fact is that the car is in pretty bad shape, with its headlights shattered, the mudguard squashed against the wheel, and as far as I could tell it would take a tow truck to move it. This morning, seeing it beaten up like that, I imagine the owner when he comes to pick it up, in a hurry perhaps, with a day crammed with appointments he had struggled to squeeze in and his car being the only instrument for honoring all of them; a simple phone number on a business card seemed too arid for the disaster he will find. Only after placing the new card on the back window did I realize the stupidity of my "Sorry"; also because, if the guy were to come for the car while school was in session, I would be there, and I could apologize all I wanted in person. But he still hasn't come, and I can't help but wonder why. Is he sick? What could be more important than realizing that someone has destroyed his car? Not to mention that —

— Pietro.

— Oh!

It's Enoch. He came up from behind me, as quiet as an American Indian, and made me jump.

— You scared me . . .

— Sorry, — he laughs. — Annalisa gave me this for you. Here, before I forget.

He holds out a folder. Contracts to sign.

— How are things?

Here we go again. How's the little girl, nice out here, you're doing the right thing, be as close to her as you can. I have to be patient, there's not much else I can do. Now it's Enoch's turn. I'd seen him at the funeral and heard from him once on the phone — like everyone else, he called to make sure I hadn't lost my mind — but I never thought he would come. He's the head of human resources: right now, he should be the only person who's really working at the company; he needs to be there to reassure and to placate overwrought employees — things for which, according to Jean-Claude, who put him there, he has a mysterious talent . . .

— Jean-Claude is out, — he says.

Here we go. It had happened sooner than he thought.

— Yes, — I reply.

— You knew about it?

And sooner than Jean-Claude thought.

— Yes.

— When did you learn?

— About ten days ago.

Enoch nods, surprised, and to tell the truth I'm surprised, too: since when have I been so sincere?

— Who told you about it?

— He did.

Since last night. What happened last night was useful for something.

— Ah . . .

He nods again, without trying to hide a certain bitterness. It's understandable: in a situation in which information is worth its weight in gold, he had come to me with the most loyal of ideas — namely, to inform me that while I was stranded here living out my grief, the boss had been fired — only to find out that I had already known for ten days. In other words, he discovers all at once that the whole business is far bigger than he is, forcing him to deduce that it must have always been so and that despite the sudden power that his appointment as the director of human resources had granted to him — him, who came from the hellhole of a call center, where on a daily basis he had to invent bullshit excuses to feed subscribers who had dialed the toll-free number with a long list of complaints — he was still floundering around at a really low level of the video game. I'm sorry; really, it's not that I'm not sorry, but this isn't his problem any more than it is mine.

— So what do you think?

— What do I think . . . I think that we, by which I mean the people considered *his* guys — you, me, Basler, Elisabetta, Di Loreto, Tardioli — now we've got a problem.

He nods, nods, does nothing except nod.

— Houston, we have a problem, — he says, in a poor imitation of the line from that film, what's its title, *Apollo 13*.

— Exactly.

— Listen, — he says, — do you have a second? Can I talk to you about something?

Jeez.

Here we go again, like clockwork. If it doesn't rain — and now it's not raining — the two characters, the one waiting in front of his daughter's school and the other who's come to see him, move over to the park. The girl with the golden retriever may or may not be there — this morning she's not. The two may or may not sit down on a park bench — this time they sit. They chat for a while: the guy visiting gradually works his way into the subject, after starting from a long way off, till he spews forth on the other — the guy always there — his own worries, his own pain, his own fears. What happened last night did help me with one thing: It helped me understand that for as long as I can avoid my own pain, I have to protect myself, I have to defend myself, otherwise I'm going to be spending my nights sinking into the pain of others. So if, as it seems, coming here to grieve and to confide your secrets is for some unknown reason becoming a habit, I'm going to have to stay distant and distinct from the people who are coming, to avoid getting involved. It's important to remember that *I'm not them.* I have to listen and observe with detachment. I have to stay on the surface. I have to notice the details, hammer away at the nonessential, distract myself. Today, for example, the weather is nice again, in the sky there are a corral of white clouds and a fairly strong sun that comes and goes trying to straddle them. Enoch removes his glasses to clean them and suddenly becomes unrecognizable. He's the kind of guy who looks as if he was born wearing glasses, with furrows from the earpieces across his temples, a sore over the bridge of his nose, and when he removes his glasses he becomes completely different. Enoch, for example, looks much younger, much meaner, and cross-eyed. He's really different.

— I don't know about you, — he starts, — but when I was little I wanted to become a labor leader.

He puts the glasses back on and becomes himself again.

— A union boss?

— Yes, a union boss like my father.

— Your father was a union boss?

— He was the provincial secretary of CISL. For the province of Como, when we lived there. He was supposed to become the regional secretary, but he died . . .

His father. How odd. Jean-Claude also started out talking about his father, unless I'm mistaken. His father the military pilot, who never picked him up from school . . .

— And instead what do I find myself doing? — he sniggers. — The exact opposite of a union boss: head of human resources. And I like it, too.

Here's Miss Gloria leaving the school entrance. It's a moment when a cone of sunshine falls right there, on that doorway, like a bull's-eye, and here she is repeating exactly the same gestures to put on her dark sunglasses — by now I've seen her do it many times: purse resting on her raised leg; long rummaging through her purse; extraction and donning of glasses; leaving with that snappy gait that always makes it look as if she's sowing things in her wake. Who knows whether she realizes that she's always making the same gestures. Who knows why she doesn't put her glasses on before she leaves. She sees me, from the distance, and waves. The sun has already disappeared behind a huge rabbit-shaped cloud . . .

— Or rather, — Enoch continues, — I used to like it. It was nice being head of personnel when the personnel were doing all right, were happy, and increased in number month by month because the company was hiring rather than firing. There were two good years. Now I don't like it anymore. Now it's a kind of hell, because this merger is terrorizing everybody. Everyone comes to me, and I don't know what to tell them. Until yesterday I trusted in Jean-Claude, my only thought was to convey to everyone his calm, his security, and despite the fact that he has seemed more distant recently, and the situation was becoming more and more complicated, I continued to believe in him. It seemed strange to me that he went on vacation at a moment like this, but I trusted him, do you see? I would never have thought that he would have dumped us like this. Then last night at nine Balser phones me and says . . .

Dumped us? *Dumped us?* But it was Thierry who . . . Wait, I mustn't fall for it, I mustn't get involved. All of this is Enoch's problem, not mine; he's the one who came here, he's the one who needs to talk to me. Stop it, okay: evidently the version that has come down, at the video game level where he's playing, is that Jean-Claude dumped us.

— . . . But this morning, — he continues, — I woke up at five, filled with worries, and I couldn't fall back asleep; I thought of what we can expect in the company, of the layoffs, of the arbitration in the labor courts, of the umpteenth invasion of our offices, this time by Americans and Canadians, and then I thought of my father, of how he would have behaved in my position . . .

My telephone rings, and Enoch pauses to let me answer. I look at the display: Thierry. *Thierry.* He's phoned me only once before, two years ago, the day I was appointed director, to congratulate me. It must be something equally important, but what? It can't be anything good, I decide. I believe Jean-Claude: I believe the story that he told me right in this very place, sitting on this bench, suffering intensely before my eyes; therefore I believe that Thierry is a traitor, so I don't answer, there, done, I let the phone ring, like Lebowski, in fact I put it in my pocket, yes, like that, to tell Enoch that he can continue talking, it's nothing important, nothing that could compete even minimally with the memory of his father. But it looks like Enoch also needs a few words of encouragement, because he's clammed up, now he has an almost suspicious expression — what do you want to bet he could see on the display that the call was from Thierry, no, impossible, he can't have read it, and even if he did, what of it, I don't answer calls from traitors, is there something wrong with that, just because Thierry is a very powerful man, "one step below God," some might say, does that mean you have to answer them?

— Go on, go on, — I say, — pick up where you left off . . .

But Enoch seems really tongue-tied by the ringing that continues to come from the inside of my pocket, so, to put him at ease,
I turn the cell phone off, voilà— oh, your epic surprise in that
moment, Thierry's epic secretary with her foxlike little face and
eyes the color of amethyst, Lucille, I think is her name, like B. B.
King's guitar, you were at a minimum doing three other things
while with one ear you kept incoming calls under control with
the speakerphone, ready to pick up the handset and say hello
to me in Italian with your French *r*, and instead you heard the
sound switch abruptly from a single ring tone to the busy signal,
rather unequivocal proof that a certain Paladini, whose cell phone
number filled with sevens you had dialed a moment ago, strum-
ming the keyboard of your console with your long manicured
fingers and nails coated with — I'm going to make a guess here
— amaranth-colored nail polish, that authentic nonentity by
comparison to the elevated personalities whose unlisted numbers
you have found yourself calling more and more often lately, that
nonentity of an Italian dared, ah yes, dared turn off his cell in the
face of your omnipotent boss — with whom, like every secretary
in the world, you are secretly in love . . .

— You were talking about your father, — I say, — about what
he would have done if . . .

Oh Lucille, you refuse to believe and press the redial button
thinking the call had probably dropped, and instead you're hearing the message that the telephone of the customer you are dial-
ing *could be turned off* . . .

— Of course, — Enoch says, with an even more unsettled, almost skeptical air: maybe he read on the display that the phone
call was from Thierry, no less. He slips a hand into his jacket
pocket and takes out two sheets of paper folded into four, opens

them up, and at the same time as he hands them to me, the girl with the golden retriever makes her — sumptuous, what else can I say — entrance into the park and unleashes the dog.

— Well, this is what I wrote, — says Enoch, — this morning at five.

I take the sheets of paper. The girl with the golden retriever takes out her cell phone and dials a number. An absurd thought crosses my mind: if she were phoning me, I would never know.

— It's all inside, — Enoch adds, — everything that I know for sure.

I unfold the sheets of paper. It's three pages of drivel, written in Arial font — and riddled with bold type. The girl wasn't phoning me: the other party answered, and she seems very happy.

> What is a **merger**? A merger is the **conflict** of two power systems aimed at creating a third, enacted for **financial purposes**. It is conceived to **create value,** but the creation of value is a concept that is good for stockholders or corporate banks, but not for the **human beings** that work at the companies, for whom the merger, on the contrary, is the most violent work-related **trauma** that could be inflicted on them.

I look up. Enoch is looking at the sheets of paper from the corner of his eye, engrossed. He's probably rereading it, struggling to go at the same pace as me, to imagine my reactions sentence by sentence.

> Once an agreement has been reached on the transaction, which is not at all easy, there is a tendency to believe that the most important part is done. This conviction stems from the economic world's historical **underestimation** of the **human**

factor, and, more in general, of **psychology**. The biggest problems of a merger are not related to the document that sanctions it.

The girl bursts out into a silvery peal of laughter, of the purest kind, of which you can only say that it makes you want to be the person who provoked it, on the other line of the telephone. How did he do it? What did he tell her? Even without his leash, the dog doesn't stray very far: he seems to be shadowing her.

Rather than numbers, in fact, a company consists of **people** who work, i.e., its **employees,** and after a merger is announced the reaction of any employee at any level is **uncertainty**. What awaits me? Will I stay or will I be sent home? Will my job description change? How will my problems be solved? Will I manage to keep the privileges I've won? No one cares much about the creation of value until the new order has answered these questions, guaranteeing that it will have new **legitimacy**.

During a merger you have to speak with the employees, **bief** and **update** everyone as often as possible; the employees need **confidence**, to feel that they are not considered a mere **pawn**. Instead they are given **canned remarks,** tossed out on the street by a couple of consultants via in-house communications, which has the sole effect of making them more **worried**. Those aseptic statements about future synergies that will not affect personnel are pure hypocrisy, since everyone knows that the only concrete guarantee of creating value on the markets is the **reduction of overhead**, and **80%** of overhead reduction is achieved by laying off **personnel**.

End of the first page. I get ready to read the second, but Enoch stops me.

— Sorry, — he says.

He takes the paper and pens in a correction. When he gives it back to me, there is an *r* between the *b* and the *i* of *bief,* at the beginning of the last paragraph.

— I missed that, — he says, smiling. An ambulance races down the avenue, its siren wailing, and Enoch makes a small sign of the cross.

Hence during a merger period the employees enter into a zone of constant **turbulence**. This is a highly critical period that in the case of large mergers can last for a considerable amount of time, during which the dominant feeling becomes **anxiety**. And anxiety that, if neglected, can grow from **individual** to **collective,** and even transform into **panic**.

Experience in contact with personnel during a merger teaches that there is a double **impact:** on the **physical** level the human mechanism tends to feel greater **stress** and **fatigue** and to accentuate every natural tendency toward **somatization,** with a perceptible increase in **allergies, respiratory disturbances, cystitis, headaches, dermatitis,** and, among women, **yeast infections, aminorrhea, and dysminorrhea**. Whereas on the **psychological** level the mind is assailed by **insecurity;** any event can generate anxious emotions such as **fear, anguish, discouragement,** and **frustration,** which in turn produce grave symptoms of **depression,** which become even graver the more the subject is driven instinctively to reject them, since the culture to which he or she belongs is a culture of pure **performance,** which cannot even conceive of the existence of such illnesses.

I stop to wait for him, in case he is lagging behind me, to give him the time to spot any typos and correct them. But he wasn't behind, since he, too, looked away from the sheet and looked at me inquisitively.

— Do you need to correct? — I ask him.

— What?

— *Ame*-norrhea, *dysme*-norrhea.

— Oh, — he says, surprised. That's not a typo, it's a mistake. He takes the sheet, pens in the corrections, and gives it back to me, but his feelings are hurt. Maybe it would have been better if I had minded my own business.

> The impact is even more **devastating** in the age group of **from forty to fifty years of age,** when adaptation resources are fewer and the risk of **losing** something through the change is much greater. One has the sensation of **regressing,** perceiving a sense of **injustice**. The trauma to be absorbed is enormous: one was attached to a **company culture,** to a **team,** to colleagues with whom one worked with **pleasure,** with **esprit de corps**. It is hard to find oneself face to face with **the others**. Even if they are described as the **"victims,"** they are still the **enemy** made flesh. Until yesterday we were in fierce **competition** with them; now all of a sudden they are part of our environment. One feels **invaded,** if only physically, and feels the desire to tell them to go fuck themselves, that things were fine without them. Instead everyone has to work together and the **shock** is huge. There have been managers from blue chip companies, where titles and hierarchies were sacred, who were unable to bear being placed in working groups together with personnel from another company, of a markedly inferior ranking, on behalf of a contingent common competence.

End of the second page. Well, the concept is clear, and it's always the same: even Enoch is trying to make me feel bad. He's trying to remind me that the possibility of unemployment is staring me in the face, especially because of my known association with Jean-Claude, and especially because I have been weakened by a terrible tragedy — the famous wounded gazelle — and that for this reason I should suffer and waste away in the ways he described — probably a mix between what he observes every day in the venting of employees and what he himself is feeling. But I don't fall for it. This is too big to be worth worrying about. There's nothing I can do, I can only keep my distance, and if a few minutes ago Thierry was phoning me only to grant me the honor (or himself the pleasure) of firing me personally, well, it would be better than planning a quick flight to Paris, with the private jet, because I'm not moving from here, and I'm not answering his phone call.

The girl is still there on her cell phone. She's stopped laughing, and is not even talking: she seems to be listening, for now, engrossed, her head down, while with one foot she is drawing a semicircle on the ground.

It's a situation that is highly destabilizing, and there are only three categories of people that are able to handle it: the **loyalists,** the **turncoats,** and the **collaborators**. All the others risk getting laid off. You have to develop a huge physical and psychological **resilience** to collapsing, and only a few are able to without adequate **assistance**. But there is no assistance of this kind. So the most common outcome during mergers is that many of the best people leave their jobs **voluntarily,** even before the merger is complete; which is regarded myopically with favor since it alleviates the subsequent action of laying off personnel, but on the contrary it represents a net **loss**. Because the men and women

that leave take with them their **knowledge** and technical
capacities, and contrary to the **virtual** value that is created
in the markets, the **real** result is a shocking **impoverishment**.
This is why in the space of one or two years, every single
large merger has gone belly-up, goddamn it.

O-kay. I look at Enoch; he's definitely wondering whether I get
it, whether or not *I've already read it*. I answer in the most unequivocal way possible: I burst out laughing. I understand perfectly that
this couldn't be more serious, especially knowing that a sense of
humor is not one of his strong points, and for a second I try to
hold back; but I can't resist, no way, and I burst out laughing. He
doesn't laugh, but he does unsheathe a smile as if to accompany
my laughter until it is depleted.

— What do you intend to do? — I ask.

— I don't know, — he replies, — it doesn't matter. Or rather
it does, but something else is more important . . .

The dog suddenly leaves the girl and comes to us. Decided.
Resolute. Seeing as his master won't get off the phone, he comes
to be petted by two complete strangers. And Enoch, as if it were
the most natural thing in the world, starts to pet him and keeps
talking.

— . . . You see, I wrote these things from the heart. I wrote
them thinking of my father. These are the things that I would say,
they are *some* of the things I would say, if I were asked about this
damned merger. I identify with them one hundred percent, do
you see? They're *true* . . .

The girl, from afar, gives a surprising two-fingered whistle to
call the dog, who in fact pricks up his ears, but Enoch continues
to pet him softly and then, his hand soaked with those caresses,
he makes a short, wonderful gesture of response that says many
things at once, all of them clear, all of them reassuring — a kind

of crazy benediction to his youth, to his listlessness, to his absent-mindedness. A gesture of such protective grace that if I were that girl I would immediately interrupt my phone call and run to meet the person who performed it, to make him my shepherd. But she doesn't, and it might be pertinent, at this point, to sketch out a physical description of Enoch: tall and flabby, with a complexion of an unnatural gelatin color, big metal eyeglasses that tyrannize his face, gray crew-cut hair like no one has seen for decades, and a shabby way of wearing his dark suit that's almost subversive: he looks almost like a politically involved Presbyterian priest or an eccentric professor known for his controversial methods. It's not that he is ugly, I mean — nothing like Piquet, for example — but there's something inescapably asexual about his apperance, like a coat of mordant anaphrodisiac carefully painted all over his body, which a pretty young female might not be able to forgive. That's why the girl didn't move, she didn't even notice the beauty of his gesture; that's why Enoch is married to a woman much older than him, obese and mysterious, to whom no other man has probably ever paid attention.

— You may know that I'm a faithful and practicing Catholic.

— Yes, I know.

— Like my parents, like my grandparents, and as far as I know, like all my ancestors. It's as if we were chained to the Bible by our last name. You know who Enoch is, don't you?

— Not really.

— He's one of the patriarchs of Genesis, the father of Methuselah and great-grandfather of Noah. Thanks to Saint Paul, the Christian tradition absorbed the Jewish tradition, according to which Enoch, together with the prophet Elijah, is the only figure in the Bible who never died.

He talks to me and pets the girl's dog, but he doesn't look at either me or the dog or the girl: now his gaze is pointed in the direction of the street, where you can see my friend the traffic cop, the one who saves a spot for me in the morning, and it's obvious that he's not looking at him, either.

— Wow . . .

— Did you know I have a brother who's a missionary in Zimbabwe?

— No . . .

— His name is Pietro, like you, he's been there for thirty years. And I have a theologian uncle who teaches at the Catholic University, and a bunch of aunts and great-aunts, both living and dead, who are nuns . . .

He continues to pet the dog automatically, without realizing it, as I was doing last night with Claudia, waiting for her to fall back asleep.

— In other words, without going into too much detail, it would be correct to state that in the past, let's say, *four centuries,* — here his voice bristles with rage, and Enoch pauses, to control it, — no member of my family has ever had even the remotest desire to curse.

— All right, I don't think that —

— Now would you mind, — he cuts me off, — rereading out loud the last sentence of the text I wrote this morning?

Here we go again: the tap is open, and now Enoch is suffering like a wounded animal, too. He, too, here by me.

— Come on, Paolo, forget about it . . .

— Please, — he is undeterred, — just the last sentence. Please. Out loud.

I unfold the paper again. And now I know what the problem is. The problem is that if I reread it, I'll start laughing.

— "This is why in the space of one or two years, every single large merger has gone belly-up, goddamn it."

I'm afraid to look up, I can't look him in the face, I can't say a single word, I can't do almost anything. There's no one here to pet except this dog: that's it, I'll *steal* it, shit, I'll pull it between my legs, since he doesn't care anyway, the dog doesn't care, its mistress doesn't care, and in the meantime I'll have something I can stare at, focus on, something to keep me from bursting out laughing. Pet the dog, yes . . .

— So my question is this, — Enoch's voice is grave, solemn, — where did this swearword use to be? It came from deep inside of me, but where was I keeping it?

The dog, like all dogs, synchronizes itself immediately to the rhythm of my pats: he responds to each one with a long batting of his eyelashes.

— It was buried deep inside me, you know, because until this morning I lived with the certainty, I repeat, *with the certainty* that it didn't even exist. Where does it come from? Please give me an answer. Don't tell me it isn't serious, don't say any of the things you want to tell me, just do me the damn favor of telling me where, in your opinion, the swearword that I printed on that sheet came from.

I'm starting to feel a little better. I've started scratching the neck of the dog, who transmits some of his Olympian indifference to me.

— Please, Pietro. I'm not joking. Tell me where it comes from . . .

I could hazard a reply, because this guy really does want me to answer him. But without looking at him, of course.

— I don't know, maybe someone else inserted it yesterday. One of the many that drop by to ask you for reassurances that you can't provide . . .

— *Someone inserted it* . . . Brilliant.

I keep scratching the dog's neck, focusing on his pleasure, and my eyes fall on his tag. It says, NEBBIA 348-7667843. I look at the girl, who's still on the phone, still off in the distance: so *this* must be her phone number. Who knows how many guys would love to have it. I look back at the tag. 348 . . .

— Nebbia! — the girl suddenly calls the dog and for good measure gives another whistle. — Nebbia, come here!

. . . and all at once I realize that her number is unforgettable, dammit, because it's a palindrome. Yes: 348-7667843, 3487667-843, it stays the same even if you read it backward. *I topi non avevano nipoti.* It only takes a second, because immediately after, Nebbia pulls his neck away, with a movement more like a horse than a dog, and he rejoins his mistress in a light and measured gallop.

— Sorry! — the girl shouts, placing the leash around his neck while already heading toward the street. And in the fluidity of this exit from the scene, without even awaiting our response, she finds a spirited salute to send our way after she's already turned her back on us, certain we're still looking at her.

— Do you know her? — Enoch asks.

— No, — I answer.

But I know her phone number by heart, I could add: 348-7667843; and the natural way she just greeted us means that starting tomorrow, whenever she brings the dog to the park and finds me on a bench, we will continue to say hello to each other with the same naturalness; all of which allows me to predict that in all probability I'll get to know her.

— Nice girl, — says Enoch coldly.

Now I sense that I can turn around, I sense that I can turn around and look at him; the dog and the girl have stifled the laughter that I would have unleashed on him until a short while ago. And, in fact, I do look at him, although he continues to not look at me: his eyes still gazing in the distance, he maintains a deadpan expression that makes my blood run cold rather than reassure me. It seems impossible for a man to reach the breaking point over a swearword, but that's exactly what I seem to see in this moment.

— Listen, — I say, — I'm hungry. Do you feel like having a sandwich?

— *Ubi maior minor cessat.*

— Beg your pardon?

His eyes are lit up by a malicious gleam, and he tilts his head forward, inviting me to look in that direction.

Thierry is entering the park. He's advancing in long strides, a broad smile sketched on his face. He's wearing his overcoat, a sign he's coming from someplace much colder than here.

chapter fifteen

Here we go.

Enoch has just settled his account, and now he's on his way. There he goes, right next to Jean-Claude's presidential and soon-to-be-ex Alfa Romeo, idling and double-parked. There he is, saying hi to Lino, Jean-Claude's soon-to-be-ex driver, who as always is probably reading *La Gazetta dello Sport*. There he is, fading like a gray moon behind the bump in the street before it reaches this point. The curse that torments him is now self-evident: it's a banner that Evil has managed to plant on top of him, and it really does seem to flutter in the wind. Now that Enoch has disappeared . . .

— So, — goes Thierry. — Not bad here.

Here we go.

Thierry looks around, curious. He has the same jovial air as always, the same face creased with cheerful lines — not wrinkles, careful what you say, but genuine cracks in the clay of his flesh, like something from a tribal mask. I haven't seen him for a while, not since the last Cannes Festival, actually, where he would sud-

denly appear at receptions, walk arm in arm with people, and infect them with the elegant bonhomie of which he is considered a
sort of guru. Back then I thought he was still close to Jean-Claude,
I still believed the *outsiders* myth, but in reality he was already plot-
ting, he was already betraying. I have to remember this because
whatever he has come here to do today, he is going to do it well. I
have to remember that I believe Jean-Claude, therefore Thierry is
just another unscrupulous megamanager bitten by the tarantula
who aspires to become a *tycoon* using other people's money: more
brilliant and original by a long shot than almost all his peers, including his weasel, Boesson, but even more dangerous precisely
because of this. I have to be careful with him, no matter what he
has come here to do. But of course, what has he come here to do?

— Did you hear about Jean-Claude? — he asks me.

— No.

The hell with it, what have I got to lose?

— I mean yes, — I correct myself, — I know they've taken
away his jet, and a few minutes ago Enoch told me, to use his exact
words, that "He dumped us." That's all I know.

Thierry smiles, with a smirk that looks both spontaneous and
not in the least spontaneous. That's how it is with him: everything
he seems to let you guess about his state of mind remains plausible
even if you put a nice "not" in front of it.

— Well, — he says, — so you already know a lot more than
almost everyone else. Do you also know why the jet was taken
away from him?

Here it is, watch out, it's a trap. I shouldn't have to answer; he
should give me the answer.

— Budget cuts, — which is true, I seem to recall, it was written
in the resolution.

Thierry smiles again, and this time the ambiguity of his smirk
stems from the fact that it might or might not contain admiration

of my avoidance of his trap. He takes a deep breath, lifts his heels lightly, then lowers them back down to the ground heavily, as if to plant them there good and solid.

— Jean-Claude resigned last night from all the offices he held, — he says. — For the International, the position will be eliminated after the merger, therefore it's no problem. For the presidency here in Italy, on the other hand, he'll have to be replaced. Therefore I've come here to ask whether you would be willing to accept his position.

Boom. He seconds this bombshell with a straight, firm, expressionless face — this time. But his almost perfect Italian, consisting of short sentences peppered with *therefores*, has a strange, militaristic pace. Now I'm the one who's smiling — but rather than smiling I'd say *I feel a smile happening* on my face. And now?

— What an idea . . . — I mutter.

— It's not just an idea, it's a decision. I spoke with Boesson, and he agrees.

As a boy I wanted to become a film producer. I even started to when I was thirty, working on a project I was enthusiastic about: a film adaptation of Arthur Schnitzler's *Night Games*. I was convinced it would yield a masterpiece, and I bought what was for me a very expensive option on the rights before I had any apparent chance to use it. I was deeply convinced that the sheer quality of the idea would automatically generate all the events necessary to make me a producer — and so it went, as strange as that may seem. I had just moved to Milan, and one day at the bank, I happened to take my place at the end of a long line and immediately after me in came Vittorio Mezzogiorno, who for me always was and always will be the greatest Italian actor. In those days his popularity had soared because he was playing the part of Inspector Licata in the second season of the TV series *Piovra,* so everyone at the bank recognized him and asked him for his autograph. I was very impressed by the

fact that he didn't exploit his celebrity to avoid that dreadful line
and that he made himself so completely available to his fans, many
of whom were elderly people waiting to cash their pension checks:
he shook their hands, scribbled his signature on their pieces of
paper, and playacted like he was dodging the bullets that people
pretended to shoot at him with their fingers, smiling sweetly at
everyone without giving the slightest hint that his thoughts were
elsewhere. Maybe that's how I mustered the courage to come forward, introduce myself as a producer, and *propose* — just like that:
there, while he was waiting in line, surrounded by the fans who
continued to pester him — that he make *Night Games* with me.
Anyway, it just so happened that *Night Games* was his favorite book;
and that more than once he had entertained the idea of performing it onstage but had always postponed the project because of
multiplying commitments, but without ever giving up on it; and
that yes, dammit, if I found the money, he would do it, as actor
and as director. The next half hour — which is how long the line
took — was amazing for me, a homecoming of sorts: as if I were
a bee that, after having buzzed around Creation aimlessly, had finally discovered where to find the nectar toward which instinct
had driven it and how satisfying it was to drink. Amid constant
interruptions from his fans, we spoke for the whole time about *our*
project, and we were enthusiastic, learning that we had been won
over by the same pages of the story and that we had more or less
the same ideas about how to transpose it to our own day and age.
During those moments I was feeling none of the doubts that used
to plague me every time I believed in something: however crazy
this might sound, I was talking with Vittorio Mezzogiorno about a
film we would do together, it was really happening, and there was
a power to it that swept away any doubts: simply put, I was right to
believe in the karmic power of my idea, and I was getting proof of
it. I am remembering all this now, before Thierry, who is still enjoy-

ing the effects of the bombshell he has just dropped, because the pages of *Night Games* that Vittorio Mezzogiorno and I liked the most were the ones in which the protagonist, Wilhelm, who had gone to Baden-Baden to play baccarat, started to win like crazy, and slowly but surely, as the chips started to pile up in front of him, he lost his grip on the situation. His mind began to wander, and his thoughts galloped off freely toward all the riches that his conspicuous winnings had suddenly placed within reach — a new uniform, a new cape, a new sword knot, dinners at fashionable restaurants — and, as he started to win more and more, new clothing, patent leather shoes, jaunts into the Viennese Woods, even a carriage . . . I find myself in the same situation today, and this is why I'm keeping my mouth shut and my eyes down, staring at my shoes, which have become a screen on which to project a film filled with a pomp and magnificence I would have denied ever having desired until a moment ago: a fabulous salary, power, an ironclad multiyear contract, stock options, a private jet, artworks, vintage cars, luxury homes, driver, all kinds of perks . . . Unctuous, hairy, devious, and blood-drenched, but remember that the proposal I have just received means access to all these things, and I am actively considering it. They are the sweetest fruits — all in a bundle — that the civilization to which I belong can offer, a kind of *hors catégorie* ostentatious wealth made available to a select circle of the elite — not at all like the ordinary and even banal circle I used to be content with; of course I'm going to turn him down: this is the last thing I want, since first and foremost it's a pretty shaky proposal, maybe even a trap; but you still have to admit it's the least dirty and risky way to enter that circle, *and I am admitting this*. Obviously I'm going to turn him down, no ifs, ands, or buts, just as there was no way Wilhelm could quit the game before losing everything, but in the meantime here I am, seeing a seventy-two-foot sailboat pass slowly before my eyes, me at the rudder and Claudia sunbathing on the teak deck . . .

but a formidable mental limit keeps me from doing the right thing before indulging myself dangerously in the wrong thing, like last night when I was facing Lara's inbox.

— You don't have to give me your answer now, — says Thierry. — I only wanted to inform you of our decision so you can think it over.

Of course I'm going to turn him down, but in the meanwhile, tacitly, I give Thierry the sense I'll have to think about it, the same way that Wilhelm, by continuing to play, gave his fellow gamblers the opportunity to win back all the money they had lost. Oh, but why do I have to be this way? I don't want to be greedy, so why am I? Why do I want to be richer and more powerful than I already am? Didn't I decide to stay close to Claudia and tune out the problems at work? So then why am I thinking of what my life would be like if I were to take Jean-Claude's place?

— No, Thierry, — I hear myself say, — I'm afraid it's not a very good decision.

There, I said it: but why was it such a struggle for me? Why did I have to summon Schnitzler, Vittorio Mezzogiorno, Claudia, and Lara herself, who had become a *friend* of Jean-Claude and would never have approved of my taking his place? Why did I need the guidance of all these ghosts to do something that I already know is right in and of itself? There they are, looking at me, disappointed by my hesitation, relieved by the answer that I ultimately gave — because I said it, I said, "No, Thierry," didn't I? I didn't *imagine* it, like Mastro Cherry in *Pinocchio:* I really said it, *didn't I*?

— Pietro, don't give me your answer now. You're going through a difficult time, so it's hard for you to think about the future. But in a month or two things will change and your ambitions will come back. It happens to everyone, it'll happen to you. Trust me: you're the right man for the job, and we can wait.

So Thierry is also giving me a helping hand with his treacherous empty praise — me "the right man": what the fuck is he saying? Now I feel like I've got the upper hand again — I already turned him down, *didn't I?* — but I must never forget that when faced with the most corrupt proposal ever made to me, I was still capable of envisioning sailboats and golf courses. There is ambition in me. I'm a real go-getter.

— For that matter, — he adds, — everything is going to be at a standstill until the merger is complete.

Wilhelm didn't stop gambling soon enough. He started losing, and in the end he was stuck with a humongous debt, three times larger than the winnings that had fueled his fantasies.

— No, Thierry. If I'm here rather than in the office it's because I've already made up my mind. I don't care a thing about the merger. The only thing I care about is my daughter.

But Thierry continues to look at me the way you look at a poor widower — and it's all right, I think, as long as I answer him like a poor widower.

— And then, — I add, — I can't take Jean-Claude's place. Less than two weeks ago he was standing right where you are now, and he was hurting like a dog over the jet stuff. And he didn't "dump" us, like Enoch says: I know for a fact that he was forced out, and since I'm his friend I can't be the one sitting in his chair.

There, I've said it clearly: I didn't go looking for excuses, I didn't bring up my daughter, I said exactly what I think, yet Thierry takes it all in graciously, as if I were inviting him to the theater. On the other hand, I do have to remember that by coming here to propose a betrayal, he has gone down two levels in the video game, and what I think sounds definitive and heavy could sound noncommittal and light to him.

— Do you know what Jean-Claude did? — he asks me. — Do you?

— No.

— He stole, Pietro. He lied, he cheated and lied. And he did it *to me*. You say you are his friend, but I was his friend, too, you know, and for thirty years. He took advantage of my trust in him and he stole money from the company: a lot of money, Pietro. He cooked the books to . . .

Oh no. These are things I don't want to hear. It's obviously a pack of lies I have no way of double-checking, since Jean-Claude is gone and the others can say whatever they want. I don't want to hear it . . .

— . . . And when I found out, he blackmailed me. You don't know any of this, you have no way of knowing, since you're honest and Jean-Claude didn't involve you, but . . .

And I *can't* hear it, since I'm so weak and greedy and susceptible to praise.

— . . . Counting on the fact that right now a scandal like this would jeopardize the merger, so we were forced to . . .

After I had legally registered my production company and invested my puny savings in the screenplay, Vittorio Mezzogiorno died. An unexpected tragedy: all of a sudden I couldn't get in touch with him, the intimacy between us vanished, no one could tell me anything; and by the time I found out he was sick, he was already dead. I went to his funeral: there were actors, directors, producers, but also many ordinary people, like, all of a sudden, I had become again — people who might have met Vittorio Mezzogiorno in a bank, asked for his autograph, complimented him and joined the crowd at his funeral but didn't have even the slightest dream of working with him. So it came to be that his funeral was also the funeral for my career as a producer. I never contemplated doing the project with someone else: the writing on the wall seemed final, and I continued to be a television writer — which was decisive to my meeting first Marta and then Lara, having a daughter, and everything else that my life has been in the past twelve years.

—... It's to your credit, but, believe me, he doesn't deserve your trust. Therefore let me ask you not to make the mistake of turning down this opportunity out of your affection for him. I felt the same thing, and I was upset when I found out how dishonest . . .

No one has made the film *Night Games* yet, but a couple of years ago in Austria they did do a TV miniseries based on it; and by an odd coincidence the decision whether to acquire it for Italy was practically the first thing I had to do after being appointed — by Jean-Claude — as programming director.

— . . . The good years we spent together, our successes, the golden days of the *outsiders,* and I never saw a single trace of that dishonesty. Yet it must have been there all along . . .

I didn't acquire the series: it sucked.

— . . . Or at least a predisposition, is that how you say it? There must have been a predisposition, if he went on to do certain things later. But where was it? I asked myself for months, I couldn't sleep until I found the answer. And do you want to know what the answer is? Do you want to know where Jean-Claude's dishonesty was when he was still honest?

And three. This is interesting. Where was Enoch's swearword? Where was the greed that had made me vacillate a little while ago? And now — even if I continue not to believe in this business — where was Jean-Claude's dishonesty? For the third time in one hour I find myself facing the same question — a question that until today had never even occurred to me. It can't be an accident. And if Thierry knows the answer now, I want to know what it is.

— Where was it?

— It wasn't there, Pietro. That's the answer. *It wasn't there.*

Now there's a strange look in his eyes.

— You see, at college I majored in physics. And I remembered learning that an atom, passing from one state to another, emits a particle of light called a photon. And I especially remember the question they asked me at the exam: they asked me, where does this photon come from? How does it manage to appear? Where was it before? This wasn't in the textbook: they wanted to see whether I had thought about it. And I, who had not thought about it, said something foolish: I said that the photon is already inside the atom. So it was explained to me that no, the photon wasn't inside the atom at all. The photon appears at the same moment as the electron's transition, and it appears precisely *because of* that transition. Do you see? It's a simple concept: *the sounds that my voice is producing in this moment are not found inside of me.* That's how I've managed to reconcile myself to Jean-Claude's dishonesty without having to erase thirty years of my life: the actions he committed in the past two years did not come from inside of him. Like the photons, they appeared at a very distinct moment, due to very distinct causes. To be exact, just like any one of the atoms of which he is composed, Jean-Claude produced the dishonesty at the moment of transition from one state to another. Because do you know how long ago Jean-Claude started to steal? Two years ago, Pietro, when he married that Vaishya princess. She had to renounce her caste to marry him, do you see, and he must have suddenly felt inadequate, *inferior,* a sensation he had never . . .

Enough already. I was interested in the answer, not in the rest of the mud that Thierry had to sling at Jean-Claude. And the answer did come, a major one. Until it gets hit by a racket, a tennis ball has no speed. The judgment that accompanies our actions qualifies only what we are, not what we used to be. I was greedy only a little while ago, and only then. Enoch's swearword has existed only since this morning. Yes, this story about the photons convinces me. And now that I have a convincing answer, I can also apply it to the subject that I have thus far carefully avoided: I physically desired Marta only yesterday, only during that long embrace on this bench — because there's no point in denying it:

yesterday, while I was embracing her, I desired her, and she must have noticed; but that desire had not been inside me before, it hadn't been sitting in me from the time we had ended up in bed together, twelve years ago, like she probably believed; and since it wasn't there, that desire had not vexed Lara one bit during the life we had lived together; it had not consumed her with jealousy, nor had it killed her. I desired Marta twelve years ago, even before I met Lara; then I hooked up with Lara because I desired Lara, and while I was hooked up with Lara I continued to desire Lara; and then I desired Marta again yesterday, in a completely new phase of my life, after the transition of not one but a billion electrons radically changed my life, my condition — my *status,* to be exact. As blind and savage as you want, also considering that Marta is pregnant; but what I felt yesterday was just an impulse, a photon of pure desire generated by the immediate and unexpected and almost intimidating display of her tits, damn, before my eyes during her panic attack — full stop. Subject closed.

Thierry remained in silence the whole time. He, too, seems to have gotten everything off his chest, and now he is silent, or maybe he is regretting having allowed something sincere to escape his lips, having come here from Paris only to set into motion move number 109 of his elaborate strategy of betrayal. And now I have an opportunity: a demigod has descended to my level, he has demeaned himself to fulfill a mission, and in fact those who see us in this moment — the Pakistani, the woman with the baby carriage, the newspaper vendor — do not have the least inkling of how much more powerful than me the man speaking to me is: at the most they can think he is one grade higher, because of a mere age factor. This is what he wanted, for reasons I will never know: so if I want to resist him — and I want to, even if I did just learn that I'm weaker than I thought — I'd be better off putting him back on the pedestal from which he has descended. Anyway, this is just an act; it's just a question of not confusing roles or getting our lines mixed up. I could always rent that famous sailboat for a couple of weeks. The important thing is that he go back to being the future deputy director of the world's biggest telecommunications group and I to being a poor, recently widowed, peripheral manager.

— So then, — Thierry says, — will you think about it?

Move number 1: cash in all the chips you have.

— Tell me something, — I say, — do you really think I'm so talented?

— Yes, — he replies decisively. — Jean-Claude is not the only person in the world who holds you in high esteem.

Excellent.

— So can I tell you what I really want?

— Of course. What do you really want?

Move number 2: stake everything on something he finds incomprehensible.

— I want to stay here.

Move number 3: pause. It'll help give him enough time to think I'm laying down a condition for accepting the presidency, and to start to think of how embarrassing it would be to go back to Paris with a new president who wants to spend all day in front of his daughter's school. But before he can spell out the concept, the pause has to be interrupted — move number 4 — to remind him who he is.

— And if that isn't possible, then I want to be fired right now, by you, and not have to think about it anymore, so that we won't have to drag out this business forever. After all, I haven't been going to work, you'd have every reason . . .

Done. End of my strategy, but especially, at this point, the end of his. He's baffled, I can see, he doesn't know which way to turn. His goal had been to promote the subject to the presidency, and he had immense firepower to achieve this: how did this happen, he must be asking himself, how the hell did we end up being one step away from firing him? And why are we talking about what he wants and not about what I want? Exactly when did the subject wrest control of the situation from my hands? Hah, the old quarrels with my brother, Carlo, over how to fight the system: he was in favor of attacking it from the outside, a rebellion, I was for dismantling it from the inside, subversion; he could give a hundred glorious examples of how you could rebel against the system, I couldn't manage to come up with even one of what it meant, exactly, to subvert. Well, Carlo, this is what I meant.

— But why *here*? — he says.

Right, Thierry: how the devil have I suddenly made this place a deal breaker?

— Because I like it here.

— I know, but what else? I don't understand what you're thinking, Pietro.

Right: deal breaker for what, then?

— There's nothing else. I'm not thinking anything.

— I don't believe you. Right now you could ask me for money, you could ask me for time, you could demand conditions that are very advantageous for your future, and the only thing you are asking me is to spend all day in front of a school, which you could do perfectly well by taking one month's vacation.

— I've already used up my vacation time.

— Doesn't matter; what I meant to say this: I can't believe the only thing you're thinking about is making your daughter happy. What are you trying to pull?

— My daughter didn't ask me to stay here. It's my idea. I'm not trying to pull anything.

At this point it wouldn't hurt to insert a word whose active principle these days, for Thierry Léon Larivière, should be as stinging as vitriol.

— It's the truth, — I add.

But it doesn't produce much. Just a short pause.

— So you really don't want the presidency?

— No, Thierry, I really don't. It's not my thing.

— Excuse my frankness, — he says, — but are you sure you're feeling all right?

A first marriage to an American, an eighteen-year-old daughter who apparently is a drug addict, a new and younger French wife, two children he never sees, an even younger Canadian mistress whom everyone knows about, including me, because every now and then he shows her off to society, and one week ago up and down both sides of the Atlantic Ocean: I bet he can't believe I want to stay here *and that's all.*

— Yes, I'm fine.

— I mean to say that, after what happened, it would be understandable if . . .

I give him enough time to find the rest of the sentence, in case he interrupted himself out of embarrassment and has nothing to add. So much the better.

— I'm fine, Thierry, — I repeat, — it's just that I've changed my priorities.

He knits his brows and nods. He has to decide whether to fire me or authorize me to stay here; but above all, he wasn't prepared for this — how can I ax him, he must be wondering, after convincing Boesson that we need him alive and as president? — and whatever may happen he will not be going back to Paris with what he wanted. Not bad. Maybe he's right, maybe I would make a great shark. Or maybe not; on second thought, definitely not: I never was particularly talented, and this masterpiece is just another photon, of which there wasn't even a trace inside me half an hour ago.

Incidentally, it's time to cash in my chips before he can pull himself together.

— So can I stay here?

He smiles, looks at me askance, and gives a smirk that couldn't be more French. He's wondering, how the fuck did the subject manage to trap me?

— But not forever, — he growls.

— Done. — I extend my hand. — Not forever.

He shakes my hand, then he actually pulls me in close for a hug, and this hug may even be sincere, in his own way he may even like me. He pulls away, sticks a hand in his pocket, and pulls out a red packet with a silver ribbon. He holds it out to me.

— Give this to Lara from me, — he says.

Sure: I'll go to the cemetery, desecrate the grave, pry it open with a crowbar, and leave the packet inside. My daughter's name is Claudia, you shithead: Claudia . . .

— Thank you.

And he leaves, completely unaware of this final gaffe. I got the better of him, but he doesn't have a defeated look. He's a professional, for Christ's sake, and he knows all too well that he can live with an occasional defeat. He'll tell Boesson that I'm not up to being president and get even with me the first chance he gets.

chapter sixteen

List of the comets I've seen:

This is easy.

Halley (1985)

Hale-Bopp (1997)

But maybe I've seen another comet, too. When I was a boy, in Rome. This is what I remember: my brother and I, very little, and our father taking us outside at night to see the comet.

— Let's go see the comet, boys . . .

It's summer. The air is fragrant. Along the Ardeatine walls it's like being in the countryside. The Caracalla Baths. The Circus Maximus. My father wearing white shoes that glow in the dark. What comet was it? Or was it a lunar eclipse?

— Let's go see the eclipse, boys . . .

— Pietro!

Who's calling me? Right, left: no one.

— Over here!

Oh, a blue Yaris is flickering its headlights at me, double-parked by the park, speaking to me — and in the language of blue Yarises flickering their headlights, it seems to be inviting me over. A head pops out the window: Benedetta's mom. What does she want? No way out, I have to go over to her . . . the problem is that it's gotten hot again, and here in the shade it feels so nice. Something strange is happening, in fact: fall arrived in a swoop two weeks ago — rain, cold, wind — but then the weather corrected course and summer seemed to start over again. The temperature began to rise as if it were early May, while the sky, rinsed clean by the rain, is unveiling itself again, one layer of gauze per day. And the sun is broiling . . .

Benedetta's mother smiles at me with her small white teeth, which look indestructible. Sitting at the steering wheel with the engine running and a piece of paper in her hand.

— Sorry, excuse me, — she says, — but if I try to squeeze into that spot I'll never get out. I forgot to give you this earlier.

A leaflet. THE PARENTOGETHER SALONS. 5 MEETINGS ON TUESDAYS AT 9 P.M. . . .

— It's a parents' association, a pretty smart group of people. I've been there a few times. They do meetings, seminars, training courses. I thought you might be interested in tonight's meeting . . .

Then she turns to my dog, who's jumping between my legs. Her naked arm, still tanned, extends beyond the window.

— Dylan! Good boy!

Dylan stands up on his hind legs to play with her, but she immediately betrays his expectations, patting him hastily, granting him only an intermediate stopover of her hand, which is aiming in reality for the steering wheel, where her finger lands, pointed at one of the meetings.

— This one, can you see?

Her cell phone rings, she answers, apologizing with a grimace, and while she's speaking on the phone I read where she's pointing: "Grandparents: Help or Hindrance? Gloria Avuelo, Nicoletta Skov, educational psychologists." This may be the one subject in the world that interests me the least, considering that three of Claudia's grandparents have died and the fourth, my father, is living in his own world, almost two centuries away from ours; then I realize that her finger made a mistake: it landed on the meeting taking place next month. Tonight's meeting is on the line above: "Beginning at the End: How to Talk About Death with Your Children. Manuela Solvay Grassetti, psychotherapist and Gordon trainer." I raise my eyes, look at Benedetta's mother.

— . . . Listen, I'm in the car, — she says, — I'll call you as soon as I get there.

She casts a malicious sidelong glance in my direction, making me an accomplice to her lie; she remains in silence for a few seconds, says good-bye, and ends the conversation.

— Sorry, — she says. Then she pauses, shakes her head as if to shed some dead hair, and finally smiles. — It might be interesting for you, don't you think?

— Actually, it might.

— Listen, I have to run now, but I wanted to tell you that if you want to go you can leave Claudia with me tonight. Maybe she can sleep over. The place is a little far, in Gorgonzola, and if you go it might get late.

— Thank you . . . — and here I am overcome by an unnatural suspension, because the tone I'd used to thank her would normally be followed by the saying of her name, but as usual, I can't remember exactly what it is: Barbara or Beatrice? Claudia must have told me four or five times, but there's something in my head that refuses to imagine this woman independently of my doubt over whether her name is Barbara or Beatrice, and in the end her name for me will always be precisely that doubt. What's more, she also caught me off guard: it's obvious that she came back here just to give me this instruction, it's obvious that in her opinion I should go.

— Let me check my schedule, — I mutter.

— Take your time, — says Barbara-or-Beatrice. — I can't pick up Benedetta this afternoon, but we'll see each other later at the gym. You're going, aren't you?

Of course. Benedetta also wanted to do gymnastics, like Claudia: but she has no talent for it, she's way behind, she's on the B team with another teacher, and in my opinion it's really bothering her, especially when she sees the adoration that Claudia showers on Gemma, the junior champion.

— Yes, I'm going.

— So you can let me know then. Don't be a stranger.

— Agreed. Thanks.

Absurdly, I start to give her back the leaflet.

— Keep it, — she says. — You'll see, they're very smart people. They do interesting things.

She smiles again, Barbara-or-Beatrice: she waves, shifts into reverse, and drives backward as far as the avenue, where she is immediately caught in traffic. Even from this distance, I can see her dig her cell phone out of her purse and place it against her ear.

I return calmly to my bench. How to talk about death with your children. Why not? Maybe there are techniques, I don't know, or metaphors. That fact that Claudia has never talked about

it so far doesn't mean she never will. I have to prepare myself, so
that I don't end up improvising when the moment arrives. Especially since in all likelihood Claudia's going out to dinner with her
uncle tonight. But I don't want to think about it right now. Maybe
tonight: but not now. The only thing I want to do now is sit in
the shade and pat my dog, that's all. And I'll put the leaflet in my
pocket — there.

The fact is that in the past week, strangely enough, everyone
has left me in peace. No one has come by to tell me their problems. Marta has called only once, the office has dropped off some
paperwork and made some rare work-related visits; this spot has
stopped being the place in the world where sorrow comes in for
a landing, and I have been able to relax, let my mind wander, observe things carefully, and even get bored — as everyone knows,
exile does have its empty hours. I've waved to Claudia when she's
come to the window, talked about childhood rashes with her
classmates' mothers, watched Olympic gymnastics lessons; I've
remembered remote and potentially dangerous things by compiling a good number of lists, without ever once suffering. And
even at home, at night, everything's been going smoothly: after
dinner I have started to tell Claudia the fantastic adventures of the
Merger, a ferocious two-headed monster with a host of abnormal-
ities (two forked tongues, four eyes that inflict madness on anyone
who looks upon it, a long, scaled tail that it uses to massacre the
bourgeois population) that my daughter's imagination seems to
appreciate more than I'd expected. I've been going to bed early.
The other day in what is now Lara's former computer I found the
two e-mail messages that I'd printed out on the night of my crisis
and forgotten immediately; I threw them away without rereading
them. No pain: I continue to feel like a man who fell off the roof
and after standing back up can't stop feeling all over his body, finding it hard to believe he was unharmed. I haven't even heard from

the owner of the C3, which has been in the same spot all this time
— and, in fact, there it is, wounded and abandoned, my business
card tucked beneath its rear windshield wiper . . .

I introduced myself to the girl with the golden retriever, this I
have done: she has a surprising name — Yolanda — and she's still
coming every day; she'll be here in a little while. But I've started to
bring along my dog, too, because there's no reason not to, after all,
and thanks to this realization, now that we're talking, our conversations remain at a reassuringly superficial level since they pivot
almost exclusively on dogs (our own, but also dogs in general),
without touching on more private and personal questions. For
example, she doesn't know that I spend all day here, nor does she
know why: she didn't ask me, and I didn't tell her; by the same
token, I didn't ask what she does for a living, she didn't tell me,
and I don't know.

I also met the boy with Down syndrome, the one who com-
municates with my car's antitheft alarm: his name is Matteo, he's
eight years old, and when he grows up he wants to be an assistant
cook — and I was moved by his modest ambition. Our contact
was instigated by his mother when she noticed the little game I
play with the antitheft device every time the two of them walk by.
In reality she came to me rather aggressively, thinking I was having a laugh at their expense, but she's a good woman and as soon
as I explained that I was only trying to add a little something to
her son's life she believed me and apologized. Matteo was playing
with Dylan and didn't hear a thing, so his friendship with the antitheft alarm remained as pure and mysterious as before; indeed,
thanks to the protection of his twenty-first chromosome, which
enables him, unlike any normal child, not to associate me with
my car, now he also has a new friend to talk with: "I don't know
why," he confided to me in a soft voice, "but every time I come
by here that black car says hello to me." Ever since that morning

his mother has taken to stopping by to smoke a cigarette with me before dragging him off to the physical therapist's; but she never stays here long enough to tell me about the many misfortunes whose signs she bears on her face, and when she leaves the office she's always in a great hurry.

In short, I've got an embarrassing truth to confess: the tranquillity that has been reserved for me, together with this unexpected return of summer and — naturally — the persisting absence of grief, has made the last seven days one of the most peaceful periods in my life. Not even the end of daylight saving time — an occurrence I always considered very sad — has succeeded in ruining it, but it's also true that in a little while my brother's going to be here, and I'm afraid that his arrival will restore a lot of the noise I'd left behind in the past few days. He got to Milan last night — a surprise visit, since there's still a month to go before the fashion shows; he called me while he was on his way to a dinner party somewhere in the Brianza area, to reserve Claudia for tonight, and that's why I really can go to that meeting; then he asked me whether I'm still spending all day in front of the school, and when I said I was he announced he would be coming by this morning. From the attitude he has maintained so far in his phone calls from Rome, Paris, and Los Angeles, the persistence of this situation seems to bother him, mostly because of his own demoniacal inability to imagine spending more than five days straight in any one country, never mind in front of a school. In other words, he's going to be here in a little while and there will probably be something to quarrel about, just as in our family drama there has always been something to quarrel about with him, often bitterly, about everything, more or less, although we're almost always on the same side when it comes to substance. The point is that there has never been any real problem between us, and maybe that's what the real problem is: we were too much the same not to feel obliged to leap at any pretext to feel different; after which, by pursuing it as a life goal, we really did become different, and so everything became more confused. For example, if I were to say this in front of him, he'd probably argue the contrary and claim we're very different but we strive to find points in common, and this would be true, too — indeed sometimes I may have even taken his side. And so, with regard to my brother, I make do with a rudimentary conviction, namely that nature unites us while civilization divides us, and vice versa; there are probably better ways to describe our relationship, but since nothing requires us to define it better, I'll make do with this one and think of the two of us as what we really are, long before and apart from any definitions: two parts of a whole. And it is precisely this sense of common belonging, without even the need to specify what we belong to, that seeps through the cracks of the world every now and then and reminds us that we are brothers, that we always have been brothers, and that being brothers is a powerful mental state; take that awesome moment, for example, when we looked at each other before diving into the water to save those two women, the day that Lara died, when I really felt that I was him and that I, too, had blue eyes.

Generally speaking, however, you could say that we don't spend too much time together. He's a famous designer, a bachelor, changes girlfriends once a year, and is always traveling; I am what I am; our lives do not intersect very much, and on the long list of our differences are some that sound really strange. For example, why does he live in Rome while I live in Milan? Wouldn't the opposite be more logical, since I miss Rome so much and he works in the fashion industry? I couldn't say. I only know that ever since I moved to Milan I've been thinking about moving back to Rome, but I never have, and the longer I don't, the vaguer and more unrealizable the idea becomes. Ever since my mother died and Dad sold the house on Via Giotto to move to Switzerland, I no longer have a place to stay in Rome, and even spending a weekend there is difficult. Lara, Claudia, and I used to go for Christmas or in June, and sometimes even in August, when the city is wonderfully empty, and the fact of having a family home there — of having a family — made everything more natural, including the idea of moving back there to live someday in the future; and even when I had to go by myself for business, maybe for just a day, I felt *represented* — I don't know how else to explain it — by that house and by that bedroom; but today a notary public, Mr. Mandorlini, lives with his family at our old house on Via Giotto, and I have a strong resistance to the idea of staying at a hotel in my hometown, with the result that I don't go down there anymore. Carlo obviously disagrees, doesn't understand, and, especially after what happened to Lara, is always inviting us to his house: "Why don't you and Claudia come down to my place for a week, it'll do you good." But his words are meaningless: first, because he's never there, and second, because he lives in a studio, and there's no room for us. He's a billionaire, but he still lives at that same hole-in-the-wall in the Garbatella neighborhood where he used to live before Wynona Ryder started wearing his jeans; where he took refuge after his historic fight with Dad, officially because of the marijuana Carlo had smoked right under his nose but in reality because Dad didn't like him dropping out of university to move to London. Quaint, cool, trendy, call it what you will, but sleeping in his apartment overwhelms me with sadness. I'm saddened by his doorless closet filled with junk hanging from hooks, the row of boots on the floor, the tiny unused kitchenette, the CDs scattered everywhere, the poster of Buster Keaton in a bathroom cluttered with the fossilized souvenirs of women — lipstick, bobby pins, combs, rubber bands — left there by ex-girlfriends in the now forgotten act of marking their territory. But what makes me most uncomfortable, and keeps me from taking Claudia there, is the enlarged photo of J. M. Barrie that covers the

entire wall facing the bed. That picture gives me the creeps. I realize
that Peter Pan is Carlo's myth, and I am witness to the fact that it always has been, ever since he was little, even before seeing the film,
and he was bowled over by an illustrated volume that Aunt Jenny
gave us for Christmas, *Peter Pan in Kensington Gardens* (the truth is that
Aunt Jenny gave it to me, and I like it very much, too, but it's also
true that the one who went crazy over it was him), and I understand that it was a smart move to call his company Barrie, thereby
transferring the cult of the flying little imp to its creator, because
it gave an unexpected depth to the whole idea — especially in a
world as superficial as the fashion world; I understand the consistency, the recognition, the loyalty to the myths of childhood, I understand it all; but I can't stomach that picture, and it's impossible
for me to sleep in front of it. It's a photo of J. M. Barrie pushing fifty
but already obscenely old, playing Captain Hook in a meadow with
one of the orphans he adopted — but in reality he grips the boy, he
hooks him, to be precise, with a horrible bony hand wrapped around
the child's little arm and a ruthless diseased smirk from beneath his
gigantic hat. The child doesn't seem to be having any fun: he looks
at the man with the hesitant half-smile that precedes fear, because
evidently he senses the threat looming over him, although he will
later be forced to settle down and even feel guilty for having felt it,
since Barrie will not do him any harm, at least that's what I believe;
but even if no harm is done, they are clearly united by that harm,
as the facial expressions captured on camera will forever attest. It's
a really terrifying photo: just remembering it bothers me, and I
don't understand how Carlo can stand to have it facing his bed.

But I can ask him in person, since he has just arrived. Here he is
in front of the school getting out of the taxi — he's never owned
a car — and he looks around for me. He doesn't see me, he's not
looking in this direction. But he has seen my car. Dylan spots him
and is starting to tug at his leash. I let him loose, and he races to-

ward Carlo, making a big fuss over him. Finally Carlo looks this
way and sees me. I don't have to signal to him to join me: the
shade of these trees would attract anyone. And here he is advancing with a smile, a loose white shirt hanging over his jeans, walking like a duck because of his flat feet. I actually feel a little uneasy
around him. Always have. Don't know why. Here he is. We hug
each other. He has a wonderful scent, of the sea, of shells. He'll
want to argue, to object. Better to turn my brain off.

chapter seventeen

— You know, I was thinking . . . why do you keep that horrible
picture in your bedroom?
   — The one of Barrie?
   — Yes.
   — What don't you like about it?
   — Come on, it's creepy. Why don't you take it down?
   — I have taken it down.
   — Oh. When?
   — It must be a year now. No, more recently: in February. Ever
since Nina told me: "Either it goes or I go."
   — Well, marry her, then. She's the sanest girlfriend you've ever
had. How is she?
   — We broke up.
   — No!
   — Yes.
   — When?
   — A month ago.
   — And now you're going to put the picture back up?
   — No.
   — Thank God.

— Listen, I've got some really big news for you. Guess who was at the dinner I went to last night.

— Who?

— Guess.

— Man or woman?

— Woman. Take a shot at it.

— Do I know her?

— By sight, let's say.

— . . .

— A rather singular sight, let's say.

— . . .

— Unforgettable, let's say.

— I haven't got a clue. Who is she?

— One of the two women we rescued in Roccamare.

— No way! Mine or yours?

— Mine.

— And who is she?

— She runs an art gallery here in Milan. Francia is her last name. Ludovica, or maybe Frederica, yes, Frederica Francia.

— And you recognized her? I don't know if I'd recognize mine.

— No, I didn't recognize her.

— Did she recognize you?

— No.

— So how did it happen?

— The way it happened is incredible. People were talking about you and —

— What do you mean, about me?

— Well, it seems that you've become a minor celebrity since you planted yourself here in front of the school. From the way they pestered me with questions, I'd say that the city society is following you passionately.

— What the fuck are you saying?

— I'm saying that they all talk about you. It was the gallery owner herself who associated our last names, before she found out the rescue business, obviously, and who asked me whether I was related "to that Paladini, an executive at Channel 4, who ever since his wife died has been spending all day every day in front of his daughter's school." I replied that we're brothers and then started rectifying the erroneous information about the television channel and Claudia, thinking the story would end there, but they, on the pretext that they were expressing admiration for you (sincere and I would say almost romantic admiration from the women, more reluctant admiration from the men), they started to pester me with questions, about you, about Lara, about Claudia, with a nosiness that really annoyed me. At which point, I don't know why, rather than say I didn't feel like talking about certain things (and, by the way, I didn't know the answers to half their questions, like what was the name of this school or what was the nationality of Claudia's nanny), I thought, "Go fuck yourselves, I'll show you," and I told them the true, brutal story of what happened that morning, because it's not as if they knew. I told them everything, do you understand? That we risked our lives to save these two women while their friends stood staring from the shore, that after it was over no one said thank you to us, and that when we came home Lara was dead. I did it to shock them, for Christ's sake, because I didn't like that you had become the object of so much gossip. But at a certain point, while I was standing there talking about that shithead with the red hair, do you remember him? The one with the rope in his hands who told us to let them drown, I see this woman turning white, I mean really white: her face became like mozzarella, her eyes turned back into her head, and she fell flat back on the table, passed out cold. And it was then that I recognized her, seeing as that's basically the only way I ever saw her, you could say, being carried away unsteadily in someone's arms. It was her.

— Fuck, Carlo. Why can't you keep your mouth shut?

— How was I supposed to know? And she deserved it, this way she'll learn to stop being such a pig: because I'd already been talking for a while, do you see? And she must have caught me talking about her without recognizing her, but she didn't say shit. Her husband was there, too, a jerk who was at Punta Ala that morning, go figure, playing golf, and you should have seen how he kept his mouth shut while I was telling the story. I can tell you, even if he wasn't there he must have realized I was talking about his wife: how the fuck many times do you think his wife could have drowned a month and a half ago and been saved by an unknown guy? Who's she?

— Someone that brings her dog here.

— Do you know her?

— Yes. No.

— Yes or no?

— We say hi and leave it at that.

— She's a knockout.

— No argument here.

— How old do you think she is? Twenty-six? Twenty-seven?

— I don't know.

— Dylan's choking on his collar. Can I let him off the leash?

— No. She's just about to go by.

— Are they friends, her dog and him?

— They sniff each other's asses. So you were saying, the gallery owner passed out . . .

— So the gallery owner passes out, and when she comes to she starts crying, all pale and trembling, apologizing, and even gets in a tiff with her jerk of a husband, who acts all offended, can you believe it? He gets pissed at me, on account of, how can I put it, the colorful language I used to tell the story . . .

— I can imagine . . .

— But she shut him up, you should have seen how brutally.

She's not as ugly as she looked while she was about to kick the bucket, by the way.

— And you?

— Me? I was eating it up. Because the two women seem to have realized that no matter how fucked up they were, they hadn't been saved by their friends; apparently when they were revived, they asked who the two *heroes* were who had rescued them, but those assholes convinced them they were the rescuers, together with the surf kids. It was *awesome* . . .

— What was awesome?

— Watching her world crumble around her. I mean, it's not every day you get to see such a scene: an upper-class bitch who suddenly finds out that her best friends are lying sacks of shit and that she was saved from drowning not by them, who had convinced her of it, but by a stranger who describes her in public as "that slut."

— You called her a slut?

— Well, just once. When I was describing how she tried to pull me under rather than let herself be saved. I got carried away, you could say, in the heat of telling the story.

— I can see. And how did it end?

— It ended that she couldn't stop crying and telling me that it was her fault and thanking me and apologizing and asking about you, how you're doing, how your daughter is, what she can do to make it up to you, also on behalf of your . . .

— My what?

— Your woman, the one you saved.

— Oh. But she wasn't at the dinner.

— No. But you can bet she found out about it this morning. They're good friends, she says. And do you know who yours is, by the way? She's Swiss. Her name is Eleonora Simoncini and she's the owner of Brick Chocolates, recognize the name? The ads with the bunny rabbit eating chocolate carrots? Her father died four years ago: she's the sole heir, a billionaire, the real deal.

— Brick, you said?

— Yes. Chocolate, ice cream, candy. Incredible sales.

— That's strange . . .

— What's strange?

— The coincidence. Brick of Lugano belongs to the Canadian group we're doing the merger with.

— You? And what does chocolate have to do with cable TV?

— Nothing, but it's a huge *global* merger, and it involves more or less everything.

— Well, sure, quite a coincidence. Does this dog bite?

— *Phew-wee!*

— No, he's good.

— *Phew-wee!* Nebbia!

— What is he, a Labrador?

— Nebbia! *Phew-wee!* Come here now!

— No. A golden retriever.

— Cut it out, Nebbia! Hi! Sorry, I'll put him back on his leash.

— Don't worry, miss. He only wants to play with his little friend here.

— Hi. This is my brother. Yolanda: Carlo. Carlo: Yolanda.

— Pleased to meet you. Nebbia, get down, boy.

— Yolanda? What a pretty name.

— Pretty? I wouldn't say so. If anything it's gross.

— Why do you say that? It's old, baroque . . . And Nebbia's a great name, too. Can I pay him a compliment?

— Of course . . .

— What a pretty owner you have, Nebbia . . .

— . . .

— . . .

— . . .

— Well, I've got to be off. And sorry again. Come here, Nebbia!
What's wrong with you today?

— Bye.

— Bye.

— . . .

— . . .

— Did you see?

— What?

— Her jeans.

— What about them?

— They're Barrie jeans.

— Oh . . .

— . . .

— . . .

— Pietro?

— Yes.

— What's with you?

— Nothing.

— Are you pissed that I talked about Lara?

— What do you expect me to say? What's done is done.

— But you're pissed.

— What pisses me off is that people I don't even know are talking about me.

— Wait a second, do you really want them not to talk? You're a
celebrity, Pietro, what were you expecting? You camp out in front
of a school like a homeless man and you expect —

— Now, wait a minute . . .

— Sorry, that's not what I meant to say. What I meant to say is
that those people never know what to talk about: they invite each
other to dinner every other day and after the first little canapé a
gulf opens up over what to say to each other for the rest of the
evening. To them you're a Martian. You're doing something sen-

sational, and don't tell me that you don't know. Already the fact
that you're upset is strange to them because if one of them died
their wives wouldn't think twice about going to a beauty spa or a
little nip and tuck. Then the fact that you throw your suffering in
their faces that way, you know, they —

— Throw it into whose face? I don't know them from Adam,
these people, *I don't give a flying fuck about them*. *You're the one* that goes
out to dinner with them, not me. Like I already told you, I'm not
upset in the least, and I'm not suffering.

— No need to get worked up over it! There's nothing wrong
with feeling upset after what happened.

— Enough already! I'm not upset. I'll be the first to admit I'm
surprised, but I'm not feeling upset. In fact, I'm fine, especially if
you leave me alone!

— Listen, why do you want to continue this —

— Carlo?

— Yes.

— Look me in the eye.

— . . .

— I-am-not-upset. Get it?

— Uh, got it. So what are you doing here, then?

— I'm fine.

— You're fine sitting on a bench all day in front of a school?

— Yes.

— For a month?

— Yes.

— Now you look me in the eye.

— I'm already looking you in the eye.

— It's just a figure of speech. Are you serious?

— I've never been more serious in my life.

— At this point I don't understand you.

— Who asked you to understand me?

— I give up, Pietro.

— Good boy. Give up.

— . . .

— . . .

— I'm just saying that if you were to accept what happened without this kind of conduct people wouldn't talk about you.

— *Conduct?* Since when do you talk like a vice principal?

— Not to mention that it might not be the best thing for Claudia to see her father acting like a child.

— Right, Claudia! I hadn't thought of that! Thank God you did. Do you mind repeating it slowly so I can take notes?

— All right already. Do what you want.

— You can bet on it. Let's do this: I do what I want and you leave me alone, and any remarks about my *conduct* that may arise irresistibly from your depths you can go and blurt out at those bourgeois dinners you so despise, while you tell them my fucking business for the sake of shocking them. How does that sound? Can you do it?

— . . .

— . . .

— It's just that I'm worried about you, Pietro.

— Oh, I'm sure you're the only one.

— I'm the only one that's telling you.

— Okay, that may be the case, so let's see if I understood you correctly. You are supposedly the spokesman for a general feeling of concern about me, which could be summarized as follows: if I were grieving but I went to the office anyway and hung in there and said that life goes on and took sleeping pills and in the meanwhile Claudia were to appear indecisive and apathetic and stopped eating, you would all be happier and give me the name of a psychologist that she should see; if I were "camped out here like a homeless man," as you put it, because I was overcome by grief, you would be moderately concerned and you would give me the name of a psychologist that I should see; but the fact that I'm here and that I'm not feeling bad, and that not even Claudia is feeling bad, and that there is no need for psychologists, this you find much more troubling. Am I right, or am I right? Do we have to grieve to set your mind at rest?

— That's not what I'm saying, Pietro.

— You're not? So what are you saying?

— I'm saying this can't go on forever. Don't tell me you're not thinking the same thing.

— What I'm thinking is that all of you are attaching way too much importance to the fact that I'm staying here rather than going to the office. You really can't accept that, can you? Why not?

— For one thing, if you keep this up you risk losing your job.

— I hate to disappoint you, but you picked the wrong example. It just so happens that, with the merger under way, more or less half of my colleagues who go to work regularly, every day, are going to lose their jobs anyway, either because they're going to be replaced by their Canadian or American counterparts or because they'll be transferred, given early retirement, or simply forced to accept the golden handshake that is customarily offered to those who leave the group of their own free will. What's more —

— But there's a big diff—

— What's more, let me finish what I was saying, for Christ's sake, and try for once to listen to what I'm telling you rather than coming back at me right away with another argument; what's more, I received formal permission from my bosses to stay here, and I work from here on a regular basis, what little bit of work you can do at a time like this, without being exposed to the paranoia raging in our offices all the time nowadays, and which will continue to rage until the merger is complete and its actual consequences have been fully manifested. Which is why there is nothing, and I mean nothing, to worry about if I stay here. But now before your rebuttal, try thinking for ten seconds about what I just said; try believing that I know what I'm doing. Try, for once, to change your mind.

— . . .

— . . .

— What do you mean, they gave you permission to stay here?

— I mean it was authorized by my boss. And after he was kicked out like a dog, which was made known a week ago, it was authorized in person by his executioner. For the time being, my office is *here*. Ciao, Yolanda.

— See you tomorrow.

— Good-bye.

— . . .

— . . .

— What can I say, Pietro: I didn't know any of this. Maybe I was worried over nothing.

— Not maybe. Definitely.

— Let's not say another word about it and put it behind us. If I offended you, I'm sorry.

— Forget about it.

— I really didn't mean to offend you.

— I know, Carlo. Let's not talk about it. Do you feel like getting something to eat? They make great sandwiches here at the café.

— I'm afraid I've got an appointment, and this afternoon I'm busy till eight. But tonight I'd like to take Claudia out to eat, like I promised her. Do you mind?

— Of course not. She can't wait to see you.

— What are you up to? Do you want to come along?

— No, she'd rather go alone. She loves you. Do you know what she wrote in a composition? She wrote, and I quote, "My uncle is awesome."

— Maybe it would give you a chance to have a free night.

— A free night, sure.

— Yes. Apart from everything else, you also need to have a little fun, don't you?

— I don't feel any great need for it, to tell you the truth.

— I mean as a rule. You can't always hang around in the same place, doing the same thing, without taking a break . . .

— As a rule, I get it. I should have some fun.

— So let's do this: I'll come by to pick Claudia up at around eight, I'll take her to a restaurant, and then I'll bring her back home, tuck her in, and go to sleep myself in the guest room. And you come back whenever you feel like it.

— If I go out.

— If you go out, of course.

— I could even have fun at home.

— Why not, it's a great idea: you can stay at home on the sofa watching TV and fall asleep during the late-night talk shows.

— As a rule, I get it. You don't have to go out to have a good time.

— Of course. As a rule. Does Claudia like Japanese food?

— If you take her, she'll like anything. But . . .

— . . .

— . . .

— But what?

— Now don't go getting offended.

— Of course not. What's up?

— Go easy on her. I don't think she's ready to talk about certain things yet.

— I'm not stupid, Pietro.

— Yes, I know, but what I mean to say is that, you'll see, she seems perfectly normal, never shows any weakness, a moment of sadness, of fear, as if nothing had happened. Her reaction is a mystery, and I still haven't found the courage to deal with it.

— A mystery. Maybe she's just copying you. She sees that you're not grieving, so she isn't grieving, either.

— I don't know what it is, but it's as if she had found her own absurd, unpredictable balance, and she lives in that balance day by day, avoiding the problem. Except that, contrary to all appearances, it must be a very fragile balance. Very fragile. That's why I'm telling you to go easy on her: for all we know, anything could break it.

— Don't worry, bro. I'll be careful. Like walking on fresh snow.

— Exactly. That's exactly what you need to do with her. Walk on fresh snow.

— . . .

— At least that's what I think.

chapter eighteen

Gorgonzola. An address I would never have found without the GPS. The smell of disinfectant. A square room with neon lights, café tables, plastic chairs. Strange blue streamers hanging from the ceiling, strange red ornaments, and a banner draped over a closet, with the fading letters HAPPY BIRTHDAY, TOMAS. About fifty people, the overwhelming majority of whom are women: a ratio of roughly four or even five to one, I'd say. Women very different from Barbara-or-Beatrice — the oh-so-patrician, elegant, tanned, pampered, *elaborated* woman who sent me here. These women are more simple, more humble. They're working mothers — many of them teachers — or housewives, who wear ordinary clothes and don't worry about their figures. They've already lost their summer tans and don't take exotic vacations during the winter. In their eyes they bear the purgatorial mark of the suburbs. The only thing they have in common with Barbara-or-Beatrice is their age — an age, to be specific, when you can no longer afford to ignore death.

Two of them have just sat down at my table and started chatting about school problems, transfers, superintendents; every now and then one of them bursts into the most vulgar laugh, but oddly enough this laugh is what makes her attractive, and what's attractive is her nonchalant indulgence of the fact that she laughs this way, taking it in stride. Actually, like Jean-Claude and his Taliban beard, this relic of our animal nature forces me to notice its accompanying features: so I notice the remarkable supernatural light released by her green eyes, a light that conveys an enormous mysterious energy, maybe the same energy that fuels her laugh and confers upon her whole being the savage sensuality of the dominators. It is not beauty but rather a sidereal evolution of beauty: a way to make an impression in a superior civilization that has abandoned the cult of beauty. I ultimately can't even look at her, and the two or three times that she looks at me the effort to hold her gaze produces a strange, instantaneous, liquid sensation, as if all my defenses had melted, my survival instinct had dissolved into a deadly passivity, and the possibility of lying on a sofa, let's say, and being eaten alive without putting up a fight were suddenly not so remote. And there is no way for me to escape, to ignore, *to forget about her,* because the periodic echo of her laugh comes back to haunt me wherever I have taken refuge and to revive my perception of her superpowers. It's ridiculous, I know, and maybe it has something to do with digesting the cheeseburger swimming in sauces that I wolfed down on my way here while standing at a McDonald's, but I really do have the impression that *she's not human,* and her vicinity makes me feel apprehensive — for both myself and her friend, in the crosshairs of her stare, exposed to the kryptonite pulsing inside it, so badly that when her friend gets up to go to the speakers' table I feel relieved for her. She's actually the chairwoman, turning on the microphone (it works, doesn't work, screeches, doesn't screech, rustles), welcoming us, apologizing for the lateness of the speaker, who's stuck in traffic, and announcing future initiatives of the Parentogether association. A dinner at the Melzo Recreation Center (ARCI) next Saturday, on the second stop of the "Tastes of Old Lombardy" tour: €13 for adults and €9 for children under the age of fifteen. The Halloween party on the evening of the thirty-first, again at the Melzo ARCI, with dinner for €12.50 and entertainment for children by the Hinterland Theater Group, including fairy tales, puppet show, and masks for trick-or-treating. Next month's lecture on grandparents, "Help or Hindrance," will take place at five o'clock — one time only — at the Quartiere 11 offices in Vimercate . . .

Vulgar Laugh is looking away from me now, turning toward the speakers' table, and I can let my gaze wander around the room, although it's bringing back to me a sense of embarrassment: not because I'm such a blatant outsider to this circle — where everyone obviously knows everyone else — but more because of the total absence of other solitary spectators like me. Everyone is accompanied by someone else, even the people still arriving are always in twos or threes: I don't feel like I'm attending a lecture so much as crashing a party. Vulgar Laugh is alone, here at my table, but she came with the chairwoman, belongs to the organization, and, in fact, the chairwoman herself announces that Letizia — Vulgar Laugh, in other words — will now come by the tables to collect our e-mail addresses. She starts with me, of course, and I would rather not give it to her but I do anyway, on account of the above-mentioned melting of any resources by which to contradict her: all it takes is her heavy, green, mineral gaze and I'm only too happy to please her. Fuck. If there is such a thing as witches, she must be one of them.

The speaker finally arrives, and she's not alone either: she's actually with four people, one man and three women, who accompany her all the way to the table like an honor guard and then scatter around the room. The chairwoman immediately passes her the microphone, without further ado, and she, a mature woman with a vigorous air about her, part Grandma Duck, part Jessica Fletcher, introduces herself — "My name is Manuela Solvay Grassetti, I am a psychotherapist" — and starts by asking us a question. *How to talk about death with your children:* she wants to know how this topic was chosen, whether we came up with it or if it's part of a learning program. The chairwoman replies that we came up with it because as parents we find ourselves having to talk about death with our children, which prompts the speaker to ask her a strange question: "About *whose* death?" As if to establish that the lecture was now really beginning, a woman in the front row places a small digital recorder on the table in front of her. "How do you mean, whose death?" the chairwoman asks. "Death, the concept of death, its mystery." At this point the speaker smiles at her and explains that her question was meant to highlight the first and most significant aspect of the issue raised in the title: when we speak about death, she says, unless we are philosophers, we are usually referring to the death of someone, either ourselves or a loved one, acquaintances, or even soldiers who die in wars we hear about on TV; almost never about death in and of itself. Very few adults are interested in the mystery of death, but children are very curious about it. This is why, she insists, she was asking who came up with the title: the fact that we did, that it stems from needs related to our everyday lives with our children rather than from some theoretical program we are following, means that she should focus mainly on answering our questions this evening, because since we proposed this topic we are obviously grappling with specific, concrete problems and we hope this evening will help us resolve them. (Her words, followed by a knowing pause, prompt a long murmur of approval.) So, she continues, she will limit herself to a short introduction, after which she will be at our disposal for — and here, making an exemplary, Pavlovian contribution to the evening, the microphone goes dead. It does so in that peremptory way that objects have of suddenly dying in our hands, letting all of us know immediately that this time it's not just being capricious, a defect that can be fixed with a shake, or a mechanical failure that can be repaired, but the notorious Inevitable Event that sooner or later happens to anything that performs a function in our universe. A death, a passing away. It's so blatant that no one makes the least attempt to bring it back to life, not even the man moving like a lemur who roams around the room acting as if he's in charge, who shakes his hairless head at the chairman's inquisitive gestures toward him. At this point the speaker stands up, and in a voice surprisingly different from its amplified version (younger, it sounds, more melodious, clean), she says that she will continue without the mic. She asks if everyone feels all right, giving rise to a chorus of yeses, after which she drinks a glass of water and starts to speak again, saying her introduction will be limited to the exposition of a concept, only one, which is very simple but in her opinion very basic: we transfer our emotions to our children. Up to a certain age, she says, what children feel toward any one thing is nothing more than a reproduction or an elaboration of what their parents feel. Not of what we are struggling to express, mind you: *of what we really feel*. And so, she says, before worrying about the relationship between our children and death we have to worry about the relationship between *us* and death. The problem is thus not one of which words, artifice, or images to use to talk to them about death, she says, but rather where we stand with respect to death — how we handled it, whether the death is of a loved one — and it enlists all the so-called paraverbal forces that our behavior conveys directly to our children's subconscious, such as the tone of voice, sighs, facial expressions, crying, etc.; or, to put it more descriptively, she adds, the grieving energy

we emit. Working on how to present death to children is equivalent to working on how we present it to ourselves: that's the whole
story. End of introduction. The speaker takes a seat again, and now
it's our turn to ask her questions.

We are caught off guard. No one expected such a short introduction, and silence falls over the room. It seems almost like a
technique devised to force us to think: our brains were ready to
store up a certain amount of information before returning to our
individual worries, and now they're united in a silent labor of re-
configuration that broadens a single received concept until it has
occupied all the available space. It's interesting. As is this stuff about
the energy of sorrow. Then it would be like Carlo said this morning, and like in the end I am tempted to believe myself, although it
still seems *too* easy: if Claudia isn't grieving, it's because she's imitat-
ing me; since I'm not emitting grief, she doesn't have access to the
energy needed to grieve. So she's not the mystery: I am.

One woman stands up and asks if she can relate a personal experience; then, without waiting for permission, she starts talking
about a major loss that afflicted her family and about her twelve-
year-old son, who remained completely indifferent to it. The
woman has a lisp, which gives her a certain charm, although physically she's a harsh prism of sharp angles. Her son, she says, hasn't
egsthperienthed that death, he wath protected as much as pothible,
but he was very cloth to the detheased. Yet from the very thtart,
he behaved with total indifferenth. At the funeral he thulked. In
the graveyard he mithbehaved, throwing thones at the grave. The
speaker asks her who the deceased was, the woman answers that it
was one of his cousins, a little older than him, and the speaker nods,
almost smugly: she says that the death of a playmate forces children
to think of their own death, and since they're not ready to, out of
self-defense, they frequently adopt a strategy of denial. But is such
behavior *healthy*? the woman asks. Yes, in the short term: how long

ago did his cousin die? *Thix months.* Goodness. In that case his denial has probably already plateaued: usually the death of a child causes terrible suffering in adults, and he may have decided to reject the stereotypical behavior surrounding him, what he might see as the theatricality of suffering. He might feel a danger of being overburdened by so much grief, of *dying* himself, so he shuts the door on it. And what *can* you do? One thing is certain, signora: You mustn't insist on talking about it. You mustn't pry, you mustn't investigate, you mustn't make him think he is required to grieve. He would feel intruded upon and become even more withdrawn. Your job is to *be there* and to let him know that you are. Besides which he might already have spoken with one of his friends, girl or boy, because at that age your peers start to become more important than your parents. It's the period when hormones kick in. And if you're really intent on talking to him, use the expression "I was wondering": "You know, *I was wondering* why you never talk about Francesco. I just wanted you to know that if you ever feel like talking about him, I'm here." Words along these lines. *I was wondering* is a hypnotic message that goes straight to the subconscious. *I was wondering.* We have to show him all our uncertainty, all our imperfection, to prevent him from feeling inadequate. The child's unconscious, the phenomenal splendor he or she has inside, is still open, wide open. And feelings hurt. It's only logical that children defend themselves.

At this point, Vulgar Laugh, who has sat back down at my table after collecting addresses, turns around and starts scribbling in a notebook, as if in the grip of a sudden emergency. Except from the movement she makes in turning toward the table, before bending her head over her notebook, I notice something on her face that isn't quite right. Some blood. In the blink of an eye, because she leaned over her notebook immediately and now I can't see her face, but it really did look as if blood was dripping from her nose. I try to lower myself very slowly so that my gaze can sneak another peek at her face below the undulating mass of her black hair while she's writing — right now she's writing *hypnotic message,* but my movement is fairly obvious and I'm afraid of being noticed. But the room's attention is focused entirely on the speaker — "You have to be very careful of what you say to children, because children believe us" — meaning that it just might be possible that no one is noticing me, and I continue to lower myself, slowly. Except that, just as suddenly as she'd begun, Vulgar Laugh stops writing and turns her back on me again to follow the lecture — and once again, during the movement that she makes to turn around, I get the impression there's blood on her face. So I shift my chair a little, slowly, let my gaze wander around the edges of the table, to include at least her profile in my field of vision, but just when I'm ready to unveil it she turns around and looks at me, smiling.

There it is.

She really does have blood below her right nostril, dark, dense blood that has already coagulated slightly, but she doesn't notice. No one notices, dammit, no one notices, not even when she turns her head back toward the room to follow the lecture. A woman in the front row is talking now, and she's saying that she has the opposite problem: last year in the mountains her seven-year-old daughter experienced firsthand the death of a child who was staying at their hotel, a real tragedy, which filled her with questions. Where did the dead boy go? Can he see us? Will I die, too? Why don't we all die at the same time? Another woman interrupts from the other side of the room, saying that her daughter, who is five, has also been pestering her with questions ever since her grandfather passed away: Why did Grandpa die? Did he decide to? Will he come back? Next to her is an older woman, dressed in black, who bears a striking resemblance to her, confirming everything she says with a nod. Vulgar Laugh continues to follow attentively, ignoring me: now I can see three-quarters of her face, and obviously the blood is still there, right below her right nostril. I even have the impression that it's getting worse, that it could start dripping onto her knee from one moment to the next . . .

You have to tell her clearly there's no returning from death, the speaker says. You have to acknowledge the child's fear and anxiety, ask her to explain them, listen to her, let her talk about what's bothering her, let her create order, by herself, from the chaos she has inside . . .

— Signora, — I whisper.

You have to change your way of referring to it from *to be afraid* to *to feel afraid.*

Vulgar Laugh turns around, stares at me with her evil, alien eyes that leave so little time to do what you want.

You have to ask her what it is that frightens her about death.

— Your nose, — I say, in a soft voice.

"Are you worried that Grandma might die? Are you frightened? Why?"

The woman knits her brows, she doesn't understand.

If she cries, let her cry. Children's crying hurts us more than it does them.

— You're bleeding, — I whisper; and at this point something awful happens because of my whispering: what happens is that instinctively she looks between her legs — oh no, no — and then everything becomes worse than I had feared because, however short a time it may last, this misunderstanding *will not be a misunderstanding* in the short term, and in fact it isn't one while she's looking between her legs and continues not to be one when her withering gaze suddenly focuses on me again and now bears the indignation together with the satisfaction of the challenged demon and makes of me an unhealthy, perverse, lost, vampirish creature who dared to violate the intimacy of her vital secretions and besmirch my hands with her menstruation. It lasts only a second, of course,

truly no more than the blink of an eye, but in that second, incin-
erated by her eyes, depraved by her blood, I am pierced by pain,
physical pain, in my stomach, my head, everywhere, and at the
same time I see precipitating from her bloodied face the triumph
of absolute evil — which in the end, I realize, is just one more
of my lists, meteoric and horrible, the list of things throughout
my life that my eyes and mind have seen where there was a gap-
ing soullessness: grinning skulls, glassy-eyed sharks, gray-skinned
zombies, corpses piled up in concentration camps, the green vomit
in *The Exorcist,* the pyramid of chairs in *Poltergeist,* the infantilization
of Frankenstein, the page of *It* that explains what It is, the physical description of Mr. Hyde, Opal kicking the lame man, the bull
killing the bullfighter, Pinocchio hanging from the oak tree, Bel-
fagor, Dracula, Moby-Dick, werewolves, Morganti caressing my
face with a blade of wheat, the owner of Brick in Lugano sinking
beneath the water like a stone, my mother lying in the coffin in
a beige cardigan that looks empty, the lifeless body of Lara surrounded by slices of melon . . .

All of a sudden, a stroke of luck: the lights in the room go out,
and the fact that I can't see anything makes me feel better immediately. The speaker continues speaking in the pitch dark — make
her draw it, she says, make her depict her fear — and this makes
me feel better, too. And after a few days, she says, ask her to draw
her fear getting better. Yes, it's getting better. The pain has disappeared. It's getting much better. Ta-daa.

chapter nineteen

What an asshole. What a colossal, incommensurable asshole. What
the fuck got into me? The cheeseburger: onion, pickles, mayon-
naise, ketchup, and then the French fries — it had been a long

time since I'd eaten anything so heavy at night. It must have been
the cheeseburger. But, but, but . . . I'm not sick, didn't throw up,
and even now it's not as if my stomach feels heavy or something.
My cheekbone. My cheekbone does hurt, but not my stomach.
And if it wasn't the cheeseburger, what was it? What an asshole.
I left my nice house on Via Durini, driving my nice big black car,
piloted by a €2,000 GPS, to go all the way to Gorgonzola and faint
— *faint* — right smack in the middle of a meeting from which
a lot of nice people expected to receive good advice on how to
talk about death with their children. I interrupted the meeting, or
rather I ruined it — "Well, my friends, I think it would be better
to stop at this point." There is no redemption for this. Better to
forget all about it as quickly as possible and go on about my business as if nothing had happened. Anyway, nobody knew me there
and I'll never go back. *List of places where I'll never go back: the Parentogether salons.* Better yet: I never went there. Take a hammer to my
hard drive, DELETE ALL. Tomorrow I'll tell Barbara-or-Beatrice that
unfortunately I was unable to go because I had a small accident
in the kitchen — "I bumped my cheekbone against the refrigera-
tor door, here, can you see?" — and if she attends another one of
those meetings, maybe the one next month on grandparents, she
whose parents and husband are still alive, if I understand correctly,
from the way she always talks about her in-laws, "my in-laws,"
"my in-laws' house," so she might actually be assailed by doubts
over whether grandparents are *a help or a hindrance,* so if she does go
there and hears people talk about the mysterious shithead who at
the previous session collapsed on the floor, unconscious, halfway
through the lecture, and then, once he'd been revived, ran away,
asininely rejecting all offers to help him, get coffee, call a doctor,
or, as the enchantress with the lisp insisted on suggesting, even an
ambulanth, she will hardly think of me. Why would she? Nothing
ties me to that person, seeing as I wasn't there. She won't think of

me. No way. People think of us infinitely less than we believe. To
be honest, they almost never do.

But, but, but . . . It still happened: why? Why did I faint? Why did
I faint? Why did I faint? While I'm driving through the warm night,
this question is the only thing on my mind, and it's strange, but,
with more than a million people between me and that room, comforted by my renewed familiarity with the city, I have the impression that I know exactly why, but it's as if the reply flashed through
my mind for only a moment, a single shining moment, and then
it disappeared. It's a strange sensation, like when you're about to
remember something but the very act of remembering drives the
memory away again. I'm probably not concentrating enough, I
think, and then I pull over and stop. Where are we? Piazzale Loreto.
Good. I light a cigarette. I only want to understand why I fainted.
Fuck! In other words, my brain has suddenly turned off, abandoned
my body as if it wanted to shed it, and it happened to me, this evening, a little while ago, at a precise moment in my life (well, the
moments of life are always precise, for that matter), a moment that
I arrived at fully conscious, as fully conscious as I am now: there
must be some reason. All I have to do is concentrate, think. It could
have been the cheeseburger, as I was saying. Or a slightly brutal way
of feeling tired. This morning Carlo spoke to me about a fainting
spell, he described it to me: it could have been the power of suggestion, *sympathy*. Or else the influence of that she-devil, the sight of her
blood, the dreadful misunderstanding that was generated . . . I have
the answer, I feel it inside, but it keeps darting around too quickly
for my mind to grasp; I can't catch it, I can't even slow it down —
goddamn, it's unbearable. What can I do? Well, I'm going to have
to come up with something, because I don't feel at all well, I feel
a killer anxiety building inside me and I obviously can't go home
in this state: Claudia is there, and we transfer our feelings to our
children — isn't that what they just told me? Okay, maybe there

is a way: Where's my notebook? Where's it hiding? I used to keep it
in the glove compartment, why isn't it there anymore? I start looking for it, but while I'm looking for it the cigarette falls out of my
mouth; I jump back, afraid it's going to burn my clothes, so it falls
right on the leather seat; the tip separates from the rest of the cigarette on impact, and while it's rolling around on the floor the rest
stays on the seat; I try to brush it away with my hand, but the fucker
has already started burning the leather, what a stench, it's already
stuck; so I grab a CD cover and smack it down on top, to put it out,
and I do put it out; but now of course there's a hole in the seat, plus
the burning smell hasn't gone away but actually seems to have gotten worse; and in fact there's smoke coming from the carpet below
my feet, and it's not coming from the carpet, oh fuck, it's coming
directly *from my feet,* actually from my trousers, yes, from the cuffs of
my trousers, I don't believe it, there's an ember still burning inside
the fold, fuck, the ember that's stuck in the seat was not the only
piece that was still lit, there was another one attached to the part
of the cigarette that fell straight into the cuff of my trousers, would
you believe it, right there, and I lift my leg to help it fall out but it
won't, I shake my leg, smack it against the steering wheel, there's no
room, so I open the door, put my leg out, and kick at the air, with
my hand I shake the cuff of my trousers and finally the cigarette falls
to the ground in a flutter of sparks, and finally I snuff it out with my
shoe, yes, I crush it I disintegrate it I pulverize it; yes, it's done, now
it's completely out; yes, nothing's burning; and I start checking the
damage, you can imagine, cotton trousers, a hole as big as a finger;
and then the hole in the seat, complicated by — what's happening now? What's that horn? Oh, I've stopped in a zone reserved for
taxis, go figure, thanks for screaming at me, young cabdriver who's
probably driving with a gun under his seat, the reason why I will not
point out to you that there are much less shitty ways to — all right
already, I'll move, asshole. A roar of the engine, a squealing of tires,

my shoulders slam against the seat back, peeling out like an asshole in the middle of the road, I'm suddenly as neurotic as a monkey and I want to press the pedal to the metal, race off, peel out, scream and shout, and I shift into first as if I wanted to kill the engine and I feel my bowels twisting in my stomach and I shift into second, and if I don't cut it out right away it'll mean that I've gone nuts and then I'll be in real trouble: calm down, for Christ's sake! What are you so pissed off about? Calm down! I slow down. Drive slowly, for Christ's sake. The song that's playing on the stereo is saying the same thing at this very moment: "Hey man, slow down, slow down." I breathe. I think. What's gotten into me? What's happening to me tonight? "Idiot, slow down, slow down . . ." Idiot is right. What an idiot. What would have happened if a child had been crossing the street while I was peeling out as if I were in a Grand Prix race? Or even if a dog, a cat, a damn pigeon had been crossing? "Where the hell am I going at a thousand feet per second?" Exactly. Where the hell am I going? I have to be very careful if I want to stay out of trouble: I've already made enough of a mess tonight, all I need now is a car accident. I put on my seat belt. After all, come to think of it, almost nothing really happened; sure, a short fainting spell, a tiny hole in the seat, a pair of trousers I have to throw away: what's the big deal? Calm down. It amounts to nothing. Calm down. And that taxi driver was right, I wasn't supposed to park there, I was wrong. It was simply the wrong place, for me, too, for what I wanted to do, regardless of the prohibition: it was too *whatever*. The cabdriver only wanted to help me, that's how I should see it: his manners don't matter, he only wanted me to realize that I was in the wrong place, he only wanted to push me in the right direction — toward the place where I could stop and clear my head and regain some peace of mind before returning home. And he succeeded, that's the nice thing, *he helped me,* because all of a sudden I know exactly where to go, and I'm going there, slowly but surely, at twenty miles an hour, and I feel much better. But of course. It's close, and above all I know my way: without traffic it won't take me more than five minutes. It's really close, how come I didn't think of it before? I'll go there, it'll calm me down, I'll relax, reassure myself, and I'll go home . . .

Done. Here I am.

This is the place.

I open the car door, but I don't get out of the car. The dark school is an imposing, romantic pile. I've never seen it like this: it looks useless and desolate, like a broken toy, like everything that belongs to children and that children leave outside. It's just standing there, a mere product of spatial forces, as if it were swallowing the time separating it from its daytime glory. Everything seems to sustain it in the silent struggle to make it to tomorrow: the absurd summer tranquillity of this October night, the trees, the park, the road, the buildings across the street, the parked cars — over which the wounded and unclaimed C3 holds court. I breathe deeply, repeatedly, and although I'm in the center of Milan, what fills my lungs feels like fresh air, fresh and fragrant. I breathe, I scan the profiles of things softened by darkness, I listen to the noises coming from the avenue: everything is so completely familiar, comforting, reassuring . . . And this is truly an amazing spot, a place in the world brimming with apotropaic forces: the Longobards must have come here to honor their loutish gods, some Christian girl must have suffered the martyrdom that would make her a saint, some young Merovingian must have been transformed into a deer by love . . .

This is the place.

This is my reason for fainting. A way for me to grasp it, identify it, name it . . .

And again the song that was playing on the stereo levels the distances and leaps into the foreground with a sentence that transfixes me because it seems to be addressed directly to me: "And now that you find it," it says, "it's gone / And now that you feel it, you don't / I'm not afraid." Because this is exactly what I'm feeling: it's the same sensation as before, the same subcortical perception of a flickering light, except that it's no longer annoying and I'm no longer afraid. Because it was fear, before. Also when I fainted, it was fear. And now it's gone. In fact, I realize that it doesn't interest me anymore. Why did I faint? Afraid of what? And what does it matter? It's only one of the many questions that I can't answer. Why is sea water salty, while glaciers, rivers, and the rain are not? Why does the score in tennis go 15, 30, 40, and not 45? Why do you have to dial the area code for local calls nowadays? What happens at the ATM if I enter €250 and only €150 comes out? What the hell does common-rail engine mean? Here comes the refrain again: "And now that you find it," it repeats, "it's gone / And now that you feel it, you don't / I'm not afraid." I don't understand the rest, and the song ends.

It's starting to interest me, this strange phenomenon with the stereo. Or rather not with the stereo, with Lara's Radiohead CD that I found in the car and that I keep listening to over and over. Most of the time I ignore it, and I especially ignore the words; but there are times, like a little while ago, or earlier, when I was driving, and also in recent days, now that I think about it, quite a few times, in which a single verse or an entire refrain literally jumped out at me and allowed itself to be understood with great natural-ness, as if English were my native language; and when this hap-pens those words always seem to be aimed directly at me, and they are always wise, appropriate, perfect. As if that CD were looking at me and trying to speak with me, give me advice.

I start looking for the case. Not without reason: maybe the time has come to take this bequest from Lara a little more seriously, and if the case has the lyrics to all the songs, maybe I'll find writ-ten loud and clear the things that — here it is; unfortunately it's not the original CD, just a compilation someone burned, and on

the cover the only thing written is RADIOHEAD. *PER APPRESSARM'AL
CIEL DOND'IO DERIVO.* TO GET CLOSER TO HEAVEN FROM WHENCE I COME
— nice, wow: who is it by, Petrarch? — in Lara's round, sensual
handwriting. Or is it Marta's? They always had pretty much the
same handwriting. Of course, it's Marta's. Now I remember. Once
the same thing happened in her car. Right across from here, right
after I had smashed up the Citroën to clear the road, while she
was finishing up her striptease. I also remember what the CD was
saying: "We are accidents waiting to happen." I bet it was the very
same CD: Marta must have been the one who burned it and gave
a copy to Lara, or was it the other way around?

Now the song is over and you can hear applause, shouts. The
singer says something I don't understand — I understand only
"old selection." He must be announcing the title of the next song,
because he says, "It's called" something or other, getting an ova-
tion, after which a very sad guitar riff starts, which is repeated for a
few beats. Then the voice starts to sing, slowly, languidly.

"This is the place," it says. I swear.

"Remember me?"

Hah, I do remember you . . .

"We've been trying to reach you . . ."

Of course. It's hard not to realize, Song. What's up . . .

"This is the place / It won't hurt, it will not hurt."

It's true, Song: it doesn't hurt, I feel no pain; especially in this
place. And let me tell you something: it's fantastic to converse
with you. Tell me something: How do you see this strange life of
mine? What do you think I should do, I mean in general?

But now I don't understand anything: the singer starts slurring
the words, and the music takes over. Nice, yeah, languid and all,
but what I'm interested in are the words. "Recognition," "face,"
"empty," I can make out a few isolated words, fragments: "to go
home," "at the bottom of the ocean," and again "face" . . .

Who knows what important thing you're telling me, Song, that I don't understand. Anyway, I also realize that if I could understand everything it would be too easy; even the responses of the oracle at Delphi were impenetrable and had to be interpreted. Not to mention that to these things there is usually a dark side, terribly complicated evil things, that it's much better not to know. And then it could simply be that I understand only the questions addressed to me, maybe that's how it works. I'm hardly the only person who listens to these songs.

" 'Cause it's time to go home."

This I understand perfectly, for example, and in fact it's true: it's time to go home. But I don't get the last verses, the song ends, and yes, I do go home. The same thing is said by the nice gratifying sound of the superreinforced car window closing — *shlomp:* it's time to go home. Thank you, Song; thanks also for the applause I'm getting now, long, sincere, and passionate: I've never been applauded in all my life. Not even once. And instead sometimes a nice round of applause is exactly what you need to go home peacefully, with your heart filled with chaos and tranquillity . . .

chapter twenty

I smell it immediately, as soon as I set foot in the house. They must have turned on the fumigators, I think: with this heat there are still mosquitoes around. Or else a stick of incense, Lara had a supply, or those big scented candles that are so popular nowadays. I make my way down the hall, the house is dark and quiet, only the blue glare of the television in the living room, and in the living room the smell is very strong. I let my eyes wander around the dimly lit room, and, for a second, I don't know why, I have the impression I've come upon the scene of a suicide — that I'm one of those guys who comes home one day and finds his father hanging from a chandelier hook, or his son, or his brother. Not an accidental death, that's a feeling I know all too well; no, a suicide: like a cold touch, frightening, that makes me shiver, before my eyes make out Carlo sitting on the sofa — alive, of course — a silver tube in his mouth, fooling around with a lighter and a sheet of tinfoil. He's heating up the tinfoil with the lighter and using the tube to breathe in the smoke this operation produces. He swallows the smoke as if it were food, leans against the backrest of the sofa, and looks at me with a sphinxlike expression. I sniff at this strange, sweet, pungent smell in the air that isn't hashish or even marijuana . . .

— Opium, — says Carlo.

I inspect the room with my eyes, in the grip of a fear as big as an ox: the television is tuned to MTV, but the sound is off; on the bookshelf the fake aquarium and its painted fish are glowing; on the table the remnants of a Yahtzee game; *Claudia isn't here,* but I still feel an enormous rage building toward my brother, which I struggle to contain — and I contain it only because, seeing as it costs me so much, I think that not exploding is precious. But I still can't help thinking my brother is a complete asshole: there he is, the first time in his life he's spending an evening with a child, sprawled out on the sofa doing opium for the sake of his mother-fucking myth of —

— Calm down: she's in bed, — he says.

I continue to restrain myself but I'm furious, and without saying a word I turn and walk toward Claudia's room. Carlo's voice comes up on me from behind.

— She's sleeping like a rock . . .

In fact, Claudia is asleep. I've often wondered how children can sleep so well while adults are doing such savage things in their homes: parents leave each other, babysitters fuck their boyfriends, uncles get high, and the children? Nothing: they sleep, the way

Claudia's sleeping now, all sweaty and serene. I stand there and devoutly contemplate her as she surrenders to the alabaster moonlight of the fluorescent dinosaurs lined up on her desk. I caress her luminous skin, and the paternal gesture I am performing reminds me of my father during the historic quarrel that culminated in Carlo's final exit from our house on Via Giotto. Mom and Dad came home unexpectedly one Saturday night when they were supposed to be spending the weekend at the seaside, and they found Carlo doing bong hits with his friends. Dad went berserk, made a huge scene, threw Carlo's friends out with the bloodcurdling and objectively terrifying rage he was able to muster from his mild existence every now and then, and Carlo, high as a kite, kept laughing in his face, ferociously, repeating "A lot of talk and a badge, you're nothing but a lot of talk and a badge." It could have been a quarrel like all the others (and in those days, between the two of them, there were tons), but instead it was final, and what made it final was not the marijuana but rather our father's epic inability to accept reality for what it was — the very same unacceptability that must have appeared to him that night: Carlo would keep on doing whatever he felt like; Carlo would completely ignore his father's expectations; Carlo didn't need his help; Carlo really would drop out of university to go to London. Now that I'm a father myself, I'm sure Dad regretted uncorking all his rage that night, in front of the smoking bong, driving his son to run far away from him forever. Carlo was only twenty-two years old, and for all his bravado, he was still as tender as a bamboo shoot. But again, now that I'm a father myself, I'm feeling that same overpowering rage, directed at the same person, and oddly enough over the same offense — *drugs in my house* — as if I had inherited the role. And this is not good: it's theater, a rerun of the old family repertory — a family, moreover, that doesn't exist anymore. Yet I'm still furious with Carlo, furious and indignant, just like Dad.

Luckily I'm still caressing Claudia's moist forehead, and it's as if my hand were resting on a healing stone, because I feel a wave of her tranquillity entering me, warm, soothing, clarifying, and for starters this is *not* theater, I tell myself, and my brother is what he is, and the main thing is that I am not my father and I also smoked pot at our house on Via Giotto, also with a bong, even after Carlo left, after which he became neither more nor less than a well-to-do drug addict; today it's no longer a pose, a provocation, a rebellion, he's doing it out of need, and since he is a drug addict, he absolutely has to get high every day, he can't skip a single day, and since tonight he's at my house he has to get high at my house, but he started to smoke his opium only after Claudia fell asleep, prior to which he also devoted himself to her, he also took her out to eat at the Japanese restaurant, he also brought her home, he also played Yahtzee with her, he also tucked her in, and maybe he also told her some crazy story while she was falling asleep, and Claudia literally adores him, and the point is this: Claudia adores him and would never want us to quarrel, for any reason in the world, not to mention that one day or another, she, too, will probably smoke joints, maybe right in this house, and maybe I'll find out, and when that day comes I must not do what my father did. I'll have to control myself, understand, remember, I'll have to be ready to do the right thing, and by now my anger of a few minutes ago seems completely artificial, ridiculous, *no longer mine,* and I have to struggle less and less to dominate it, less and less, less and less — until I realize that, abracadabra, my anger is gone . . .

When I remove my hand from my daughter's face and quietly slip out through the door so the opium fumes don't get in, I feel like I've just sidestepped a deadly trap. Anything, now, anything but a quarrel with your brother.

— You want some? — says Carlo out of the blue, as soon as I return to the living room.

He means opium, do I want some opium.

Fuck, this is the last thing I was expecting. And now? What do I say to him, "No"? Is there some way I can say, "No, thank you," as serenely and normally as he asked me to partake? And then what happens? I go to bed, and he stays up smoking by himself? Not to mention that it's opium. I smoked it many years ago when I was at university and I was studying with Beppe Caramella, who always had opium around, who knows where he got it. I liked it: it was a literary drug, epic, glorious, it gave you a nice feeling of distance, of being cool — the feeling of *no longer being affected,* that's what it was, by the things that affected me — and it had no bad aftereffects. At least that's what I remember. I haven't had any since then.

Carlo takes a long drag of the smoke and looks at me.

All right already. Fuck it. A little opium won't hurt.

— Give it here.

— Have a seat, — says my brother, the expert.

I sit down on the sofa, and he passes me the tinfoil. Even though I fainted just a little while ago, goddamn it, it's still not going to hurt me.

— Careful, — he says. And he shows me how to hold the tinfoil, at the center of which is a small, fingernail-sized brown ball.

— I know, I know, — I say, even though I don't know shit. Beppe Caramella and I used to smoke opium in a kind of pipe, and he would take care of everything. All I had to do was inhale. Carlo clicks the lighter underneath the tinfoil, and right away the little ball starts to melt, releasing the fumes. It slithers smoothly like a ball of mercury down the folds in the sheet, leaving behind a thin brown trail. Just moving it around and looking at it is so —

— Come on, inhale, — says Carlo.

I place the tube in my mouth, I inhale.

— Everything, — says Carlo, — inhale everything.

I look at Carlo and nod; he really wants me to get high, it really

matters to him. In fact, my first toke was a little timid: more smoke
is floating in the air than went down my throat. Carlo clicks his
lighter again, and I inhale again as soon as the smoke starts to rise,
and this time not a single wisp gets wasted: everything enters my
mouth, with a surprising taste of barn, resin, bread, fruit, wheat,
milk, paper, and incense — good but verging on disgusting; and
from my mouth some goes down, warm, into my lungs, but most
goes up, cold, into my brain. Carlo passes me the lighter, inviting me to do it by myself. With the tinfoil in my right hand, the
lighter in my left, and the tube in my mouth, I light up again and
move around the slippery little ball and I inhale the smoke for
the third time, taking a deep breath — what the fuck; I repeat
the operation another time, and then I break away, pass him the
whole arsenal, and lean against the back of the sofa. Then he starts
smoking again, and while he's smoking I look at him in the partial
darkness that is slowly becoming glassy — or is it grainy — or is
it chalky: he's very adept at sliding the little ball down the creases
in the tinfoil and chasing it down with the tube in his mouth, betraying an ability I almost envy, despite what it signifies. He takes
a couple of long tokes, then he leans back, too, smiles — the imp-
ish dimples — and now it's my turn again, and then I take one,
two tokes, and there's tenacity in my tokes, I don't want to say
it but there's grit, rivalry, and then him again, and then me, and
then him, yeah, the curse of being brothers, one-half for each, one
each, first one then the other, like when we were little, on the po-
nies in the park, or on the flying saucers at the EUR amusement
park, next to Dad, and we never won, ever, sometimes we would
manage to stay on till the bitter end but in the final duel we were
always beaten, and I've been carrying this one-on-one trauma
around for years, I'm not kidding, I've always been scared of duels,
I've always thought I would lose them so I've always avoided
them, not only at the amusement park, I mean, but in life, always

carefully avoided them, the duels, the head-to-heads, as much as possible, until three years ago, until that wonderful epiphany at the merry-go-rounds at Castiglione della Pescaia, when Claudia insisted that I take her on, what else, the flying saucers, and I got up my courage and took her, already feeling the humiliation I would suffer when some fucking daddy together with his chubby daughter would beat us ruthlessly, undeservedly, because you're not going to tell me those flying saucers really shoot — and if they do, *what* do they shoot? — it's the woman down there in the ticket booth that decides everything, she's the one that decides who wins and who loses, whether there is a pulsar or not, I've never understood, and cutting to the chase, we got on the flying saucer, and I'm already thinking what excuse I'm going to make after we've lost one, two, three, four times, when Claudia starts to feel bad about always losing, and instead we win, yes, the others fall one by one, we are the only ones left flying along with another saucer shooting at us for an endless second and in the end we win, incredible, we even win the final duel, they go down and we stay up, and not only do we win that duel but we keep on winning and we never stop, we are always the ones still flying, we are always the ones that win, against any and all adversaries, no one can beat us, and it's really fantastic to win this way, there's really nothing better, winning effortlessly, undeservedly, and *endlessly*, because you win a free ride and the woman in the ticket booth has chosen us tonight, she's decided to let us into the remarkable, magic, victory–free ride cycle — another victory, another free ride — and maybe those were the best moments of my life, yes, the moments when I was happiest, that evening, at the Castiglione della Pescaia rides, when the last adversary who dared to go head-to-head with us sank into the abyss and the only ones left were the two of us, Claudia and me, up there, surrounded by the coastal lights punctuating the blackness of the sea and caressed by the night-

time breeze ruffling our hair, both certain, by now — and this is
what's so unprecedented — that in a little while it would happen
again, and then again and again and again, her because she's convinced her father is unbeatable, me because I know this is a kind of
miracle, that we have been *chosen*. In the end Claudia gets fed up; I
swear: after ten or maybe fifteen victories in a row, she got fed up
and wanted to go on the bumper cars, and we gave the free ride
to another father-child couple, leaving the field unbeaten, like
Rocky Marciano . . .

   Carlo looks at me, smiles, passes me the opium again. A drug
addict. I knew it, it's not as if I didn't, it's just that seeing it with my
own eyes has an effect on me. Carlo is a drug addict. Everything
is cold in my head now, everything frozen. The words *drug addict*
are frozen, and once again I am my father, I am my father in the
Arctic chill of the word *father,* who was right, back then — an icy
reason — because it was true, it has always been true, the use of
soft drugs leads to the use of hard drugs, it's so easy, how the hell
did my sons — look at them there, the rebel and that other guy,
the passive-aggressive one — how the living hell did those two
fucking assholes ever manage to claim the opposite? Do you want
to know what the best moments of *my* life were? What's that you
say? I say: do you want to know what my best moments, the best in
my life were? Stop, everyone, hold it right there: this is telepathy,
how the fuck did Carlo manage to — Do you remember when
Mamma took us to the park at Villa Celimontana? Do you remember when I got on the swings and you twisted the ropes? Mamma
didn't want us to, but we waited for her to get distracted and when
she was distracted you twisted them around and around so tight I
couldn't fit on the swing anymore, I had to lower my head and sit
there all hunched over waiting for you to stop and release them.
The ropes started to unwind and on the swing I started to spin, I
spun and I spun, faster and faster, do you remember? And when

Mamma realized, it was too late, there was nothing she could
do to stop the spinning, and at a certain point the ropes stopped
unwinding, because by then I was spinning so fast that after a big
yank it started winding up from the other side, and so on until
the swing stopped and Mamma got mad and she made us leave.
Right, it was when the first unwinding, the fast one, came to a
stop, when there was that yank, before the rope started to wind
back up in the other direction: that was such a fantastic moment. I
never felt anything like it again, it had everything I wanted in life:
an immense and unstoppable force, speed, fear, and courage, too,
and adrenaline, followed by dizziness, of course, because with all
that spinning I didn't understand shit; and at the moment of the
yank it was all unbearably intense, do you see? So intense that I felt
great, fantastically great, that I could experience it, *contain it*. I've
tried to re-create that moment a thousand times: through surfing,
parachuting, bungee jumping, drugs, and even though I get close
— because the force is there, the adrenaline is there, the dizziness
and the fear are there — but something is still missing. You might
say that what's missing is the fact I'm not a boy, but I swear it's not
that, I swear that when you throw yourself into thin air from an
airplane, or when you shoot up for the first time with a powerful
unknown drug, you *are* a child. So it's not that. What's missing is
quite simply something that is no longer there. What's missing is
you; what's missing is Mamma.

Silence.

Just a second, just a second. Why is Carlo saying these things to
me? And how could he read my mind? Silence. A heavy silence —
I don't know what else to call it. It's strange, all at once I can no
longer distinguish between me and him. Damn, Carlo, what a sensation, what a moment: I feel almost as if I were you. Everything is
so sharp, the television, the sofa, the bookshelf, but I can't distinguish myself from you. It's the opium. No, don't be so superficial,

don't be so *arid:* it's one of those moments, it's got nothing to do with the opium. It's the opium, I'm telling you. Come off it: do you really think a little brown turd can change things so much, can generate such a mess? Couldn't it be that things were already different and the mess was already there? What mess are you talking about? What do you mean, what mess? *This* mess: one head that contains two. Every muscle in the face slackening and drooping down. Subaqueous gaze, sweat, naked word, gray surrender. High school finals, Dylan Thomas, the ardent miseries of youth. What do you mean, what mess? Plus, to give you the whole picture, I have the clear sensation that I'm neither me nor you; that I'm, how can I put this, a fly. Exactly: it's the opium. And earlier? Earlier you were reading my mind, in case you hadn't realized. Since when does opium enable you to read minds? And that humidity stain shaped like Corsica on the ceiling? Why have I never noticed it before? Shaped like Corsica with a little finger. And the finger is pointed at the bookshelf, it's indicating something. The toy aquarium on the shelf, to remind me to turn it off otherwise the batteries will run out? The television on with the sound turned off? The fly that's shuttling between the TV screen and me — granted that I'm me, to be clear, and not it? Look: I shoo it away, and it goes to the TV screen; it spends a couple of seconds on the screen and comes back again; I shoo it away again, and it goes back to the screen, always to the same spot. It's trying to tell me something. What's written in the captions? Radiohead. *Radiohead!* Hah! Where's the remote? Quick, we've got to turn the sound back on, where's the remote? You're sitting on it. Where? Here it is. Man, you are totally fuc— Shhh! Listen: what's he saying? The guy over there, the one with the squint, the one pressing the microphone between his hands as if it were a dead chick, what's he saying? "I am up in the clouds / and I can't and I can't come down." That's what he said: I understood perfectly, right? Well, I have to tell you some-

thing really important I just found out tonight, Carlo: Lara com-
municates with me through the songs of this band. It was her.
Don't laugh, dammit, I'm serious. Do you hear them? "I can watch
but not take part / where I end and where you start." Did he say
that or didn't he? It's her. Don't ask me how. I have no idea, but
that guy with the bad eye must be a kind of medium. Look at how
he twists and turns, look at how he suffers. Listen to him. Lara
speaks to me through him. Right now you can't understand a
thing because every now and then he swallows his words — *but he
only swallows the ones that aren't meant for me,* do you see? When they're
meant for me, he suddenly stops swallowing and you can understand him just fine. When I'm driving my car too fast and he tells
me to slow down, I swear I understand him just fine. And when I
understand, he's always saying something about what I'm doing:
how else can you explain it? Look, you've got a hole in your pants,
I know; and the CD that Lara left in the car, maybe because a
fortune-teller predicted she would die soon, and she also wrote
something very poetic on the cover like I'm going to heaven, I'm
close to heaven. It's her way of continuing to speak with me, I finally realized. Come on, stop laughing already. Do you want more
proof? They're broadcasting a concert, right? Let's try another test.
Let's listen carefully to the next song. Here it is, it's started: listen
and you'll see. Sooner or later something will make sense, and
that something is meant for me. It'll be Lara speaking to me. Now
the squinter is swallowing his words, but — Shhhh! I was only
saying that — Shhh! This isn't meant for you, bro, it's meant for
me. What do you mean meant for you? Shhh! Let me hear *the whole
thing.* Okay, let's hear it all. None of this makes any sense, wouldn't
you know; but if you want to hear everything then let's hear everything. Forget about it, he's swallowing *all* the words. There, it's
done. Can we talk now? It was "Pyramid Song," bro. Do you know
it? I practically know it by heart. Oh, yeah? So what does it say? It

talks about a girl who throws herself into the river and while she's drowning she sees the moon and the sky filled with stars and black angels descend to her and she relives all the things she's done and rediscovers all her lost lovers. And why was it meant for you? Because a girl I went out with jumped into the Thames twenty years ago. Wow, that's fantastic. In the sense that not only Lara, but all dead people speak to the living through these guys. She let herself fall and, *puff*, she was gone. And tell me something: were you maybe thinking of her when I arrived? Yes. Aha! You see, I'm right? Listen up: first point, tonight you remembered that girl after all these years and instantly she communicated, through *them*. I was thinking of her, like I have every night for the past twenty years. Oh. Every night and even tonight. Now the fly goes toward him, and he leaves it alone, he lets it walk over his face, like an African child dying of starvation. So the coincidence doesn't impress you? And so? Yes. Well, so let's see if this will impress you: second point, first, when I entered the house and you were thinking of that girl, for a second I had the impression someone had killed themselves. I swear. I felt the chill of a suicide, how do you explain that? I'm telling you it's the opium. Oh, then you're obsessed. Think: when I came in *I hadn't smoked yet*. It doesn't matter, opium has a retroactive effect, it changes the past: that's why I smoke it. What are you talking about, retroactive effect, I'm telling you the opium has nothing to do with it — also because, by the way, it's not having any effect on me, if you really want to know. Why the fuck are you laughing, if I tell you that it's having no effect on me it's having no effect. Okay, my muscles have collapsed, and the air is like solidified, and suddenly I remember even the tiniest details of my high school finals, and I have the impression I'm speaking without opening my mouth, and vice versa, and in my head there's a huge block of ice, and vice versa; but all things aside I swear your opium is having no effect on me. None. Go ahead, laugh, in the meantime

they slipped you this fake opium. They ripped you off. And if I
were you — because there's still this crazy possibility, which
would explain our otherwise inexplicable telepathy, for one —
then they would have ripped me off, too, and I would find nothing
at all funny about it. Old Rudy doesn't rip anyone off, bro. Inexplicable, just to get this straight, as long as a guy continues to pene-
trate the deep darkness of human experience with the feeble light
of reason and expects everything taking place outside his flickering
cone of light to be just a coincidence, or the effect of a substance,
or to be not even happening. The truth is, the world is a ball of
magic, my friend, and this is the only reason the water doesn't fall
out of the oceans while the earth is rotating. Really? I didn't know.
Right: I know because Dylan Thomas said so, and I did an essay on
Dylan Thomas for my finals, and for some reason my finals are the
thing that right now I remember better than anything else in my
life. All that poetry I learned by heart, you see. "I have been told to
reason by the heart, / But heart, like head, leads helplessly; / I have
been told to reason by the pulse"; and so on, that's all I can remember, but on the other hand I couldn't remember at the exam,
either — but I remember the last line: "The ball I threw while
playing in the park / Has not yet reached the ground." The ball.
The ball of magic. Opium's the least of it. Good going, guy. The
only thing I know by heart is a shitload of lines from *Star Wars II
— Attack of the Clones*. "You wanna buy some death sticks?" "You
don't want to sell me death sticks." "I don't want to sell you death
sticks." "You want to go home and rethink your life." "I want to go
home and rethink my life." Well, at least now I get it: I never liked
Attack of the Clones, it bored me to death and I was never remotely
tempted to learn the dialogue by heart. Life seems easier when
you're able to fix something. Now at least we know the *Attack of the
Clones* guy is Carlo, and so I must be me. You're asking me to be
rational, but I can't. He's the one that's grieving, and I'm the one

that's not grieving. When I'm close to you my mind doesn't belong to me anymore. Right, he is Carlo, and I am me. There's a strange spring between us right now, a kind of thaw. Maybe something unrepeatable has happened, not maybe, definitely: something unrepeatable has happened. Carlo spoke with me. Even if I insisted on arguing — arguing's the only thing I know how to do with him, for that matter — tonight my brother spoke with me. He told me why he's grieving. The difference between knowledge and wisdom, Obi-Wan: the difference between knowledge and wisdom. I look at him avidly, fiercely; I've never looked at anyone more *intensely* than this. He's handsome, he's rich, he's famous, he's *cool,* but he's also one of those desperately not-simple people who need many gifts from life just to be able to put up with it. And to grieve. The fly continues to buzz around, to alight here and there on his sweaty face, and he continues to tolerate it with an age-old patience; but all of a sudden — I can't believe it — *he smacks it* and knocks it flat. Out of the blue, like that. Seeing him do it makes it look like the easiest thing in the world, but it's almost superhuman, like fishing with your hands. The fly isn't dead, it's flopping around on the rug, half dead, in a daze. Carlo picks it up, looks at it. "Master Windu," he says, "you have fought gallantly, worthy of recognition in the archives of the Jedi Order. Now it is finished." And he crushes it — gross — between his fingers.

Yes, Carlo is grieving, and he spoke with me — but does it *count* to speak this way? I didn't even realize, I'm realizing only now. We were high: does it count? Does it count even if tomorrow I will have forgotten everything? I'm already starting to forget, I feel it: oh, why didn't I realize earlier? Help, Carlo, tell me those things again. I'm falling asleep, I'm passing out again, they're slipping away: tell me again, quick. Tell me about the girl who drowned in the Thames and broke your heart. Are you sure she killed herself and it wasn't an accident? Have you really thought about her every day for the past twenty years? Do you miss her so much? What was her name? And do you really miss me when you get high? Yes. Yes. Yes. Tracy. Yes . . .

chapter twenty-one

Now things are going decidedly better, but this morning . . .

This morning, before dawn, when I woke up on the sofa, Carlo was gone and with him the opium and the paraphernalia used to smoke it. I got up to go to my bedroom, but I realized that I felt like shit and had to run to the bathroom to throw up. And while I was there throwing up, hugging the sides of the toilet bowl, I saw Dylan looking at me from the doorway — perplexed, I would say. It was just for a moment; Dylan disappeared immediately; but in that moment I felt more ashamed than I had ever felt in my life, and it seemed literally impossible to live with that shame. I felt so filthy in that moment, so stupid, even unworthy of the compassion of a dog. I would rather have stuck my head down the toilet bowl into my own vomit, like in that scene in *Trainspotting,* than leave the bathroom and maybe catch the eye of Mac, Claudia's nanny, who always gets up before dawn and is pure of heart. To wake Claudia up, have breakfast with her, take her to school, and wait in front for her like all the other days suddenly seemed like a paradise lost. Everything was clear in that moment: I was unfit to take care of my daughter; sooner or later the truth would come out; sooner or later I would do something awful.

Then, as happens, this sensation began to get weaker, much fuzzier, I stopped throwing up, and when I stood up I realized that my legs were steady and I still had a future ahead of me. A click of the flush, and the vomit disappeared in a greenish whirlpool; despite myself, I started to think I might get away with it. I locked the door, filled the tub with warm water, got undressed, stepped into the tub, and scrubbed myself with a vengeance, using every product within reach. Then I dried myself in my soft bathrobe, shaved very carefully, put on fresh underwear and a shirt, a perfectly pressed gray suit, shiny shoes, my nicest tie, and in this way, drawing on all the best things I had available, I started to feel the courage to move forward. It was a way of fooling myself, of course, but it worked: you *can* judge a book by its cover. In the meantime the sun came out — a violent sun, absurd this late in October. I looked out the living room window, down to the street. People were hurrying on their way to work, and I felt worse than all of them, I did, but not to the point I could no longer mingle. I took Dylan out, watched him take a shit in the trembling, ridiculous pose dogs adopt when they shit, and while I was picking up his shit from the sidewalk I thought that when it came to inconvenient postures, as a matter of fact, he was the last one that could act morally superior to me. Back home I went in to face Mac, in the kitchen, and her legendary silence helped me to think she hadn't noticed a thing: not a word, just a single protective gesture, filled with womanly compassion, when with her hand she fixed the collar of my jacket bunched up below my neck. Then I was able to go and wake Claudia up, and everything began to go smoothly as usual. We had breakfast, she told me about dinner with her uncle — at the Chinese restaurant, because the Japanese restaurant was closed — we left early so we could play "Unfortunately" with the GPS, and in front of the school we saw all the others arrive, like we always did, until the bell sucked her and the other children into the classrooms, leaving us parents outside to chat about the heat. At that moment you'd never know the mess I'd gotten into the night before, and it's not as if this amounted to not having gotten into it, but it made me feel better: it was a little like getting €50 in change after you'd paid only €5, I realize, but compared to what I was feeling when I was hugging the toilet just three hours before, the sense of shame was perfectly bearable. I'll redeem myself, I thought.

Then Carlo arrived. In a taxi, at around eleven thirty, on his way to the airport, he stopped by to say good-bye to me and to leave a package for Claudia. He was serene, placid. I exclude categorically that he had to pull himself together quickly, like me, to be presentable: him, he must be used to certain reawakenings. We practically didn't say a word to each other, but we hugged, hard and long. The fact that I had struggled so much to take my distance from last night didn't mean I didn't remember what had happened: we had gotten high together and he had talked to me about how much he missed the girl who had drowned in the Thames, how much he missed Mamma, and *how much he missed me*. No, we didn't say anything about it, but it was the most tender moment between us since . . . since forever, is what comes to me: since forever. Yolanda was there, too. She had arrived with Nebbia and waved hello right while I was hugging Carlo in my arms, and when Carlo left we stayed there for a little while to chat about the weather. It must have already been higher than ninety, and she said that she had heard on the radio that the lowest temperature last night had been seventy-five — an absolute record for this time of year. She was wearing the same Barrie jeans as yesterday and a yellow sleeveless T-shirt with the wording GRAVITY ALWAYS WINS practically on her tits; I thought it was really funny, rude but also desperate, after all, because she's young, yes, but come to think of it, there are not that many years separating her from the reality that right here and now her tits are denying so defiantly, and I felt authorized to comment on the fact: "Wise words," I said. "They're from a song," she said. "Oh yeah, by who?" "By Radiohead." And she left to pick up some certificate or other from the vital statistics office.

So I was left alone, in the shade, to think, and I am still here. To think, yes; but no longer about what I did last night and about how I can redeem myself — which is why I say that things are going decidedly better; but about this umpteenth coincidence. Maybe there's really nothing to understand, maybe it's really just chance and its stubborn little touches, but it sure is strange: these Radioheads really do seem to be pursuing me. So I jump in the car, grab the cover of Lara's CD, and scan all the titles to see if there's one that has something to do with gravity, but there isn't. It's hot as hell in the car, so I get out, and to my own surprise, I call Marta on my cell: if I had had to look up her number in my little black book and go to a phone booth, I would definitely never have done it, but with the cell it's just a matter of touching a couple of keys, and in the time it takes me to realize this, Marta has already picked up.

— Hello?

— Hi, Marta, how's it going?

— Fine, and you?

— Me, too. Where are you?

— At the gynecologist's.

— At the gynecologist's? Oh, right, of course . . . everything's okay, isn't it?

— Everything's fine, yes.

— Listen, I wanted to ask you something, but if I'm interrupting I can call back later.

— No, that's all right, I'm waiting for my turn. What do you want to know?

— Nothing, it's that here in the car I found a CD by Radiohead, except that it's not an official CD, it's a compilation that someone burned. On the cover are the song titles that look like they were written by Lara, but since you and she always had the same handwriting, I was wondering which of you made it: you or her?

— I did.

— Oh. Are you sure?

— Sure I'm sure.

— But did she ask you to, by chance? Or was it all your idea?

— It was my idea. Why do you ask?

— Um, no reason. And this phrase on the cover, *per appressarm'al ciel dond'io derivo:* who wrote it, you or her?

— It was me. I did.

— Of course. In fact, it's the same pen. And what gave you the idea?

— It's from a poem by Michelangelo. When I burned the CD I had just read his sonnets, in Vigevano, and they made a big impression on me.

— Ah, I see.

— Why are you asking?

— No reason. Just to know.

— To know what?

— Nothing, just curiosity. Since I like that CD, I was wondering where it came from. That's all.

— That's all?

— That's all. Hey, when can you come over for dinner, you and the kids?

— I don't know . . .

— Are you free tomorrow night?

— Yes . . .

— So come over tomorrow night.

— . . .

— Deal?

— Okay. Thanks . . .

— No biggie. See you tomorrow, then.

— Pietro?

— Yes.

— This phone call is weird.

— Weird? What's weird about it?

— I don't know, but it's weird.

— No, it's not. It's normal.

— Oops. It's my turn. Gotta run.

— Why am I not surprised? Go. See you tomorrow. Bye.

— See you tomorrow. Bye.

I hang up. Marta's right: in fact, it was a weird phone call, but it was also decisive, because if Lara didn't make the CD, then all this pileup of coincidences doesn't really mean anything. What sense would it have? It's all well and good to abandon logic, but in that case Lara has nothing to do with those songs: she left them in my car only as an intermediary between Marta and me. And I can't figure out why a dead woman would act as the intermediary for the songs of a band to act as an intermediary between two living people who could just as easily communicate with . . .

— Excuse me, Dottore?

I turn around instinctively, even if around here no one ever calls me *dottore*. Nothing, there's not a living soul.

— Dottore, up here!

I look up and see a little man waving his arms from a window in the apartment building across the street. He looks older. He waves his arms and nods, smiling: he is speaking directly to me; and now that he's sure he's got my attention, he makes a hand gesture; a gesture I can barely make out but that even from a glimpse has a clear meaning in Italy, unmistakable . . .

— Are you in the mood? — the little man says.

Due spaghetti, a little spaghetti, it means. The little man is rotating his hand downward, with the index and middle fingers making a V sign; he's inviting me to have *due spaghetti.*

— Tomato and basil! — he shouts. — I'm just about to toss the pasta in. Come on up!

It's surprising — isn't it? — the number of things that can happen to you while you're waiting in front of a school. A complete
stranger invites you to lunch from a window. And I accept, of
course I do: because although this invitation might seem absurd,
it is certainly no more absurd than the metempsychotic theory
that my sister-in-law just sent up in smoke, or the dogged coincidences that had led me to formulate it to make sense of the coincidences, or the conditions in which I formulated the theory,
last night, while smoking opium with my brother on the living
room sofa; on the contrary: in this company, you could say his
invitation was the least absurd thing. So I voice my thanks and
accept, yes; the little man gestures that I should come up to the
second floor (the middle and index finger *V* that a moment ago
were the prongs of a fork have turned into the number two), and
here I am crossing the street, and I pass an entrance of anodized
aluminum and I climb the unadorned stairs, filled with the smell
of all the sautéed onions in Milan. First floor: a dog barks hysteri-
cally behind an apartment door. Second floor: the little man is at
the door, with his hand outstretched and a big smile stamped on
his face. The first thing is he's not a little man: he's bigger than me.

— Come in, Dottore. — He shakes my hand. — My name is
Cesare Taramanni, I'm Roman like you.

He closes the door and guides me down a gloomy, plum-
colored hallway crammed with boxes, to a room that turns out
to be big and bright, with two large windows facing the street.
Except that the room is also crammed with boxes, dismantled
furniture, packed-up armchairs, objects wrapped in plastic . . .

— I apologize for the mess, but tomorrow the movers are
coming. I'm going back to Rome, you see, after thirty-six years . . .

He heads toward a table set for two, right next to one of the
windows, across from which shimmers the white mass of the
school.

— Over here, Dottore, have a seat. From here you get a good view of the school.

From the window, I see the spot in the world where I spend my days, for the first time without belonging to it. My car, the school door, the park: from here it looks like any other place.

— Excuse me, Dottore, — the man says, — I'm going to go check on the sauce.

And he disappears past the door on the other side of the room. Now it's obvious that my mind is swarming with questions (who is this man? why did he invite me to lunch? how does he know all these things about me?), but his dismantled life all around has such a strong impact that it stifles any inquiries. I've done quite a few moves in my time, but they were *my* moves: I have never happened to find myself in the midst of a stranger's move. It's sobering. Despite the care with which everything's been packed, many objects can be recognized through the cellophane and the newspaper — pots, pan handles, lampshades — and there's something imploring in their popping out of their boxes, as if they were calling for help to escape. The depressing outlines of paintings impressed on the wallpaper, nicks from unknown corners on the wall, the brutal interruption of domestic piety that for years must have made this dining room inviting; everything lends itself to creating the impression of suddenly landing *on the other side,* in an imaginary space bristling with symbols to interpret, as in dreams; an impression made even stronger by the table carefully set amid the boxes — white tablecloth, shiny silverware, separate glasses for water and for wine — one of those image-symbols that a person usually dreams, as I was saying, and then spends months at the psychoanalyst's trying to figure out: *I was there, dressed all elegantly, in the midst of moving boxes, and a stranger was cooking spaghetti for me, and outside the window was the window of my daughter's classroom, and it was October but it was as hot as August, but the most incongruous thing was the set table that held*

*court from the center of the scene. What does it symbolize, Doctor? The normality
that persists in my overturned life? The domestic warmth that survives in the cold air
of change? The quiet chaos that I have inside?*

Here he is again, with a carafe of wine in his hands. It's been
years since I've seen a carafe of wine.

— Excuse me for being so bold, but I've been wanting to invite
you up for some time, and here we are down to the last day. It's not
good for you to eat sandwiches, you know? A nice plate of spaghetti
al dente, with fresh tomato and very little oil, is much better for
your health.

He fills the two little glasses with wine, to the lip, like the
peasants do.

— Drink a little of this, please. It's nothing special, but it is
genuine.

He offers me the glass, takes his own, lifts it up.

— *Salute!* — he says.

He takes a long, hard gulp and downs half the wine. I drink a
little less. It's one of those strong, bitter wines that leave you wondering whether they were made this way deliberately or by chance.

— How do you like it?

— It's good.

— Frascati. My sister sends it to me from Velletri. Or I should
say she used to send it to me; from now on I'll pick it up myself.
Have a seat. If your daughter comes to the window, you'll be able
to see her from here.

I struggle not to show on my face too much curiosity or even
amazement, dismay. Who knows if I'll manage.

— In reality I only wanted to meet you, Dottore, before going
away. I wanted to meet you and offer my sincere condolences: I am
very sorry for your wife.

— Thank you.

— I know what it means, believe me, because my wife also

passed away, two years ago. I, too, found myself alone from one day to the next. I know what it means . . .

He shakes his head, smiles. He must be about seventy. Gray hair that's still thick, nice plebeian features, like a character out of a Pasolini movie, in contrast to his unaccented speech. The opaque teeth of a smoker, even if I don't see so much as a single ashtray — he must have quit.

— Because it's easy to say you're a widower, but things are much more complicated, — he takes a second gulp from the wine glass, emptying it. — Mourning is very complicated. It takes time. And you need something to focus on. Luckily for you, you have that splendid little girl that fills your life, but us, for example, Rina and I, we didn't have children. And then I was already retired, I didn't have anything to keep me busy. It was just the two of us, me and the time that was supposed to pass. Do you know that for a year I did nothing except sweep? I swept the floors of the apartment like a madman, as many as fifteen, twenty times a day. I was overcome by the obsession that not even one fleck of dust should remain, and that's how I got by, do you see? I swept . . .

. . . And his tired, forlorn eyes stare at a specific spot in the room, corresponding to a tower of boxes, where he seems to see something that I don't see — maybe it's the sofa on which he used to watch television with his wife — but before he abandons himself to the opiate of reminiscence, they come back to rest on me . . .

— Don't worry, Dottore. I'm not going to tell you the story of my life. It was just to tell you that I think I know how you feel. And I understand perfectly why you spend all day out front. But now I'm going to go check on the spaghetti, with your permission: I wouldn't want it to get overcooked.

And he goes back into the kitchen with a light, agile step.

— Aha! We're ready! — he shouts through the door. —

Another thirty seconds and we would have had to forget about pasta al dente!

Through the door come the sounds of the steps he is taking, so sharp and precise you can almost see them: the spaghetti poured into the colander, the pot placed in the sink, the spaghetti drained thoroughly and then turned out into the pan with the sauce and placed back on the still lit stove. And now the scent of the tomato sauce comes from the kitchen, passing beneath my nose and drifting out the window, so strong and good that I feel as if I can also see it — thick and wavy like in a cartoon.

— Would you like some Parmigiano, some red pepper? — still through the door. I hesitate, don't know what to say, but he immediately comes out of the kitchen, holding the pot full of steaming spaghetti, and sets it down in the middle of the table.

— I don't use them, but many people do. If you like, here they are.

With a kind of sleight of hand, he makes two little glass bowls appear and sets them on the table: one contains red pepper and the other the grated cheese.

— No, — I say, — I don't use them, either.

— Bravo. Because tomato has a delicate flavor, and if you put red pepper on top of it, forget about it: you wind up tasting only the pepper . . .

He starts filling the plates: first mine, a huge portion, then his, a huge portion. I know what this is: it's the purely Roman cult of abundance, quantity becomes quality. They don't practice it in Milan, they think it's vulgar.

— . . . Parmigiano, on the other hand, doesn't kill the flavor of the tomatoes, but it changes it. And when the tomatoes are fresh and raw, only lightly braised and peeled, of course, braised and peeled, and they're good, from the garden, like these, well, I

say they could never have a better flavor than what they already
have, so everything you add is a step backward . . .

And while the man who called me dottore *fills the plates, the tomato sauce
starts to drip down from the serving fork, staining the white tablecloth with red. It
symbolizes blood, doesn't it, Dottore? But whose blood?*

— I put a drop of oil on mine. Would you like some?

— Yes, thank you.

I hand him the bowl that he has just given me, and with the oil
he draws a *C* on top of it. Then he does the same with his own, sits
down, and tucks the napkin into his shirt collar.

— Well, *buon appetito,* — he says.

— Thank you, the same to you.

He starts in on the spaghetti with great vigor, as if he had to
finish it by a certain time. He doesn't twirl it: he shovels it like hay,
using the fork to accompany it up to his mouth. This, too, is the
healthy gesture of the Roman plebes — like Alberto Sordi eating
macaroni — which here in Milan is mistaken for bad manners.

— And so tomorrow you're moving back to Rome? — I say,
for the sake of saying something; but I say it right when he's asking me whether I like his spaghetti, so our questions overlap. A
moment of embarrassment follows, in which we try to figure out
whose turn it is to speak. And since the spaghetti is really good, to
get things moving again, I speak up.

— It's really good, I mean it.

— Thank you, — he says, — before last year I wouldn't have
known how to make it this way. Then I signed up for a cooking
class and . . .

And that's it, his sentence ends there. I say nothing, because,
strictly speaking, now it's his turn to answer my question of a little
while ago, but he keeps devouring forkfuls of spaghetti, and so I
limit myself to eating, too, Roman-style, like him, in silence, like

him — that silence at the table that is usually broken by someone saying, "Listen to that silence: it means the food is good." And, in fact, this *spaghetti al pomodoro* is really fantastic: there seems to be a hint of orange, somewhere between the taste of tomato and that of the basil, which must be the secret they taught him in that class. Even though there's a lot, I think I'll eat everything. Yes, and then I'll ask him to teach me how to make it, and he'll tell me, he'll reveal his secret, in the name of the immense respect he has for me, it'll be his good-bye gift before returning to Rome, and I'll tell it to Mac, and she'll make it whenever we feel like, and it'll taste like this, exactly like this . . .

Do you see? I was eating that mountain of spaghetti and I stopped thinking of anything else. I only thought about how good it was and how I could manage to eat it again and again and again. What does this mean?

But all of a sudden everything changes. My gaze falls outside the window, down to the street, right while Matteo and his mother are walking past my car — by surprise, since this wasn't their usual time. The boy looks at the car without the least suspicion that today it can't say hello to him, and even when he's already walked past it, the car doesn't greet him, he keeps walking with his head turned backward, his mother dragging him along by the hand, waiting for the beep of the antitheft alarm. Yes, all of a sudden everything changes; because of this boy and the unshakable faith he has come to nurture in that greeting (which depends on me, on my ability to set it off), I feel miserably out of place: I should be down there, dammit, not up here, I should already have taken care of the daily obligation to him I've assigned myself, and it doesn't mean shit that this isn't his time slot: am I or am I not the man who spends all day in front of the school? And so? What does it matter whether someone comes by at nine or at one? I should have been there . . . I dig the key chain out of my pocket and press the antitheft button: maybe it'll work from up here, I think. Nothing doing. I press the button again, once, twice, before the questioning gaze of the man, who has stopped chewing out of surprise. Come on, alarm: this is important. *Work!* You're still in time, the boy still believes; he's starting to be a little dismayed, for sure, he stops, yanking his mother backward, turns toward her, who can't help him, however, because she doesn't have a shred of his faith, she only has troubles, worries, appointments, but then he turns toward the car again — you see? — with that slowness that for him is speed, and he starts walking backward, because he still believes . . . I lean out the window, goddamn it, take aim, and press the button and keep it pressed, forcefully, all the way down — and finally: *beep,* the car alarm works. The boy doesn't seem to react, but it's just his slowness, he does react, does he ever, and in fact here he is raising his hand and waving hi to his friend the car, and then he turns toward his mother, who has stopped. Now she's the one who looks dismayed, because she doesn't see me in the vicinity: she turns and turns, looking toward the park, toward the school, she doesn't understand. I hardly know her, hardly at all, but I have the sense I know what she's thinking: she must be wondering how the devil I came up with the idea of playing hide-and-seek, me, here, at this hour, and *with her,* who if she doesn't break down crying at any moment in the day it's only because she manages with all her strength to postpone it to a later moment . . .

The man who called me dottore *is looking at me with growing amazement, almost incredulously.*

— Oh, it's nothing, please excuse me: I left my car unlocked, — I mutter.

But our lunch really is over, because, while the mother and child disappear toward the avenue, here comes a half-eviscerated blue Twingo parking near my car. Is it Marta's car? Yes, it is, and as a matter of fact, Marta gets out, dressed like a teenager — miniskirt, tank top, boots — not at all like a pregnant mother. She looks one way, then the other, then toward the park, then inside my car, then toward the tables at the café where we had a cappuccino after her panic attack the other day, then at the park again, she, too, dismayed like Matteo's mother was at not seeing me anywhere — indeed, even more: dismayed like Matteo was when my car wasn't greeting him . . .

— Marta! — I lean out the window, whistle. — I'm up here!

Marta raises her eyes, shields them with her hand like a visor over her forehead. I don't think she can see me against the sun like this. But she can hear me.

— I'm up here! — I shout. — I'm coming down!

Then my sister-in-law arrived, Doctor, and I dropped everything; I dropped the man who had called me dottore, *the excellent spaghetti, the apartment over-run by boxes, I made up an excuse, said thank you, and ran down, and while I was running down the stairs I understood something that I already knew, namely that the only reason that no one considered me crazy even if I waited in front of a school all day was the fact that they thought I had always been there, nailed to that spot in the world by pain, and this fact had become one of the few certainties of their lives, maybe the only one, and in that strange way I reassured them, the reason why, when they stopped by to visit me, they also found the courage to face their own pain, to admit it, above all, and then to touch it and to talk about it and to rid themselves of it for a moment, pouring it out on me, flooding me with the secret, rotten substance it was made of, because at that spot where according to them I had chosen to grieve we were all mysteriously strong, but if I started to be there off and on, if I acted like I, too, needed to move around, to be away, to get high, to eat spaghetti, in other words if I started to act like them, and it just so happened that they came looking for me and I wasn't there, then we were all weakened, they became dismayed and I became nothing more than a mentally unbalanced man who couldn't accept real-ity, and I think I can figure out by myself what this means, Doctor, because when someone decides to stay in one place then he should really stay there, always, no ifs, ands, or buts, and in short the dream ended with me going out into the street*

and the sun blinding me and the October smog melting me and I felt an immense
love for everything that came into my visual field and I decided that I would never
go away again, never again, never again.

chapter twenty-two

— Where were you?

  — At the home of a guy who lives across the street.

  — You have a friend who lives right here? What luck.

  — No, I just met him today. What about you, what brings you
here?

  — Nothing, I was in the area . . .

  — . . .

  — Okay, I came by because of that phone call earlier. I want to
know why you asked me that stuff.

  — About the CD?

  — Yes, about the CD.

  — I told you: it was just a whim, a curiosity.

  — It was not a whim. Don't try to bullshit me: I'm a sorceress,
you know.

  — You're no sorceress, Marta . . .

  — You called me for a specific reason having to do with that
CD, and then to throw up a smoke screen you invited me and the
children to dinner. If you don't want to tell me, fine, but don't
deny that you phoned me for a specific reason.

  — All right, I'm not denying it.

  — So what's the real reason?

  — What if it doesn't concern you?

  — If it didn't concern me, you wouldn't have called.

  — Listen, can we at least go in the shade? The heat is crushing me.

— Speaking of being crushed: don't tell me it's been here the whole time.

— It has. No one's come by. You see? My business card is still on the windshield.

— But it's almost new . . . let me see the license plate. 2004: it's new.

— Yes. You can't see now because of the reflection, but it's only got 850 miles.

— Maybe it's stolen.

— I used to think so, too, but not anymore.

— Tell me I'm right: it's stolen.

— No, it's not. Because it's locked. See?

— Oh, yeah.

— A thief doesn't lock a stolen car when he unloads it. And the car alarm is on, see the little light?

— Yes. How weird.

— It's very weird. Hello!

— Hello!

— Who was that?

— Claudia's English teacher. Come on, let's go in the shade. I'm sweating like a pig.

— Well, of course you're sweating, dressed like that.

— I always dress like this. It's my uniform.

— No, today you're dressed more elegantly than usual. Another thing you must have a reason for; but this time it's definitely none of my business.

— As a matter of fact, you're right. There, much better.

— Wait a second, let me see . . .

— What?

— You've got a bloodstain on your shirt. Two, three.

— . . .

— Four. What did you do?

— Oh . . . it's not blood. It's tomato sauce.

— Tomato? From where?

— Up there, at that man's house.

— You were . . . *having lunch?*

— No, we were done.

— Wait. Come here. I'm not going to bite.

— What are you doing?

— I'm removing the stains. Stand still. And who is this guy that invites you to lunch here, of all places?

— He's just a nice guy. He made some great spaghetti. But tomorrow he's moving. Are you sure this isn't just making it worse?

— You're right. I've made it worse.

— Look . . .

— Sorry. I got a zero in domestic skills.

— Exactly: I didn't ask you to —

— Look at the mess I've made. And now? Wait, I've got some mineral water in my bag . . .

— Come on, don't insist. It's okay like this.

— Listen, I can't possibly make it worse. Is that your phone?

— Yes.

— . . .

— It's Carlo. Sorry, I have to take this.

— Go ahead and answer. In the meantime I'll try to fix this.

— Look, it's not a problem. All I have to do is keep my jacket buttoned.

— Let me do it. Go on, answer.

— Hello?

— Hey, bro.

— Hi, you're home already?

— Yes. Do you know how hot it is in Rome?

— No.

— Ninety-three. You can't breathe.

— Well, it's pretty bad here, too.

— Listen, I forgot to tell you something fantastic that Claudia told me last night.

— There, the spots are almost gone.

— Really? Good.

— Good what?

— Oh, sorry, I was speaking to Marta.

— It took a lot of water.

— Is Marta there? Tell her I said hi.

— Carlo says hi.

— Hi, Carlo!

— She says hi, too.

— Yes, I heard her. How is she?

— She's fine. Just a second: I think that should do it, you know. You're getting me all wet . . .

— Don't worry, with this heat it'll dry right away.

— Yes, but that's enough for now; then we'll see. Sorry, Carlo, you were saying?

— I was saying that last night Claudia told me something fantastic.

— Yes? And what did she tell you?

— We were at the Chinese restaurant because the Japanese place was closed, and I suggested she get the Peking duck, the crunchy one, which they'll cook for a minimum of two people. And do you know what she told me?

— No, what did she tell you?

— *She told me that she doesn't eat meat from* Looney Tunes.

— She doesn't eat meat from what?

— From *Looney Tunes*. The cartoons: Daffy Duck, Bugs Bunny, Wile E. Coyote . . .

— Really?

— You didn't know, did you? She told me it's a secret.

— I knew she didn't eat rabbit, but the truth is I never asked her why.

— Well now you know that your daughter doesn't eat rabbit *or duck or coyote or canary* because of *Looney Tunes:* so she won't eat their meat. Isn't that fantastic?

— Nice, yeah.

— I wanted to tell you, even if she asked me to keep it a secret.

— You were right to tell me. It's such a beautiful thought.

— She's amazing, that little girl, truly amazing. Spend half an hour with her, and you want to be just like her.

— Yeah.

— And you're a great father, Pietro.

— Come on.

— Yesterday I was wrong. You're doing the right thing. Hang in there, and if you need to call me, it doesn't matter where I am, I'll get on a plane and I'll be there.

— Thanks, Carlo, but you saw for yourself: we're getting by just fine.

— Yeah. You're strong. I only meant in case of an emergency.

— Let's hope that doesn't happen.

— Of course not. At any rate I'll be back soon all the same. I want to spend more time with you.

— Whenever you want. We're here.

— That'd be nice. You'll be my guests. In Cortina, why the fuck not? No, better, Saint Moritz.

— Right. Saint Moritz is better.

— Okay. Bye, Pietro. Talk to you soon.

— Later.

— . . .

— . . .

— There's a little bit of a circle, compared to earlier . . .

— You did a great job, Marta. Thanks.

— . . .

— . . .

— What is it?

— Nothing. That phone call was weird, too.

— Why?

— He had a specific reason for calling, and he talked about something else.

— Did you understand what the reason was?

— Maybe.

— And now do you want to tell me what your reason was? Why did you ask me those questions?

— Now you're pushing it, but I swear it's not . . . Oh, all right. Fuck it, I've got nothing to be ashamed of.

— It's about Lara, isn't it?

— Of course. About Lara and that CD. Because you see, I've been listening to it ever since I started waiting here in front of the school, and at a certain point it seemed . . .

— . . .

— . . .

— It seemed what?

— Well, considering that I'd never heard Radiohead, and of course it seemed weird to find that CD inside my stereo. I immediately thought that Lara must have put it in there, at the seaside, when she used my car because she had lost the license plate of hers, or they stole it, do you remember? You were still there, weren't you? Or had you already left?

— I remember.

— Come to think of it, I'm going to have to deal with it sooner or later, because the car is still there, without a license plate, and a report has to be made to the DMV, and it's going to be a mess because the car is in her name . . . Well, to get to the point, I found the CD inside my car stereo, and I thought Lara had left it there.

And I didn't remove it, you see? I left it in, so every time I started the car it would play, and I listened to it, maybe absentmindedly, but I listened to it. When I was here, I mean: because at first, to be honest, I didn't notice, not when we came back to Milan behind the hearse, not in the early days, in all that madness, even if the CD was obviously already there. No, it was here, early in the morning when I was coming here, and then before I knew it I was spending my days here: it was here that I noticed the CD. And I listened to it.

— Do you like it?

— Yes, it's really beautiful. But the fact of the matter is that after a certain point I started understanding the words, too; never a whole song, don't get me wrong: isolated words, scattered phrases, but without trying. I know English pretty well, but usually, if you ask me what a song is saying, by ear, without even looking at a singer's lip movements, I don't understand a thing. Plus, this singer slurs his words, even if you try you can't tell what he's saying. Yet every now and then, I could understand certain verses easily. Again, right then and there I didn't notice: I understood them, end of story, maybe they struck me because they were nice, I didn't give it a second thought. But after a while I couldn't help but notice that every time I understood something it was always related to what I was doing at that moment. I don't know, like *idiot, slow down* when I was driving too fast, or —

— "The Tourist" . . .

— What?

— I said that *idiot, slow down* is a line from "The Tourist." The song. The title of the song.

— Oh. At any rate it happened a few times, and to tell you the truth, it's still happening: I do something, and at that very moment the song speaks to me about the same thing. Sometimes the verses that I pick up are so pertinent they sound like commentary, do you see? Commentary or advice on what I'm doing. And then there's that verse written on the cover, the one by Michelangelo. How does it go?

— *Per appressarm'al ciel dond'io derivo* — to get closer to heaven from whence I come.

— Exactly.

— And so?

— And so, but like this, by suggestion, at a certain point I started thinking that . . . that they might not be just coincidences.

— Meaning?

— Since Lara is dead, I mean. As if . . .

— As if?

— Come on, it's obvious what I mean, isn't it? As if Lara . . .

— As if Lara were speaking to you through those songs? Is that what you thought?

— I didn't really think it. But a doubt did cross my mind.

— What doubt?

— The doubt that in the endless number of phenomena we tend to consider impossible, rationally speaking, there may be some that are not, which might include some unfathomable form of communication we could call out-of-body, between the living and the dead.

— Through Radiohead?

— Come on, reason isn't everything.

— *You* are wondering whether Lara is continuing to speak to you from the other side through Radiohead songs?

— Listen, you wanted to know why I asked you those questions, and now I'm telling you. Don't go getting cynical on me, you of all people, who believe in everything. What does it matter through what medium? I don't have that doubt now anyway, so . . .

— Why not?

— Because she didn't make the CD, that's why not.

— And what does that have to do with anything?

— What do you mean what does it have to do with anything? If Lara had made the CD, and had left it for me in the stereo when she died, on top of everything else writing that line about *appressarmi'al ciel* on the cover, I could have even come to think, however absurd it might sound, that it had some connection with what happens to me when I listen to it. But you made the CD, so . . .

— So what?

— So there's no connection, and the whole story makes no sense.

— But she was the one who left you the CD, Pietro. In your car.

— She didn't leave it for me. She put it in when she took the car, seeing as she couldn't use her own.

— So what? What was she supposed to do, put it in her will?

— She was listening to it. It was something between you and her, if anything: you who made it and she who listened to it. I don't fit in.

— You don't fit in? You fit in so perfectly that you've been listening to it for a month and a half.

— Listen, let's change the subject. Enough already.

— Come on, help me to understand: you develop the sensation that your dead wife can communicate with you through Radiohead songs (a sensation that, by the way, casts a *definitive* light on their music: that's coming from someone who knows them by heart and was never able to understand where their mysterious energy came from), and then, right when we get to the good part, when this sensation is about to make you one of the chosen, of the elect, you take it all back? All because the computer that made that CD didn't belong to Lara but to me? Don't you realize what you're saying? You've managed to discover something really important, now all you have to do is believe in it, all you have to do is believe in what you yourself realized, and what do you do instead? Look for an excuse and retreat?

— Fuck me for telling you.

— You just finished saying that reason isn't everything. So what does it matter how many moments can't be explained rationally? Doesn't the suspicion ever cross your mind that there are some things you can't explain simply because you don't know them?

— But *what* things? What am I supposed to know?

— Okay, be that way. Let's start with the license plates, since you're the one who brought them up.

— What do the license plates have to do with anything?

— They have everything to do with it. Lara didn't lose them, and they weren't stolen. I removed them.

— You did what?

— I removed them. I had to, since she couldn't make up her mind to do it. The night before leaving I unscrewed them and threw them in the creek near your house.

— You threw the license plates in the Tonfone?

— Yes.

— Are you nuts? Why?

— To help her get rid of her obsession.

— What obsession?

— Lara never told you she was obsessed by the license plates, did she?

— What are you talking about?

— I'm saying that Lara was obsessed, anguished, terrified by the license plates of her car. So badly that toward the end she couldn't even sleep. But she never found the courage to get rid of them. It's as if she were imprisoned by those license plates.

— I can't believe it. You threw the license plates in the Tonfone . . .

— Do you at least remember the number of her license plate?

— No, I don't remember. Why should I?

— It was your wife's license plate, after all.

— Exactly. I can't remember my own, never mind hers.

— YA666AL. That was her license plate.

— Meaning?

— You know what the triple six means, don't you?

— Of course I know. You don't expect me to believe that —

— And you also know that Satanic messages are always written backward, right?

— Satanic messages? What are you talking about?

— I'm talking about reading her license plate backward. Give it a try . . .

— I told you that I don't remember.

— YA666AL. Read it backward.

— LA666AY. And so?

— Decipher it.

— Decipher *what*, Marta?

— But you have to pretend you're Lara. Pretend that your name is Lara and try to decipher her license plate read backward: LA666AY.

— Listen, Lara wasn't obsess—

— LARA THE ANTICHRIST AWAITS YOU.

— . . .

— . . .

— You're joking, right?

— You don't believe it?

— Come on, tell me you're joking.

— The fact that you don't believe it doesn't mean it doesn't exist, you know.

— Come on, tell me you didn't remove the license plates and you didn't throw them in the Tonfone.

— I'm sorry, but I did.

— Okay, you did, but *as a joke*. Nothing wrong with that, after all, how could you know that Lara was going to die: you just wanted to make me spend a nice afternoon combing through that garbage heap to find them. Admit it.

— You're fucked up, Pietro, do you realize that?

— Oh, so *I'm* the one's who's fucked up?

— Yes, you are. Two hours ago you were on the verge of believing that Lara was speaking to you through Radiohead songs: if she had been the one who burned the CD, or rather, if *I had told you* she was the one who burned it, then you would have believed it, and now you're making jokes about an even more obvious sign. How does it work, explain this to me: Radiohead yes and Satan no?

— Satan no and Radiohead no, that's how it works. And I was an idiot to tell you about —

— Obvious and dangerous! Apart from what it means, because I'll grant you that if someone *doesn't believe,* like you, hah, they can pretend nothing's wrong; but the danger she was facing, you don't consider it a danger? There are people who do a lot of terrible things because of the triple six, just read the papers: you have to admit it's no party to run around with that number branded on your rear bumper, an invitation that any fucking Satanist would accept instantly, maybe he'll follow you, carjack you, and take you to one of their covens . . .

— Covens? What are you talking about?

— Black masses. Astral guinea pigs. Human sacrifice. That's what I'm talking about. It could have happened any time with a license plate like that, don't you get it? "Excuse me, I couldn't help but notice your license plate . . ." and who knows where it would lead. Did you ever wonder how they begin, certain happenings?

— No, you really are nuts. Now you're going to start tearing your clothes off again and I'll have to cover you with my jacket.

— . . .

— . . .

— . . .

— I'm sorry, Marta . . .

— You're a fucking asshole.

— I apologize, I really do. I didn't mean to offend you.

— Leave me alone.

— Come on, I'm sorry. I was just kidding, I didn't mean . . .

— The only thing I have to say to you is this, Pietro: if you had the slightest idea of what it means to have to fight every day against certain forces, if you could only imagine what it means to have a night filled with demons, spirits, and suffering souls that persecute you, you wouldn't think it was so funny.

— I said I'm sorry, okay? Please forgive me.

— That's the problem right there: you don't realize. Even with Lara, *you didn't realize* . . .

— Marta, listen to me. I love you, a whole lot. You're about to — let me get a word in edgewise, please: you're about to have another child by another man who won't take care of you for even one minute, just like the other two. And now that Lara is dead, you feel alone. So remember what I'm going to tell you: you are not alone as long as I'm around. You can count on me, always. I'm not joking, listen to me: you can even call me in the dead of night if you wake up afraid of Satanists, vampires, or zombies: I'll protect you. I won't act like an asshole anymore. And whenever you feel lost, weak, unattractive, alone and desperate, all you have to do is call me; I'll come, and I'll tell you how whenever a man sees you, whenever one meets you, he falls in love with you instantly, zap, like lightning; I'll show you that famous picture in front of Krizia and then take you to the mirror and force you to see that you're still as beautiful today as you were then, amazingly beautiful, I'd even say, because it's as if time had stood still for you. And if your washing machine, your car, your computer, or your cell phone breaks, and you feel like dying at the very idea of wasting energy to fix them, don't worry: call me, and I'll take care of it. I'll take care of you whenever you need me to, every day of the year, every year that comes, until you've met a fantastic man who will love you deeply for the rest of your life, and then he'll do it much better than me. I'll do all of this, Marta, I swear, I'll be *proud* to; but please, I beg you, can you please stop talking about Lara and me? Do you get it? Never again.

— . . .

— . . .

— . . .

— Come on, stop crying.

— But how can you not feel guilty?

— Guilty of what?

— You never said anything like that to Lara.

— Maybe I didn't say it, but I did it. I did it every day.

— No, Pietro, you didn't.

— I took care of Lara.

— Not enough, you didn't.

— Please, Marta, let's not start up again.

— Her life was filled with evil . . .

— Can we please stop talking about this . . .

— Filled with evil . . .

— Can we please stop talking about this . . .

— Like mine . . .

chapter twenty-three

List of the times I've moved:

From Viale Bruno Buozzi to Via Giotto (Rome)

From Via Giotto to Via di Monserrato (Rome)

From Via di Monserrato (Rome) to Piazza G. Miani (Milan)

From Piazza G. Miani to Via R. Bonghi (Milan)
From Via R. Bonghi to Via A. Catalani (Milan)
From Via A. Catalani to Piazza G. Amendola (Milan)
From Piazza G. Amendola to Via Buonarroti (Milan)
From Via Buonarroti to Via Durini (Milan)

— What are you writing?

Enoch is one of those people who should never go jogging. It should be compulsory for him to wear a jacket and tie, no matter how sloppily he always seems to wear them; in his soaking-wet sweatshirt he's almost monstrous, so exhausted, blue in the face, huffing and puffing, his glasses fogged up.

— Are you off today?

— I took one of my vacation days.

— Good idea. But you're going to kill yourself doing this.

He snorts.

— Forty minutes in the hot sun without stopping.

— Exactly. Sit down.

Enoch sits down. He gasps for air. He takes off his glasses, and in the time it takes him to fog them up again he turns into *that other guy* — the cross-eyed, evil one; then he puts them on again and becomes himself again, but his glasses start fogging up immediately.

— This weather sure is unbelievable, — he says. — What do you think it's about?

— You mean in the sense of greenhouse gases and stuff like that?

— Yes. Or divine punishment.

— Well, as punishments go, I'd have to say it's my favorite.

— Wait. Maybe it's just the beginning. Maybe we're going to be roasted on a slow flame.

He takes his glasses off again, wipes them, puts them back on.

— God is very patient, — he adds.

Right, and while we're on the subject: who knows what ended

up happening with that swearword and whether he ever got over it — from all appearances he didn't, seeing as he's talking about divine punishment.

— I came to tell you three things, — he says, suddenly changing tone. — First thing, Piquet is badmouthing you.

— Piquet?

— Let me rephrase it: he's been talking about you all the time, for weeks now, every chance he gets, even at meetings, even when you're unrelated to the business at hand, he talks about you, you, you. It's as if he were obsessed with you, and he's ending up contaminating the others, like Tardioli and Basler: seriously, you're far and away the thing they talk about most in there, that's how much Piquet talks about you . . . Except a few days ago he started badmouthing you, too.

— Really? What is he saying?

I asked because I figured I was supposed to, but it's amazing how little it matters to me. I didn't realize.

— He says you're sneaky. Or rather, what is it he says you are? A *smartass*, that's it: he says that you're a big smartass. He says that with this business of you being in front of the school, you're going to get the better of everyone, each and every one of us. He says it's all a plot.

— You're kidding. And what is it I hope to achieve?

— To get Jean-Claude's job, he says. It's sheer paranoia, I know, and I wouldn't have even brought it up if it weren't for the fact that he's always coming here to see you and you might just happen to confide in him, I don't know, tell him something he could use against you. And then I feel a little responsible for this, you know, because he started to obsess over a plot when I told him Thierry came here the same day I was here. I didn't think it was a big secret, and I didn't think I was causing any harm: I was just talking about you because, as I was saying, you're the only thing people talk about at the office, and Piquet was wondering how Thierry would take it when he found out you were hanging out in front of the school, so I told him Thierry already knew about it because I had seen him coming to you, with my own eyes. But like that, I swear, I told him like it was the most normal thing in the world, precisely because I thought it was the most normal thing in the world. You're friends. Well, from then on Piquet started saying that you're a smartass, that you're angling for Jean-Claude's job, that you play like you're a zombie but instead deep down you're working on Thierry to become president. This is why I told you: to warn you not to trust him, that's all.

Enoch's eyes look dead tired, and not just because of the jogging. He keeps floundering about at a lower level of the video game, where players are beset by distorted, false, and incomplete reports, but now he's also giving me the impression that he realizes it, finally, and he's sick of it. The first thing he had to tell me, including the pinch of guilt he wanted to unburden himself of, doesn't interest either of us in the end. The reason why I won't offer him any comments, to explain, for example, that Piquet doesn't *always* come here, that he came only once, or to remind him that he had already manifested this hostility when he was jealous of my being appointed director and spread the rumor I was about to be fired — the bit about my being a dead man walking dates back to then — and more than anything else I won't start telling him that deep down, guided by his flaming paranoia, Piquet didn't stray too far from the truth — seeing as Jean-Claude's desk was actually offered to me. These are all things that don't matter to me, here and now, much less to Enoch.

— Well, thanks, — I limit myself to saying.

— I thought you should be aware of all this. That way you'll know how to act.

— Of course. I'll be careful.

I suddenly lower my eyes to check my watch — three twenty-five — and Enoch notices. You should never look at your watch when you're talking with someone.

— Do you have to go somewhere? — he asks.

— No, no. Claudia's coming out in an hour. Please, continue.

Enoch lifts his head and looks upward, toward the foliage of these trees that still look alive and well, although the ground below is covered with a thick carpet of dead leaves, because it's fall, *fall*. It's been like this for a while, as if up there they couldn't find an appointment or even an inspiration for us.

— The second thing I wanted to tell you is that this merger is really suicidal. A huge mistake. Not only for the reasons I tried to explain in that, er, *document* I showed you the other time. Apart from the reasons, which hold true for all mergers, I'm talking about *this particular* merger, which, because of the way it's conceived, is a huge blunder. Want to know why?

— Yes.

— So listen to my reasoning. We have two large industrial groups, right? One European and one American, which have decided to merge. The European one is owned by a certain number of banks, companies, and single investors, and it's controlled by Boesson; the American one is controlled and owned by a single family, at the top of which sits Isaac Steiner. Obviously this intention to merge presupposes the existence of a mutual benefit, which allows me to hypothesize that both groups, Boesson's, which henceforth I shall call *Us,* and Steiner's, which I shall call *Them,* stand to earn at the end of the process. The things I wrote a few days ago, and which you read, confute this same assumption, that is to say, they claim that the wealth generated by the merger, all things considered, will be inferior to that which was generated by the original groups; but at this point the merger is a done deal, so that's not my point. My point is that when two colossi like Us and Them face off, even just to merge in the mirage of a mutual benefit, one of the two ends up prevailing over the other. Despite the fact that they come to a laborious agreement to prevent it, the Us and Them idea persists and will never be completely eliminated. It might disappear at our level, but it will definitely not disappear at the level of Steiner and Boesson: the two of them will never merge, they will always be *Me* and *Him*. Do you follow?

— Yes.

— Actually, this is how the meaningless expression, technically speaking, to *win* a merger originates: no matter how meaningless it is from a technical point of view, in fact, it's justified, given that we are dealing with two human beings driven by boundless ambition, and at the end of the day, one of the two will control the other. No matter how little, even at sidereal heights, *one will be on the bottom and one will be on top*. Good. Now, everyone knows that in our case, to use the technically meaningless expression, We are the ones that will win the merger. True or false? Have you arrived at the same conclusion?

— Yes.

— Good. This means that, independently of what happens to the other 200,000 or so employees of the resulting group, in the end Boesson will be above Steiner. *Effectively* above, I mean. Well, we're going to have to forget about that. I've had the chance to study the details of the merger, the documents that for months have been negotiated, discussed, fine-tuned, approved, rediscussed, renegotiated, reapproved, etc., to make way for what will be the final structure, and I can tell you that that's not how it's going to go down. The merger won't be won by Us, it'll be won by Them. Even if in the end the most important posts will go to Boesson, the winner will be Steiner, and do you know why? Because of the standard that was chosen, Pietro: the structural model.

Enoch must realize that his argument is getting complicated here, because he pauses. Then, noticing I'm not asking him any questions, he continues.

— Take the fact that both Boesson and Steiner are known to be religious. Boesson is a Catholic, Steiner is a Jew; Boesson, because of his extremely sober life, his strict everyday observance, mass every morning, fasts on Friday, etc. — the things that everyone knows, in other words; and Steiner, although he's dissolute, because of the well-known, historical commitment he made to attain the restitution of assets taken from the Jews during the Nazi period. Each in his own way, therefore, the two big leaders are champions of their respective religions. Two *different* religions, am I making myself clear? Each with his own standard: the hierarchical and immutable Jewish model and the elastic and complex Catholic one. Well, which of the two do you think inspires the merger?

He stops, looks at me, but it's clear that he doesn't want my reply. He's only teasing a little before moving in for the kill.

— The Jewish model, Pietro, not the Catholic one. When Boesson will be God on Earth, president and general director of the biggest telecommunications group in the world, he will be the god of his enemy. And then he will have lost. To seriously win this merger he should have structured it differently, he should have followed the Catholic standard.

— And what would that be?

Enoch lights up, visibly satisfied by the answer he is about to give me. Then he puts his index fingers together and moves them slowly in the air, drawing a triangle.

— *The Trinity,* Pietro: Father, Son, and Holy Ghost.

With the tip of his right index finger he touches the three vertices of the triangle, and now it's as if the triangle really were before us, hanging in midair from his touches.

— For himself he shouldn't have planned the highest seat of all, that of the ancient solitary god of the Jews. He should have planned three seats at the same level: one for the Holy Ghost, the neutral and powerless divinity, who doesn't count; then one for the Father and one for the Son. And since we all know what happens to the Son, — at this point, Enoch slowly opens his arms and leans his head to one side, mimicking a languid crucifix, — rather than his own omnipotence Boesson should have anticipated the rivalry with Steiner for the role of the Father. A rivalry to be consumed slowly, every day, with patience, humility, discipline, leaving Steiner the conviction that he could prevail, without, however, giving him time to do so: because Steiner is seventy years old, has had three bypass surgeries, and is a drinker, womanizer, and cigar smoker, while Boesson is forty-five, a teetotaler, and in excellent health. It would have been enough to sit next to him, Pietro. Not above him: *next to him*. Wait for a while, and one fine day Steiner's seat would be occupied by his son. The Son, as I was saying . . .

Again he opens his arms and mimics a crucifixion, but much more quickly than before. Then he drops his arms and smiles.

— Then he would have won.

Enoch is satisfied: satisfied and dazed, as if following this line of reasoning to the end had been a huge exertion. I remain sincerely struck by his words, and I feel on my face a dazed expression similar to his, mostly a kind of plastic amazement: I thought that the merger didn't matter to me at all, and instead, putting it like this, I discover that in the end it does matter to me.

— That's very interesting, Paolo, — I say, — it's far and away the most sensible reasoning I've heard about this affair. Why don't you try it out on one of the big bosses?

— I tried it out on you so that *you* could try it out on one of the big bosses. Like Thierry, for example, seeing as you're friends.

— Come on, who am I? I could never have thought up something of the kind. No, you have to tell it to Thierry. Here it's not
about being friends or not. I don't think Boesson has ever thought
of framing the issue in those terms, and if someone were to make
him notice what you have just —

— And then there's a third thing, — he interrupts me, pulling
out of the back pocket of his sweatpants a piece of paper folded
in four, crumpled and soaked in sweat. He holds it out to me and
I am forced to take it, even if I'd gladly forgo it: it's sacrolumbar
sweat, the most disgusting kind. I am forced to take it, unfold it,
and read it because obviously the third thing Enoch has come to
tell me is written there. And while I'm unfolding it I have to choke
back laughter at the thought of finding myself before another
huge swearword in Arial typeface.

> I hereby present my resignation from my present position as
> Chief of Human Resources for this company. My resignation
> is irrevocable and will take effect immediately.
>   Sincerely,
>   Paolo Enoch

I lift my eyes from the sheet and look at him. He always manages to surprise me, Enoch does, with the things that he writes.

— Did you already send it?

— No, I'm going to tonight.

— If I tried to dissuade you I would be wasting my time, right?

— Yes. I've made up my mind.

— Okay. But then don't do it *like this*.

— How do you mean?

— Not like this, not with this letter. Speak with them first.

— Okay, but with whom? I'm the person people speak with
when they want to hand in their resignations. I see three or four

people a day. Jean-Claude is gone, and the new president still
hasn't been appointed.

— Speak with Thierry. Go to Paris and speak with him. Explain
your reasons, at least, and tell him that stuff about the merger.
This is a critical moment, and if you leave like this, out of the blue,
you risk creating a . . .

What am I saying? What am I trying to defend? Thierry is a
traitor, the moment is exactly the way he and Boesson wanted
it, and Enoch can't hurt anyone. He doesn't count. Like me, like
everyone. We are all just monthly bank transfers issued automatically. As far as they're concerned, the more people who quit
the better.

Enoch smiles, enjoying the silence on which I've beached. Then
he goes back to looking upward, the treetops, the sky, nodding
imperceptibly.

— Friday morning at dawn I'm leaving for Zimbabwe, — he
says. — If all goes well, on Monday evening I should be at my
brother's mission on the Zambezi River, on the border with Zam-
bia. Imagine, it's flooded six months out of twelve but they don't
have drinking water because the water they have is rotten with
malaria. They have to bring it by truck from Victoria Falls, which
are more than 125 miles away. Except the truck they had in the
village has died on them and is beyond repair. So I sold some stocks
I had and bought a new tanker truck for the Firefighters of Como,
where I did my military service as a boy. In exchange they gave me
their old tanker, and I shipped it to Harare, which is the capital of
Zimbabwe. It should arrive today or tomorrow. Friday night I'll be
arriving in Harare, too, and Saturday morning I'm going to climb
into the tanker and drive, accompanied by a young Portuguese
priest named José, a friend of my brother. There's almost 620 miles
of roads to the village, dirt roads for the most part, but if we don't

run into any landslides or detours we should make it in three days and two nights.

All of a sudden, the image of Enoch in a khaki shirt, sandals, and Bermuda shorts, at the steering wheel of a tanker truck in the dusty heart of Africa, blows everything else away. Yes, I think, in those clothes he would shine — in those clothes *he will shine*. Much better than in a jacket and tie.

— I don't know what to say, Paolo, — I mutter. — I imagine you've thought about this carefully.

— Yes, Pietro. I've been wanting to do this for a long time. I'm not cut out for this life: I had to lie every day, I only did things I didn't believe in, I made too much money. That swearword opened my eyes. For me it'll be like being reborn.

— And your wife?

— She feels the same way I do. She'll join me in a couple of weeks, after she's taken care of things for the sale of the house, which is in her name. We won't come back. Do you, by any chance, need a cell phone, or rather, a *videophone*?

He pulls a silver cell phone from his pocket, giggling, and shows it to me.

— You don't, eh. So take a look at what I'm going to do. I could smash it, believe me, there's nothing I'd like to do more, throw it on the ground and watch it fly into a thousand pieces, but I've got a better idea.

He stands up, crosses the park, and goes as far as the trash receptacle on the other side of the street. But rather than throw it inside, he rests it delicately on the lid and leaves it there glittering in the sun. Then he comes back and sits next to me.

— We'll leave it there. I bet before your daughter gets out of school someone will see it, stop, take a look around pretending nothing's up, and slip it in their pocket, convinced they've had a stroke of good luck. I would love to stay and enjoy the show with you, but unfortunately I've got an appointment in twenty minutes and have to run. I gave my car to the doorman of my building, and I have to go fill out the papers for handing over ownership.

He says this last sentence with a perky enthusiasm, the same that many men of his age use to confide in you that they've rented a studio apartment for their mistress. Home, stocks, car, cell phone: stripping Western man of his possessions. That's what it was: Enoch had looked tired, exhausted, even at the end of his rope, and now he was simply free. I go back to reading the sheet of paper, those four throwaway lines written, it sounds, as if he were already in Zimbabwe, drawing on a collection of badly spoken primitive languages.

— Not that it matters, — I say, — but there's a repetition: did you see it?

Enoch stretches his neck like a camel to look at the sheet.

— "*Present* my resignation from my *present* position" . . .

— You're right. Do you have a pen?

I give him my pen and he crosses out the second *present*. Then he writes *current* above it, gives me back my pen, and folds the sheet in four.

— Thanks, — he says, and sticks the sheet in his pocket. Then he stands up, forcing me to do the same thing.

— Well, I'd better be off. Otherwise I'll be late.

I look at him: it's probably the last time I'll see him, so I should give him a hug, but all that sweat and baggy flesh really turn me off, and I limit myself to holding out my hand. He barely shakes it.

— You've been a loyal colleague, Pietro.

— You, too, — I say. — Keep in touch.

— By letter. It's the only way to communicate. What's your address?

— Via Durini 3. Want me to write it down?

— No, I'll remember. — He touches one of his temples. — I've freed up a lot of space on my hard drive.

A woman passes close to the cell phone resting on the trash bin. She sees it, hesitates, but then walks straight past, and we'll never know how badly she wanted to take it.

— Safe, — I say.

But Enoch doesn't seem to be so confident, and he follows her with his eyes until she disappears down the side road. Then he looks at me and smiles.

— Listen, — he says, — the decision I've made makes me suddenly feel wise, so let me give you a piece of advice, if you don't mind.

I don't know how it happened, but suddenly we're too close — I smell his body, his breath, this isn't good — and I have to take a step backward.

— Not at all.

— Just for the sake of it, even if you probably don't need it.

— Good advice always comes in handy.

— Well, then, my advice is this, — he takes another step forward, and there we are again, too close — as soon as you feel like you can't take it anymore, get out. No matter where, no matter when, just get out. Don't fight it, ever.

Enoch, the man who was cast down to Africa by a curse. He stands there for a few moments staring at me, still too close, reeking, let me just come right out and say it, as if to sculpt his words through this proxemic assault — and perhaps to enjoy my embarrassment; then he withdraws, shrugs his shoulders, and leaves. He's walking quickly, yes, but he gives no sign of breaking into a run. He passes by the cell phone without looking at it, crosses the street, becomes a gray hoodie gliding past the wall of parked cars, and in the end disappears down the side road, he, too, like the woman who a few minutes ago didn't take his cell phone.

Forever, I would say.

chapter twenty-four

This is not good: I'm in the gym, my Zen temple, where everything is dedication and childhood and lightness and harmony and movement and space and time in perfect balance, and the girls are actually practicing on the beam, both physical location and symbol of balance, and nevertheless I am as unfocused as a — Ooops! Claudia has dismounted with a somersault, but she's too close to the beam and *she grazed it with her head.* Gaia, the instructor, pointed it out to her, but very calmly, shaking her head without the least concern — "Farther away!" — as if it had been some ordinary error and Claudia hadn't risked splitting her head open. But maybe it's because in reality she hadn't risked splitting it at all; maybe she was a couple of feet away from the beam; maybe it's me who, like I was saying, is unable to empty my mind and drive away my thoughts as I usually do. One in particular: I'm not doing enough for Claudia. I'm not doing *anything,* I feel like saying. Carlo did more in one night than I have in all these weeks. He made her dream, and I don't make her dream. I'm jealous, to tell the truth. The thought of the two of them on top of a golden cloud at the Chinese restaurant last night demoralizes me: she asking him questions about fashion shows, collections, Hollywood, famous actresses, and he answering with his reassuring calm, already treating her like the girl she will become in a few years and giving her a glimpse into the world that fills her with an emotion she will disclose with the simple sound of the magic word — *uncle;* the thought demoralizes me. I'm mortified by the closeness between the two of them, who never see each other, and precisely because they never see each other, Carlo ends up becoming, in her eyes, an invaluable asset, while the truth, banal like every truth, is that Carlo thinks of her only on those rare occasions when he sees her, when he sets about playing the part of the magnificent one, uncle as myth, uncle as husband, uncle as the person you can tell everything to, the adult Alpha, a grownup on the outside and a boy on the inside — and for the rest of the time he doesn't think about her at all; he stops thinking about her as soon as she shows the first signs of falling asleep, and he immediately goes back to devoting himself to himself — the only true great love of his life — and to his grief, to his drugs. I'm jealous of him, dammit. It pisses me off that day after day, for years, I'll do all the work, I'll follow her progress at school, in sports, I'll accompany her everywhere to comfort her and make her feel as little as possible the emptiness of no longer having a mother, and then her future is something she'll go looking for to him. The joy, the emotion of feeling grown up, confiding a secret to someone, the hope of doing what most excites her in life, she's going to go to him looking for it. Not to her father: to her uncle.

He gave her a cell phone, the dog. That's what was in the package for her he left me this morning, when he came to say goodbye before leaving: a cell phone. He didn't ask me whether I was okay with it, he simply took for granted that I was — but it just so happens that I am not okay with it and you shouldn't give cell phones to ten-year-old girls without first asking their parents' permission. A rich person's cell phone, with a video camera: *just like his* is what Claudia said when she opened the package (excited, yes, but not surprised, because evidently they had talked about it at dinner last night, come to an agreement), this way they can see each other even when they're far apart; just like Enoch's, I'm saying; and it's clearly not irrelevant that first I saw Enoch get rid of his in such an exemplary fashion and I kept an eye on the trash bin where he had placed it until, just as he had prophesized, not even a quarter of an hour later, another woman passed by, and this one took it and slipped it into her purse, convinced that today was her lucky day — a *woman,* that's what struck me, not a little girl: an ordinary middle-aged woman, neither pretty nor ugly, the perfect representation of all the women and all the men of this city on intimate terms with an object deposited there to represent all the evils of the world; it is clearly not irrelevant, I was saying, that first I witnessed this disappearing act and immediately afterward I saw practically the same cell phone reappear in my daughter's hands. For the one person who freed himself of it before my eyes there were two people, one of whom was my daughter, who before my eyes had yielded to it and I could do nothing to stop them. So there was the problem: I cannot electrify my daughter like Carlo can by talking to her about fashion and the jet set, and he doesn't try to buy me off with the latest-model cell phone, but I can't even protect her from the power these types of things have over her. Which is why I say I do nothing. I'm neither fish nor fowl. What I do for Claudia could be done just fine by a nanny or by a particularly scrupulous grandfather; what Carlo does, on the other hand, those three or four times a year he remembers he has a niece, can be done only by him, *the uncle.* And I'm jealous, because seeing as I can't save her from fashion, from glamour, and from cell phones, all the better that I be the one, not him, to make her dream with these things. But the idea of buying her a videophone never even crossed my mind, while Carlo woke up with an opium hangover and with all the naturalness in the world, before getting on a plane that for a few months would make him disappear like a legend — London, Berlin, New York — and he thought about it and he did it. Yes, I'm jealous of him, and I'm ashamed, and I don't know what the remedy is, because when you're jealous of your own brother the cause is always the same, obviously, and I've run out of time to deal with it, seeing as our mother is dead . . .

— Claudia has really improved.

Benedetta's mother. Barbara-or-Beatrice. I didn't see her at school this morning or at the end of the day, and at the beginning of gymnastics class she showed up just in time to deliver the girl to the instructor, dashing off immediately afterward. I had hoped to escape her, but here she was anyway, sitting next to me . . .

— Yes, I have the same impression.

— Benedetta's struggling, though. I don't think she's cut out for it.

There Benedetta is, in the group of the least talented girls, lining up for the vault. It's her turn: she does her run-up, pounds her feet down on the springboard, and for better or for worse her vault takes her home, though she falls back on her ass on the mat. The instructor — Giusy is her name, I think, even more acid than Claudia's instructor — immediately shakes her head.

— That butt, — she crows, — do you want to keep it straight or not?

With her pelvis she makes a vulgar, derisive movement, making the error macroscopic. Benedetta nods and keeps listening, in case Giusy intends to humiliate her a little more; but Giusy limits herself to sending her back to her place with a nod of the head.

— Did you end up going to that meeting in Gorgonzola last night? — Barbara-or-Beatrice asks me.

— No, I wasn't able to.

— What a shame. If it was because of Claudia, you could have left her with me, like I told you.

— No, it's that my brother came by to see us, and then . . .

— Your brother, the one that runs Barrie?

— Yes.

— Well, the next time you see him tell him he's my idol.

She gets up and with what looks like a can-can step shoves her ass in my face — a solid, sinewy ass, solid and sinewy the way she is all over, for that matter — so I can read the magic logo printed on the back pocket of her jeans: BARRIE.

— See?

And if I were to squeeze that ass right now? With both hands? Who could blame me?

— I see.

She sits back down on the bleachers, satisfied, and shrugs her shoulders.

— Lorenzo teases me, but I ignore him.

Lorenzo is her husband: a little tyrant with an air about him that is tremendously smart-alecky, vain, effeminate, loaded with arrogance and money, who teaches God knows what at the LUISS Guido Carli University and is a consultant to God knows what cosmetics multinational. Last year he was mentioned in *Class* in an article on Italy's most important business consultants, and to celebrate it he hosted a dinner to which Lara and I were invited. The invitees included the journalist who had written the article.

— So now you're a member of the MTV generation, he says, but he's way off, because I never watch TV. I really like your brother's clothes, *I'm enthusiastic* about them, and if Jennifer Lopez wears them, too, there's nothing I can do about it. Tell him: I'm ready to get a divorce for him.

She's obviously joking; she laughs, of course, showing off the sharp white teeth you'd never want to be bitten by; but in the meantime she's said the word, and it's the first thing that comes to mind when you meet her husband. And then, now that I see her better, dressed — or rather, undressed — like a fifteen-year-old, with her jeans and more by my brother, a low waist with the elastic of her underwear and more peeking out past the belt, skin-tight and faded and torn with the letters LLEVANTA on the thigh and more, but also with a teeny-tiny sleeveless T that comes half-way down her stomach — this is Barrie, too? No, she would have told me, she would have shoved her tits in my face, too — two dozen black rubber bangles on her wrists that actually look like washers for a drain, and purple Converse sneakers on her feet — in other words, if I were her husband I might have a few sarcastic comments to make as well.

— The next time he comes to see us I'll invite you to dinner, that way you can tell him yourself.

I'm not her husband, and I couldn't care less how she dresses.

— Really? Do you mean it?

After all, she's hardly the only woman her age to dress this way, especially in summer — or in this inexplicable return of sum-mer in the midst of fall like the one we're living now; indeed, if it weren't for the fact that all the women her age are doing more or less the same thing, even thirty-year-olds like Marta and twenty-five-year-olds like Yolanda, if Barbara-or-Beatrice were an isolated case and the target consumer of Barrie were only girls that watch MTV, no way in hell could Carlo get people to spend €120 or €180 for those jeans and sell as many pairs as he does.

— Of course I mean it.

Her cell phone rings and a rumba starts: she rummages for it amid the chaos of her Freitag bag made from recycled tarpaulins (I know because Annalisa, my secretary, has the same one), she finds it, looks at the display to see who's calling, makes an apologetic grimace, answers, stands up, goes off to the side to speak, looks for a corner in which the reception will be better . . . But Lara wasn't like that. Lara wasn't always on the phone, and she would never have taken Enoch's cell if she'd seen it on top of a trash bin. Lara dressed soberly, and she didn't buy into Carlo — in fact, there was always something off between them: they were wary of each other, uncomfortable around each other, not close. It was pretty easy for me to be in the middle because I was never ignored, in any circumstance. But Claudia adores him, her uncle, worships him independently of me, and this is harder to accept. My brother, her uncle. The secret she told me a few days after her mother's death: "Do you know what upset me most in my life? It was when I discovered that *my* grandmother was also *your* mother . . ."

I have to stop thinking, that's the point. Here I have to look and leave it at that. I have to breathe, relax, empty myself, and pay attention to my daughter, who is practicing on the balance beam. Period. Here she is, practicing her dismount again. She's motionless, as taut as a slingshot. Her feet at a slight diagonal try to exploit every possible inch of the narrow beam. Her arms pointed upward. Her hands that seem to be hanging from her wrists. Her arched, flexible back, charged with potential energy ready to be unleashed. She's trying to focus. She has to do something *difficult,* something few girls in the world are able to do, and she has to do it perfectly, otherwise she'll be scolded. She's waiting for the right moment to jump, the split second in which she'll be in control of all her strength and ability. She concentrates, waits. But she knows that she can wait only a few seconds — four, five, no more — after which she'll have to jump regardless. I'm up here, and I can't help her. Or can I? Of course I can, my little sweetheart. I can help you if you hear me. Can you hear me? Do you remember the poster that was in your first-grade classroom? It was about a little boy who is trying to lift a big block in front of his mother. He tries and tries, doggedly, with all his might, but he can't. So he tells his mother, "Mamma, I can't," and his mother tells him, "Use every ounce of energy in your body, and you'll see that you can." The little boy tells her he did, he used every last ounce of energy, and his mother answers, "No, honey, you still haven't given it your all. You still haven't asked me to help you." Think of that poster, sweetie, and before you dismount, look at me. For just a moment, without losing your focus. Look at me as if I were part of your routine, and take my energy, too. If I survive in you at the moment in which nothing exists except your body and the movements it has to make, then I can help you, you'll see. And then your mother will survive together with me, and she can help you, too. *Come on,* sweetie, look up. Let's play the romantic game you are never supposed to play in real life (do you remember the time in nursery school when they asked you to define your fathers with an adjective, and all your little friends said, "big," "good," "handsome," "important," and you surprised the teachers by saying "romantic"? You didn't even know what it meant. You thought it had something to do with Rome, the city that I was always talking about, where I was born and where I took you for Christmas every year. But what you said about me was that I was "romantic," and from that day on, the teachers started to look at me differently . . .). Let's play the game that Newland plays with Ellen in *The Age of Innocence* when he sees her from behind, leaning against the rail, underneath the pagoda at the end of the wooden pier, lost in contemplation of Newport Bay at sunset, and a catboat glides slowly in front of her, and Newland prays that Ellen will *feel* his presence behind her and turn, but Ellen does not turn, and so he says to himself, "If she doesn't turn before that sailboat crosses the Lime Rock light I'll go back," and the sailboat crosses the Lime Rock light and Ellen does not turn and Newland goes back . . . Let us play this game, too, my sweetheart, let us risk everything *right now.* If you don't look up before jumping, you won't make it. If you don't look up before jumping, I will always be jealous of your uncle. If you don't look up before jumping, then it really will be true that I am doing nothing for you. Come on, look up. Look up. Look up . . .

Ah, she looked at me: a perfect look, if I do say so myself: all eyeball, without the least movement of her head, quick as a flash, intense, and romantic, exactly, which no one else was able to intercept. The pure look that a child gives a parent, still untainted by the creases caused by guilt and incomprehension that sooner or later will appear to damage that look when, for the first time, for some bullshit reason, I will have hurt you or you will have hurt me. But also the unforgettable look that a woman gives a man, fraught with erotic tension, which you will repeat in exactly the same way on the day you lose your virginity under a plaid blanket in the freezing cold of an empty, unknown country house, when, all collected in your own body like today, you will lift your eyes in the same way toward the eyes of the trembling boy who will be entering you, and if you find them closed you will know you were not wrong, and you, too, will close your eyes. But more than anything else a very brave look, because at that point, if you had not found my gaze, if your gaze had come up empty because I was, let us imagine, back there talking on my cell phone like your best friend's mother, or even sitting down here, yes, but intent on chatting with her rather than looking at you, then you would have lost the energy rather than found it. But instead you found it because you trusted me, and there you go, exploding with a power that doesn't seem to belong to you — so slender and tiny — and you jump upward and forward like a grasshopper — clearing the end of the balance beam much more than before. Your front flip is huge, abundant, outlined in all of its roundness by the paintbrush of your ponytail, and the landing is perfect, you nailed it to the mat, without wobbles, hops, or hesitations. You did it. You're on your feet, amazed, and you look at me again. *Brava,* sweetie, you did it. It came out perfect, and even our game came out perfect, and so will our life. It will be a successful life. Gemma, your older schoolmate, your ideal girl and gymnast, gives you a hug, shares your happiness, even if at first she felt something break inside, the first shadow of a doubt that will start to accompany her from now on, the doubt that in the future her supremacy in the gym will no longer be uncontested, that one day you might surpass her . . .

Even Gaia, the instructor, seems happy this time. You look at her like a puppy dog, waiting for a well-earned compliment.

"Very good," she says, "but don't look at your father before jumping. Look at him after."

chapter twenty-five

There, they did it: they've disassembled the freight hoist. When we arrived, they were still bringing stuff down, and Claudia and I were enthralled by the cage coming down filled with boxes and going back up again empty. There really is something fascinating about the way it works: despite its simplicity — a freight hoist, as I was saying, that glides up and down a stairwell — it conveys a very reassuring idea about the achievements of progress and prosperity, due to the heavy labor it has replaced, which no one will ever do again. The movers, two Slavic guys and an older Italian, probably the boss, were as synchronized as an assembly line — load, send down full, unload, put in truck, send back up empty — like the gears of a much bigger machine, suggesting something powerful, unstoppable, superior. At least that's what I liked to think while I was watching; who knows what Claudia was thinking.

Then I accompanied her to the lobby, waited with her for the bell, killed time talking to the father of one of her classmates, and now that I'm back outside the job is done. The back door of the truck is still open, the guys have disassembled the hoist and packed it up, the boss and the man who calls me *dottore* come out of the building at the same time and exchange a few words — they're probably scheduling an appointment at the Roma Nord tollbooth in about seven or eight hours; then the boss goes over to the guys and the man who calls me *dottore* comes over.

— We're all set, Dotto', — he says.

I smile, nod, can't figure out what to say. One thing for certain, however, is that everything is much less sad than yesterday, much lighter, less awkward, and I suddenly feel as if I understand the reason for this evolution: yesterday this man, bound and gagged, was still facing the past tormenting him with its horrendous groaning; now, though, he's facing the future, and this is the giant machine whose gears have been turned by the movers: of the future, to be precise; of his future. A future that chases away any weariness in his brown eyes, holding as it does a return home after thirty-six years, his golden years close to the sister who sent him cases of Frascati, the phenomenal tomato sauce prepared with the secret recipe he learned at cooking school, the bitterness of widowhood diluted by the language of childhood (he's already rediscovered it: he said *dotto'* like a Roman), and the serene acceptance of all the other things that will come willy-nilly, which the man who calls me *dottore* finally feels prepared to face thanks to the unique and perhaps final condition placed on his life: *I'm out of here.* I'll accept everything, even solitude, even disease, even agony, but in Rome, not Milan, the city where I lived only because she was here, and when she passed away I found myself sweeping the house like a lunatic in an immense effort to pass the time. Because there are people who migrate once and for all and people who leave and then return, and that's who I am, I'm the type that leaves and then returns.

Am I projecting? Am I projecting myself onto him, am I maybe attributing my feelings to him? I don't think so, I wouldn't say so: I'm not risking madness because my wife is dead — I'm not even grieving; and I don't need a future somewhere else, because I already have one, not in another place but in another person. I have Claudia, yes, and she is carrying my future on her back.

— This is good-bye — shaking my hand — I'm sorry I didn't invite you up sooner, but I'm shy.

— Good luck, — I answer, who knows why. — And give my regards to Rome.

— I'll send you a postcard sometime, if you give me your address. One of the classic views: the Coliseum, Saint Peter's, the Imperial Forum . . .

— Via Durini 3. Want me to write it down?

— No, it doesn't matter . . .

And now he does something surprising. He takes a felt-tip pen out of his pocket, probably the one he used to write his address on the final boxes he packed up this morning, and writes my name on the back of his hand, like a schoolgirl. Then he looks at me, smiling.

— And remember, — he says, — the darkness lasts for one year. Our ancestors were right: twelve months of mourning. Once they've passed, everything will clear up. You'll see.

No, I'm not the one who's projecting: it's him. He suffered like a wounded animal, and he thinks I'm suffering like a wounded animal. Who knows how much sympathy he felt day after day, looking at me from the window, ever since the neighborhood gossips clued him in to what had happened to my wife; who knows how much sorrow he imagined coloring my every gesture in the hours I spent out here feeling no pain. Who knows how much he spoke about me with his only friend — was it the newspaper vendor or the café owner? — telling him every detail of how I felt and how long it would last . . .

— Thank you, — I tell him. — I guess this is good-bye.

— Good-bye, Dotto'. Hang in there.

He turns around and goes back to the mover, who's waiting for him by the back door of the truck. I stand there looking at him for a while, thinking how wrong we can be about the things we're most sure of. Is this also happening to me? With reference to what? Then I hear a *pssst*. I turn around quickly and find Piquet in front of me.

— Hello. Were you in a daze?

— Oh! How long have you been standing there?

— Five minutes. But you were speaking with that man . . . Who is he?

— A guy who used to live across the street. He's going back to Rome.

The back door of the truck closes, the engine starts, and the man who called me *dottore* returns to his bare and despairing home. Another half hour in that hole, maybe only twenty minutes, and it'll all be over. He makes a last nod of the head in my direction, and I reciprocate.

— Feel like a coffee? — says Piquet, pointing with his chin toward the café where, in fact, I usually have my coffee around this time.

— Sure.

— Can you believe this weather? On the radio they said today will be even . . .

He's unable to finish his sentence, because all of a sudden there's the sound of a brutal collision behind us, followed by a sinister rattling. We both turn around. The truck. In reverse. It made the wrong maneuver and hit a parked car dead center.

I can't believe it.

The car it hit is *the very same* parked car.

I dash to the scene of the accident, ignoring Piquet — without regret, since he's been badmouthing me. The rear corner of the truck backed into the C3, bending it backward and smashing in the rear windshield. All hell breaks loose: the elderly mover gets out to check, scratching his head — he must have been at the steering wheel — immediately joined by other people, including the man who calls me *dottore* and the traffic cop who saves a spot for me every day; everyone gathers to see the results of the train wreck, but only the rough and primordial understanding they're afforded. The economy of their movements betrays the certainty that they are facing a simple, indisputable fact; no one seems to suspect that all this simplicity might be concealing a trick. No one, for example, is attaching due importance to the little card whose whiteness shines through the shards of broken glass on the trunk; no one seems to even vaguely suspect the truly exceptional nature of what they have witnessed, the amazing statistical incongruity; everyone is convinced they have seen a moving truck badly damage an almost new Citroën C3. Yet for at least as long as the truck is stuck in this position, it would still be easy to reconstruct the arabesque that fate has drawn over its unhappy carcass, because the damage I did more than two weeks ago is visibly incompatible with the latest damage and with the unfortunate reverse maneuver that caused it. For Christ's sake, how can no one see it? To strike the car from that angle, the truck *cannot* have smashed in the whole side — I did. It's right there before their eyes: all they have to do is notice. It'll be another matter entirely once the truck has been moved to free up the roadway — which seems imminent, given the traffic jam forming; but someone should notice right now, dammit. But it looks as if no one will: no, for them everything happened a few minutes ago. I look at the man who calls me *dottore,* who's talking to the mover: maybe *he* knows; maybe when I crushed the C3 to clear the road he was looking at me from his window — if, that is, he already knew my story, which I can't assume; and it was raining that day, it was cold, it wasn't summer like it is today, there was no reason to sit down and linger by the window; but the accident did cause a terrible racket, and maybe he ran to the window and got there in time to see that I was the cause . . .

Here we go, the time has expired: the trapped cars start to honk their horns, and the traffic cop has lost control over them. The mover is an expert in these things — a professional traffic obstructer — and he realizes the time has come to move the truck. He excuses himself, climbs back in, starts it up, and shifts gears while the crowd of curious bystanders scatters, freeing up the street, and the traffic cop starts to get the traffic moving. At least the dynamic of the accident is clear . . .

I'm still standing next to the C3, in the grip of a joyful and boyish relief. No one is looking at me, no one is noticing — like when I got out of the water the day Lara died, and I had just saved that woman, and even there no one noticed. I could reach my arm into the trunk, grab my business card, and be gone.

Who would notice?

Maybe Piquet would see me. He's still here, and he's looking at me: he'd notice. But it wouldn't be a problem; he's so paranoid he'd never imagine what he's seen. Why did you stick your hand through the hole in the rear window? I was removing a dangerous shard of glass. I was afraid someone might get hurt. Oh . . . No: the problem is the man who calls me *dottore*. He might know. He's coming back now, he's coming straight toward me. He opens his arms and says, "Some way to start, eh?" — with my address written on his hand. But if he knows, he should tell me and give me the chance to save face: for the love of truth, he should say, maybe addressing the traffic cop, who represents authority, the only damage my mover did is this part, here in the middle, while the damage to the taillights, here, and around them, to the bumpers, all the way to the broken mudguards and the awful crumpling of the sheeting pressed against the tires, that was caused by the gentleman over there a few days ago, wasn't it, Dotto'. And then I would say yes, he's right, it's a very strange coincidence, I did it with my sister-in-law's car, and I even left my name and phone number to pay for the damage, there it is, can you see? Between the bits of broken glass? That's my business card: I stuck it under the windshield wiper, with my phone number and everything, but the owner never called me, and the car has been sitting here . . . But he doesn't say a thing and doesn't even give me a dirty look to insinuate that he knows but doesn't want to be a snitch; forget about it, he walks away again, it's all the same to him. For the traffic cop, too: like it or not, the crushed rear axle of that car has been staring him in the face every morning for more than two weeks, yet he doesn't notice, or he doesn't remember, or he acts like nothing happened. And especially the mover, who parked his truck in a no-standing zone and immediately came back here to check, to touch, to explain that his clutch slipped; he doesn't give the least indication that he realizes his fender bender cannot have generated all that damage, that it must have been there before — which is already less obvious now that the truck is gone. No: the only element that continues to connect this car to what truly happened — the famous *truth* — is my business card; once that's gone, it will simply have been struck by a moving truck doing a maneuver — as all of us here are ready to testify.

What should I do?

I count to ten: if by ten no one says anything, I'll take it back and forget about it.

One. Two. Three.

Which in the long run doesn't change a thing for the mover. He did his damage, plain and simple, the penalty on his insurance will kick in regardless, and by one of the many quirks of insurance policies, the extent of the penalty has nothing to do with the extent of the damage, therefore . . .

Four. Five. Six.

Nothing will change for anyone, and that's the truth. The truth is that no one cares a thing about this car because *it doesn't belong to anyone.*

Seven. Eight.

And no one is looking at me.

Nine.

And stealing from insurance companies isn't the same thing as stealing.

Ten.

Done.

Today will be even hotter than yesterday, they said on the radio. I heard it myself.

chapter twenty-six

— Aboveground swimming pools are tacky.

Cassowary Man downed his coffee in a single gulp, removed from his pocket a little black notebook, its pages all creased, and read this strange sentence. I was about to ask him why he had started badmouthing me again, but he caught me off guard.

— Beg your pardon?

— My sentiments exactly, — he answers, pleased with himself.

— That's exactly what Nicky said: "Beg your pardon?" Nicky is a friend of ours, and he was showing us the swimming pool he had built in his yard, aboveground, of course. "Beg your pardon?" And the answer was . . . — He reads from the notebook, — "Whenever I see a swimming pool I feel better."

He takes a cigarette from the pack on the table, sticks it in his mouth, and doesn't light it. He stares at me.

— Francesca? — I ask.

— Who else? — he says, a little too loudly. — She's in a kind of acute phase, listen to this, — he reads from the notebook, — "A ponytail means your hair is dirty." We had just gone into Hi-Tech on Saturday afternoon, and the salesgirl asked if we needed any help. She had a ponytail, of course.

— And what did she say?

— Who, the salesgirl?

He pats around his pockets, evidently looking for a lighter that isn't there. I pass him mine, and he lights his cigarette. He inhales deeply and speaks while exhaling all the smoke.

— What do you think she said? The same thing anyone else would have said: "May I help you?"

— And Francesca?

— What Francesca said is . . . — He looks at the notebook again. — "No, thank you. Just browsing."

He takes another long drag on his cigarette and assumes a difficult to decipher expression of vigilance, of expectation.

— Well, at least you're back together, — I say. — Last thing I knew, she had moved out.

Here we go: as if invoked by my words, a savage paranoia starts beating in his eyes. We're back in the savannah, surrounded by all kinds of danger.

— She came back because I begged her on my knees to come back, Pietro, — he whispers. — *I told her I was sorry,* do you get it? me to her, and I promised her I would never bring up the subject again. That's why she came back.

— And did you keep your promise?

— Of course. If I dare to even mention it again, she'll leave and never come back. But I write things down, I write everything down.

He squeezes the black notebook between his hands, which seems to calm him down. Maybe I can still change the subject and ask him why he's coming here to confide in me if later in the office he goes around telling everyone I'm a smartass. But the truth is that I'm much more interested in the behavior of his Francesca, and his ashen face, disfigured by the blade of apprehension, tells me he's about to tell me a real doozie.

— I'm trying to figure it out, Pietro: it's a mechanism of a per-

fect simplicity. At this point she can say anything, and everyone
ends up thinking they've misheard . . .

He closes the notebook, throws away his cigarette.

— The secret is, *she doesn't realize it*. That's what makes it all work:
that's the beauty of it; because Francesca is *beautiful,* and beauty in-
timidates people. You remember Francesca, don't you?

— Yes.

— You remember what a nice piece of ass she is?

Boom. She's pretty, sure, but not as pretty as he thinks. In
other words, she's got a few flaws. Her front teeth are too long, for
example, what orthodontists call an overbite. I noticed because
Claudia has the same thing, and in a year or two she'll have to
wear a retainer.

— Yes.

— And can you envision her? I mean, can you imagine her face,
her expression, when she says certain things?

— Yes.

— Her *own* special expression, I'm saying. The way she smiles
curling her lips, the light that shines in her eyes . . .

I get it: he wants me to say no.

— Well, not really. I've seen her once or twice.

He shakes his head, disappointed, looking down.

— Well . . . then you won't understand. You won't get it.

He goes back to staring at me, but from the change in his expression you can clearly see he's working on an idea.

— Maybe you can imagine someone else, — he says, with sudden enthusiasm. — Let's try this: think about a very pretty girl
you know well.

— Why?

— So you can understand.

— But I do understand.

— Pietro, for you this stuff about Francesca is just a story, just words. But what I want is for you to *see* it, if you can. Otherwise you'll never understand what I'm going through. Come on, think of a hot piece of ass you know . . .

He continues to stare at me wide-eyed, his pupils dilated to the point of invading his whole iris. Maybe he does coke. Maybe he did a line this morning, half an hour ago, before coming here.

— Come on, — he insists, — what'll it cost you?

Fuck it, he's right: what'll it cost me? We're never going to get around to why he's been badmouthing me anyway.

— I have to think of a pretty girl I know?

— Right. But really pretty.

— Done.

— What's her name?

What difference does it make? What kind of simian curiosity can drive him to ask a question like that?

— Just so I can give her a name while I'm describing the situation to you, — he adds, because I must have tensed up. — You don't have to tell me who she is. Just her name.

— Marta.

— Okay. Marta. Now imagine the scene. It goes like this: Marta is at a restaurant with friends. The restaurant has only recently opened, and it belongs to a friend of her friends, who for the record is gay, not a minor detail. The owner approaches their table and asks how everyone likes the *culatello*[*] with Parmigiano sorbet: he asks everyone, but by sheer accident, he's looking straight at her when he asks, making her feel obliged to answer. And she answers . . . — He looks at his notebook, — "It's delicious, my compliments to the chef." But the owner doesn't understand. "Beg your pardon?" he

---

[*] *Culatello* is a Parma ham made from the rear of a pig's hind legs. Its name incorporates the common word for ass, *culo,* which is also a derogatory term for gay men.

says. "It's delicious," Marta repeats, "my compliments to the chef."
Okay? Can you imagine the scene?

— Yes.

— Can you visualize the expression on Marta's face while she's
saying this? Her tone of voice, eyes, everything?

— Yes.

— Now I want you to focus. Don't underestimate the power
of a mind focused on building a truly complete image. Marta, we
were saying: try hard to *envision her*. Her face, her way of smiling,
of moving her hands. She's beautiful, all dressed up. Her earrings,
her makeup . . .

This is getting ridiculous: suddenly Piquet looks me in the eyes
and speaks to me slowly, articulating his words as if he wanted to
hypnotize me.

— Close your eyes, you'll see how many things appear . . .

Here we go: what's even more ridiculous is that I do close my
eyes, here, sitting at the café near the school, under the guidance
of a paranoid cyclothymic who looks like a cassowary; the most
ridiculous thing of all is that this farce really does manage to trig-
ger my imagination in the end. There she is, Marta, sitting at the
restaurant: she's all dressed up, wavy hair cascading over her forehead, soft red lips with slight veil of lip gloss, bare-shouldered, luminous, an asymmetrical neckline, troubled chestnut eyes with
only a hint of eyeliner; she bursts out laughing, drinks red wine
in small sips, and leans forward slightly to whisper something . . .

— The owner arrives, asks how they like the *culatello* with sorbet, and she says, "It's delicious. My compliments to the chef." . . .

Except that — I realize — I'm not imagining it at all, I'm *remembering*: yes, it's my memory of when I took her out to dinner at
that restaurant near Torre Velasca thirteen years ago, right after
her audition for Canale 5, when she still didn't know she'd passed
with flying colors, which is why she was so seductive, so excited

and available, because I had tickled the most secret and burning ambition in the fog of her nineteen years — to work in television, become famous, be desired and admired — and she felt one step away from fulfilling it . . .

— Are you there?

. . . And two hours later, there she is, dancing naked to "Dance Hall Days" by Wang Chung at my walk-up on Via Bonghi, slightly drunk but still in control of herself, in a lethal mix of naughtiness and naiveté, determined to discharge into me, *a television writer,* all her pulverizing beauty and thus falling short of the bull's-eye she doesn't realize she's already scored. Here she is coming closer, circling around me, and with her lips she grazes my ear, and suddenly she sinks her teeth into my neck as if she really did want to suck my blood — that seminal bite I have repeated so many times since then, on the neck of every other woman I have found in my arms, but that was unfortunately never again inflicted on me . . .

— Pietro, are you there?

— Yes, I'm there.

— Good. Now the only thing you have to do is change the first thing Marta says. Everything you have just imagined stays the same, except her first line is no longer "It's delicious, my compliments to the chef." Her first line, the thing she says right after the owner looked at her asking "How is it?" now becomes . . .

But it makes no sense to remember these things. Marta is crazy in a totally physical, sexual way — something much more dangerous. Marta doesn't say things without realizing it; without realizing it, Marta gets undressed; without realizing it, Marta goes to bed with people and gets pregnant. I have to stop thinking about her. I have to stop immediately.

— "Who's the fairy that made these portions?"

I open my eyes again.

— Now do you understand?

Of course. Piquet is as pale as a sheet; he seems to be still hanging on to the question he just asked, and all I have to do is say something to him. Any little thing about this Francesca who's tearing him apart. Not about Marta, Marta has nothing to do with this.

We're talking about Francesca.

— Come on, now, you can hardly blame her, — I say. — Built-in swimming pools are much classier than the ones aboveground; when women put their hair in a ponytail it's almost always because it's dirty; and the portions in restaurants are always tiny. If you ask me, her only problem is that she's too savvy in a slightly brutal way, but I wouldn't worry if I were you.

I know exactly the kind of smile I'm struggling to adopt — reassuring, ironic, knowing — and my sense is that it's working; but it's useless, because suddenly we're no longer in the hypnotist's office, we're back in the savannah, where irony has no citizenship, and a cheetah must have also appeared, because the cassowary hunches over with a wild look in his eyes.

— Ah, no? — He gets pissed off. — So listen to this. Tuesday night, opening of a photography show at Studio Elle. — He lowers his voice. — "It looks like black dicks are bigger than white dicks after all." — He raises it again. — Do you know the color of the hand she was shaking? Do you know *who* it belonged to?

This syndrome is really remarkable. *If it's true,* it's really remarkable.

— No, who?

— The South African consul, who had come all the way from Rome to inaugurate the show.

— And what did you do?

— I ran away. I said a big hello to the air, as if I'd seen someone I knew, and left it at that. I waited on the other side of the room for five minutes staring at the brick wall painted white, and then, when I mustered up the courage to look at her, she was chatting happily with a friend of hers and the consul was gone.

— And she didn't realize what had happened?

— Of course not.

— So we'll never know what she thinks she said.

He grabs my arm.

— Pietro, the problem isn't what she thinks she says, the problem is what she says. And in reality it's *my* problem, not hers. Because in the end I understood, you know. In the end I understood everything.

Here we go. Sooner or later a paranoiac understands everything. Otherwise he wouldn't be paranoid.

— What did you understand?

— Exactly what I said: that the problem is mine, not hers.

He lets go of my arm, thank God, and lowers his voice again — and a good thing he does: the trees might be bugged!

— Follow my line of reasoning: who is she really dropping her bombshells on? Who is she talking to when she says those things? To herself, no, because she doesn't even realize she's doing it. To other people? They're a revolving cast of characters: friends, salesgirls, waiters, consuls . . . Can you believe that now, even as she's doing it more than before, she never does it twice to the same person. Never. No, actually there is one person who is always there, who refuses to believe he misheard, who *knows* what's going on; and that person is me. She's doing it to me.

Naturally. He is the epicenter of the things happening around him, so things are always happening to him, all of them, even when they happen to other people; and he is the only one who can understand them.

— Now she's in a lockbox, — he continues. — To get her to come back to me, I promised not to talk about it anymore. Now she knows she can blast away, and does she ever. Listen to this one,

— he starts reading from the notebook, — "If I don't take a piss I'm going to explode." "I lost my virginity to a friend of my father's." "This *sgroppino* tastes like cum . . ."

Awesome . . .

— All in the past week, Pietro, and all in front of different people; the only constant was me.

— Okay, but how do you know she doesn't do the same thing in front of other people when you're not around?

— I tell you, she's talking to me: she's saying all of these things to me. My son's psychologist thinks the same thing.

— What psychologist?

— The psychologist my son is seeing. I told you about him, didn't I? Saverio's had a lot of problems since his mother and I separated: nervous tics, stuttering, allergies. Now he's started to count rather than speak, and we took him to a psychologist.

— What do you mean, he counts?

— Rather than talk he counts. So we took him to this psychologist, but naturally the psychologist wanted to speak with the two of us more than anything, also because of the fact that Saverio has stopped speaking. So to make a long story short I told this psychologist about Francesca, and she —

— Wait a minute. — I raise my voice a little, too, and I hope he understands *why.* — What do you mean, your son counts rather than speaks?

— Look, it's very upsetting, it makes me want to cry just to think about it. Rather than speak he counts. "Saverio, how did it go at school today?" "17,616; 17,617; 17,618 . . ." *Theatricalization of rejection* is what the psychologist calls it.

Theatricalization: what do you want to bet she's the same psychologist I fainted in front of the other night . . .

— And he doesn't say a word?

— Who, Saverio? No.

— Does he do this with everyone?

— Everyone.

— Even at school?

— Even at school.

— For how long now?

— A couple of weeks.

— You mean a single count that's been going on for two weeks?

— I think so. Last night on the phone he shot out some huge numbers, like 100,000.

I'm baffled: he said that it's upsetting, that it makes him want to cry just to think about it, but in reality he's talking about it with an almost dismissive detachment, as if it were foot-and-mouth disease or heartburn.

— And what does the psychologist say?

— What do you expect her to say? She says to leave him alone, not to lay a guilt trip on him, and to tone down the conflicts between us parents, because, in her opinion, that's what he's rejecting. That's why she wants to talk with the two of us, together and separately. Like I was telling you, the other day, when I was seeing her alone, I told her about Francesca, so that she would understand the situation I'm in, too, and to ask her what this stuff means . . .

Forget about it. Nothing doing. *Piquet wants to talk about Francesca.* No matter how hard I try to keep the focus on his son, he'll always find a way to bring it back to Francesca. He could count as high as a billion, poor Saverio, and he would still never get this guy's attention . . .

— . . . She's saying all those things to me. She's devised this way to force me to see her hidden aggressiveness, the part that frightens her, that she can't accept and she represses, so she can see whether I can accept it.

— You mean Francesca.

— Yes.

— And why is she supposedly doing this?

— To test me. To see if I really love her.

All of a sudden, without even looking at his watch, he must have decided it's late, because he takes the check, glances at it, and puts two €2 coins on the table.

— It's insecurity, — he adds. — It's the fear of losing me.

— Is that what the psychologist said?

— Yes. I mean no. The truth is, she only asked questions and listened. But it was while I was answering her questions that I realized it: she's testing me, do you see? She wants to see whether I accept the part of herself that she rejects. I realized it and I said it, and the psychologist didn't object, so . . .

He fusses with his hair for a while and gets up, in a commotion of cracking joints. I get up, too, while he's already walking toward the school.

— Um, your notebook . . . — I say.

He stops in his tracks, looks at me, then looks at the little black notebook that is still on the table.

— Oh, — he says and with two long strides goes back to recover it. The waitress arrives, takes the money, and starts clearing the table. He ignores her, but I say hello, because by now we know each other. Her name is Claudia, too. Once she asked me if I knew a good acting school.

— The last thing I need is to lose this, — says Piquet, slipping the notebook into the rear pocket of his jeans.

— Is the psychologist the one who advised you to write down everything she says? — I ask.

— No. It's my idea.

— Why are you doing it?

He starts walking. I trail him.

— Francesca is sick, Pietro, — he says in a serious tone of voice.

— For the moment she doesn't want to hear about it, but sooner or later she's going to have to get help: and when she agrees to get help, the fact that I've written everything down will end up being useful.

No one is left in front of the school. The movers are gone, so is the traffic cop. I look at the window of the man who called me *dottore,* and it's closed. Only the C3 is still there, shining in the sun — twice as crumpled now, but with only one culprit for the damage.

— Because I won't give up, do you understand? — Piquet starts up again. — She's testing me, and I don't want to have to lose her just because I'm not strong enough to take it. I *am* strong enough. I'll pretend nothing's happening, she'll keep dropping her bombshells, and I won't bat an eye. "You piece of shit," "Beg your pardon," "Way to go," how hard can it be? By now I know how it works. It's a disease, after all, like incontinence, but I love her, I can't live without her, and if she were incontinent and refused to admit it, I'd learn to change her underwear without her realiz . . . — he stops, overwhelmed by the sequence of verb tenses — . . . well, without anyone noticing, in other words.

He stops and with the remote activates the alarm on his car. A huge Mercedes SUV parked in front of the park responds with a beep — very different from mine, shorter and sharper. What would Matteo think?

— And in the meantime, — Piquet concludes, — until she agrees to see someone, I'll continue to stay close to her, and I'll protect her, yes, I'll *cover* her when she drops her bombshells in front of other people: I'll pretend nothing's wrong, I'll smile like she does, and the people in front of her will be practically forced to think they've misheard. How hard can it be?

He looks at me, smiles. On his face I can see forming, literally, a warm, blatant sigh of relief, as if the formulation of this last idea had made his problem disappear in an instant. Bingo! He spent half an hour sinking before my eyes beneath the weight of an unbearable pressure, and now he's settled everything simply by deciding to put up with it.

— Eh? How hard can that be? — he repeats.

— Easy as pie, — I say. Ignoring the fact that, in my opinion, Francesca won't be exactly enthusiastic about this change.

— Well, I've gotta get going. I bought this awesome laptop, directly from the manufacturer in Taiwan, but I have to pick it up from DHL because the idiots sent it to my house. I told them to send it to the office, I specified it expressly on the order form, since I'm never home, but forget about it: they sent it to my home address, so it went back and now I have to go pick it up.

I wonder what I can do for him. If I were his psychologist, I could convince him to start some kind of therapy. If I were his wife, I could demand a court-ordered test or have him committed. If I were Enoch, I could take him to Africa with me . . .

— On the positive side, I won't be going to the office this morning. The less time I spend in that nuthouse, the better. Things are getting worse and worse there. Worse and worse . . .

And if I were his CEO — if I had accepted Thierry's foul offer and, while continuing to spend my time here, I was already the boss — I could fire him, yes, making sure he has a nice golden parachute, which together with his severance would be sufficient, I think, to give him enough time to fall flat on his face and pull himself back up, slowly but surely, without in the meantime getting himself fired for serious misconduct and hitting the skids.

— Bye, Pietro. — He shakes my hand. — Thanks for the advice.

What advice?

— Bye.

But I am who I am: the dead man walking, the smartass who's got everyone fooled; and no matter what I might do to try to dissuade him, he would immediately think I was doing it to screw him. There he is, starting it up — *vroom,* a little heavy on the gas pedal — he lowers the window, waves good-bye to me again, and exits the parking lot, brushing past the trash bins. No, there's nothing I can do. There he is putting on his turn signal and entering the side road. Who knows how high his son is counting now.

chapter twenty-seven

And she's crying, this woman, sobbing on my shoulder . . .

Yolanda stares at us, curious, from the nearby bench. Something authorizes her to do so. It must be that she has already seen me hugging a statistically improbable number of people — Jean-Claude, Marta, Carlo, Enoch, Thierry: who the hell is he, she must be wondering, The Hugging Man? Maybe I'm the one who authorized her, by my attitude. Of course: I have a woman crying on my shoulder and I'm standing as still as a statue. It must be funny, but I have no idea what else to do. Nothing comes to me naturally . . .

The woman keeps sobbing.

The fact of the matter is that right then and there I didn't even recognize her. It might sound awful, but when I lifted my eyes from my notebook, right after hearing my full name called out, and I found her in front of me, me sitting on the bench, she standing, the only thing I could see were her tits: they inflated her jacket so forcefully they seemed to be calling me. Only when I stood up, too, freeing my visual field from the dictatorship of her bust, did I notice the violent commotion gushing from her eyes — and right then and there I recognized her: eyes of a blue I'd never thought I would see again, because I had thought the only thing that could make them so languid and watery was to drown to death in front of your children on a late summer morning, but it's evidently their natural color. Immediately after, without my having said a word, the woman threw herself on me and started sobbing, and she stayed that way. That's how it happened. That's why doing nothing comes naturally to me. But even doing nothing isn't natural: on the contrary, it might be the most unnatural thing of all, and if the woman doesn't break away from me sooner rather than later, I'll have to do something.

The woman doesn't break away. Yolanda continues to stare at us, and the woman doesn't break away . . .

So I begin to caress her, but softly, careful to keep our contact as far as possible from any real physicality, since I can't help but remember what happened to me the only time I touched her. So no neck, no hair, no hips or any other part of the soft and maybe naked body in which the maternal and somehow yielding abundance of her flesh could make something happen again. Her shoulders. Which aren't naked; which are hard; and which I touch softly, just enough to register my presence. To do anything less would be not to touch a woman at all. And I breathe softly, to limit as best I can the effect of her scent — the scent of the sea, of juniper, almost of curry — which I can already tell is dangerous from the tiny amount that reaches me. All the same, while she keeps crying vigorously, as if the very act of crying gives her the energy needed to fuel it, and I am thinking that all these tears are getting to be a bit much — yes, I saved her life, and at the same time as I was saving it my wife was losing hers, which according to the romantic version concocted by Carlo with his society stories is the cause of my subsequent inability to budge from here, and I realize this can all be very emotional, but to be perfectly blunt, not *so* emotional — and all of a sudden, to top it all off, as if struck by a blowpipe, I'm pierced by an excruciating revelation concerning none other than Carlo, who connects the drowning of an unknown woman, which he prevented two months ago, to a drowning in the Thames he wasn't able to prevent twenty years ago, of a girl named Tracy, whom he hasn't stopped thinking of since, which casts a completely new light on the energy I reminded him of when he was jumping into the water to rescue those women — dragging me along with him, let's face it, because no matter how you slice it, the truth is that he was the driving force behind the rescue, all I did was follow him — and now I understand why he did it, now I understand why he catapulted himself into the water that way, I did it only because he was doing it, but now it's clear that he did it because no one else was supposed to drown in the world anymore, ever again, anywhere, my poor brother — nevertheless, as I was saying, while I'm thinking of all these things that would seem to set some distance between me and our already minimal carnality, *nevertheless,* here it is happening all over again. Another hard-on. Another savage, powerful hard-on. Another hard-on caused by contact with this woman, as if my testosterone had always belonged to her.

I shift my eyes, looking for Yolanda, in case she's still staring at me, but luckily she's stopped: now she's wandering in a circle as if she were curled up around the telephone, shoulders hunched, head low, hair falling over her face like a curtain, and she speaks with the air of someone telling a secret. The one who's staring at me now is Nebbia, whose sixth sense has definitely alerted him to this manifestation of an animal nature that momentarily unites us. I really need to get a grip on the situation.

I break away from the hug with the greatest possible delicacy. The woman allows herself to be moved over, removes her hands from me, and immediately lowers her head, continuing to sob in this position. She has beautiful natural dirty-blond hair, thin and shiny. She's dressed elegantly, in black, no T-shirt or tight jeans or exposed midriff: trousers and a lightweight jacket, probably Armani, like every rich forty-year-old woman should dress when it's this hot; and she's quite short, and from the waistline down also clearly deformed; and the main thing is we've stopped touching each other; yet my erection gives no hint of subsiding. It's her tits, dammit. They're such an abuse of power I can't stop looking at them. She must have had them done, it's impossible for them to be so firm at an age in which nature, despite its past generosity, reclaims all firmness . . .

And now her face is turning upward, slowly, shyly, still wracked with sobs: it's luminous, ample, a constellation of freckles, a face of a Medicean beauty that some women manage to attain only when they are truly rich.

—I . . .— she mumbles.

A slightly flat nose — this I remember well; watery red eyes, swollen with tears; a string of pearls around her neck, two pendant earrings studded with diamonds that capture the light and shine.

—I . . .

And here I go making a crazy gesture completely against my will — conceived, one would say, not by my brain but by my feverish dick, with all the inevitable banality this entails: index finger to the lips (*my* index finger to *her* lips) with a soft, brazen sensuality, the perfect prelude to what I worry I intend to do next, which has now become possible, near, even natural (I wanted nature: here it is at my command), in other words, to grab the cheeks of her fat ass, pull her so close that she feels my erection on her belly, and kiss her till she's breathless. It's definitely what Brother Nebbia is hoping to see, but maybe she herself expects something of the kind, since she's so congested with humors and emotions, her breath already catching in her throat, a visible prisoner of the erogenous bubble around us.

But I'm not an animal, let me be quite clear about this. I'm ashamed.

Away with the finger.

— Ssshhh . . . — I say. — No need to say a word, signora.

Big mistake. Calling her *signora* sounds even more sexually charged. Damn. On the other hand, *everything* becomes erogenous when your dick is hard, pulling at your pubic hairs so much it hurts.

— Please sit down, — I say.

Maybe if we change position . . .

The woman sits down, docile, and I sit next to her.

— Don't cry, — I say.

The woman nods. Her hands start fumbling around in her purse, and she takes out an immaculate handkerchief with which she starts dabbing her eyes. She's stopped crying, but she continues to heave big sobs that make her tits jiggle.

— I'm happy to see you again, — I say. — How are you?

She catches her breath, but rather than answer me she starts sobbing again: louder this time, as if being no longer on my shoulder had turned up the volume of her commotion. Yolanda turns around for a second stare, but this time, as soon as her gaze crosses mine, she looks away. Nebbia, however, keeps staring at us, disappointed.

From the street a braying of car horns distracts the whole crowd. A long line has formed for something that's happening farther ahead. There's a traffic cop — another one, not the usual guy — but the people at the other end of the street don't see him and they honk like mad. In the middle of the road a tow truck keeps cars from passing. The cop is telling the drivers to be patient. *The tow truck is hoisting the crushed C3* — shit, now of all times. The cop heads down the street to try to calm the hotheads, but the racket shows no sign of dying down and it ends up dampening the commotion made by the woman, who suddenly quiets down.

Despite the cop's efforts, the clamor keeps getting louder and the line longer: now it goes as far back as the side road. I want to stand up, to see if the car owner has turned up, and discover finally who he or she is; but I can't, of course, because although my cock is still hard as a rock, things have been getting better since we sat down, and if I were to stand up again she might, too, which would put us back into the earlier situation . . .

The tow truck finally has the C3 hooked up and drives off in a cloud of carbon dioxide, pulling the whole line of traffic behind it. Gone. I'll never know who owns that car.

The silence returns. The woman took advantage of the interruption to fix herself using the handkerchief: now she simply has the swollen and sensual features — here we go again — that all women have after a crying jag, but she seems to have regained control, is breathing normally, and is looking at me with a certain audacity. Maybe she can even speak.

— Are you feeling better? — I ask.

Her forehead creases: I know these creases, they signify compassion. Lately I've seen them form on many foreheads, because human beings really are all equal in some things.

— I'm sorry, — she says, — I only found out yesterday, and I can't tell you how much . . .

Will she start crying again? No, she holds steady. But to hold steady she has to hold her tongue. She swallows.

— . . . It upset me, — she concludes.

— Forget about it. Don't say a word.

She blinks her eyes, locks her jaw, as if she were gathering her forces.

— I know that it's no use thanking you now, — she insists, — but I at least want you to know that I didn't do so before because . . . — her voice breaks again, and again she stops for a moment to keep from crying. It must be tough.

— It doesn't matter. I mean it.

The strain ripples across her face, as if it were a digital picture being edited and someone had hit SHARPEN.

— I didn't know you were the one who came to rescue me, — she says. — Do you believe me?

— Of course I believe you.

— I don't remember anything about that morning, and my friend doesn't, either. We believed what everyone told us when we regained consciousness. And no one told us you were the ones who brought us to safety.

— Well, there was a lot of confusion, — I say, — and nobody knew our names.

Another touch of the SHARPEN button, and her face is drained of all the signs of human weakness it showed just moments ago. Incredible how little it took. Now no one would ever think that five minutes ago she was weeping like a fountain.

— No, — she says bluntly. — Confusion has nothing to do with it. They didn't tell us anything about you. Otherwise we would have looked for you, even without knowing your names, and we would have found you.

It's really extraordinary how much she's transformed: quite simply, *she is no longer* the same woman who was crying on my shoulder a little while ago.

— You have a house there, too, don't you?

— Yes.

— Precisely.

Of course, from what Carlo said, she must be Eleonora Simoncini, the chocolate factory industrialist, more accustomed to giving orders and chairing board meetings than to shouting "Don't leave me!" or bursting into endless tears; and the black Mercedes S500 that I notice only now on the other side of the street, double-parked with its hazard lights on, is definitely hers, and behind the wheel there is definitely a superefficient driver who is definitely taking notes of the urgent calls arriving on her cell phone . . .

— Listen, — she whispers. — I have to ask you an important question. Would you mind answering it?

This is the way people must know her: cold, authoritarian, controlling. That she comes equipped with a certain personality is hardly a surprise, but the speed with which she's recovered it is nothing short of miraculous: like Superman in a phone booth.

— Not at all.

She places the handkerchief back into her bag and stares at me, with the same crease of compassion on her forehead.

— What exactly happened when you and your brother went into the water to get us?

For the record, my dick is hard as a rock, but events have quite decisively overtaken this phenomenon.

— I'm not sure what you mean.

— No one there said anything to you?

— No.

— You didn't speak with anyone? You just went and threw yourselves into the water?

— Yes. We just went ahead and threw ourselves into the water.

Her expression grows a little sharper, and even the crease disappears.

— Didn't anyone try to stop you?

— Stop us? Oh, maybe you mean that idiot who —

Uh-oh. Now I get it. A surge of blood rises to my temples while my heart literally jumps into my throat. That's why she was crying so hard. I understood everything *one second before* she took out of her bag the picture that confirms I was right.

— *This* idiot?

Oh no. It was her husband. This is really bad. Listen to how fast my heart is beating. The red-haired genius who told us not to go in and rescue her *was her husband.* Look at him there — their wedding picture, no less — in a morning coat, tall, with a sunlamp tan, a worldly gaze stares out from beneath the hand he has held up to shield himself from the showers of rice, a long aristocratic arm around her waist in a vaguely protective pose — hah — and she's not buying it one bit, truth be told, a luminous smile aimed elsewhere, an ardent gaze that is also distant, almost nostalgic, her body at least two sizes smaller than it is now and therefore looking really fantastic in her wildly embroidered cream-colored dress, gorgeous but — you can't miss it — totally unrelated to his pompous outfit, as if it were tailored for another wedding.

I look up from the photo. The same person who still believed in the future back then is now staring at me with a bone-chilling hardness and doesn't believe in it anymore.

My erection, needless to say, has melted.

— Please tell me, yes or no, — she's giving an order, — when you and your brother jumped into the water to rescue us, did this man try to dissuade you?

Now we have it. And now there are several ways I could answer, far too many to be able to choose the right one. I could start, for example, by no longer being so sure of what pretty boy said, or I could consider the eventuality that the rope he was tossing toward the two women was not as short as I remember, that it might have only *looked* short — that's it! — and only because he had decided to use a different rescue system from ours, certainly less heroic, less showy, but if the rope had been long enough, certainly much safer and more sensible, considering the risk of kicking the bucket that Carlo and I had actually run, because unlike us, whose rescue instinct rose from our Freudian subconscious — Carlo from the legitimate need to break the chain of drownings that seemed to be persecuting him, and me, as I was saying, so as not to be outdone by him — unlike us, as I was saying, this man might have been acting out of a broader intelligence about things, worrying about his wife but also about his children at the same time, for example, wanting to at least protect them from the danger of losing both parents in a single shot . . . But if I were really to venture into such a thicket, toward which I can already feel my age-old, deadly inclination moving me, I'm sure I would never get out of it, or if I would it would not be through the yes-or-no answer this woman is demanding of me. And this is not what I want, because I'm sick of being this way, I can't take it anymore, for my whole life I've been playing the losing card of reasonability, of deeper reflection, of fucking mediation, and I can't even remember anymore when it was that I decided to be this way or why, and whether it's too late to turn back and do what my brother did — tell everyone I see to go fuck themselves — I can always change, of course, there are even people who change at forty, why not, and even if later on the change turned out to be only temporary, if I were to answer this woman right here and right now the way Carlo would, with the rashness, clarity, insolence, courage, confidence, sincerity, fatuousness, and acceptance of the risk of being wrong that I have always envied him — well, who gives a fuck: it would still mean a lot more than trotting out my usual bullshit doubts.

— Yes.

In fact, Carlo, let's do this: why not let me *be* you, like it happened the other night for a long fantastic moment when we were getting high, and get the most out of this story. The syllable that I just pronounced is already quite a mouthful, but it doesn't give me a leg up, does it? And this is, in fact, an ideal occasion to get a leg up. Am I right? So let's do this: I'll accompany her with one of your long gazes, hard and lustful, no holds barred; she can handle it, see? She's just heard the proof that her husband tried to do her in, imagine how that must be pissing her off, yet she doesn't drop this brazen look, because deep down it's a huge boost to her ego, a precious compliment to her fading beauty. You see, Carlo? It works. It works even if I do it. She's a woman, after all. And — you see? — here's my erection again, and this time it's not at all surprising, illogical, or unheard of; on the contrary, it's the natural consequence of the pleasure that we're reading into the back of each other's eyes — and we don't give a fuck whether it's really there or not, right? For us it's convenient to read it into each other, and we do read it into each other, that pleasure, while our gazes are saying, "Fuck it, you make me horny as hell," in other words, something we have established as the only thing truly capable of consoling us in the shitty situation we're in, and we can afford it, pay attention, we are irreprehensible, irreproachable, *innocent*, we alone in all the world, since we are those-who-while-her-husband-was-letting-her-drown-like-a-rat-saved-her-life-risking-our-own-and-immediately-after-lost-our-wife-and-suffer-in-silence-dedicating-ourselves-body-and-soul-to-our-daughter-so-much-that-we-spend-all-day-in-front-of-her-school, and so, for Christ's sake, if we do it — that's how it works, doesn't it? — *if we do it* that means it's all right.

Done: Eleonora Simoncini lowers her eyes, and in that gesture is the proof that yes, it really does work that way. But of course. And what a relief for a change not to just watch it happening. How nice for once to be the hostile dominator who takes his fucking bigger piece of the pie. How liberating for me to be the asshole this time.

What happens now is a secret, Carlo, a solemn secret. Yolanda sees everything, of course, but *what* does she see from over there? She sees the fat broad who after all that crying takes a few steps away and suddenly stops, stoops, looks down, and then lifts her head to check whether The Hugging Man is looking at her, and in fact yes, The Hugging Man is looking at her, and then she low-ers her head again, touches the ground with her hand, delicately, foolishly. Then she stands back up and goes back to him.

That's what she sees — in other words, *nothing*.

Now I'll tell you what's really happening, Carlo, which no one else will ever know, because it's being done for our benefit alone, and only we can see it, and it's a secret between her and us. What's happening is that Eleonora Simoncini raises her filthy-rich hands in front of our eyes, and with her right she slowly slips her wed-ding band off the ring finger on her left, and in her eyes there is a clamor of evil and good — not only of evil, Carlo; and the good is what we just put there. And then what happens is that she turns around and seems to be leaving, but after a few steps she stops, because on the ground there is a drainage hole, slightly hidden, you know, with its nice rusty grate covered with dry leaves, and what happens is that she stops and stoops down, and stares into the unspeakable blackness you can see through the openings, and then she looks at us, and smiles, and, smiling, she lowers her hand to the grating and seems to touch it, but, in fact, she doesn't touch it, no, because there's no need, and smiling she throws her wedding ring down the sewer.

chapter twenty-eight

In the end they told me. "You'd better go see a doctor," they told me.

Sure, why not; it's an encumbrance that's been hanging over every encounter, contact, conversation, or simple exchange of greetings that I've had in the past two months: the anomaly of my behavior, its basic unacceptability; my need for therapy. In the end they told me, and the one assigned to tell me was Marta; in other words, the weakest individual of the lot, the most unstable and the one most in need of therapy herself.

She came to dinner, at my invitation, together with the children, and we ate happily with Mac, who had cooked up a fantastic risotto and an equally exquisite meat loaf; and we observed the new posttrauma dynamic settle over the relationship between our children, which is much more nuanced and mature than before: Claudia no longer tyrannized her little cousins, and the two of them submitted to her just the same and without any resistance, so the hierarchy remained in place — Claudia on top, Giovanni below her, and Giacomo below Giovanni — but without even the shadow of conflict. Little things, of course, details — Claudia allowing her cousins to go first on the PlayStation, while the two of them gallantly offered it to her in turn — but with an eloquence that only children display in their little actions. Lara's name was never mentioned, but the three of them offered a clear homage to her by behaving the way that she, unheeded, had always asked them to behave when they were together. And the two of us, Marta and I, observed all this and said how nice and even moving it was to see that the children's reaction to Lara's death was *to obey her*. Then Marta also informed Mac of the fact that she was pregnant again and exhibited her bare stomach, smooth and just starting to show, which Mac examined with shamanistic attention, prophesying that it would be another boy; in short, everything seemed peaceful, in keeping with the situation, everything seemed to be going fine; and we even decided to go to the seashore together the next weekend to try to understand whether what had happened in that house meant that it was over, which is possible, or it wasn't, not necessarily — obviously the really important reaction would be Claudia's, as well as mine, in part, since it's *our* house, where *our* mother or wife died, and where as a result we might discover that we can no longer spend a single happy hour; but the fact that

Marta and her children are also going to come along, cushioning us when we face the impact with the place, seemed very generous on her part, very protective — and I really didn't expect to feel protected, me, by her. And she was beautiful, Marta: simply, normally, *familiarly,* as sometimes happens to her, too, a beautiful girl in a beautiful home, at her ease surrounded by children, wine, and leftover food, without any sense that something is chasing after her. It really seemed like one of those rare moments of order and peace that every now and then manage to impose themselves on even the most chaotic lives, and the impression we then got was that the two of us would make it, that we would manage to raise our children without the stain of misfortune in the backs of their eyes, helping each other to keep alive in our children the warm idea of family that for various reasons was absent from our own lives. If Marta really needed the energy of smiles to get through the day, this was certainly a good occasion to stock up on them.

But all of a sudden, in the midst of this nice comforting quartet, Marta spoke to me about this Dr. Ficola. A psychoanalyst, no less: excellent, she said, Freudian, *serious, traditional* — emphasizing these last two adjectives ironically to reassure me that, although the advice was coming from her, he wasn't a vampire or a samurai, in other words, I didn't have to worry about finding myself outside the pool of dead Aristotelianism in which she seems to think I'm flailing. She went on to explain that she doesn't know him, so I didn't need to worry about breaking the rule against going into therapy with someone who has treated, is treating, or is even simply acquainted with your friends or family members. She only said he had been recommended by a psychotherapist friend, and she handed me a piece of paper with the name and telephone number on it. End of story. The reason why I should go to this Dr. Ficola was magisterially taken for granted. After which it suddenly got late, and the children were tired, and for a few days now they've been sleeping too little, and tomorrow morning she had an audition and had to rest up so she wouldn't look like a monster, and in other words in five minutes she was on her way home, leaving me here with this piece of paper in my hand. Mission accomplished. "Go see a doctor": in the end they told me without even telling me . . .

So in the next half hour I struggled mightily to stay focused on the adventures of Pizzano Pizza — which in my immense spiritual nobility I continue to read to Claudia one chapter a night despite the fact that its insane, paranoid, hard-core-drug-addict-and-secret-friend-of-Lara author considers me a *fucking yuppie* without ever having seen or met me; I forced myself to browse through those idiotic pages, but I was royally pissed off, and I couldn't wait until Claudia fell asleep to focus on my rage. Result: Claudia doesn't fall asleep. Usually she falls asleep right at the end of the chapter — one thing that schizoid does know how to do: he knows how long the chapters of children's books should be — but this time, nothing doing: as wide awake as a cricket. Despite our feast of risotto and meat loaf, she said she was hungry, and so I took her to the kitchen to have some milk and cookies and then to the living room sofa to watch some cartoons: the few other times she had trouble falling asleep it had always worked, but this time, nothing. *Samurai Jack, Spider-Man, Scooby-Doo!* It's been going on for a while now, but Claudia still isn't sleepy, and I'm sizzling with rage. Now that I understand that the reason for her agitation is *my* agitation, I realize this, but Marta's advice has really pissed me off, so sneaky, immediately backing off, and I can't find peace again by watching a cowardly Great Dane jumping into his master's arms. I think of Marta's gall, the nerve of her telling me to see a shrink, as if I were the one who had broken down in the middle of a parking maneuver; but then I also realize she's not the only one who thinks I need help, that, in fact, it's a kind of tacit understanding that everyone around me shares and that the environmental pres-

sure, for lack of a better term, generated by this collective thought
has simply broken the weakest link, inducing her to take action
on account of the crowded cupola of instigators who can't accept
the way I spend my days — or, to a lesser extent, who don't know
how to mind their own fucking business. The Band of the Creased
Foreheads: my brother; Thierry; Barbara-or-Beatrice; Annalisa,
my secretary; Miss Gloria and Miss Paolina; Maria the custodian;
Enoch; the man who called me *dottore;* even my father from his
arteriosclerotic cloud; even Eleonora Simoncini, the uxoricide
survivor; and maybe even Yolanda, who one day I will discover has
been assigned to check up on the progress of my illness. But then
I realize that I'm always having to justify Marta, to absolve her,
all the time, even at the cost of plunging into paranoia, and I get
even more pissed off, since my indulgence toward her nails me to
my responsibilities more than does her aggressiveness toward me;
because while it's true that after going to bed with her that first
night, I didn't call her up again and, in effect, *I ran away* — back
then it was easy, in the pre-cell-phone era — leaving her there
like a morsel of beef among the piranhas, but it's also true that
unlike all the other guys who did exactly the same thing after me,
including the fathers of her two and soon to be *three* children, what
I did, rather than say "fuck it" and disappear into a world that was
certainly big enough for me never to have to see her again, was to
hook up with her sister, yeah, and I didn't run away and I practically got married to her and had a daughter by her and built a
family before her eyes, and if a woman had done the same thing to
me, I think, if she had dumped me down the toilet and then gotten married to Carlo right after and had stayed with him forever,
well, in that case I think I would have considered that woman
eternally responsible for everything bad that happened to me and
to the world, including, obviously, the fatal aneurysm that one
day would take away her poor unfortunate little hubby; and not

just that — seeing as things still have to be explained, goddamn it,
it's not that people do them for no reason — then I would have
believed and continued to believe that she has always been in love
with me but because of some formidable kink in her diseased brain
she preferred to humiliate me rather than try to make me happy,
which is why I would have advised her — here I go — to see a psychoanalyst as soon as she could, and a good one, if only to offend
her, at least make her lose sleep if only for one fucking night . . .

Fuck. It's amazing how many things I can be accused of.

And Claudia won't fall asleep. She wants to see the *Samurai Jack*
cartoons again, and she asks me if she can switch to the +1 channel, which broadcasts programs with a one-hour delay: of course
you can, sweetheart, even if you'll never understand how exceptional it is for someone like me that you can even do it. Especially
because when I was little I wasn't allowed to be up at this hour,
and if I couldn't fall asleep it was my problem, I had to stay in bed
anyway, quiet as a mouse, and count sheep; and then simply because *there were no* cartoons on TV back then, especially not at this
hour. They were shown only at lunchtime on Saturday ("Today
the Cartoons") and sometimes on Sunday afternoon, and anyway
they were always those fucking social realism cartoons like *Gustav*
and *Professor Balthazar;* but especially because of the real novelty not
only that cartoon channels are now on 24/7 but also that they all
have an alternate channel, allowing you to see the same thing one
hour later, we added it to our package only a couple of years ago,
when the French arrived, and to be perfectly honest I was actually
against it, go figure, it seemed like too much, it seemed perverse,
I couldn't believe that children, in the chaos of a life lived entirely
in the present, could plan on seeing a repeat if for some reason
they missed a date with their favorite cartoon, or that they might
want to see the same cartoon a second time one hour later, or that
parents would actually allow them to — and to lay it all out there,

even though it was my job, I didn't understand how the hell Disney, Fox, or the Cartoon Network could make money by paying billions to have a second satellite channel without changing the program bundle and the subscription price. And this is precisely why, my dear, the most exceptional thing of all, the most abnormal, because in the long run they make out like bandits with this little trick, *they lose* but they also make money, and this isn't normal, just as it isn't normal to go to McDonald's and discover that if you order a Happy Meal with a burger + fries + soft drink you spend less than you would had you ordered just a burger and a soft drink *without* fries — in other words, you take the fries, throw them in the wastebasket, and you spend €1.50 less than if you hadn't ordered them. I can't explain what's abnormal about all of this, or about the +1 channels, I can only pretend that it's normal just the way it is for you, and hug you and hope that you'll fall asleep quickly; but *it's not normal,* goddamn it, just as it's not normal right now that your mother isn't here with you, except the first abnormality is one you share with all the other children in the Western world, while the second isn't . . .

Samurai Jack, quiet and invincible, is doing the same things he was before, in the same dark future into which he was projected by the forces of evil: he meets the same talkative Scottish cyborg in the middle of the same endless rope bridge, who refuses to let him pass, as always. With the same attention you observe the frenetic battle that results, your whole body tense and emotional, as if it were the first time, as if you didn't already know that in the end, exhausted and unable to beat each other, you find out that they were both cursed by the same dark lord — and thus, in reality, they are friends . . .

It's the world that's not normal nowadays, sweetheart. Polymers, hormones, telephones, benzodiazepine, debts, supermarket carts, restaurant orders, eyeglass shops, A is in love with B but B is not in love with A, the money always ends up getting stolen, every death has a culprit. That's the way the world turns. *It's not normal anymore.* And they want to send me to Dr. Ficola . . .

chapter twenty-nine

Oh, the tragedy of a phone ringing in the middle of the night . . .

Oh, the warmth of that kiss . . .

I had fallen asleep.

The telephone ringing. The cartoons. Claudia is sleeping on the sofa. She's alive, breathing. Oh, that kiss. The phone keeps ringing. 2:05 in the morning. Something must be wrong. My father? Carlo? Marta? What kiss?

— Hello?

A buzzing, a crackling. Music in the receiver. Marta's children. The kiss in my dream, I was dreaming. I've got a hard-on . . .

— Pietro?

The voice of Jean-Claude.

Silence.

A torrent of clicks from an intercontinental phone call.

The music on the receiver is an Elton John song.

— Yes?

Silence. Clicks.

That fantastic kiss.

The song is "Sacrifice."

— How's it going?

— Okay. And you?

Silence.

2:05 *in the morning.* Now Jean-Claude will apologize for waking me up — what time is it over there? — and give me some bad news.

I put the TV on mute.

I'm ready.

Silence.

Clicks.

"Sacrifice."

— Hello? Jean-Claude?

Silence. Clicks. "Sacrifice."

That kiss in the dark, among the hotel's dirty laundry.

— Yes?

— Is everything all right? Are you in Aspen?

Silence.

Now he'll apologize for calling so late and tell me.

What hotel?

Silence.

He doesn't know how to tell me. It's definitely something awful.

The inclined vacuum . . .

— Yes.

Silence. "Sacrifice."

Yes, he's in Aspen or yes, everything's all right.

Clicks.

Or both.

In my dream I was in a huge building.

— Jean-Claude, can you hear me?

Clicks. Silence. "Sacrifice."

Claudia moves, turns onto her side. Could she fall off the sofa? In my dream I was looking for her in this huge building and I was filled with anguish. No, she can't fall. But why won't Jean-Claude talk? He called me, I didn't call him!

— Hello, Jean-Claude. What's going on?

Silence. The volume of the music is lowered. "Sacrifice" be- comes a meowing. What's going on?

— My father was an *airplane* pilot. — A quick cough. Or is it a sob? — Did you know that?

He's drunk, that's what's going on.

— Yes.

Silence. Clicks. Meowing.

— And maybe he worked for the secret services.

Drunk as a skunk, yes. Good God.

— *Maybe*.

Jean-Claude had had a drinking problem years ago. But he got over it. At least that's what he said.

— Did you know that, too?

— Yes, you're the one that told me.

In my dream I was filled with anguish because I was afraid that Lara had kidnapped Claudia.

— That's why he never came to pick me up at school.

Silence. Clicks. Meowing.

— He couldn't, do you see?

Silence.

— But he loved me.

Click.

Silence. No more clicks, no more meowing.

— Hello?

He hung up.

What now? What's he going to do? Will he call me back? Will he call someone else? Should I call him?

I've got a lump in my throat now. Actually, I've got several lumps: the lump from waking up, the lump from the dream resurfacing, the lump from that kiss, the lump from my hard-on, the lump from the awful news suspended in that phone call. What happened? Claudia turns over on the sofa again, mumbles a few incomprehensible words — *"saraginò," "perestimo"* . . . But then she says "Three!" and this she says very loud, clear, and sternly, as if it were an order. Then nothing. Three what? What's she dreaming about?

In my dream, she was in danger, and the danger was Lara.

I pick her up. She's light as a feather, as usual. As usual she doesn't relax, collapse in my arms; she stays rigid, stiff as a board, with her legs as straight as breadsticks. Like a magician's assistant during the levitation act. As if her coach were tormenting her about perfection even in her sleep.

In my dream Lara wasn't dead. We had divorced, and I had been awarded custody of Claudia. I found myself in this huge building/ city and I was filled with anguish because I was afraid that Lara had taken her away. Everyone was in this building, it wasn't even a city anymore, it was the whole world, a covered world. I ran up and down this building/world and asked every person I met about Claudia, but no one knew anything. They looked at me with a wrinkle of sympathy on their foreheads, their eyes creased with compassion. No one confirmed my doubt that Lara had taken her, yet I was more and more sure of it, and my anguish grew . . . This was the dream; so where had that kiss come from? Where was the inclined vacuum? Why do I have a hard-on?

I deposit Claudia on her bed, slowly, to keep from waking her up, and I cover her with the sheets, although it's really hot. I stand there for a second watching her sleep, as usual, but I keep my ears pricked to hear the telephone from the living room, in case Jean-Claude calls back. What should I tell him if he does? And what should I do if he doesn't? Should I be worried? Should I call 911 in Colorado? From here, 500,000 miles away? Can you?

That vacuum, that kiss. Where did they go?

I turn off the IKEA star, and I slip into the living room again to wait for Jean-Claude to call back. Maybe he just got loaded to snap out of a difficult moment. Maybe he just wanted to unwind, but then he was embarrassed. He's a tough guy. He's a billionaire. He's got a three-year-old daughter, a noble and beautiful Indian wife. He could redeem himself in a thousand ways. If I call him

back, he might feel humiliated. I can only wait for him to call.
The cartoons continue without the sound. *Fat Dog Mendoza.* They
make more money broadcasting them round the clock than they
would by shutting off the broadcast and starting up again later.
How many children are watching *Fat Dog Mendoza* right now? How
many adults, not counting me? And how many adult males with
hard-ons?

On the coffee table is the piece of paper with Dr. Ficola's phone
number. Of course. "You need to go see a doctor . . ."

At one point I found myself in the lobby of a grand hotel that
was filled with elegant people going to a party. There was a wooden
gazebo in the center of the lobby, a kind of information kiosk, from
which a woman was exiting whom I couldn't see, because I was
looking down; the only thing I could see were her boots, and they
were the kind that were fashionable when I was a boy: brown,
leather, tight around the calves, with a zipper and without the long
pointy toes like today. I wasn't quick enough to see the woman
because her hand grabbed one of my arms and with an immense,
superhuman but also natural force — a force that responded to
a law — she dragged me past a big security door, setting off the
panic exit device with a karate chop. Once again I could only see
her 1970s boots, which she cracked in the air like a whip; once again
I wasn't quick enough to see her, because we were now beyond the
door and beyond the door was the darkness — and what's worse,
the vacuum . . .

Of course, *that* vacuum.

Jean-Claude hasn't called back. By him it's six fifteen in the evening. Aspen in the off-season must be terrifying, like every other
place in the world in the off-season. If his father died, today, at
some hospital in Marseille, and he just found out, and he has drunk
three or four whiskeys in a row by the fireplace feeling guilty about
letting him die alone, and he felt like pouring out his sorrows to

me out of the blue, because it's a moment in which he doesn't have many friends left, then his phone call would not be so strange . . .

That vacuum. It's not the absolute vacuum, like Torricelli's; it's a solid vacuum, so to speak, pneumatic, elastic, and above all — here we go — it's *inclined;* in this way, even if the ground suddenly gives way beneath our feet, the woman and I don't fall but we start to slip through the air, diagonally, rapidly, and high on adrenaline like at a water park. It's a fantastic emotion, takes your breath away: we spin downward, shooting through that alleyway of black air — an air that holds us up at the same time as it pulls us down, that restrains us but also accelerates us, that has no consistency but also has some — and the woman keeps holding me by the arm, and her grip is *talking to me* now, saying trust me, don't be afraid, don't resist me, don't resist anything, ever . . .

But Jean-Claude's father died when he was twenty, and even his mother passed away some time ago. So why did he call me then? Why hasn't he called me back? What's the bad news?

Our nosedive ends when it has to end, a second before my heart bursts in my chest, with a long soft landing on a sea of cloth, and the hand that grips me says that it's a pile of dirty laundry from the hotel above us — the hotel/city, the hotel/world. It's still pitch-dark, and now the woman in the boots helps me to stand up, even if there's no longer any up and no down, and rather than stand-ing up we're actually swimming in this placenta of dirty laundry that swallows us and supports us, and we're standing up but we're also lying down, we're the astronauts floating in the cosmos, and we breathe the intimate odor of the world, the acrid, penetrating but also reassuring odor of all the underwear and pillowcases and socks and T-shirts and tablecloths and slips and dirty linens in the world. And now the woman is hugging me and she's as liquid and hot as mercury, and I feel like that, too, I feel like her I feel that I am *her,* and the kiss that we give each other — here it is — is the

natural evolution of this consubstantiality. Terminal, oxyhydro-
gen, definitive, it's the absolute kiss, the *ur-kiss,* that melts us and
glues us inside each other and scatters us in the chaotic beauty of
the universe . . .

Wow, what a dream. Who knows whether I would have remembered it tomorrow morning, if Jean-Claude hadn't called.
The almost full moon shines with its obtuse face, peering through
the window frame. No, I never do remember my dreams. Tonight
Jean-Claude did something for me: he woke me up, he allowed
me to remember forever that inclined vacuum, that wild kiss. By
contrast, I have done nothing for him. He's over there, orphaned,
drunk, defeated, listening to Elton John, and even if the moment
of reckoning were to come, the moment when he climbs the stool
in the bathroom and slips his head into an electric wire noose, I'm
sitting here, on the sofa, with a hard-on, watching *Fat Dog Mendoza,*
and I can't do anything to stop him. That's the truth. Oh, Dr. Ficola, why can I always do so little for others? Who was that woman?
Why do I keep getting horny rather than grieving?

chapter thirty

—Hello?
— Hey there, brother.
— Oh, hi, Carlo.
— How's it going?
— Fine. And you?
— A little tired but fine.
— Where are you?
— In Rome, the equatorial metropolis.
— Of course, but tonight you're going to be on the MTV
Awards. I read the interview in *La Repubblica.*

— What interview?

— What do you mean, what interview? The interview in to-day's *Repubblica*. The one where you call yourself the outsider on the inside.

— I didn't do any interview.

— Perfect. So they made it up.

— Unless . . . In *La Repubblica,* you said?

— Yes.

— Not in *Corriere della Sera*?

— In *La Repubblica.*

— You're sure?

— Sure I'm sure . . .

— It's only because a lot of people confuse *Repubblica* with *Corriere*.

— What are you talking about? I never confuse them.

— But I do. I think that I spoke over the telephone with a re-porter from *Corriere,* not *Repubblica.* And I didn't realize it was an interview.

— So in other words you haven't seen it.

— No, I haven't read the papers.

— Excuse me, don't you have a press office that gives you clip-pings every day?

— I do, but today is Saturday and there's no one at the office.

— Of course. You're right.

— Never mind. Tell me how Claudia is doing. I called her on her cell phone, but it's off.

— She's fine. She's here on the beach with me.

— On the beach?

— Yes. We're in Roccamare.

— Really? Since when?

— We came last night.

— Alone?

— Marta was also supposed to come with her children, but at the last minute she couldn't make it.

— And so it's just the two of you.

— And Dylan.

— Ah. What's it like?

— Beautiful. It's like July. We're on the beach, and there's a ton of people. You can go swimming, the water's warm, and —

— No, I mean what's it like for you being there? It's the first time you've been back, isn't it? After the . . .

— Everything's fine.

— Claudia, too?

— Yes. She's here playing by the water with a friend of hers.

— Yes, but at home? How did she take it?

— Calmly. As if nothing had happened.

— You've got to be kidding. In the house where her mother . . .

— I don't know how, Carlo, but that's the way it is.

— Are you sure? Don't you think it's a little soon to be there alone?

— I told you: Marta was supposed to come, too, but then at the last minute she couldn't make it.

— I get it, but you were hardly obliged to —

— Yes, sweetheart! I saw! Good girls!

— . . .

— Sorry, I was speaking to Claudia. They're making Dylan jump through a hoop. Look at that! Good girls! . . . You should see Dylan jumping: he's excited because he never gets to go to the beach in the summer: dogs are not allowed. They are not supposed to be allowed now, either, but since it's October there's some kind of suspension of the rules, and everyone has brought their dogs . . .

— . . .

— We had to do it sooner or later anyway.

— Do what?

— Come here. To see how it would affect us, both of us. Better to do it when it's eighty-six degrees out and you can be on the beach and go for a swim as if it were summer.

— Yes, but not alone.

— Relax: if I get the sense something's off, I'll get in the car and leave.

— But you might not sense it while she does.

— What are you trying to say, that I'm an idiot?

— Come on, Pietro, what can I say? I don't like the thought of the two of you being there alone, that's all. I've got half a mind to come join you.

— Great. And the MTV Awards?

— Who cares about the MTV Awards?

— You have to present the prize for best alternative musician.

— And instead I'm going to come there, go figure.

— A prize that according to the interview you'd really like to give to Björk, but you're sure it's going to go to Franz Ferdinand instead. By the way, who the hell is Franz Ferdinand?

— It's a group. *The* Franz Ferdinand.

— Ah. And how can you be so sure they're going to win? Are the MTV Awards fixed?

— Pietro, I'm serious. I don't like the fact that you're there by yourselves in that house.

— I believe you. But you can't come anyway. You're inside the system now.

— At three o'clock I've got an appointment, but as soon as I'm done I'll get the car and come.

— They're coming to get you. You have entered the Matrix.

— I'll be there by seven.

— At seven you have to go play the outsider on the inside.

— Come off it! We can go eat fish at Anna's.

— And those guys will come to get you at Anna's. They have SWAT teams, helicopters, spy satellites. And Anna's is closed.

— Or else . . . Of course. Why don't the two of you come here? It'll only take you two hours. You'd make it in time for the concert at the Colosseum.

— Carlo, you have no idea how nice it is here.

— Come on, try to make it! I can have as many tickets as I want. For the award ceremony and for the party. Think of how happy Claudia would be. Britney Spears is going to be there.

— Precisely. The less she sees of her, the better.

— Enough already! Do you remember who you liked at her age?

— Me? I liked Pino Daniele.

— Besides him. I said when you were her age. You don't re- member, do you?

— ABBA?

— No, worse! You liked ABBA when we were already living on Via Giotto, so you were at least twelve. I mean when you were nine.

— Let me remind you that Claudia is ten and a half.

— Okay, when you were ten and a half. You don't remember who you liked?

— I didn't like anyone when I was ten and a half. I played Lego and left it at that.

— You don't remember the Rotary Club party, when Pippo Baudo called you to the stage and had you do that quiz?

— I don't know what you're talking about.

— And naturally you won. You won a book, *The Adventures of the Red Corsair*. You don't remember what you told Pippo Baudo when he asked you who your favorite singer was?

— I refuse to believe that I was ever interviewed by Pippo Baudo.

— There's a photograph of it, buddy: I have it in my album of family pictures. You standing there with the book in your hand, and in front of your mouth the microphone held with a professional flair by Pippo Baudo. You don't remember your answer?

— I must have repressed it.

— "Ricchi e Poveri," that's what you answered.

— Go figure. I must have said it just to throw him off track.

— When you were Claudia's age your favorite singers were Ricchi e Poveri. Come clean.

— What about you, then? In your bedroom you had a poster of Gabriella Ferri.

— I used to beat off to Gabriella Ferri, which is another thing entirely.

— You beat off?

— I beat off, I beat off! I can't tell you how horny she made me with that throaty voice of hers. I would put "Rosamunda" on the record player, look at the poster, and beat off. It was awesome.

— You're the only guy in the world who ever beat off to Gabriella Ferri, do you know that?

— Says you. Cucca did, too, for example.

— Some pair, you and Cucca.

— She was our ideal woman. Energetic.

— She died not long ago, didn't she?

— Yes, she killed herself. And it really upset me. I had just seen her on television again, after so many years — on the Pippo Baudo show, of all places: immense, high as a kite, beyond good and evil. Beautiful. It made me feel like getting to know her, I swear. To call her up and say, "Ms. Ferri, when Cucca and I were little we used to beat off thinking of you."

— Some consolation.

— Better than nothing. I won't say that it would have changed anything, but —

— All right already. I'm coming! Dylan . . . over here! Sorry, Carlo, Claudia wants to go in the water again and I have to put Dylan back on the leash, otherwise he'll follow her. Come here, boy. Come. No, no, no: not in the water. Come. Stay, be a good boy. Like that. Good dog.

— . . .

— . . .

— Pietro, are you there?

— Yes.

— I'm serious, why don't you come?

— Because we're here now, Carlo.

— Exactly. You're close. Drive down. It's better.

— We really can't. We've got Dylan. Where are we supposed to put him? Plus Claudia already has plans with her friends here. It's Halloween, and they're going out trick-or-treating.

— Let her decide. Pass her the phone.

— She's in the water.

— I'll call back in a little while.

— Come on, stop insisting. Everything's fine, believe me.

— No, Pietro, that house is not fine . . .

— Listen, sooner or later we had to deal with it. No —

— And Halloween is not fine, either, if I may say so. You go down there to spend the weekend on the feast of the dead?

— Halloween is not the feast of the dead.

— It's the feast of the dead, witches, and ghosts.

— It's Samhain, the ancient Celtic New Year. The feast is an exorcism to defeat winter and famine, which the Irish immigrants in America mixed up with the legend of the jack-o'-lantern and the masked games that people play.

— There you go, Mr. Know-it-all. If you want to talk about Halloween nowadays, you have to have a degree in anthropology.

— The reason I know is because it's written in today's paper, right next to your interview. It doesn't matter, anyway, because that's not how we should see this.

— See what?

— The fact that Claudia and I are going to stay here tonight to celebrate Halloween.

— So how should I see it?

— As something that happened and that's that. It's a critical transition, I know, and we didn't plan to be alone, but that's how it went. The fact that it's October 31 is sheer coincidence. That's how it went. You also have to trust the way of the world every now and then. Or don't you? Yes, sweetheart, I'm coming! Listen, Claudia's waiting for me in the water, she wants to dive off my shoulders. With the somersaults she's learned she's amazing everyone . . .

— I saw her this summer. Be careful she doesn't bump her head on the bottom! I know people who because of a dive ended up —

— What's gotten into you? You've got an album of family pictures, are afraid of ghosts, and are predicting accidents: you sound like Aunt Jenny.

— I don't know, Pietro. I don't like the thought of you two there alone, and I told you. In fact I was actually going to propose that we sell the house, go figure . . .

— Let's see. Let's see how Claudia reacts.

— We can buy another one somewhere else. In Sardinia. In Liguria. In Greece. An even nicer house.

— Of course we can, but let's not do anything hasty. We're all tied to this house. It would be better if we could save it. There's always time to sell it later.

— Well, in any event don't worry about it. As far as I'm concerned you could sell it tomorrow.

— Thanks. We'll have to figure out what the best thing to do is. Hey, I've got to go. Claudia's waiting for me.

— Give her a big kiss from me.

— Of course.

— And tell her to turn on her cell phone. I sent her something.

— All right, I'll tell her. What is it?

— It's a secret between me and her.

— Ah. Okay then. Talk to you tomorrow.

— Yes. Tomorrow.

— And stop worrying. Everything's under control.

— All right. Have fun.

— You, too. And say hi to Björk for me.

— Bye, Pietro.

— Bye. Here I am, Claudia, I'm coming!

chapter thirty-one

I didn't tell my brother the whole story. Nooo . . .

Yes, it's true. Marta did pull out at the last minute yesterday morning with a brief phone call, leaving me with the choice of whether to go to the seaside alone or not to go at all; and it's true that the decision to come was a little iffy — alone, here, Claudia and me, at the house where Lara collapsed before her eyes (I've tried to imagine the scene many times, but I've never been able to get past the moment in which Lara suddenly collapses and the tray of prosciutto and melon ends up on the ground and shatters into pieces; Claudia's reaction, her probable cry of shock, her definite running, kneeling down, and repeating "Mamma, Mamma" to the inanimate mannequin that Lara has become, and above all the sense of abandonment she must have felt realizing that her mother was no longer with us, that I was still on the beach, and that I wasn't even answering my cell phone . . . now, that's something I'll never be able to imagine). And it's true that it seems like July, it's true that it's really nice out, it's true that Claudia is actually mysteriously peaceful even here and that after dinner she walked around the neighborhood with a mask over her face, together with a multitude of other children trick-or-treating; it's true that Maria Rosa, the woman who comes from inland to take care of the house, made a compassionate attempt to hide every trace of Lara, sticking her clothes in a trunk, washing all the linens, deodorizing the closets, getting rid of every product or object that might be connected to Lara, from the diet crackers that she alone ate to the moisturizing creams and hair-removal strips. All of this is true; and deep down it's true that in coming here, as I told Carlo, I followed the way of the world, allowing circumstances to make my decision for me; but I didn't specify what the decisive circumstance was, the last stone over which I skipped before ending up here. This I didn't tell Carlo, nooo . . .

The fact of the matter is that I doubted whether I should come here or not for only a few minutes, and the reason I let go of it so quickly has nothing to do with Claudia, and it's the same reason I would never have allowed Carlo to come here and didn't even entertain for a moment the idea, which per se was not all that strange, of getting back in the car and driving Claudia to Rome to enjoy the big MTV party. The fact of the matter is that while I was sitting there, on the bench in the park opposite the school, right after the phone call from Marta saying she couldn't come, I received a visit. Of course. From Eleonora Simoncini. Dressed in white, this time, of a much more aggressive, almost predatory elegance, with an intriguing neckline under her jacket, a brazenly tight skirt over her generous buttocks, and a pair of cream-colored boots that were very different from those of the woman in my dream but equally hypnotic and surprisingly vulgar. She was wearing her hair wrapped in a kind of brown turban, from which a few rebellious locks hung over her face that looked carefully studied to reinforce the impression of a tremendous inner tension. Her return was fatal: her appearance certainly didn't surprise me as it had two days ago, yet it disturbed me even more because it expressed something truly obscene, it was a kind of free and savage growl in the face of every reason that should have restrained her within the limits of the composed and vaguely sorrowful apparitions with which, for two months, my days in front of the school have been punctuated.

She came, Eleonora Simoncini, and she told me some things of an embarrassing intimacy. She informed me that she'd thrown the bastard out (that's what she called him: the bastard), and while she was saying it she was light-years away from the solemnity with which two days earlier I had seen her drop her wedding ring into the sewer; she was lighthearted, instead, and oozing energy from every pore, as if in the past forty-eight hours she had realized that the only thing she ever wanted was to be saved from an uxoricide in order to get rid of her husband for all the right reasons; and it was a totally physical energy, as if the rebound from that discovery had been released into her flesh, freeing her from an ancient mortification. She told me that she had presented the bastard with a draft agreement for a consensual separation, prepared by her Swiss lawyers, according to which she would keep the houses and the children, as the more well-to-do spouse, and would pass him the risible sum of €1,032.91 a month, equivalent to the net salary of a sailor named Oreste, who took care of the yacht she had given the bastard as a present on the occasion of their fifteenth wedding anniversary, which represented his most prized personal property; she cheerfully listed all the expensive vices that the bastard would no longer be able to afford (from collecting modern art to sponsoring a speedboat team) and even the measures of total ruin — economic and, above all, legal — that would come down on him if he dared to reject the proposed agreement. But then, as if it were related to her revenge, and without my having minimally hinted at the question, she told me that she was going to spend the weekend at her house in Roccamare, and if by chance I was going, too, we could see each other. All her energy, which until then had been directed against her husband, came to focus on me, establishing through a few primal elements — her perfume, the artfully lowered gaze, the predatory clothing, and, precisely, that simple sentence in the conditional — a formidable sexual force field that made her seem like a kind of blank check slipped into my jacket pocket. Keep it, fill it in, and deposit it. Here it is, the way of the world . . .

So now I'm here, in a T-shirt, smoking on the veranda of the house in which just two months ago my woman died, with a full moon shining in the tropical heat and the warm wind rustling the branches of the pine trees, ready to send a text message like a damn teenager. Here it is, shining on my cell phone's display in all its ravenous, hormonal absurdity: *Coast is clear.* But I still haven't sent it. I'm keeping it here, for now, in the barrel, and I'm not sending it. In reality I'm not at all undecided; I know full well that in the end I'll press the button and the message will go, but at the same time I'm struggling to delete it from my mind, for a moment, and to think of myself in the way Carlo thinks of me, lost like a trumpet soloist in this marvelous night, melancholic, good, and focused on my grief and on the task of keeping it as far away as possible from the bed where my daughter is sleeping — all the more tempted to knock back two or three glasses of rum to lighten the heavy load pressing down on my shoulders. American movies are full of heroes like this: Gregory Peck. James Stewart. Henry Fonda. Kevin Costner. After all, till now I could be that hero, too. I still haven't done anything they wouldn't do, and if the grief were to pounce on me, here, now, if it were to stop circling me, lurking behind the lives of others, and once and for all sink its hooked claws into my stomach, I could really become that way. I'm ready for this, I've been ready for two months, I've been waiting to grieve . . .

Coast is clear.

I replay the Radiohead CD in the stereo, which I've brought outside. It doesn't surprise me anymore. I know all the songs by heart, but now I'm the one interrogating them. Track 2. "Pyramid Song." Here's the piano's lament, the pained voice howling before it starts to sing. "I jumped in the river and what did I see / Black-eyed angels swam with me . . ." How many nights did Carlo spend grieving while he was listening to this song? Thinking of all the things he could have done with that girl if she hadn't jumped in the river? Until he couldn't stand it anymore, until he delivered himself forever to little scales, syringes, rolled-up banknotes, and sheets of tinfoil?

Coast is clear.

Track 17 now. "Big Ideas." The song that I consulted imme-diately, the other day, as soon as Eleonora Simoncini was gone, because I remembered that it contained some wise, liquid words very appropriate for me, and that I listened to over and over again during our trip last night, coming down from Milan, with Claudia asleep in the backseat, and then again tonight, while she was out celebrating Halloween in the moonlight, until she came back with a bag full of Mars bars, Kit Kats, chocolate eggs, and other junk, tired, dirty, and ready to go to bed. I must have listened to it a hundred times by now, recognizing each time the absolute truth of what it says, yet without ever erasing the thought of my blank check. Here it is: "She kisses you with tongue / And pulls you to the bed / Don't go you'll only want to come back again." It's true, Song. You're right. That's how it would happen. "So don't get any big ideas / They're not gonna happen / You'll go to hell for what your dirty mind is thinking." It's true. That's how it'll happen.

I get up, go into the house. Claudia is fast asleep in her room.

Carlo sent her on her cell phone a picture of a pumpkin whose
teeth are clattering with fear. She liked it a lot, but she showed
it to me right away — so it wasn't a secret after all. I go back out
on the veranda. Lara's Golf is shining in the alleyway under the
moonlight. Parked there without license plates it has a sinister,
ghostly air. In the end Carlo was right, Halloween *is* the feast of
the dead. According to the article in the newspaper, the Celts
feared that on the first of November the spirits of the dead could
join the world of the living, thereby provoking a temporary disso-
lution of the laws of time and space: anything could happen then,
even the return of dead people from the afterlife, to join the living
and celebrate with them.

  Coast is clear.

  There, I've sent it. The way of the world has nothing to do with
it. I acted deliberately.

  I'll never be one of those kinds of heroes.

chapter thirty-two

Cheekbone, corner of the mouth, lip, earlobe, earring . . .

  I'm kissing details.

  I keep my eyes open, I want to see what I'm kissing: details of an
exciting whiteness, disconnected body parts, outsized, because this
woman can't fit inside my eyes in one piece: as if she had become
infinite, imaginary . . .

  And I breathe deeply through my nose, I inhale all the perfume
she's wearing, but also the human odor beneath it, which will grow
little by little, through induction, secretion, friction, until it pre-
vails over the perfume once I'm inside her. Because this will happen, it's for certain: you could question anything except the fact
that in a little while I'll be inside her and her natural mammalian

odor will prevail over the delicate marine essence she has sprayed all over herself to cover it. And it is this certainty that excites me, even if I haven't done anything, I haven't started anything — oh, it's a truly unbelievable moment: it was worth the lying, pretending, text-messaging, the skin is unbelievable, the mouth is unbelievable, the hair, the neck, the neck is unbelievable — or, rather, the single parts of the neck, the tendon, the vein, and the tender saddle formed at the juncture with the shoulder is unbelievable, as unbelievable as the promise contained in every part of the body that I'm squeezing in my arms, in the hips, down there, that I limit myself to caressing softly, in the tits that I haven't yet even brushed against but that press, solid, against my chest; and even the outdoors carries the same promise, in the smell of the grass, the earth, the hot night, the shimmering darkness of the moon, the sound of the wind, of the fucking nightingales warbling, of the frenzied nature surrounding us, because it's October 31, let's not forget, and this is not the way all of this should be . . .

I press my chin against her skin, my one-day beard is like an electric charge to her sensitive parts, and in fact she is grabbing my shoulders, panting, giving herself up, and here we go, here, her head is leaning to one side, her hair flowing back, her neck is mine — the moment has come. I open my mouth and wrap my lips around her flesh, place all my teeth against her skin and inhale slowly to find the perfect suction; she still doesn't know why, can't imagine, sighs and moans as if this were everything, but this is not everything — she can't imagine the bite I'm about to give her. But I know, because I tried it once, and since then I've never been able to touch a woman without thinking of Marta. Love has nothing to do with it. It's more like a vampire instinct: one day she did it to me, and since then I do it every chance I get. Here we go, in fact: I do it. I bite down, yes, and I start to squeeze, and right away I feel a shiver go through her flesh, the muscles surrender, the nerves

pop, and from the puffs of her breath a long "aaahhh" arises sub-
merged in dismay. Yes, dismay. Because my bite is not made by my
incisors but by my *canines,* they're the ones sinking in, dramatically,
as if they wanted to puncture her jugular and suck out her blood
— and it's strange but you're never ready for this: despite all the
vampire movies we've seen we never imagine that someone could
bite us this way, nor how great it would feel . . .

The bite keeps sinking in — "aaahhh" — but it doesn't hurt, I
know, because there's something anesthetic about the pleasure it
gives. What's making her stiffen is fear, not pain: fear that the jaws
will not stop — I know this, I've felt it — that they'll keep biting
down until they've torn off a mouthful of flesh. And then I stop
sinking them in. I continue to squeeze, but I don't increase the
pressure, because I don't want to hurt her, I only want to hold her
between my teeth and hear her moan, inert, moan, moan, and
now dissolve into an abandonment that is truly legendary, dramatic, luminous, insane: the abandonment of the hungry when
they faint, of the stunned prey dangling from the leopard's mouth
— the abandonment of the girl who was drowning and fought
with Nosferatu, who had come to the rescue, but preferred to die
rather than be saved by him, and tried to drag him underwater
with her but didn't succeed, and so she gave up and allowed him
to take her, rescue her, kiss her, and suck away all her blood . . .

"*Aaaahhhh*" . . .

Done: I start to let go gradually. Eleonora Simoncini has felt a
pleasure she will never forget, which would be enough for her to
go home fulfilled without any need to feel something more. But
instead, obviously, as soon as I take my mouth off her neck she
takes the initiative, almost as if she had to redeem herself from
the narcotic passivity into which my bite had plunged her, and
she starts kissing me furiously, squeezing me, licking me, and her
hand suddenly goes down, as precisely as a karate chop, until she

grabs my cock through the fly of my trousers — a gesture that I've always appreciated enormously, to tell the truth, because in its insolence it maintains something modest, adolescent, 1970-ish, like Patrizia Pescosolido, my first girlfriend, with whom I had enervating make-out sessions in the attic of Gianni Albonetti, nicknamed "Futuro," with its idiotic red and blue lights, walls covered with egg cartons, and a Brian Eno record playing over and over ad infinitum . . . In the same way, while she is pressing my cock against the cloth of my trousers, and squeezing it harder and harder as if she wanted to break it off and take it with her, I can finally devote myself to her tits, and I start fondling them with both hands as I've wanted to ever since the first time I saw her, the other day, in front of the school; but I, too, out of a kind of romantic, dutiful symmetry, limit myself to doing it from the outside, without violating the veil of cloth in which they're wrapped. And basically this, too, is an unbelievable moment, because Eleonora Simoncini is not wearing a bra, no, just like Patrizia Pescosolido at sixteen, the definitive proof that she's had them done, and in fact they react with a truly inhuman elasticity — *boing:* they seem to have springs — a kind of blind cyborg obedience to the order to stand tall, round, and solid no matter what happens, and so amid the countless pleasures generated by contact with this miracle there is also room for the hot and perverse pleasure of second thoughts, because I've always been very critical of the idea of sticking two bags of silicone into the chest of a woman for the sake of *improving her,* but if these are the results then I had better rethink my position . . .

Naturally we keep kissing, but at this point they're kisses without flavor, a cover, while our minds are someplace else. We are no longer one, that's what it is, as we were a moment ago during the bite; that vegetal surrender is gone, and we've gone back to being two distinct individuals pumping adrenaline from the grim caves of the ego and are outdoing each other in the struggle to placate the greediness that remains — almost in competition with each other, yes, almost in combat. And she's the one who ups the stakes in this competition, taking the step that Patrizia Pescosolido took an entire winter to complete, namely to move from outside my fly to inside it. I feel her hand yanking at the buttons, almost tearing them off, and slipping quickly through my underwear to grab my cock like a hammer. And then I — again for the sake of symmetry — lift up her jersey as far as her neck, revealing the absolute whiteness of her tits, and I grab them, yes, I fill my hands, squeeze them, I feel them overflowing between my fingers — *I use them,* you could say, for the final purpose for which they were made. It's gratifying, I can't deny it, but something mechanical has entered into the correspondence established between her hands and mine, and if she scratches my pubes with her nails I immediately squeeze her nipples even harder, as if the nonexistent dialogue between us were to suddenly appear in this stubborn and primitive form, with no tenderness, no liberty. And since this woman is not Patrizia Pescosolido, and we're not sixteen, and we're not in the attic of Gianni Albonetti, nicknamed "Futuro," and we can't stay like this all night, like when it used to be so nice to stay outside, whole afternoons kissing and pawing each other's precious parts, well today this gratification is no longer enough for me, and it generates a sense of squalor — brilliant, if this were actually a competition, but undeniably arid and mortifying at the thought that it was supposed to be a communion — since I'm the one, this time, taking the next step, hurling myself on her nipples with my mouth and starting to suck them, first one, then the other, then *both at the same time* (since it is possible to huddle together this weaponized flesh and turn it into a single, remarkably towering critical mass), but with a brazenly tactical lust, because it's not any better this way, in fact, it's worse, the distances are cleared once again and the mythical vision of her tits bursting out of her rolled-up jersey has disappeared — so then why, if the mechanism that governs us works so well, does she always respond to my movement in the same way. Oh, I know, Eleonora Simoncini: I know the norms that govern these things between sophisticates like us, I know that the first time you never take it in the mouth; I won't say that I agree, because personally I think it's useless, senseless, and even hypocritical, but I know the rules and I assure you that in the past I've always respected them, for what it's worth, or maybe I've only been subjected to them, but whatever the case I accepted them; but tonight is different and now I want to violate them, tonight is an exception to all the rules and now I want you to suck my cock, and the canine lust with which I'm sucking your nipples is neither more nor less than an order to do so. You have no choice, get that in your head: I'm sucking on something that a little while ago I held in my hands; in your hands you're squeezing my cock, and now it's your turn to suck it: what else could you do?

And she does it. Neither remissive nor unsure, without giving the least impression that she is submitting to a coercion: on the contrary, she's in complete control of her actions and is even happy to be performing them, judging from the playful look she gives me before lowering herself over my belly; there she is, lifting my T-shirt, and so begins a tortuous approach consisting of kisses and sucking, from my chest to my hips, then between the hairs surrounding my belly button, then directly on my belly button — as long as she doesn't overdo it, because it's a kind of torture, and there are women who don't realize how unbearable it can become . . . But no, she doesn't overdo it, she keeps working her way down, little by little, and when she finds my cock pointing straight at her throat she interprets it correctly as an end-of-the-road sign, and she stops tormenting me. Here we go: she gets up on her knees, finishes unbuttoning my trousers, pulls them as far down as she can, and in the same way lowers my underwear, all with the requisite solemnity, because she is evidently aware of the surge of serotonin that this ceremony produces in a man's brain. But then she does something strange that I didn't expect: she takes my cock at the root and lifts it up, toward the air, as if she knew how good it feels to have the breeze of this tangerine night blowing over it, and she spends a few seconds looking at it, motionless — airing it out, I feel like saying, like you do with a good wine before drinking it; then she blows away a lock of hair dangling over her eyes and she sticks it in her mouth.

Oh, the *start* of a blow job — Oh. Every time I'm amazed that such a simple thing can be so infallible. A mouth that opens, and off you go: what does it take? Anyone can do it. So why doesn't it happen all the time? Why do we make it such a rare treat? We're crazy, all of us.

I close my eyes: everything's perfect, light, foreign, and I'm only a visitor to my life, an alien that has fallen from a superior civilization into the hot mouth of this woman. Oh, it's fantastic to stay like this, without thinking of anything, floating in a present that is so pure and absolute that not even I can be a part of it . . .

. . . But unfortunately, as if summoned by the absence of malcontent, the inhabitants of my brain start appearing, surprised, annoyed, *envious,* each with his or her own fucking comment. Lara: "How can you?"; Marta: "You see? You're a pig"; Carlo: "You see? You lied"; Piquet: "You see? You're a smartass"; Piquet's girlfriend: "I'm much better at it than she is"; Piquet's son: "78,603,614 . . ."

I open my eyes again, and the crowd disperses. In short: I'm not doing anything, the one that's doing is this woman kneeling on the grass. I'm only a meal being carefully consumed, mine is the fluid state of a venerated idol — pure sentient inertia, innocence, unconscious, dependence . . . By keeping my eyes open, I can *see,* and what I see is pure pornography — the head bobbing between my

legs, the tits crushing my thighs, the cheeks hollowed by sucking
— which once again incites the demon of competition, of dissatis-
faction, giving me a huge desire to . . . to . . . Oh, but how do they
manage to get fucked up so quickly, these things? If I close my eyes
everything is reduced to a crowded sexual fantasy, if I keep them
open the desire comes back to grab, to possess, to give pleasure
rather than to receive it. *To give pleasure:* what idiocy. I've already
done much more — I've got to think, goddamn it — I've saved her
life: without me she would be dust in an urn, forget about pleasure,
mourned, cremated, and buried next to her dearly departed father
in the family chapel in some sparkling Swiss cemetery, and the
fabulous riches that she left to him, not to mention the positions
to which he succeeded her in the various companies belonging to
the group (first and foremost Brick chocolate, powdered milk, and
instant puddings in the dessert department, the historic company,
together, of course, with all the holdings and lending institutions
and trusts that make the money disappear, but also more recent
acquisitions in the dog-eat-dog world of globalization, like fitness
machines, I think, and even inflatable structures for playgrounds),
all of this would have already landed in her bastard husband's
hands; the reason why, to put it simply, I *deserve* this blow job, and
she is the first one to acknowledge it, otherwise she wouldn't put
so much devotion into it, so much —

What's she doing, stopping?

No, she's not stopping, she's kissing my balls. And here comes
that breeze again, wow, but this time, with my skin all moist with
saliva, it feels cooler and makes me shiver . . .

— I want to suck your cock all night long, — Eleonora Simoncini declares loudly, squeezing my cock an inch from her lips as if
it were a microphone. And this is a beautiful thing to hear, it really
is: beautiful and decisive, because it's as if she had invited me to lie
back on the grass, in *savasana* position, to look at the pine branches

if I really can't close my eyes, and at the blurry stars, and the fiery moon, while she finishes pursuing her idea of virtue rewarded. But as reassuring as the meaning of her words may be, there was something in their *sound* that disturbed me, something raspy, yes, and sharp, like a kind of sacred, excruciating lash whose length ran across my entire body — the most intrusive physical sensation I've ever felt in my life. It's gone now and lasted only an instant, and she has started to suck again, concretely, productively, in the now blatant attempt to make me come in her mouth; but the discovery you can also feel *that* throws everything off balance all over again.

— Say it again, — I hear myself order.

Eleonora Simoncini stops again, lets my cock slip out of her mouth, flips her hair back with a beautiful shake of the head, and looks at me, amused. Then she repeats the bit with the microphone, now more excessively, taking my cock with both hands and talking above it with her eyes closed, like the torch singers she probably likes.

— I want to suck your cock all night long, — she repeats.

This time it's even louder, almost unbearable. The vibration, yes, the vibration that her voice emits an inch from my dickhead, the *u* and the *o* more than anything, the vibration of the *u* and the *o:* like a downward shot that penetrates the very symbol of penetration, the pitch of nails scratching a blackboard, and then the cavernous echo of a deadly lament that resounds in the most remote depths of the loins, the reverberation of a distant and desperate sadness — what the fuck kind of evil mantra is this, achieving the opposite effect of its meaning? Because I can't control myself anymore, it's obvious; it's no *savasana:* my situation has gotten out of hand and I've become a blind force, recrudescent, and I'm even fighting to subdue the valorous resistance with which this mouth refuses to break away from me, and of course I win, and I pull myself up on my knees, there, I've done it, and I pull her

up, too, forcefully, ruining a blow job that was a sure thing in exchange for what? For this knot of imperatives, this chaos? Hug her,
from the top, squeeze her, fondle her, my tongue on her neck, my
tongue on the prongs of the magnet, on the battery, on the electric socket, opposite charges attract, equal charges repel, if your
adversary attacks you with a slice you always respond with a top
spin so the rotation of the ball will stay the same, *grab ahold of it,* yes,
the difference between subversion and rebellion, the slap of the
wave against the cliff, the cracking of the egg that opens up, and
then turn it around, certain that it's worse this way but the point
is that I want it to be worse, I want the worst, yes, Satanism, sey,
tsrow eht tnaw I, *turn it around,* the great struggle that people have
admitting that they masturbate and the miserable figure cut by
those who admit it without difficulty, in other words she doesn't
want to turn around, but sex is manipulation, especially during
exceptional heat waves, and then immobilize her, Keanu Reeves
stops the bullets in midair, basically I already had to do the same
thing to rescue her, basically what else is Om besides a powerful
vibration, what do you mean a previous life, every day you see
so many of those faces that when you do meet a person and you
have the impression you've met them before you probably *have* already met them, there, like so, immobilize her and then turn her
around, I know, song, you told me, the only thing you'll want to
do is go back home, of course, the three stages of alienation, I'm
at work and I dream of being at the seaside, I'm at the seaside and
I dream of being at work, *I'm at the seaside and I dream of being at the seaside,* of course, the sea, the rough seas, hold her still with only one
arm, now, free the other, up this skirt, down with these panties . . .

— No, no. I can't.

What?

— I can't . . .

Oh, no, no, no. I said down with these pan—

— I can't . . .

So then I must have gravely offended some powerful lunar deity, because it's not possible that every time, goddamn it, *every time* it's always the same story: it's practically the only thing I remember, from the time of Patrizia Pescosolido, to be precise, and our simultaneous loss of innocence, at the apartment on Via Severano, which remained empty after the death of her aunt, always the same inexhaustible river of murky blood that drives me back every time I try to work my way into some pussy (*list of the girls that couldn't the first time: Patrizia; the German camper at Palinuro; what's-her-face, the one that came in third for Miss Punta Ala, Barbara Bottai; the one from Channel 4 with the absurd last name, Luisa Pesce-Delfino; Lara, of course, go figure; and even two of the four women I cheated on her with, Gabriella Parigi and the French PR agent with the pierced tongue, who looked like Isabelle Adjani and without a shadow of a doubt is the most beautiful girl I ever fondled*). And now? These words paralyzed me, my hand turned to marble in the act of squeezing her snatch like Pluto in "Rape of Proserpina," the kisses turned to stones — that's why she so brazenly took it in her mouth — that's why she wanted to suck it all night long — *the only thing she would do* — she'd had a blow job up her sleeve ever since she arrived — but I defused it — and now how can we go forward? Going backward is out of the question, because now the blow job is unrecoverable, it's gone, it's the turnpike ticket that flies out the window, the Ping-Pong ball that falls off the balcony — *how can we go forward?* Forget about fucking her anyway, that's a dirty trick you can play only on a woman you really love (*list of the women I've really loved: Patrizia Pescosolido, Lara*), and okay, all right, also with French PRs who look like Isabelle Adjani, but on a totally exceptional basis and above all if it's glaringly obvious that there will never be a second chance; give up, then, raise your arms and be done with it: that would be wise, for sure, but there's still this hard-on in the way, always the same, permanent erection that apparently accompanies every

minute spent in proximity to Eleonora Simoncini, turned to gran-
ite by the events of the last few minutes and not at all debilitated by
the last few seconds — I should get over it, but how? By focusing
on disgusting things: warts, verrucas, pus, corns, Berlusconi showing a bug to prove that he's being spied on, the face of his lawyer,
Previti, swearing to uphold the Constitution, the cassowary face
of Piquet, Enoch's sweat, the Oil for Food scandal, the price of gas
rising while the price of oil drops, the financial consultants who
sell Argentinian bonds to retirees, Enron, Parmalat, Alitalia, Fiat,
Telecom, paying for incoming calls, Tim Vodafone Wind Tre the
forced repatriation of illegal immigrants the bridge over the Strait
of Messina the merger of groups that should be competing the antitrust authority that backs the way Jean-Claude was forced out
Thierry's proposal to take his place the ridiculous salary I continue
to pocket without doing shit — but nothing happens, all this has
the opposite effect on me, it gets even harder and imprisons me
even more, increases my energy, and although from a purely logical point of view a shitload of time must have transpired, if only for
the quantity of things that have crossed my mind since she said "I
can't," in reality very little time has transpired, almost none, I don't
know how, she *just* said it, and I haven't even begun to hesitate, it's
a kind of miracle, it's like the Samurai Jack video game on Play-
Station when you've filled up on Zen energy and you hold the R2
button down — the Sakai attack mode, it's called — and it slows
down by five times the action time of your adversaries while your
time is cut only in half, so as to give you a devastating, Einsteinian
superiority, and in fact here we are again with the same sensation of
inviolability we had when I rescued her, together with the amazement, the exhaustion, the rage, and the fear — of what? — here it
comes again, the enthralling awareness that I'll manage — to do
what? — because there's all the time and the room in the world
to do it and I'm infallible, and the unconscious is really a preci-

sion device, goddamn it, look at how the rescue scene has been replicated, it's unbelievable, even the position is exactly the same, up ahead is her discombobulated body, full of flesh fleeing in every direction, and behind is mine, composed, compact, bearing order and control, which contains it and governs it through an erection smacking against her milky-white buttocks . . .

I've got it, Eleonora Simoncini: I've figured out how to move forward. I touch the R2 button, time has almost stopped: I finish removing your panties, which were halfway down, and I start to stick my middle finger up your ass. Naturally you stiffen — a finger in the ass at this moment can mean one thing only — and you moan, but you don't repeat your no, you don't say you can't, and I bet that your heart jumped into your throat, *boomboomboom,* because suddenly you think it's going to hurt and you weren't prepared for pain, but what do you expect, we're the first ones to do it, we're in prehistoric times — at the bivouac, as you see, without even a grotto for shelter — two coarse sylvan creatures disliked by the God of the Moon, two Cro-Magnons, freshly landed from the biological leap that will lead us to conquer the world but still thousands of years from the refinement of using oils and balms to make this act less bloody — so yes, it's true, you'll feel a little pain. There, my whole finger is inside. You see, once, several years ago, Lara and Marta went to a lawyer in Bellagio — Alessio Romano was his name — about a lawsuit they'd inherited from their deceased parents, something about the house on the lake that they owned around there. The lawyer listened to the story of their local nuisance, said he would be happy to help them, but claimed that to do so he needed to fuck them in the ass, first one and then the other, best if done immediately, right there, on the couch in his office. Since Lara and Marta were still upset by the deaths, in quick succession, of their father and mother, I convinced them to forget about him and let me take care of it; after which, before reporting him to the authorities, I decided to confront him in person, made an appointment, and when I was facing him, not at all intimidated by his massive, bearlike bulk, I asked him fairly aggressively to account for his behavior toward my wife and sister-in-law, at which point he caught me off guard, saying that he wanted to fuck me in the ass, too. The point was, he told me, for reasons too long to explain but historical and indisputable, sodomy was the only instrument that could make a relationship truly solid and lasting, establish an inexpugnable oneness that he called the "symbiotic bond," before which any adversary was destined to succumb; and since he liked winning lawsuits, even as modest as the one we had proposed to him, behold, the act became necessary — otherwise, as was his custom, he could not accept the case. I started pulling my finger out. He didn't manage to convince me, old Alessio Romano, but once I'd left his office, in the placid glare of the lakeshore, I was so thunderstruck by his madness that I decided to leave the job of reporting him to the next client. I limited myself to keeping an eye on him, through the discreet solicitude of my friend Enrico Valiani, a Milanese lawyer, who by the way also has a house near here, right beyond that hedge, of whom I asked the favor of gathering information about him and checking every now and then to see whether he had been disbarred; and — listen up, here comes the good part — *no one has ever reported him.* What I learned about him is that he is a strange man, son of a Fascist who was executed by partisans, a former member of the Monarchist Party, who in the 1990s arrived in a remote Luddite community in Valbrona, where they live as if it were the early nineteenth century, and he became one of the top authorities, even representing it on a television hookup during a summer episode of *Uno Mattina,* but no reports, complaints, or disciplinary measures of any kind have been filed against him by any prosecutor or professional order in Lombardy. On the other hand, since

the day he theorized the need to fuck me and the rest of my family
in the ass, Alessio Romano has continued to practice the profes-
sion at the courthouses of Como and Lecco, on behalf of small
landowners from the Lariano Peninsula in property litigation
against the public administration — scoring an enviable number
of successes. Do you understand what this means? Either one or
the other is true: either he proposed it only to us, for some reason
that can have to do only with us, in which case I'd like to know
what that reason is, or else there's an unspecified number of inhabitants of the Lariano Peninsula who found it eminently reason-
able to allow themselves to be butt-fucked by their lawyer for the
sake of winning a lawsuit; in which case, you'll have to admit, it
would be a fairly interesting phenomenon, also considering the
sociogeographic proximity of that corner of Italy to the Canton of
Ticino, your birthplace. Now my finger is almost out, but — I'll
grant you this — I'm going to stick it in again, to help you prepare
a little better, because you're not ready, look at how stiff you are,
still, terrified, but you moan and keep not saying no, so I'm going
to continue this way, still in Sakai mode, toward the symbiotic
bond that was evidently our destiny from the start, ever since I
saved your life to the beat of my cock on your ass, and even more
if you consider that in this moment you and I are *merging* publicly,
you see, me in the belly of the French Whale with my little high-
tech office, my yuppie salary, and my unlucky secretary, you in
the belly of the Jewish Shark who with all your empire of luxury
goods, which is so small compared to his but has remained whole
and independent because Steiner, contrary to his behavior with all
of his other partners, swallowed you without chewing, and this
for the sake of a much-gossiped-about relationship between the
two of you, I repeat, much-gossiped-about, gossip to which on
principle I paid no attention but after having had a sample of your
concept of gratitude I have to admit takes on an attractive credibil-

ity, and in short we were merging anyway, you see, and according
to the news leaks about the outcome of the merger negotiations,
it seems that I would have fucked you in the ass anyway, that's it,
because I send my finger up a third time, deeper, now, more aggressively, and I move it, I turn it around and around, and at this
point it's impossible for you not to remember when I rescued you,
and above all *how* I rescued you, maybe you're not aware but it's
unquestionable that somewhere inside you conserve an indelible
memory of every single instant of that morning, otherwise in this
moment you would not be saying oh Pietro oh Pietro, you would
not invoke me by calling my name, and you would never agree to
be fucked in the ass like I am clearly about to do, on the grass, like
a goat; something would block you — the fear of pain, perhaps, or
shame over the inevitable stench of shit that has prevailed over
your now dissipated perfume, or even the thought alone that
Claudia might wake up and come looking for me, because I even
told you that she's asleep in her room, and even if she has the misfortune to be my daughter, and as you can see I'm an absolutely
satanic father, bad enough to go and recover Lara's license plate in
the Tonfone creek and nail it to my forehead, *you're a mother,* for
Christ's sake, I've seen your children with my own eyes cuddling
close to you after I went all the way to Hades to bring you back to
them, and it's shameful, let the Devil himself tell you, it's really
shameful that you, a mother of two, don't feel the minimum protective instinct toward my poor little orphaned and innocent
daughter, who could come out into the yard any moment, confused, afraid, and see us, there we go, I'm pulling my finger out for
the third time, and the next time it won't be my finger, you know,
and it will hurt much more, you know, and all the same you're
not running away, and you don't even put up any resistance, only
your oh Pietro repeated in the moonlight like the howling of a
wolf, which means that you're worse than me, or even, like Marta

says, that you're *like* me, which means that what happened two months ago awakened something repressed and unavowable in you as it did in me, and it shocked you and excited you and made you numb to everything else as it did me, and it will always be one of the most terrible and at the same time most amazing experiences of your whole life, because it's not as if we can choose these things, not as if we can choose with whom to share them, it would be nice but that's not the way it is, they are the ones to choose us, and from that moment on the only thing they want is to be replicated, replaced, relived, and so they chain us to the worst thing we're capable of doing, making us dangerous, yes, making us nothing more than accidents waiting to happen . . .

Here we go, Eleonora Simoncini. It's obviously no longer my finger pressing against your ass. And obviously I'm not using violence, even though in all probability I'll break it. Obviously we both want it, and the reason why is also obvious. Everything is obvious. For that matter, this is what's nice about the Sakai attack mode: everything becomes clear. But now the R2 button has to be released, the moment has come for time to start running normally again, to celebrate this absurd ritual so saturated with destiny — our merger, on the night of the spirits, our symbiotic bond: *plug in* . . .

part three

chapter thirty-three

No fall this year. With an epic storm that flooded all the basements in Europe and a trail of cold, fog, and humidity that dragged on for weeks, the gangrene of winter finally began and erased even the bare memory of the fantastic Indian summer from which we had come. The message was clear: "The good times are over, kids"; maybe a little rough, but without any of the catastrophic phenomena that people had associated with the persistence of the exceptional heat. It was a gift, that climate, nothing more, nothing less: now everyone realizes it.

With the change of seasons people's habits have changed, too. I'd never noticed how much we tailor our habits to meteorological conditions: our schedules, trips, stopovers, everything. Neighborhoods that had been so familiar to me that I could see them with my eyes closed became new and almost unknown. Some people disappeared completely — the Pakistani who cleaned windshields, for example — others changed their schedule and their behavior, but without conveying the impression they were improvising: as if, together with their heavy clothes, they had also taken their winter habits out of storage. As a result, the other time, Chronos, has lost out and is reorganizing new concatenations. And me, spending all day here, I can feel it in my bones. At first a series of movements that seemed casual turned out to be quite rigidly structured, so rigidly, in fact, that it could be expressed in mathematical terms (for example: Matteo and mother going to physical therapy session + old man coming out by the main door, lighting a cigarette, and going on his way + dwarf walking by with her grocery bags − traffic cop gone home + arrival of the trash removal truck − Matteo and mother leav-

ing the physical therapy session + the first two travel agency
employees taking their coffee break — the trash removal truck
driving away + the other two travel agency employees taking
their coffee break = arrival of Yolanda and Nebbia). The same
thing kept happening afterward, too, in the way new or modi-
fied elements were put together. Hence a downsizing of the role
of Yolanda, who no longer stops by the park and limits herself
to walking by, shivering, with Nebbia on a leash (they are both
obviously creatures of the summer); the disappearance of the
dwarf and the transformation of the employees' coffee break
into the fleeting appearance of one of them (they take turns),
who orders four coffees to go and takes them back to the office;
it all seems to be a function of the increased importance of the
elderly smoker: now he no longer disappears immediately after
lighting his cigarette and has taken to lingering under the can-
opy of the kiosk, exposed to a humidity that cannot be very good
for his health, in an effort to engage the vendor in conversations
that are pretty formulaic. Matteo and his mother come by only
on alternate days and have changed schedule: now they come
between the departure of the traffic cop and the arrival of the
trash removal truck. All the extras on bicycles have disappeared,
and there are far more people standing around outside the stores
smoking cigarettes. These are small things, I know, but not as insignificant as I had thought, because the lives of all these people,
including my own, seem to depend also on the order that we are
able to give them. And more often than not, the only order we
can envisage is the repetition of the same actions to the bitter
end, performed in the same way at the same place at the same
time; only outside forces compel us to change, but we adapt to
the change and start repeating ourselves all over again in our
new actions. Take me, for instance: now I'm in the car, with the
heat on and the windows fogging up, but when I see the arrival of

the minivan bringing meals to the school I get out and go to the café, so as to avoid running into Claudia's teacher, who comes out a few moments later (Gloria on Mondays, Wednesdays, and Fridays; Paolina on Tuesdays and Thursdays); and when I return, after having had a sandwich (chicken salad), a glass of water, and a coffee and then reading *La Gazetta dello Sport* from cover to cover unfolded on top of the ice cream counter, Claudia almost never fails to stick her head out the window on her way back from the cafeteria, see me, and wave. And if one day she happens not to stick her head out, or she looks out when I'm already back in the car, I get the feeling that something isn't right, and my mood suffers the consequences.

Together with winter many other things have arrived. A phone call from Jean-Claude, first of all, reassuring me that he was all right; he asked me a ton of questions, about me and about Claudia but also about the situation at the company, so many questions that he made me feel like I was the only news source he had left. I told him that Thierry had offered me his position, and he said, "Typical"; but I didn't tell him about the accusations they're throwing at him, in part because he obviously already knows them. The only thing he told me himself is that he likes Aspen in the off-season, he's at peace, and he's reading *Coriolanus*. Not a word about the late-night phone call that had so worried me: as if he had never made it.

Then a couple of postcards arrived, one from Enoch, from Zimbabwe, and one from the man who called me *dottore,* from Rome — and, oddly enough, they both arrived on the same day. Enoch's was a composite of photographs (of Victoria Falls, a majestic African elephant, a herd of gazelles) plus a map of the Victoria Falls National Park on which, in the upper right corner, there was an arrow with the inscription, in felt-tip pen, *"Nous sommes par là."* The text was a simple *"Auguri."* The postcard from the man who called me *dottore* was the classic view of Saint Peter's from the perspective of Via della Conciliazione, and the text was an equally classic *"Saluti."*

And some people came by, of course, but they, too, had changed, as had my manner of receiving them. Before there had been Piquet, Enoch, Marta, and Carlo; now there were my secretary, Basler, and Tardioli. Before we used to converse perched on the park bench or sitting at the table outside the café or standing in the shade of the plane tree; now we have to sit inside the car, and everything seems more artificial, including the fact of my being here. With the new people have come new problems, new stories, and new suffering, but now I'm much more distant than before, which increases the misunderstanding of my presumed suffering — or, depending on the point of view, my presumed sneakiness. Annalisa, my secretary, who when the weather was nice never brought me the documents to sign, preferring to use a messenger service instead, has started coming by with a certain regularity, even for ordinary things, proving, as I see it, the purely wintertime fragility that afflicts some women, driving them to go outside and defy the rain rather than spend time alone in a dimly lit room without being looked at by anyone. On the other hand, she still doesn't have a boyfriend, and I can't figure out why. Apropos of Annalisa, I realized that the story about my refusing to become president had been leaked, or at least rumored — and here there are two possibilities: it was either Thierry or Jean-Claude — but I steered clear of either confirming or denying it, which must have disappointed her. Basler, the head of the press office, came by one day to inform me that the day of reckoning had arrived and that things for the men close to Jean-Claude were looking pretty bad. He said that the French had started breaking balls, in a strategic, systematic way; and he also told me about Elisabetta Oberti, another one of Jean-Claude's pets, who had been literally crucified through a series of pretexts regarding the weekly film program she headed — details that in their time had all been decided on by Jean-Claude himself, such as the font and size of the captions and the use of jump cuts to shorten interviews — until, he said, having reached and surpassed her tolerance limit, she rebelled against the two hired guns sent by Paris to inspect the books and told them to go fuck themselves, screaming "You've got nothing to teach us, you fucking Gauls. Back when your ancestors were still living in caves we were already flaming faggots!" But despite all his efforts to be funny and prove his complicity, Basler reeked like a barrel of sardines: go figure, the same man who was at the switchboard of information flows inside and outside the office didn't even broach the subject of my refusal to take Jean-Claude's place, as if he knew nothing about it — which was impossible, since even Annalisa knew. The impression I got was that he was on some kind of a mission, although I have no idea for whom or for what purpose; so I kept my mouth shut, without expressing a single opinion, playing to the hilt the part of the traumatized widower. But one thing is true: together with the coming of winter, the Shakespearean era that Jean-Claude talked about truly has arrived, the era filled with betrayals and paranoia, which will empty the company of its residual humanity and, in the end, justify the fateful curse used by Enoch.

And while we're on the subject of paranoia, I was just starting to wonder what had become of Piquet when Tardioli arrived with the story of his spectacular exit — the story of the cassowary man and the sliding cup holder. He says that Piquet had bought a laptop computer online directly from its Taiwanese manufacturer — and I knew this was true, because he had gone to pick it up one of the mornings he had been here; and he says that it was a real monster, that laptop, with something like a 160-gigabyte hard drive, a superflat screen, wireless, Centrino, everything: all for the royal price of $3,000 or so. He says that Piquet was gloating because, among other things, the laptop also had a sliding cup holder, which seemed to excite him more than everything else, since he talked about it all the time. According to him, that little device was a tribute to the magnificence of our decadent age, when such a refined accessory can be designed for the sole purpose of preventing the formation of a white ring on the top of your desk. But it was an accessory that no one ever saw — they heard him talk about it, that was all — because Piquet never brought the laptop to the office, he kept it at home. Well, this sliding cup holder almost immediately began to give him trouble: it wasn't the right size, and it would close unexpectedly, knocking over the soda can, until one day Piquet appeared in the office all agitated and asked for help from just about everyone because he had to write an e-mail in English to the help center in Taipei — his English is atrocious — to inform them that the sliding cup holder was broken: an hour and a half wasted to find out how to say *"porta-lattine estraibile"* in English, the entire second floor involved, everything at a standstill. First of all, how do you say *"porta-lattine"*: "cup holder," "can holder," or "bottle holder"? Heidi, Tardioli's secretary, is German, but she speaks perfect English because her mother is Australian, and she was definitely leaning toward "cup holder," but Piquet was fixated on soda cans and insisted on "can holder," until Giananni, the one who handles the rights for sports events, went down to the garage to check the instruction manual for his Pontiac, which is filled with such doodads, and he ended the discussion: "cup holder." Then there was the problem of the adjective, *"estraibile,"* in part because no one understood how the device worked: but in the end Piquet made a drawing on the conference room blackboard and they realized that it was a kind of molded tray that went into and out of the side of the computer, and then Heidi established that in English it should be called "sliding" — "sliding cup holder." And so Piquet sent an e-mail about the broken sliding cup holder to the online help center in Taiwan, which was supposed to answer in real time, but since it was night over there the reply didn't come in until the next day — and the reply was "What sliding cup holder?" He says that Piquet had a meltdown and kicked the watercooler, swearing at the people at the Taiwanese online service who didn't even know the accessories in the computers they were supposed to be providing help for; and everyone in the office should have understood right then and there that Piquet had snapped, because his reaction was so over the top, like a real neurotic; but he says that by then all of them were caught up in the business of the sliding cup holder, and they calmed him down, and Heidi went over and sat next to him to trade e-mails in English with the Taiwanese to explain the situation more clearly. The two of them write: "The sliding cup holder that comes with your portable computer"; and the Taiwanese answer back: "According to our records this model has no accessory of this kind." And the two of them write: "Nevertheless, you just so happen to have sold me one, but the sliding cup holder broke immediately, in addition to the fact that the diameter of the soda cans it is supposed to hold does not correspond to Western standards"; and then the Taiwanese, whose curiosity had been piqued: "But where exactly is this cup holder located?"; and the two of them (at this point everyone, the entire second floor, is gathered around Heidi and Piquet): "It's located on the left side of the object"; and the Taiwanese, still in real time, from Taipei: "At what point, exactly, with respect to the CD/DVD tray, which in that model is located on the left side?" And here he says that Piquet blanched. He turned literally into a ghost, he says. "*What* CD/DVD tray?" he said. He says it was a major embarrassment, growing worse as it slowly started to dawn on everyone; but before anyone could say anything Piquet ran away, and he says that since then no one has been able to find him: cell phone turned off, answering machine unplugged, no way of contacting him.

Tardioli came back to see me other times — many other times. He's a shy, insecure guy with a visible tendency toward depression, but also lucid and creative; on my recommendation, Jean-Claude retrieved him from the dead end of corporate imaging to place him at the head of major event planning, which is why he had to work closely with Piquet; and as crazy as it might sound, for him Piquet had been the last point of reference in a company being devoured by the merger, the reason why he now feels so lost and alone. I tried to put myself in his shoes, and it can't be easy: the executive who appreciated you stuck like a post in front of an elementary school; the president who trusted you ousted and accused of embezzlement; the head of human resources, with whom you shared your problems, fled to Africa to become a lay missionary; the more experienced colleague, with whom you worked, vanished after mistaking a CD drive for a cup holder. There's plenty of room for despondency. And since I trust him, because he's not on a mission and he's coming here only because he needs *normality,* with him I did talk. Not that I had some speech to give him, but I answered his question about whether it was true that I had been offered Jean-Claude's chair and refused it, and I gave him the advice that I thought he needed: accept the severance pay that's going to be offered to everyone after the merger and find another job somewhere else. But here, too, a misunderstanding was generated, because I gave him this advice thinking exclusively of what was best for him, while he must have thought that I had access to who knows what confidential information regarding the group's future projects, and he got scared. Even though he trusts me, in fact, he probably didn't believe me when I told him that I don't give a shit about the merger and that I refused the presidency out of pure regard for Jean-Claude; but the very fact that the seat was offered to me in the first place must be flashing in his brain as proof that I am deeply involved in the maneuvers related to the merger — a signal confirmed also by the absurd privilege that I enjoy in being able to spend my days here doing whatever the fuck I want rather than sweating it out in the office like everyone else. So in the end I think that he took my advice more as a warning that he was about to be canned, and I'm sorry about this; just the same, I have no doubt that a change of air would be good for a kid like Tardioli, so it doesn't matter that he took my advice for a threat: what matters is that he get busy looking for another job and put this situation behind him as quickly as possible. On the other hand, I'm also sure that however much I might try to explain the way things really are, if I had spoken to him sincerely about the confusion generated in me by the grief that continues not to arrive, all it would have done is increase the misunderstanding, like in the film *Being There,* when Chance keeps repeating that he's a gardener and everyone takes it as confirmation that he really is an éminence grise, terrifying and powerful. This is the direction things have taken, and there's nothing anyone can do: Tardioli himself admitted to me that at the office they're talking more about me than about the merger, and for that matter the two subjects are considered closely related, the story about the rejected presidency having become the fulcrum of every discussion, the key to every conjecture, the subject of Byzantine interpretations on a daily basis.

Within the realm of possibility, I still try to talk to him about Piquet: I ask him whether he's dropped a line or there's any news of him, acting as if I were worried about him when what I really want is news of Francesca, his woman, and of Saverio, his son. That Piquet had dropped everything I already knew, and frankly I didn't care all that much, but I can't bear to see the simultaneous disappearance of those two giants, about whom I would like to hear more: I especially would like to know whether they're really the way I imagine them every day, floating in the amniotic fluid of their psychotic bubble, one in the act of hurling abuse at the doorwoman of her building, the other ceaselessly shepherding the infinite flock of natural numbers; or whether, instead — *unfortunately* is the word that comes to mind — Piquet invented the whole thing, and the splendor he hacks out for them in the blackness of their woes is nothing more than a loving tribute dreamed up by his burned-out mind. But Tardioli is a very reserved kid, he doesn't unburden himself, and I had to be more and more explicit until I could ask him whether he had thought of calling Piquet's girlfriend, at least, or his wife, so we could stop worrying about him, and he answered that although he had thought of it, he couldn't, because he didn't know the girlfriend's last name and he had never seen or met the wife. I don't know Francesca's last name, either, but I told him the name of the design studio where she works, because that I do know — it's the Elle Studio on Corso Lodi — and Tardioli assured me that he would call her there. I also tried to get him to talk about her, I asked him how long he had known her, what she was like, and he told me that he had seen her only once, when he'd had dinner at their house last summer. "A beautiful girl," he said, "real nice and everything." That was it. He gave me nothing that would help me understand whether "and everything" included the memory of her asking Piquet to throw the clothes out the window.

And then Eleonora Simoncini arrived. And everything about her has changed, too, but it has nothing to do with the change of season. Of course, her winter garments make her much less attractive, but that's not why she no longer has the same effect on me as before. The fact of the matter is that the theory of Mr. Romano the lawyer didn't work: no symbiotic bond was established between us; on the contrary, there is an embarrassing feeling of

complicity in what was unquestionably the most savage and reck-
less act of our lives. This immediately became very clear when she
showed up a couple of days later, accompanied by the outbreak
of a deafening storm, and neither of us knew what to say, sitting
there in the car, the world hidden behind a thick blanket of rain,
the crash of thunderbolts setting off car alarms. I'm sure that if
we had written the scene for a movie it would have been intense,
sensual, and even romantic; but we had to live it, which was something else entirely. We could literally see our thoughts condensing
around a single crucial point: we had done something really nasty,
it was ridiculous to try to sweep it under the rug and transform it
into a relationship, because we had done it a quarter of a century
too late, that's the point, and while it might be gallant and maybe
even constructive to get fucked in the ass in the backyard with the
risk of being caught by your parents, it becomes idiotic and almost
criminal to do it at the age of forty-five with the risk of being surprised by your children; and although the primary responsibility
was mine — my house, my initiative, my daughter — she had
done it just as much as I had: like me, she had shown that she was
ready to gamble with a little girl's sleep, and like me, she still had
the calluses on her knees to prove it. Here we were, and it was
right for us to be here, in the grayness of a front seat drowned
out by the rain, with no promise to exchange, no word to say,
no future, and even the simple act of looking at each other was
painful. Rigid, perched on the edge of the seat, her patrician eyes
obscured by the veil of humiliation, she, too, realized that there
was nothing we could do, because it was as over as over could be
between a man and a woman. "And now?" she said. "What's your
plan?" Obviously no attempt at irony could straighten things out,
but I think that at that moment nothing better could be said, and
the silence was hard to bear. I may have smiled while I pointed
with my chin toward the dark mass of the school, beyond the

natural car wash that was swallowing us. "There it is," I said; and I remembered a story to tell her, something that had happened to me many years ago and seemed perfect to make her understand how I felt. But the story was too long, and for us the time was up. "I'll see you around," she said, and got out, getting hopelessly drenched as she ran to her Mercedes under the pelting rain that the raging sky hurled down at her.

chapter thirty-four

Once, almost twenty years ago, as I was coming back to Italy from my first trip to the United States, something strange happened to me on the plane. I had a seat in the last row, where there are only two side seats, and when boarding was over, the seat next to mine was still vacant; I was already savoring the thought of a comfortable trip by myself when I saw a steward coming up the aisle, pushing a wheelchair carrying a paraplegic woman. The seat that I thought was free was assigned to none other than her, and the steward asked me to give up my place, by the window, because obviously she wouldn't be able to get up to let me pass if I had to go, let's say, to the bathroom. It wasn't as though I could say no, and so the paralyzed woman was deposited heavily in my window seat, and I moved to the one next to it. She was American, more or less the same age as I am today — which back then made her seem old to me — and her legs dangled grimly during the transfer from the wheelchair to the seat: this is all that I know about her, because for the entire trip I avoided letting our gazes even cross, and when it was just plain impossible, I managed to make sure that our visual contact would last only as long as strictly necessary: a moment or two. If you really must, you could say that I ignored her. And in short order we took off, we ate, I got up to go to the bathroom. We watched the movie.

Every now and then a stewardess came by and asked the woman whether she needed anything, but the woman never did, until everyone on the plane fell asleep and the stewardess stopped coming by. I tried again and again to find a position that would allow me to sleep, but it was difficult, because the woman was monopolizing the armrest we shared; until, I don't know how, by turning my back on her and propping myself up on the other armrest I was able to nod off. I slept for about an hour, and I could have slept some more, but at a certain point the woman woke me up. She did so delicately, patting me lightly on the shoulder, the same way my mother used to every morning back then. And, just like my mother, the woman *was standing up.* She had to go to the toilet. I stood up to let her pass — "Thank you," she said — and I observed her taking the ten steps needed to reach the bathroom: she walked perfectly, like a normal person. I looked around the penumbra of this belly of a whale, but no one had noticed: everyone else was curled up asleep, and there wasn't even the shadow of a stewardess. The woman stayed in the bathroom for quite a while, then she came out, took ten steps to reach her seat, I stood up again to let her pass, and she sat down. "Thank you," she repeated. Then she rested her head against the pillow and closed her eyes immediately. After that I was unable to find the position in which I had fallen asleep, so I didn't sleep anymore; she, on the other hand, slept like a rock until the lights were turned on for breakfast and the stewardesses started coming and going again, asking her whether she wanted anything. The woman ate her whole breakfast, had two servings of coffee, then started reading a book for the rest of the flight. During our landing her hands gripped the armrests tightly, because she must have been a little frightened. Now I could look at her as much as I wanted, because she was the one avoiding my gaze; and I did: I looked at her constantly, but I didn't look at anything specific about her. In fact, as I was saying, I wouldn't be able to tell whether she was a blonde or a brunette, pretty or ugly; I was simply trying to make her feel the full brunt of my eyes pressing down on her, I wanted to make her feel embarrassed — but even if I succeeded, she gave no sign of it. Then, when the plane stopped at the terminal, they asked us to remain seated over the loudspeaker. Immediately afterward a steward (another one, not the same one) arrived with the wheelchair, and the transfer of the woman was repeated in reverse. When the steward lifted her, I looked carefully at her legs: they really did seem limp and lifeless, with no muscle tone — the legs of a marionette; and when he started steering her down the aisle, walking backward, she was no longer able to avoid my gaze and was forced to smile at me and wave her hand.

Well, Eleonora Simoncini: what I wanted to tell you is that in front of you I felt the same way that woman must have felt in front of me.

chapter thirty-five

— Hello?

— . . .

— Hello?

— Good morning, may I speak with Pietro Paladini, please?

— Hi, Dad. How are you?

— Pietro, is that you?

— Of course it's me.

— Your voice sounds different.

— I swear, it's me.

— But very different. It's someone else's voice.

— But it's me. How are you?

— No, that can't be. You're not my son.

— Come on, Dad. You called my cell phone. It has to be me.

— That has nothing to do with it. I know my son's voice. You're someone else.

— I recognized you immediately, didn't I? How else could I, in your opinion, if I were someone else?

— You saw the name PAPÀ appear on the display, that's how you did it. Now please pass the phone to my son.

— There was no name on the display. Just the words UNKNOWN CALLER, because you're in Switzerland and your number is blocked.

— Listen, I have no idea who you are, and I don't know why you want to pass yourself off as my son, but please pass the phone to him immediately, otherwise I'll call the police.

— All right, I'll pass him to you.

— . . .

— Hello?

— Pietro, who was the guy that answered the phone?

— A colleague.

— Did you authorize him to answer your phone?

— Yes, of course I did. How's it going?

— You must have your head up your ass, because he tried to pass himself off as you.

— Really? Thanks for telling me. How are you?

— Fine. Claudia?

— She's fine, too.

— And you?

— Great.

— Are you still spending your days in front of the school?

— Yes.

— Cover up, it's cold.

— I'm in the car, Dad.

— Good boy . . . Listen, what was it I wanted to tell you? Oh, yes, I wanted to invite the two of you to lunch. Mamma is dying to see you.

— Who?

— Mamma.

— . . .

— And me, too, of course. But as you know, it makes her sad to see so little of you. Can I tell her you're coming?

— Yes . . .

— She said that she'll make you baked pasta with eggplant. And meat loaf.

— Fantastic. Can you pass Chantal to me, please?

— Who? Oh, Chantal. Of course. Chantal! Carlo wants to speak with you. Why do you want to speak to her?

— I have to ask her for something for my backache.

— Ah. Did you put your back out?

— Obviously.

— All right. See you soon.

— See you, Dad.

— Here's Chantal. I'll pass her the phone. It's Carlo. Bye.

— Hello?

— Chantal?

— Carlo?

— No, this is Pietro.

— I thought so.

— Can you talk?

— Yes. He's gone to the other room. How are the two of you doing?

— We're fine, but I get the impression that he . . .

— He what?

— Well, he just told me that Mamma wants to make me meat loaf.

— Oh, of course. Every now and then it happens. That he sees your mother, I mean, that he speaks with her. But the doctor says there's nothing to worry about.

— And he mistook me for Carlo. And earlier he called me on my cell and didn't recognize me. He forced me to say I was someone else.

— Forced? That's a big word.

— Well, in other words, he insisted on saying that it wasn't me. And to cut it short, I had to —

— And you did the right thing. There's nothing in the world worth contradicting him over.

— True. But I was wondering whether this, um, whether this ongoing deterioration might lead to some . . .

— To what?

— I don't know, to some *strange act*. Who knows what happens in his head.

— I know. The only thing your father needs is every now and then to see reality as something different from what it is. Exactly like you or me. Except that unlike us he has a much better chance of doing it.

— That's one way to put it. Another way would be to say that he's completely lost his mind. Excuse my brutality.

— Your father hasn't lost his mind, Pietro. He's sick, not crazy. Let me assure you that most of the time he behaves in a completely normal manner. He's just fighting to survive, and if you're not riding him all the time, repeating that his wife is dead or that one of his sons doesn't want to see him anymore, he manages to get by quite nicely.

— So let's put it like this: when he invites me to lunch at Mom's request, I worry, and when you tell me not to worry, I relax.

— You can put it however you like, but in the end try to stay calm. Your father is fine.

— Did he finally give in and install the dishwasher?

— No, he donated it to the Red Cross.

— The dishwasher? What's the Red Cross going to do with it?

— Oh, they accept everything.

— The only reason I was saying it is because if I understood him correctly, he would like Claudia and me to come to lunch one of these Sundays, but I don't like the idea of you having to wash the dishes by hand afterward. It seems so absurd.

— Sorry to be so blunt, but what do you care how I wash dishes? Come to lunch and don't worry about it.

— Okay, you're right. So I say we come next Sunday. Not this Sunday, the following one. Is that all right with you?

— Of course it's all right.

— Is he still convinced that Lara died in a car accident?

— He hasn't mentioned it lately, but I think he is.

— In that case could you please help me to change the subject if he starts talking about it in front of Claudia?

— Don't worry. I'm an expert at changing the subject.

— I don't want to confuse her, you see.

— Of course. How is Claudia doing? Is she suffering a lot?

— No, that's just it. She's calm. I don't know how, but she's calm.

— Check her hair.

— Beg your pardon?

— Check her hair. See whether it's turning white.

— At the age of ten and a half?

— Yes.

— Why?

— Trust me. Check her, and if you find even one white hair, tell me.

— White hair. Okay.

— So we'll see you on Sunday.

— On Sunday.

— . . .

— Chantal?

— Yes?

— Can I ask you something?

— Yes.

— It's a little indiscreet.

— Go ahead, ask me.

— Why are you doing it?

— Doing what?

— Why are you devoting your life to my father?

— What the heck kind of question . . .

— I told you it was indiscreet. If you don't want to answer, it doesn't matter.

— Because I love him, Pietro. That's all there is to say.

— . . .

— What, you don't believe me?

— No, I believe you. It's just that, well, it can't be very easy to love him at a time like this.

— On the contrary: Your father is a wonderful man, even with his illness. And loving him is a privilege.

— I meant with his character. And the need for constant care, and his obsession with saving money . . .

— I like being near him, and while I'm near him I take care of him. I was a nurse for thirty-two years, for me it's normal. And anyway your father is much better than he might seem.

— Thanks to you.

— No, Pietro. No one can make you feel good if goodness is not already inside you. That's what I've learned.

— You're right. So we'll see you next Sunday.

— Good-bye, Pietro.

— Good-bye.

— Hello?

— Hi, how are you doing?

— Hi, Marta. Fine. And you?

— Little Giacomo has a temperature, but it's not very high.

— Hmm. There's a lot of that going around lately. And your belly?

— It's growing.

— Do you already know whether it's a girl or a boy?

— It's another boy.

— Hooray! Congratulations!

— Thank you. Even if I would have preferred a girl.

— Really? Why?

— Take a wild guess.

— Because you already have two boys? What does that matter?

— Let's just say that if he turns out like the other two they'll have to commit me.

— Come on, they're good boys.

— Yeah, right. Two little angels.

— No, it's a good thing there's another boy, you know? Have you decided what to name him?

— I was thinking of Aldo.

— What? You must be kidding.

— Why? Maybe it's not a beautiful name, but it's my father's name and I think —

— Marta, *you can't* call him Aldo.

— Why not?

— You can't have three sons named Aldo, Giovanni, and Giacomo. They're the same names as the comedy trio!

— Oh, I hadn't thought of that. Aldo, Giovanni, and Giacomo, you're right . . . Even if in reality it would be Giovanni, Giacomo, and Aldo . . .

— Look, you just can't.

— . . .

— . . .

— No, I guess I can't.

— You're doing the right thing.

— . . .

— . . .

— I was just getting used to the idea, fuck. You always ruin everything.

— Oh, so now it's my fault.

— But why, for Christ's sake, *why* does everything always have to be so complicated? A woman can't even call a son by her father's name. Why not? Why do things always have to turn out this way?

— They don't always have to turn out this way, Marta. Just this time.

— Well, that's the way they always turn out for me. For some fucking reason I can never do the things other people do day in and day out.

— Don't go playing the victim now.

— All I wanted was to call him Aldo. I really did. And now I can't. Can you tell me why?

— Maybe that's not meant to be his name, plain and simple.

— It was my father's name, for Christ's sake. I loved that name. Don't I have the right to give it to my son?

— Then why didn't you call one of the other two Aldo?

— Who cares, when they were born my dad was still alive.

— Exactly. What was it, were you afraid of giving him the satisfaction?

— . . .

— Hello?

— You're a real asshole, you know that?

— Come on, I'm sorry. I didn't mean it.

— And when you apologize you're an even bigger asshole.

— I was serious.

— Exactly. People who realize they've been assholes a second after the fact are even bigger assholes.

— Okay. The next time I'll let two or three days go by.

— As a matter of fact, the biggest assholes are the ones that make a joke after apologizing.

— Marta, I don't want to fight. It's just that I can't stand it when you play the victim.

— Oh, so now I'm the one that has to apologize. Did I hurt your feelings?

— All right, I take back what I said; call him Aldo and forget about it.

— . . .

— What difference does it make? "Nice, are they all yours?" "Yes." "What are their names?" "Aldo, Giovanni, and Giacomo." "You're kidding! Like the comedians?" "Yes, like the comedians." End of story.

— . . .

— Call him Aldo.

— You know that's exactly what I'm going to do.

— Come on, it's not a real problem? Am I right?

— Yes, you're right. Oh, by the way, I wanted to ask you something.

— Fire away.

— Did you ever call that psychoanalyst?

— No, I didn't call him.

— But are you going to?

— No, I'm not going to.

— So you're not going to do analysis with him?

— Marta, I don't think I —

— So do you mind if I go?

— Beg your pardon?

— I said if you're not going to go, then I could go. I want to go back into analysis.

— But didn't a friend of yours give you his number?

— Yes.

— And didn't you say that this analyst is really strict?

— Yes, and what of it?

— Isn't it against the rules to be analyzed by a friend of a friend?

— My friend is not a friend of his, she's a colleague. She recommended him. It's against the rules to be analyzed by a friend, that's why I'm not going to her; and so is going into analysis with the same analyst as your sister-in-law, and that's why I'm asking you to think twice, because if I go you won't be able to.

— Marta, I don't have to think twice. Go ahead and do therapy with him, I don't mind.

— Analysis, not therapy.

— All right, analysis.

— So should I call him?

— Yes.

— Okay, thank you.

— For what?

— So I'll talk to you later.

— Marta?

— . . .

— . . .

— No, it was nothing. Talk to you later.

— Bye.

— Bye.

— Hello?

— It's snowing!

— Where are you?

— In Rome. And it's snowing!

— Here it's raining.

— And here the snowflakes are coming down and it's beautiful. It's snowing on me right now, do you want me to give you the weather report?

— No, thanks. But is it sticking?

— You bet. The city is paralyzed. Airports closed, buses skidding on the streets, everyone outside throwing snowballs like in '86.

— What do you know about '86? You were in London.

— That's what everyone around here is saying: "Back in '86, back in '86." . . . Did it snow so much in '86?

— A lot, yes.

— It's fantastic. No one's working.

— I can imagine. Lucky you.

— Come on, maybe tomorrow it'll snow up there, too.

— But here it's different, in the sense that everything gets paralyzed, too, but people get pissed off.

— God only knows what you're doing up in Milan.

— I work here.

— Okay, but don't go telling me you wouldn't be able to find work in Rome. I've got a plan, hear me out: sell your dollhouse up there and buy a nice little apartment here in Garbatella, where unfortunately the prices are sky-high by comparison to ten years ago, but it's still one of the most convenient neighborhoods in Rome, in addition to being the hottest. Then we'd be close.

— That's your plan?

— Yes.

— What about work?

— You could work with me. I've got half an idea to open a radio station. You could manage it.

— Tell me the truth, the half an idea just came to you.

— Okay, but it's still a great idea. Radio Barrie: you like the sound?

— Come on, what are you going to do with a radio station?

— Music. Community. Image. I'm serious, Pietro.

— Do you have any idea how much frequencies cost?

— Listen, I'm loaded. I don't know what to do with my money anymore. The more I try to get rid of it, the more I make. I could even make money off a radio station.

— If you don't want to make money, the safest thing would be to avoid commercials.

— Perfect. Radio Barrie: the only commercial-free radio station in the world. So do you accept?

— Yes.

— When do we start?

— Saturday, when you come up here.

— Oh, now that you mention it: I can't come. This weekend I have to go to London, I'm afraid.

— What a shame.

— But next Sunday I have to change planes at Malpensa, and I could take a later connection, that way we could have lunch together.

— The Sunday after this?

— Yes, with Claudia, of course. How is she?

— Fine. But we can't that Sunday. We're going to have lunch at Dad's.

— At Dad's? How come?

— He invited us.

— Oh. And how's he doing? All right?

— Well, he's completely off his rocker. Chantal says that he's fine, but I'm not so convinced of it; sometimes she sounds crazy, too.

— Like I've always said: She's the crazy one, not him.

— Why don't you come along?

— *Where?*

— To Dad's. Since you're passing through.

— Are you kidding?

— Look, he's not feeling well. The other day on the phone he thought I was you.

— Can we not go over this again, please?

— Come on, what did he ever do to you?

— Pietro, please.

— He's old, he's sick. He says that he speaks with Mom, that he sees her . . . He told me that Mom is going to make us baked pasta, do you get it? How can you be so hard?

— Me, hard? He didn't give me the time of day for twenty years, and if I hadn't been the one to go back to him, when Mom got sick, he would still be that way.

— Yes, but then you made up.

— Made up, my ass. Do you know what he told me on the day Mom died? Her body was still warm, and do you know what he said?

— What did he say?

— He said, "Well, now we're the two bachelors of the family." That was his way of making up . . .

— Tact never was his strong point, you know that. It was a gaffe.

— A gaffe? What would you call hooking up with the nurse that took care of Mom, another gaffe? For your information, they were already together before Mom died.

— So what? You think he's the only man who ever cheated on his wife?

— At the age of seventy? Before her eyes while she was dying of cancer? With her nurse? You're right, the world is full of men who cheat . . .

— It wasn't before her eyes. Mom didn't know what was going on.

— *She didn't know* . . . How can you talk like that? How can you go to lunch with those two?

— No, how can you hate him so much? He's your father, for crying out loud.

— It's precisely because he was my — Listen, can we just drop the subject? Shit, why do we always end up talking about him? We had an agreement, fair and square: no more talk about Dad. After that you do what you want and I do what I want, but *no more talk about him,* I'm begging you.

— All right already. We won't talk about him.

— . . .

— . . .

— By the way, did that woman you rescued ever contact you? A note, a phone call, a thank-you . . .

— . . .

— You there?

— I'm here. You were saying?

— I was asking whether the woman you rescued ever contacted you. Seeing as she was a close friend of the one I saved, I thought she might have.

— Not a word.

— Go figure. Hey, I've got to get going. I want to throw some snowballs.

— Have fun.

— Bye, Pietro.

— Bye.

— Yes?

— Hi, Pietro.

— Hi. How's it going?

— Fine, and you?

— Fine. Any news?

— Yes. They're here.

— Who?

— The gods.

— What gods?

— Boesson and Steiner.

— Where's here?

— Milan.

— Oh, really. Why?

— What do you mean why? To sign.

— To sign what?

— The merger. Don't tell me you didn't know.

— Know what?

— Pietro, you're kidding, right?

— No. I don't know what you're talking about.

— You didn't know that they'd decided to come to Milan to sign the merger documents?

— No.

— Come on, everyone here knew about it.

— But I'm not there. The only person who tells me things is you, and this is something you didn't tell me.

— I thought you already knew.

— I didn't, though.

— They decided to sign here.

— Here? How come?

— To be a little more discreet, they say. To be a little less ostentatious.

— What? They create the biggest group in the world, and they want to be less ostentatious?

— What can I say, Pietro? They're signing here. They've already arrived.

— Boesson and Steiner . . .

— Yes, with wives and children in tow. Boesson is at the Principe di Savoia, and Steiner is supposed to be on Lake Como, at the Villa d'Este. They're doing a little shopping over the weekend, Tuesday night they're all going to the opening of La Scala, but in the meantime on Monday, on the feast of Saint Ambrose, when all the offices in Milan are closed, they're coming here to sign. Sorry, but I was sure you knew.

— It doesn't matter, nothing serious.

— Maybe you could come by the office.

— Me? Why?

— For the sake of it. To show your face. The office is packed with these unbelievable brownnosers, French and American. We've been physically invaded.

— Exactly. I'll spare myself.

— They've occupied the conference room. They order pizza every twenty minutes and tell jokes. You can hear their laughter all the way over here. And they stick their noses into everything.

— It'll pass.

— And Basler is a big kiss-ass.

— He's just doing his job, to kiss ass.

— And everyone around here is going nuts.

— That's their business. They're just using the merger as a pretext to misbehave. Don't let them infect you. In the meantime, while we're on the subject of people going nuts, did you ever find Piquet's girlfriend?

— Yes, I spoke to her over the phone.

— And?

— They broke up.

— *Really!* And she didn't tell you where he is, what he's doing?

— No. She says she hasn't seen him in more than a month.

— Ever since the cup holder incident . . .

— Exactly.

— And how did she sound to you?

— Her? Normal. How was she supposed to sound?

— I don't know, it depends on her tone of voice. What exactly did she say?

— She said that they broke up one month ago and that since then she hasn't heard anything from him.

— I know, but was she aggressive when she said it? Was she sad?

— What do I know, Pietro? We were on the phone.

— Did she ask you any questions?

— Questions? Ask *me*? No . . .

— Did she remember who you were?

— Why should she?

— Well, you had dinner at her house.

— Yes, but I wasn't going to say it. It was already embarrassing enough to ask her about Piquet. Do you know I couldn't even re- member what his first name is?

— Piquet? It's Federico.

— Yes, but I couldn't remember. Here everyone always called him by his last name. I had to ask her whether she was the com- panion of Mr. Piquet . . .

— Who's vanished, if not worse. Did you tell her?

— No, I didn't feel like it . . .

— All right, then it's clear she didn't tell you anything. You were too impersonal.

— She told me they broke up, what else was she supposed to say? What do you mean too impersonal?

— Too impersonal. Maybe she knows things and didn't tell you because you were too impersonal. Maybe she knows where he is. Why don't you call her back and tell her that you're Marco Tardioli, that you've met because you were at dinner at their house, and —

— Listen, I'm not going to call her back. It was already embarrassing enough the first time.

— Okay, okay. Forget I said anything.

— Why don't you call her instead? Besides, I couldn't do it even if I wanted to: she'd realize that I was the same person who had called before, and she'd get suspicious. Even if I don't understand why she'd have anything to hide.

— You're right. I'll call her. Did you find her at Studio Elle?

— Yes. I don't have the number with me now, but it's in the phone book. Let me know how it goes.

— Sure thing.

— So in other words, you're not going to come to the office?

— I wouldn't dream of it.

— Not even tomorrow, when Boesson's coming?

— Especially not tomorrow.

— But aren't you afraid of getting canned?

— If they can me they can me, Marco. Nothing will change if I come or not.

— This is true. Except I don't understand how you can be so calm.

— You're the one saying I'm calm.

— You act like you don't care about anything.

— You know what the Americans say? Keep cool.

— Those are just words.

— Exactly. They don't cost a thing.

— Yes, but you seem — No, forget about it, it's none of my business.

— Stop worrying. So in other words they're signing on Monday?

— On Monday, yes.

— Well, you'll see that everything will get better after that.

— Let's hope so. I'll keep you posted.

— Thanks. And tomorrow say hi to God for me.

— Amen.

chapter thirty-six

I do spinning.

Yolanda's cell phone starts ringing just in time: it forces her to walk a few steps away from me to answer it, and I can regroup, try to better understand what she has just told me — because even a vacuum can be dizzying. *I do spinning.* Okay. A little while ago, while she was walking by with Nebbia during a fleeting winter appearance, I started to talk with her. I don't know why, and I especially don't know why this morning, but I felt the need to break the pattern. I stopped her and practically forced her to engage in conversation. A few words about the cold, a few about the sky that really did look like snow today, then about our dogs — and up to this point nothing new, they're the same things we've always talked about; but then, for the first time, I went further and remarked on her change of habits: before, thirty-minute strolls through the park; now, instead, a single hasty walk just long enough for the dog to take care of its business. I didn't ask her why (the reason is obvious: because it's cold), but bringing it up was enough to prompt her observation that I, on the other hand, had not changed, that I'm still here, even without the dog; and at that point it was as if the distance between us and our unsatisfied curiosity, which had remained constant over the past few months, had been reduced to zero: we were finally authorized to ask each other what we had always wanted to know. She went first: why was I always here, every day, even without Dylan, even in bad weather? I didn't want to delve into whether she already knew the answer, maybe through the neighborhood grapevine; it didn't really matter. I told her the truth, but in two stages: in the first stage by telling her that the company where I work is in upheaval because of the merger and so I prefer to stay here, in front of my daughter's school, waiting for the tensions to simmer down; and then, realizing it really was too little and especially that it didn't explain all those hugs, I added that I got into the habit of staying here rather than, let's say, going home, or going to play tennis, or doing something else, because my little girl — and I pointed to the whole school, in a loaded synecdoche — had lost her mother not long ago. Immediately after, I observed her carefully and saw her imperious beauty soften into a smile that was sad, sympathetic, and yet, maybe precisely because of her beauty, still fairly enigmatic. It's always so hard to imagine what beautiful women are thinking. Did she understand? And if so, *what* did she understand? At that point it became interesting to find out what she would say; and after a short pause, what she said was: "Wow. What a great father." Besides a warm, violent wave of satisfaction, fairly hypocritical per se (would she have said it with the same tone of voice if she had seen me a month ago, in Roccamare, on the grass in the backyard with Eleonora Simoncini, guarding my little girl's sleep in such a manner?), her comment sparked a sudden acceleration in my curiosity. I remembered when Carlo, here in the park, complimented her on her name, and she replied that she hated it; offend thy name, I had thought, and thou will have offended thy father. Maybe Yolanda had problems of her own. So when I asked her, "And what do you do?" I found myself rooting for an answer that would bring her father into play, if such an answer existed. And I also told myself yes, it existed, it existed in spades, because she might have replied, for example, "I work with my father" — a lawyer, let's say, who hires his lovely and listless daughter to work in his office and shows her off, surrounded by leather-bound volumes — part-time, of course, and with a symbolic paycheck that still represents her sole source of income, so as to keep her on a tighter leash than the one she has around Nebbia's neck; but I would never have expected the answer that, with an astounding innocence, Yolanda actually gave me: "I do spinning." I looked at her in shock: she must be about twenty-seven, she's beautiful, obviously rich — she has a dog that costs a bundle — and she does spinning for a living. At that moment her cell phone rang, she stepped away to answer it, and she's still there, about twenty steps away from me, speaking intently into her cell, head bowed, while I'm wondering: maybe she meant to say she *teaches* spinning? She's a former volleyball player? A phys ed major who never got her diploma? Courses at some fitness center owned by a friend? She's certainly got the physique for it. But on the other hand, if I was looking for a critique of her father, what better answer could I expect? It's as if she had said look at me, look at how many opportunities could come my way; beauty, for certain, but also satisfaction, wish fulfillment, social status, jobs, money, love; and instead the only thing I do in life, besides walking my dog and talking on my cell phone, is spinning. And I have a shitty name, and of course I'm stupid, and before long someone will get me pregnant, and even if we get married we'll get separated immediately, and it'll be an awful struggle for me to be a mother, truly awful, and I'll have to go to my parents for help, and everyone will have the confirmation that I'm useless, and guess whose fault all of this is going to be . . .

There, she's put the phone back into her pocket and is walking toward me. In five seconds she'll be here again. What do I say to her now? *I do spinning*: if she had told me she had leukemia, maybe I could have found something to say, but as it is, I can't think of anything. Better to say nothing, then, better to close that door immediately; at any rate, her answer was a full stop, and the interruption to take the phone call was the beginning of a new paragraph. Bye, see you later, and so on. But now she's the one with a shocked expression on her face, and she takes her last few steps in my direction, staring at me with her mouth wide open, as if I was the most surprising thing she had ever laid eyes on; and this is impossible, seeing as I've turned into one of the most predictable sights in this neck of the city. In fact, now that she's reached me, her shocked gaze goes right through me because it's aimed not at me but at something behind me. With a nod of her chin she invites me to turn around, and I do, and what I see makes me gape, too: two big black cars with diplomatic plates have double-parked, one in front of the other, right outside the park. One's a Mercedes 400 CDI, and the other is actually *a Maybach* — until now I've only ever seen them on the Internet, never in real life — so beautiful and immense and shiny that all the other cars suddenly look as if they're out of focus. Two young giants who emerged from the Mercedes are opening the door of the Maybach, from which steps an elderly man, also enormous, who starts walking in our direction.

— Who's that, Marlon Brando? — whispers Yolanda, because at first sight that's exactly what he looks like. But it's Isaac Steiner. I recognize him immediately because he's one of those men you only have to see in a photograph once and you never forget him. Yes, there's no doubt: it's really him, the lame god of our blessed merger. He even has a cane, no less. And obviously, absurdly — here he is — he's come to me.

— Mr. Paladini? — he says in English.

— Yes.

— Steiner. A pleasure to meet you.

He holds out a surprisingly thin and tapered hand, completely disproportionate to his bulky wrestler's build. I shake it, and it's also soft, smooth, which manages to increase my shock.

— My condolences.

— Thank you.

Nebbia starts sniffing at his legs — very aristocratically, I have to say, as if he knew this was the richest and most powerful man he would ever get the chance to sniff. Steiner pretends not to notice.

— Am I interrupting something? — he says, and focuses a very discreet gaze on Yolanda, which is still just enough to send her running.

— Oh, no, — she mumbles, and dashes off, literally, pulling Nebbia behind her. Who knows, for a second there she must have been afraid of getting involved in the introductions and maybe being forced to repeat to Steiner, and in English, to boot, her occupation: *I do spinning . . .*

— I hope I didn't interrupt anything important.

— No, no. Nothing important.

— Will you understand me if I speak English?

— Yes.

He points toward my car with a barely perceptible wave of his cane.

— Is that your car?

— Yes.

— Can we sit inside? — he says. It's actually starting to snow: big flakes, as scattered and heavy as cotton. — I'd like to speak with you.

— By all means.

We get into the car. Steiner plops heavily into the passenger's seat, and the springs squeak beneath his weight. The front seat has suddenly become too narrow, as if my Audi had turned into a Panda. Steiner settles in, arranges his cane between his legs, and gives a noisy sigh, while I feel the strange desire to touch him, since his presence here is totally unreal, larger than life in every sense. Seriously, I might be dreaming. I start up the car to get the heat going, and Radiohead has the same idea, because before I can turn off the stereo, the song manages to find the time to say "Just 'cause you feel it doesn't mean it's there." How true. Things shouldn't only exist, they should also mean something; and what is the meaning of him being here?

— Well . . . — he says.

All of a sudden I understand: Eleonora Simoncini. Of course. They met, she told him God knows what, he got pissed off and came looking to stick it to me. Now he'll say a couple of things and hand me over to his henchmen, who are going to work me over . . .

— A lot of people are saying that this merger is the first failure in my life, — he says, still speaking in English. — But they're wrong.

He doesn't even look me in the face: he looks down at the dirty floor mat. What an idiot I am. *I knew* she was his lover, everyone knows . . .

— First of all, — he continues, — it's not a failure. Not necessarily. The Frenchman only won the first round.

Round . . . The snow has started falling more heavily, and it's covered the windshield. The only defensive move I can think of is to turn on the windshield wiper for a couple of swipes and restore visibility again; but it's only made things worse, because the two arcs of clean glass reveal the goons stationed in front of the car. In their hands, umbrellas look like Barbie doll accessories.

— In fact, he only won the draw to choose his side of the field . . . No matter, even if it winds up a failure in the end, it wouldn't be the first, or the worst.

He looks up, stares at me. Here we go. Maybe he'll punch me out himself, crack my nose with his cane, here in the car. He's a self-made man: he must have done all kinds of shit when he was young . . .

— I came here to tell you about the time I really failed.

Yet he's not threatening me. In his gray eyes there isn't a shadow of rage, and his legendary face expresses no aggression. His voice is quiet, warm, and it even sounds like he's speaking more slowly than usual, articulating his words with a limpid, scholastic pronunciation, to enable me to understand everything. So far, in fact, I haven't missed a word.

— How much do you know about the story of reparations paid to the victims of the Shoah? — he asks. — Are you aware of how it ended up?

On the other hand, what do I know about how he usually talks?

— To my knowledge, Switzerland had to fork over a huge sum of money, — I say.

Steiner goes back to looking at the floor mat.

— 1.25 billion dollars. Not Switzerland: the Swiss banks — there's a difference. And since I am well known for having dedicated my life to this lawsuit, when the banks agreed to pay such a large sum I was considered one of the protagonists of the victory. But the opposite is true. I was the loser.

He shakes his head gently, still looking down. No, he doesn't seem to be mad at me, he almost ignores me — which, rather than calming things down, only makes his appearance more mysterious.

— You see, — he continues, — I'm Canadian, not American. My parents immigrated to Toronto, and I was born there. I'm a Canadian Jew. In business I learned not to make too much of the distinction, but when it comes to matters of conscience it's absolutely crucial: because the Canadians have a conscience, and the Americans don't. And it's this conscience I have that led me to failure . . .

While he's saying this last sentence he raises his eyes to me again, and his face is brimming with a radiant pride that remains luminous even during the silence that follows. Now he looks like an enormous boy who has aged, and Yolanda saw right, he really does look like Marlon Brando: the same uncombed white mop, the same inhuman combination of animal magnetism and bodily mass. The snow has covered the windshield again, but I no longer feel the need to remove it: I might be wrong, but I'm no longer afraid of being inside the car with him.

— Eight years ago, — he goes on, — when the American undersecretary Stuart Eizenstat published the report that bears his name, all he did was to certify facts that had long been known: the Swiss banks continued to hold on to gold and funds derived from Nazi plundering of German Jews, and the report nailed this down definitively. But at the moment in which 1.25 billion dollars was set as the amount of the restitution to be paid to the heirs of the victims, I smelled something rotten: this was an outlandish amount, more than double the largest estimates that had been calculated up until that moment, and I realized that a big chunk of that money would end up in the pockets of people who had nothing to do with the Shoah.

Now, if anything, there was a slight vibrato of anger. But not toward me, that much seemed clear.

— On the other hand, until Germany's declaration of war prevented it, trade in gold of questionable provenance was official United States policy, as attested to by countless other reports before and after Eizenstat. The size of that request, therefore, gave off the appearance of also shifting American responsibilities onto the shoulders of the Swiss banks. Which, for their part, had done a historical audit from which it resulted that the value of accounts in Swiss banks that had lain dormant since the end of the Second World War and were traceable to victims of the Ho-

locaust amounted to a total of 10 million dollars; therefore that
was the sum they were making available. Do you see? Ten million as opposed to 1.25 billion. On the one hand, the banks' offer
de facto denied that tens of thousands of German Jews had been
robbed in addition to being exterminated, while on the other, the
Americans' demands were a kind of tribal war cry for the specula-
tors, besides being a *final solution* of their relationship to the disappearance of the Jewish gold. We had worked forty years, and for
what? Restitution for the victims? No. To wage another war, to
assert once again the law of the jungle; and however tough the
Swiss may have acted — and they were tough — this time we
were the stronger ones: on our side we had the government of
the United States, the Israeli government, the Jewish associations,
multinationals, magnates, diplomats, historians, movie stars, not
to mention the press throughout the free world. In the event that
the Eizenstat report was not accepted, a plan was already in place
for a total boycott: not only of their banks but also of every single
Swiss product — chocolate, milk, watches, everything they make
in Switzerland.

He picks his nose. Quickly and with a certain elegance, owing
mainly to a hand with a diamond cutter's grace, but he is still
picking his nose. Then he disguises the gesture by rubbing his
chin with the back of his hand and acting vague, but between his
thumb and his index finger he's holding something. I'm curious
to see where he's going to stick it . . .

— But not everyone agreed. I wasn't the only one to think the
settlement was really a form of blackmail, ignoring the reason for
all our efforts — to pay reparations to the victims of the Shoah.
I could give you the names of Jews who think the way I do, but
they probably won't admit it, although they're very influential —
Israelis, Canadians, Europeans. We were a minority, of course, but
a minority that could not be ignored.

There: on the side of the seat. A classic.

— So I decided to put my own reputation on the line. It was up to me. I was able to convince the Israeli government that with the Eizenstat report we risked endless legal wrangling, and I got it to give me a mandate. To negotiate.

He picks his nose again. No, this time he's just scratching.

— The decision was made that if I managed to get 400 million, the whole affair would be concluded right then and there: forty times as much as what was being offered and only a third of what we were asking. It was tough but feasible. I had a certain influence in Switzerland, since my group's transactions went through many of its banks. Plus I was a close friend of a gentleman who is, sadly, no longer with us, Enrico Simoncini, with whose daughter, I am told, you are acquainted . . .

Here we go. He looks up and pierces me with a sidelong stare, terrifying. I was just starting to relax and had even begun to fool myself into thinking that he had appeared for no reason, *a miracle,* like an apparition of the Madonna; but, in fact, this is the reason, and I suppose it's the most I could have expected. His beady eyes bore right through me, and suddenly I can't move, I'm weak, slow, heavy, as though it were his turn to use the Sakai mode. How much does he know? What does he want *to do to me*?

— Besides being a big player in the confectionary industry — he looks down again — Enrico enjoyed a certain clout with some members of the Swiss federal government, who could put pressure on the bankers . . . In short, it was a big gamble but not a desperate one. Not nearly as bad as the situation of the Swiss if they refused to accept my mediation.

I turn on the windshield wipers for another swipe, and the gorillas are still there, dark, motionless, standing beneath the snow; but without their eyes on me I feel free to defend and to explain myself, if necessary.

— I spent months setting up the playing field. The hardest thing was making the Swiss see me — me, Isaac Steiner, *the Jewish Jaws* — for what I actually was in that case, namely, a righteous man. And the difficulties got worse when my friend died in such a bizarre way. Do you know how Enrico died?

No sidelong glances this time. No Sakai mode. It's a question, pure and simple.

— No.

— Decapitated by a Ping-Pong table that flew out of a truck in front of his car on the highway.

He stops speaking, allowing this additional absurdity to sink in. I'm going to be seeing that Ping-Pong table in my dreams; I'm definitely going to be seeing it.

— In short, it was very difficult, — he continues, — but, I repeat, it was in the realm of the possible. And so one day seven years ago I landed in Zurich at eight o'clock in the morning. I didn't sleep a wink on the trip over. I stared out at the black ocean and the stars. I felt invulnerable because I was doing something righteous. I was working for others. For the dead. And when I found myself before the Swiss I gave the most important speech of my life. I didn't even touch on the risk they were running if the talks broke down and the financial embargo that would result in numbers three times as high as their country's budget. It was probably the most convincing argument I had, but I didn't use it: I wasn't there to blackmail them. I made it clear that I didn't share the ultra-aggressive stance of the Americans, which is why my mission should be considered a true mediation; and that anyone that came after me would be much worse. I gave them the figures and I focused on the main idea, namely that for rich Jews the Holocaust had been a Holocaust twice over, because it had annihilated both their people *and* their possessions. It was a speech that would have been difficult to deliver in any other forum, since it might have

sounded cynical, but before the greediest money managers in the
world I was able to do it: in the Shoah, poor Jews lost their lives
and their loved ones, but the rich lost their lives, their loved ones,
and their wealth. They suffered an additional defeat, and it was
our duty to pay them restitution at least for that. It was the only
remaining possibility for setting the world right . . .

Pause. Although I can see only his profile, since he's luckily
still staring relentlessly at the floor mat, he seems to be becoming
more absorbed in his thoughts, more reminiscent.

— It was the most important speech of my life, the best, the
most inspired, and when I concluded, I even got the impression
that I had convinced them. I don't know why. I hardly expected
them to tear off a check and place it in my hand, but I did believe
I had given them the nudge they needed to be convinced to add
at least one more zero to their offer. And I said *to be convinced,* not *to
be forced.* Anyway, it was their only possible salvation: give in, yes,
but not to the blackmail that would come after me but rather to
the greater good, while at the same time saving themselves 850
million dollars. It was not hard to understand, and I thought that
they had.

I turn on the windshield wipers again — it's the only action I
can still perform — and this time he raises his eyes and looks at
the snowstorm that is surely electrifying Claudia and all the other
children at the school; he seems astounded, as if he were seeing it
only now.

— Let me tell you, — he says, — if someone were to propose that I live my life over again, I would refuse, I would say no,
just to avoid having to relive the five minutes that followed that
speech . . .

So it wasn't astonishment, it was pain. And he wasn't seeing the
snowstorm: in that white whirl moving in time to the windshield
wiper, he sees what he is about to tell me, so intensely that it's as

if he were projecting it, and in fact I can see it, too: curtains shut tight, an enormous rosewood table, leather chairs, plants, unused plasma TVs, four or five middle-aged bears in dark suits, and there he is in front of them, wearing a linen suit and the same adolescent pride on his face that I'd seen a little while ago — huge, immensely rich and powerful, yet never so exposed, so vulnerable, so defenseless . . .

— One of them, I don't think he was even the president, took the floor and complimented me on my speech, telling me how deep the personal esteem for me was among all his colleagues, and he dwelt in particular on my moral qualities, after which he said, however, that their offer of 10 million dollars was final and nonnegotiable, because it was the result of their fucking historical audit.

He turns and looks at me.

— Do you see? They didn't give me a thing. I didn't make a red cent off the biggest deal in my whole life. Ten million it was, and 10 million it remained. The airplane waiting for me on the runway had already cost me 7 million. Shitheads.

Look, he's really suffering; just like all the others who have come here, he, too, has ended up unleashing an amazing wave of sadness before me. This spot is truly miraculous: a wailing wall without a wall. Milan is a holy city, and no one knows it . . .

— Once I got back to New York I immediately tendered my resignation to the World Jewish Congress, but the same American friends who had assisted me in my attempt begged me to withdraw my resignation and I did. By then I was putty in their hands. They also begged me not to handle this matter anymore, not to take any initiatives related to it, and not to speak with anyone. In exchange they would maintain the strictest silence about my failure, and they did, they did it so well that from that moment on my attempted mediation was understood *to never have happened* . . .

He goes back to staring at me.

— So if tomorrow you, for example, were to decide to sell this story to a newspaper, I could sue you and the newspaper, and I would win, and I would take possession of both the newspaper and you.

This is obviously a threat, and a pretty obnoxious one, but this time he doesn't scare me. First, because I'm not the kind of guy who sells stories to newspapers; second, because for him, after a lifetime of abundance, it's a knee-jerk reaction — a kind of decompression that will let him go back to being *the Jaws;* maybe if he'd left without saying it, he would have risked an embolism.

— A year after the attempt that never took place, the banks gave in to the Eizenstat mediation and agreed to pay the sum of 1.25 billion dollars. A big New York law firm was placed in charge of the payout, and in the past six years it has distributed to the account holders 125 million dollars. Approximately 200 million went to other Jewish survivors. 145 million went to the Jewish organizations and the lawyers. In all, to date, 473 million dollars — in other words, after the legal fees, the same figure for which I had fought. But it's less than half the amount that was actually disbursed: the rest of the money still hasn't been distributed, and no one knows where it will end up.

He takes a deep breath.

— That's the whole story, — he says.

And he sits there, motionless, watching the end credits rolling down my car windshield. Then he turns to me, says, "So long," shakes my hand, opens the door, and begins the laborious operation of hoisting himself out of the car; it is only now, seeing how he struggles, that I realize the truly immense consideration he had shown to me, lowering himself into this tub rather than ordering me to join him in the Maybach. There, he made it, he's outside. A gorilla immediately shelters him with an umbrella, but it's impossible to shield a body like his with only one umbrella: another one has to step in — and in this manner, escorted by two gorillas and protected by two umbrellas, Steiner limps to his car, leaning on his cane far more than before. The Maybach swallows him up as if he were a boy — the world is back in scale — and when the door of that wonder car closes again, it makes one of the most beautiful sounds I've ever heard.

Why did he come here? Why did he tell me that story? Was he really Eleonora Simoncini's lover? Is he still? What does he know about her and me?

The cars take off, leaving behind two black rectangles that are as neat and precise as votive symbols. The one left by the Maybach is enormous, and its very enormity is the proof that a god has just visited; but the snow is already erasing it, and I, enchanted by the scene's perfection, am unable to do anything but watch it disappear, watch it disappear, watch it disappear . . .

The phone rings. It's Annalisa.

— Hello?

— Dottore, — her voice is electric, excited, — you won't believe who's on his way to see you!

But at this point it's easy: what does it take?

— Boesson, — she says. Mystery begets mystery.

chapter thirty-seven

*In the dark wilds of Illinois, among the tall grass and across the ancient deer trails, drift the howls of wolves. Ancient predators huddle in the dark night seeking prey and being sought by their own hunters. It is not the glittering lights of Chicago but is instead something primeval, something that has existed with little change for thousands of years. A hunt that is always on. A hunt where at any time hunter can become hunted. Nestled in the center of this **quiet chaos** is the town of Tuscola. Here dwell dark beings who struggle to survive the ancient battle.*

You know those things you begin with the certainty that any minute you're going to be interrupted? And then you're not? And so you soldier on, and it starts to get interesting? Well that's what happened to me.

I have just verified that there are 2,180 sites on the Internet that mention quiet chaos. I tried to open some of them, but they were too big and my cell phone couldn't handle them. The only one I was able to open is this one, and now I have a definition of quiet chaos: a hunt that is always on, a hunt where at any time the hunter can become the hunted. What does this have to do with my life? It would be interesting to think about it. But first it would be interesting to think about how I got here.

Boesson is supposed to come, right? So to kill some time while waiting for his arrival, I got the urge to do something, just for fun: I connected to the Internet with my cell phone, went to Google, and typed in ISAAC STEINER: 54,800 results popped up. Then I typed PATRICK BOESSON, and there were 53,600 results. True, I thought: for what it matters, these two divinities who will merge their empires in three days have almost the same importance on the Web. *Almost:* and for the one who'll be coming out on the bottom that difference should not be underestimated. If Boesson had shown up at that point, it would have simply been a positive thought I could keep in mind while shaking his hand. But he didn't come, so I continued my interrogation of Google. I typed JEAN-CLAUDE SANCHEZ, and the results dropped to 317; this was also true: Jean-Claude had always preferred to stay out of the limelight. THIERRY LARIVIÈRE, and we went back up to 19,600. PIETRO PALADINI: 111. Perfect. An improvement on the thought I had to keep in mind while shaking Boesson's hand. But there was still no sign of Boesson, so I kept on Googling. It turned into a kind of game, and in fact I started to copy the results in a notebook. CARLO PALADINI: 185,000. BARRIE: 4,470,000. GIORGIO ARMANI: 1,050,000. FEDERICO PIQUET: 113 (two more than

me, grrrr!). PAOLO ENOCH: 9. ELEONORA SIMONCINI: 207. ENRICO SIM-
ONCINI: 493. MARTA SICILIANO (my sister-in-law): 101. LARA SICILIANO
(my wife): 0. RADIOHEAD: 571,000. ELTON JOHN: 2,160,000. SILVIO BER-
LUSCONI: 571,000 (the same as Radiohead). COCA-COLA: 9,240,000.
PEPSI-COLA: 1,110,000. MAFIA: 4,280,000. BILL GATES: 7,100,000. WIL-
LIAM GATES: 51,100. BIL GATES: 5,770. BILL GATHES: 92. BRILL GATES: 142.
BILL GRATES: 242. BILL GAITES: 159. BILL GATSE: 450. BILL GGATES: 24. BILL
GSATE: "TRY BILL GATES." GEORGE BUSH: 7,510,000. GEORGE W.: 415. BUSH:
15,900,000. BIN LADEN: 5,290,000. SADDAM HUSSEIN: 17,000,000. DEVIL:
30,400,000. GOD: 63,900,000. DEATH: 115,000,000. SEX: 183,000,000 . . .

It was at this point that I came up with the idea of typing QUIET
CHAOS — and a whole new stage of the game began; 2,180 results
was the last thing I expected. I had thought I was the one to invent quiet chaos, do you see? I thought *it didn't exist*. I was expecting to find something, because I know that in this world you can
never really invent anything: but finding 2,180 sites that use the
expression really amazed me. I tried in Italian and Spanish: 8. In
French: 9. In English: 2,180. So it's something Anglo-Saxon, probably American. And I got the urge to open those sites, to see what
they had to say about quiet chaos — and above all, to see *what it is*.
But my cell phone couldn't open almost any of the sites, because
they were always too big. The only one I did manage to open is this
one, called "Tuscola: Buried Destinies." There must be an illustra-
tion, a graphic of some kind that my display can't show, and then
this short text: dark beings, primeval creatures, ancient battles;
hunters becoming hunted; and, *nestled in the center of this quiet chaos*
— meaning that quiet chaos must be the summary of all these
things — a town in Illinois. Then there's the icon to click to enter
the site, but no way, my cell phone can't handle it, when they sell
it to you they say you can surf the Internet but then you find out
that everything is always too —

Here he is. Boesson. He's arrived. On foot. Alone. He's coming

up the side road, he's *rising* — in the sense that every step he takes
reveals another part of his body. He looks like a boy. He's walking at a swift pace, unafraid of slipping on the snow-covered sidewalk. It's stopped snowing, but the storm has turned everything
white, and the cars struggle up the hill leading to the school. Not
Boesson: he walks quickly, as if the snow were grass. He's dressed
in black, with a tight overcoat that comes down to his knees. He
sees me and actually waves from the distance. We've met only
once, at the Cannes Film Festival, last May, during a dinner with
four hundred guests: one of the thousands of hands he shook half-
heartedly at one of the dozens of fancy occasions he had halfheart-
edly attended, because I hear he is phobic; how did he recognize
me? I wave to him, too, and we meet in front of the park.

— Hello, — he says, smiling, and extends his hand. He's surprisingly young for a god.

— Hello.

His handshake is loose, friendly. He's smiling, relaxed. Smooth,
pale, unwrinkled skin. Jet-black hair.

— How's it going, Pietro?

He calls me by my first name. I'll have to do the same. Who
knows how it sounds.

— Fine, and you, Patrick?

Smooth, natural.

— I had a nice walk, — he says. — When it snows I can't resist
it, I have to go out for a walk. Ever since I was a child.

His perfect, accent-free Italian is striking. Not even a French *r*.
Usually only spies learn languages so perfectly.

— So this is where you spend your days.

His shoes are drenched. One of his laces is untied.

— Yes.

He looks up at the snow-covered trees, embracing them with a
gaze that radiates approval.

— You're doing the right thing. I would do the same thing in your place. Even in *my* place, but the only problem is that I have four children and they go to three different schools. So I wouldn't be able to. I could take turns waiting in front of all three, but it wouldn't be the same.

And he smiles, encircled by the steam of his breath. What a situation: there was only one man in the world who counted more than the guy here two hours ago, and now he's here, too, and he's talking to me about his children like someone I went to university with, and I'm not even surprised. I couldn't have made all this happen if I tried.

— Do you know Steiner well? — he asks me abruptly. — Is he a friend of yours?

Oh no. That's why he came. But of course: *he knows*. What a disappointment. It's not true that mystery begets mystery, it's just romantic nonsense. Mystery begets logical consequences, like everything else.

— Never seen him before.

— Seriously? So what did he come here for? — Still smiling. No threat, no authority. He really seems curious: young, relaxed, and curious.

— He came to tell me a story.

Now he's going to want me to tell it, goddamn it. And I'll have to decide whether or not to please him, because his courtesy tells me that I have to do it not out of necessity but out of choice; and it's definitely an important choice, because there's a big difference between telling and not telling — but the fact of the matter is that I have no idea what's at stake, nor a single criterion for my decision.

— A story? What story?

— A very private story, — I answer, — but what I can tell you is that it has nothing to do with the merger.

— Uhm, — he murmurs, curious. Not a word. He seems to be

thinking. I look around, puzzled, as if I were asking this place to tell me what to do. Help me, place! But it's deserted, all the snow has erased any human presence. Wait, one second: an employee of the travel agency comes out of the bar with espresso in little paper cups. So this must be when Matteo and his mother leave therapy — that is, if they've come today. What day is it? Friday. So they were supposed to come. I didn't see them arrive, but I was inside the car with Steiner two hours ago, and it was snowing heavily — so let's do this: if they come out, even in the snow, with the buses paralyzed and the subway packed with people, then in a little while they'll be leaving by the main door, and I won't tell Boesson a thing. If, however, they don't come out, because the mother saw the weather and decided to stay home, despite recommendations not to skip any sessions, especially now that she's cut them in half, if, in other words, the woman gave up today, then I'll give up, too, and I'll tell Boesson what Steiner told me. At least it's a criterion.

— And you'd never seen him before, — says Boesson, and he smiles again.

— No.

His immobility is impressive: stock-still like a cypress. Not just his body: his head, his legs, his arms, his hands: everything is motionless. Right now, for example, he moved his eyes, he lowered them for a moment and then raised them again, but they're the only thing he moved. I don't think he can stand still like that spontaneously, not with this cold. It's control.

The door of the building where the physical therapy studio is located is closed.

— You know, — he says, — in *The Wealth of Nations* Adam Smith claims that capitalists rarely meet with each other, even "for merriment and diversion," and that their conversation still always ends up in a conspiracy.

— But I'm not a capitalist, — I say.

— Of course not. — Boesson nods, he seems amused. — Nevertheless . . .

He removes a piece of paper from his pocket and reads.

— From 10:22 to 10:46, — he raises his eyes again, smiles, — one of the biggest capitalists in the world was inside your car with you. And he told you a story. Without ever having seen you before. — He nods. — Strange, don't you think?

— Yes, it's strange.

But no, it isn't strange. Steiner came here to suffer, like everyone else, because this place attracts suffering. End of story. The main door is still closed.

— Oh, of course you weren't the person being watched, — says Boesson, and he puts the piece of paper back in his pocket.

God is patient, said Enoch: How patient is he? How long can he drag this out? How long until he can say that Matteo and his mother didn't come?

— Does this mean that right now he's watching you? — I ask.

Boesson laughs, but he looks around — first to the right, then to the left.

— Could be, — he says. — Who knows . . .

He bows his head and stays that way, eyes lowered, in a pose that would be very sensual if he were a woman. Of course, what a difference between him and Steiner: one parading his greatness, the other one hiding it. *His head bowed before me . . .*

— You know, Pietro, — he says, and looks at me, — I'm like Lieutenant Columbo: when people do something strange my head is filled with questions and I can't get rid of them until I find an answer. And now the question in my head is this: Why did Steiner come here to tell you a story?

They're here. The first to come out is the mother: she looks at the sky, realizes it's stopped snowing, then lets Matteo out, all bundled up. Now let's see if you've got balls, Pietro Paladini . . .

— I have no idea, — I say.

Matteo is wearing two fantastic red snow boots that stand out from the white snow like blood. The mother is holding a big black umbrella in her hand. They start walking toward us and cross the street.

— Maybe if you told me the story we could understand.

Once they've reached the sidewalk, the mother holds the umbrella by the tip and Matteo grabs on to the handle, as if it were the hook of a ski lift, skidding over the snowy sidewalk in his boots. From the ease with which everything is done, with no preliminaries, no discussion, it seems like the enactment of a specific agreement: "Please, Matteo, if you come I'll let you do the ski lift."

Now the mother is walking backward, dragging Matteo along with her umbrella. And Matteo is good at sliding without losing his balance, in an awkward but stable position, scooting down with his rear end and leaning forward with his shoulders to compensate. Now he sees my car, parked in the usual place — halfway down the street, between us and them. I put my hand in my pocket and press the remote.

Beep.

— Maybe you're right, — says Boesson, — but in the meantime you could still tell me.

Matteo absorbs the greeting but doesn't risk returning it with his hand, like he usually does, because what he's doing now is taking all his effort. Now Boesson is looking at him, too: rather than get pissed off he looks at the child with genuine interest, and he keeps looking at him for a while before turning back to me, smiling. Except that now I know what I have to do, and with his Franciscan humility he ends up making it easier for me.

— I'd rather not, — I say.

Boesson doesn't bat an eye, as if for him it was normal to hear a

refusal from the subordinate of a subordinate of a subordinate —
and he doesn't even stop smiling.

— Why not? — is all he says, in the most serene way.

Yes, why not. Because this woman who is waving back to me is
heroic, that's why not: she came out this morning, too, despite the
snow, to take her son to a physical therapy session that will never
make him like other children but that is good for him anyway,
and now she's dragging him behind her, slowly, *literally,* not like a
burden but like a human being who with a little bit of hard work,
and patience, and extra attention, can have even more fun than
everyone else. That's why I won't tell you. For that matter, this
thing you want, a logical explanation, it doesn't exist.

— Hi, Matteo, — I say, while the boy slides past me.

— Hi, — he answers in his nasal voice. He's as happy as a clam.
Boesson must only now be realizing that the boy has Down syndrome, because his smile becomes brighter, astonished.

— You guys are the greatest, — I say, and Matteo closes his eyes
the same way Dylan does when I stroke his throat. The woman
shoots me a glance brimming with gratitude for including her
in my compliment, and so, still walking backward, with her son
sliding in the snow holding on to the umbrella handle, she walks
toward the side road accompanied by our smiles: as Marta's theory would have it, her batteries have just been recharged. Except
that now the incline of the street is steeper, and you can see that
she doesn't trust it, and she stops, decreeing an end to the ski lift
game. Matteo doesn't protest: he lets go of the umbrella handle
and, holding his mother's hand, as always, he disappears step by
step behind the hump that the road makes as it descends toward
the side road, the same way that Boesson rose up from it a little
while ago. Boesson, who has started looking at me again, mild,
conciliatory, motionless, *normal.*

— Listen, Pietro, — he says. — Why don't you want to tell me?

And he keeps smiling. He really seems like an exquisite person, well mannered and humble. If Claudia were to look out the window now, she would see me with a friend of mine. But Jean-Claude says he's a paranoid megalomaniac, and I believe him. I can't let myself be fooled by what I see: this man is not what he seems. He's not humble, he's arrogant. He's one of those individuals who believe that everything that happens has to do with them — like Piquet, except that Piquet is a nobody who mistakes a CD drive for a cup holder, while Boesson is a tycoon who wants to conquer the world.

— Because it has nothing to do with the merger, I told you. It has nothing to do with anything. It was just a meaningless secret.

He thinks he's omnipotent, yet he will never know what he wants to know, the reason Steiner was here. And since it would seem that I've got the balls not to tell him, he'll never even know why I won't tell him. Hah. It would appear he has gotten too small. Eh, the trappings of power help, do they ever: the big cars, the luxury, the drivers, the bodyguards, the snarly character — they help. It's no accident that now, while he's silent, he's probably reflecting on the fact that it's too late to order me to do what he has so far limited himself to requesting kindly, that I'm thinking the same thing I thought about Steiner, word for word, but that I wasn't thinking when I was in front of him: I'm thinking that with all his power he himself doesn't know the reason why he himself is here. If Lara weren't dead, I'm thinking, he wouldn't be here. If she hadn't died while I was rescuing Eleonora Simoncini, he wouldn't be here. If the first morning I hadn't joked to Claudia that I would wait outside for her until school was out, and if I hadn't decided then to really do it, and if the day after I hadn't decided to tell her the same thing again and then to do it, and if in doing it I hadn't felt so good, then he wouldn't be here right now. And he wouldn't be here even if six years ago we

had enrolled Claudia in the private school where she had gone
to preschool and where she would have been enrolled today if
Lara's parents hadn't both died, in the space of six months, of the
same rare form of glandular cancer — since they, relentless sup-
porters of private schooling, had paid the tuition as a gift to their
beloved grandchild, and it would have been impossible to enroll
her in a public school without upsetting them. And if, even after
Lara's parents had died, we had enrolled her in the other public
school we liked, Rossari-Castiglioni, which was more convenient
because it was closer to home, and because Marta had enrolled
little Giovanni there, but, apparently, according to hearsay we've
gathered in bits and pieces and never really double-checked, is
much more disorganized than where she goes now, which is why
we were undecided until the last minute; and if in the end Lara
hadn't told me to make the decision, and to make my decision
I did something that I never told her about, namely I went to
Annalisa, my secretary, and asked her, without any explanation,
"Which of these names do you like better, Cernuschi or Rossari-
Castiglioni?" and if that morning Annalisa, without the least idea
of what I was talking about, hadn't answered, "Cernuschi," with
her usual bewildered expression, *he would not be here right now* . . .

     — Listen, Pietro, — he resumes, without losing a thread of pa-
tience, — I understand your discretion, and I appreciate it, even.
But let me explain my point of view. On Monday Steiner and I
have to formalize the biggest merger in the world — because
that's what we're talking about: the biggest merger in the world.
The negotiations lasted nine months, and in the end the agreement provided that I would be president and he would be vice
president. Now look at me, please, look at me . . .

     He raises his arms and does a full turn, voluptuously, glorying
in the humility he thinks he's fooling me with but that is actually
fooling him.

— Can't you see that I'm not like him? Can't you see that I'm the same as you? *Infatto,* I could be you.

There it is, a Gallicism — *infatto* rather than *infatti* — an imperfection like that could cost a spy his skin.

— What did your father do for a living? — he asks.

— He was a lawyer.

— Really? Don't you see? My father was a lawyer, too. We're equals. And starting Monday, I, I mean you, will be one rung above Steiner. He's the *Jewish Shark,* Pietro, and that's what he was when you and I were kids. He's the master race. He's never been the number two of anything: never, in his whole life. But this time he wasn't tough enough to stay on top, and he had to agree to be on the bottom.

He pauses, which allows me to notice something: Steiner's name has gone the way of Spielberg's movie, from *Jaws,* in English, to *Lo Squalo* — *The Shark* — in Italian; now Boesson is using the same name I would, the *Jewish Shark.* I don't think it's an accident. I think it derives from the fact that Steiner didn't just see the movie, like the rest of us: *he produced it.*

— Look, — he goes on, — I don't know about you, but I was born in a town of 13,000 inhabitants. A tiny city where everyone knew everyone else. And when my father took me to the Bastille Day festival, I saw the mayor onstage, and I thought he must be the person with the most worries in the world. I thought he must have had a minimum of 13,000 worries, one for each of us. Coming back to the present, our merger affects about 210,000 employees, and for them I will be like that mayor. Starting on Monday, everyone, from the lowest errand boy at our Bangalore office on up, will have the right to become one of my worries. I'll have to worry that everyone feels invested in the energy generated by the merger and that they're optimistic, that they hope to improve their condition. I'll have to worry that they work and produce,

but also that they're aiming for a specific personal goal. And I will,
I'll be a good mayor.

He stops speaking, smiles. What's he trying to tell me? *I know
all these things*, dammit, I've heard them all before: I'm a good boss,
you've got to trust me, I have a lot of energy, understanding, if my
dog gets hit by a car it's my fault . . . Is this how he cast a spell on
an old devil like Thierry? Is that how he convinced him to sell his
soul, with this rhetoric about the good provincial mayor?

— And in this way every employee will generate pressure on
his immediate superiors, you see? He'll push them with a force
that they will absorb and emit, in turn, to their respective superiors, and so on, from one level to the next, from one company
in the group to another, all the way to the top. Everyone will be
filled with this flow of positive energy, even you: someone below
you will hope to get your job, while you'll be hoping to get the
job of the guy above you. The things I'm talking about are very
simple, Pietro, very human: testing yourself with important tasks,
buying a nicer car, moving to a bigger house or a fancier neighborhood . . . Now try to imagine the pressure that will be generated:
try to imagine this accumulation of 210,000 individual aspirations
in a single collective tension, from the rank and file on upward;
this is something I know how to produce.

But of course, that's how he convinced Thierry. What people
say doesn't matter, what matters is who says it. And this is how
he'll convince us, too, we the mercenary managers, at the conven-
tion that will be organized in a couple of months in Biarritz, or in
Palma de Mallorca. We'll arrive there gloomy, pessimistic, wracked
by doubts about our future that has suddenly become uncertain,
and in the instant luxury that five-star hotels know how to deliver
he'll transfix us like thrushes with loud demagoguery about the
healthy capitalism of days gone by, which in his speech will sound
as sweet and inviting as an orchard. And we won't be able to help

but believe him, of course, because with our own eyes we'll see that he himself believes it, that Steiner and Thierry believe it, and the only one who doesn't believe it has turned out to be an embezzler and a thief. But there's one thing I don't get: How does he think he can convince me, here and now? And above all, convince me of what?

— Except that in this grand scheme, I'll be the only one who can't emit anything to a person above me, because above me there will be no one. While Steiner will be below me, and he has never been below anyone; and Steiner, like everyone else, will be able to exploit the great collective pressure that will bear up on him to try to improve his own position: namely, to take *my* position.

So this is what he was driving at. He's afraid. Of course he is: he, too, must have seen that Steiner's name appears on the Web more often than his; he, too, must have felt the formidable awe that Steiner commands simply by showing up — an awe that only those stupid Swiss bankers ever resisted, for which they were punished by fire and brimstone. To make a long story short, he, too, came here to suffer: welcome, Boesson, to the land of sorrow.

— Now do you understand why anything that Steiner says or does is important? Especially if it's strange?

Of course, the same thing was said on the site I opened a little while ago: the hunt is always on, the hunter becomes the hunted; and nestled in the center of this quiet chaos is a little man dressed in black who can't get someone to tell him a story that means nothing.

He has lowered himself too much, that's the point.

— Yes, I do, — I say, — but what Steiner told me has no pertinence to this business. What if he only came by to pull a jealous scene on me?

— This is no laughing matter, — Boesson sneers, suddenly

turning in the other direction. It's the first gesture of impatience
he has made in a situation where a guy like Steiner would already
have mowed me down with his Maybach. And to think the idea of
a jealous scene is not even as absurd as he believes.

— I was just giving you an example, — I insist. — I understand
your doubts, but let me assure you that Steiner's reason for coming here is a mystery. A mystery, believe me. Mysteries can happen, and we have to accept them.

Boesson's smile creases with sarcasm.

— Of course, the mysteries: the Immaculate Conception, the
Holy Trinity; and Steiner coming here to tell you a story . . .

Enoch! That happened a month ago, in this very place: he told
me to tell the big bosses his beautiful idea! And Boesson is the top
dog . . .

— By the way, — I say. — Do you mind if I change the subject
and tell you something about the merger?

— Of course.

— Something true? As if I were a friend?

— You *are* my friend, Pietro. The friends of my friends are my
friends.

This is getting hairy, really hairy.

— Because you were right, — I say. — It's true: starting on
Monday everything will be dumped on your shoulders, and you
won't be able to dump anything. And Steiner won't settle for
being vice president, it's logical, and he'll try to do you in. But all
of this is provided for by your structure for the merger; and if you
don't mind my saying so, that's what's wrong with it.

How was it that Enoch put it? He didn't say *structure*, he used
another term . . .

— What do you mean, wrong?

Model, he said *model*.

— It's a question of the model. Of the model you adopted.

— There's not so many models to choose from for a merger like this.

— It's not a choice among many but between two. I'm talking about models of power. Of power hierarchy.

— It's the most advantageous model, Pietro.

— It might be the most advantageous in theory, I don't question it; but when they talk about you and Steiner, as people, then it no longer is. You've just finished proving it.

I surprised him. I always surprise people when I turn their arguments against them.

— You're religious, like they say, aren't you?

— I don't know what they say, but I am religious.

— You go to mass every morning, they say. You pray. You spend your vacations in monasteries praying.

— Yes, it's true.

— So I'm sure you'll understand what I'm about to tell you. Because you see, Steiner is also attached to his religion, starting with his last name; of course he's not observant — hardly. But he is perceived as a Jew to the same extent that you are perceived as a Catholic. Am I right?

— Yes.

— So try to imagine if instead of merging your two groups you were merging your religions. Even then, despite every effort to do things equitably, in the end one would be on the top and the other would be on the bottom. It would be inevitable. Jesus would be either in or out, right? Well, if Judaism and Christianity were to merge like we're merging with Steiner, it would be the end of Jesus. That model, the model that you chose for the merger, is missing Jesus.

He's shaken. He keeps smiling, but his smile seems plastered on his face in horror.

— Because it's the Jewish model, Patrick. — *Patrick:* I called him by his name. — I'm no expert, but one thing I do know: the one all-seeing, all-knowing God in a vertical relationship to his people is the Jewish God. He's inflexible, heavy-handed, completely lacking in the amortization measures perfected by Christianity, which by no coincidence is much more recent, more modern . . .

It's all coming out so wooden: oh, where is Enoch's graceful touch? His lightness?

— The God of the Jews is alone, — I continue, — like you will be starting on Monday. But he is God, let us not forget, and he can manage just fine on his own. But you are a human being, and no human being can bear the pressure that was meant for God. So what you said is true, and starting Monday your life will be a living hell: a constant, gnawing suspicion that in dealing with any of Steiner's actions you should have been more prudent, more astute, more farsighted, more alert . . .

At the same time Boesson seems very taken by my words. He listens carefully, almost worried, his smile has become a shadow of its former self — little more than a memory.

— But now try to think what the merger would be like with a Christian model.

He tries, hah, he struggles, but he still *doesn't see*. He looks like a monkey staring, cross-eyed, at the mystery of human evolution . . .

— You said it a little while ago: *the Holy Trinity* . . .

And here a triangle should be drawn in the air, slowly, marking the vertices carefully, like Enoch did, and at more or less the same spot where Enoch did, for that matter, because we were right here, in front of the park. Enoch, who, as we speak, is loading tanker trucks in Africa.

— Father, Son, and Holy Ghost, — and this has to be pronounced with solemnity, with the luminous gaze that accompanies true revelations. — Not a single vertex, and not even two, but *three*. Because together with Jesus came this boisterous invention of a third deity that we Christians have all to ourselves: neutral, abstract, powerless, which stays in its place, uninfluential yet necessary, to safeguard the relationship between the other two. And since we all know the destiny of the Son . . .

Here a pause should be taken to mimic the crucifixion, spreading the arms and leaning the head to one side — like this. It doesn't matter how infinitely less languid it is than Enoch's gesture: it's still effective, of that I'm sure.

— . . . You and Steiner could fight as equals to conquer the role of the Father. This would still be stressful, of course, but not nearly as much as the other way, and the main thing is that it would be stressful for the two of you: Steiner, at his seventy-odd years, and you, forty . . . ?

Now I've astounded him. Literally. Despite my awkwardness he's fallen for it hook, line, and sinker.

— Forty-five . . . — he mumbles.

— And you at your forty-five: how long could this go on? How long before *the son* of Steiner, the jet-setting playboy, appears in his place?

Yes, I've astounded him. Except I realize that in his astonishment there's something astounding me. I realize it suddenly, looking into his eyes immediately after I've finished speaking: he's seeing something illuminating in my words, clearly, *but he's also taking for granted that I am the Holy Ghost of the situation* . . .

— That's the most intelligent thing I've ever heard in my life, — he says.

Yes, it's incredible — in those dismayed little eyes is the certainty that I, Pietro Paladini, have just nominated myself for the role of the third vertex in the triangle. But of course: they're the eyes of someone who has just heard the most unexpected, brash, crazy — and intelligent, of course, and even providential, for him, at this point — of proposals: make me a god, I will save you.

— You're a genius, —is his verdict.

Hah. A genius, no less. He no longer needs to lower himself: I've suddenly become a genius. So that's what I was thinking, he's telling himself, that's why I refused the presidency and extorted from Thierry permission to stay here . . . Yes, not much you can do about it anymore, *that's the way* things are now: it doesn't matter that all I did was parrot things that someone else had told me, and it matters even less that, while I was doing it, the thought never even crossed my mind that what I was saying might apply to me personally. I suggested the solution to his problem, and in exchange I asked for a third of the loot: what's so strange about that? It makes perfect sense for someone like him: it's the only thing he can think of. I'm a fucking genius, and I'm asking for the compensation I deserve. I'm not a smartass: I'm the king of smartasses . . . And it's hard not to ponder the meaning of *this,* and in fact I can't avoid it: what a shame I didn't tell him before, I think, before it was too late. To have known that he would swallow the bait . . .

— Thank you, — I say. — Even if unfortunately it's too late for —

— It's not too late, — he says resolutely.

Oh God . . .

— Are you saying you could still change it? You're not, are you? It's too late to change now . . .

— I can do whatever I want, — he utters, lost in thought.

Oh God, he's thinking about it. Unbelievable. He's seriously thinking about sending everything up in smoke and sticking me in the spot for the Holy Ghost. This is completely crazy: me, a titan, a god. Powerless, of course, a superbonehead, an empty shell, a puppet on a string, but who gives a fuck, my life would still become fabulous. Just like that, zap, from one day to the next. Hear the latest, sweetheart? We're moving to Paris. Private jet, Maybach, driver, a sudden downpour of medieval abundance. The cover of *Fortune* magazine: Pietro Paladini, the new face of international finance. Roman, 43. Astrological sign: Cancer. Widower, father of Claudia, 10, gymnastics champion, son of a well-known lawyer in the capital, brother of the famous designer/founder of Barrie — the very picture of a successful family. Degree in philosophy from the University of Rome, magna cum laude. Master's from Harvard. Twelve-year apprenticeship in television production, then the big leap into high finance, and today he's seated alongside Isaac Steiner and Patrick Boesson at the helm of the biggest telecommunications group in the world. He's an eccentric: at the last World Economic Forum in Davos he reportedly spent all three days skiing with his daughter. Other hobbies: horseback riding, surfing, and sailing. How long was the boat that passed before my eyes when Thierry proposed the presidency to me? Seventy-two feet? Phooey! *One hundred and sixty-five* feet: a three-masted schooner, fifteen-member crew. Claudia! Claudia! CLAUDIA! Forget about it, she can't hear me, this damn boat is too big, I'll have to have an intercom installed . . .

All of a sudden this is what we're talking about. *This* is what Boesson is driving at.

— But of course, — he says, laughing. — You're right. It was a little graceless, this operation — he's already talking about it in the past tense — and the Holy Ghost *is* grace.

Wilhelm's winnings at baccarat were nothing compared to this: now I really could produce *Night Games*. In America, holy shit, in Hollywood. Annalisa, can you get me Spielberg on the phone, please. Hello, Steve? Hi, this is Pietro Paladini. Me? Fine. And you? Fantastic. Listen, we've got a project for you. I was thinking we could do it together, us and Dreamworks, fifty-fifty. *Night Games* by Schnitzler: you know him, right? I know, I know . . . Let's just say that I'm well informed. Awesome, yes . . . A sword straight to the heart, yes . . . Well, now the rights are in our hands and . . . Beg your pardon? Stanley? Oh, yes, of course: no, no, I never met him, but I'm not surprised he made you read it. After all, *Eyes Wide Shut* was adapted from *Traumnovelle* . . .

— But of course . . . — he repeats, and looks at me, and laughs, and reflects. — *Maintenant l'Esprit a le droit de cité parmi nous et nous accorde une vision plus claire de Lui-même* . . .

I could give Matteo and his mother a life of leisure — because you can see she's struggling. Anonymously, of course: the unknown benefactor . . .

— *Ici il ne s'agira donc de l'Esprit Saint que dans l'économie divine. L'Esprit Saint est à l'oeuvre avec le Père et le Fils du commencement à la consommation du dessein de notre salut* . . .

I could also support Marta and all three of her children, that way she could keep up with her acting without earning a red cent and she wouldn't be so stressed out. She might even get better . . .

— The biggest merger in the world, inspired by the Catechism of the Catholic Church. Can you imagine how badly the Shark is going to take it . . .

I could step down in five or six years, once the holy mission is complete, and live off the interest . . .

— Of course I'd have to have blind faith in this Holy Ghost, — Boesson says, in a different voice, more sharply. I look at him: all the riches that had been dancing before my eyes dissolve into his ordinary, simple, and yet stingy features, which are nowhere near as fresh and relaxed as they were when he arrived.

— It's logical, — I say. — But if you take a normal, reserved, and sufficiently intelligent man and you turn him into a god, he'll have no alternative but to be loyal to you.

I had meant to reassure him, but instead his gaze suddenly darkens, as if a flock of crows had just crossed overhead.

— Is this stuff about the Trinity something Steiner suggested to you? Is that why he came here?

No way out, the night has fallen. Now he really does look like the cassowary man in the middle of the savanna.

— Come on, — I protest. — Don't be so paranoid. This is the best way for you to screw him: why the hell would he want to give you instructions how to do it?

— If the Holy Ghost is with me, then I screw him. If it's with him, then I'm the one that gets screwed.

— I'm not sure I understand: you turn an ordinary man into a kind of god and he's going to turn around and join forces with your enemy?

— It depends on his character . . .

And here he breaks his immobile pose and walks around me slowly, staring at me, unsmiling.

— Can I trust you? Can I trust you? Can I trust you?

He enunciates this triple question and stops, continuing to stare at me with a crazy look on his face.

He's a little bit frightening like this.

But then he melts into his usual smile and returns to his aplomb, with theatricality, to indicate that he was acting; but I get the impression instead that he's acting now and that we've both been acting the whole time, except for a moment ago. If we want to talk about what someone's really like . . .

— Do you remember who said it? — he asks.

I dunno. It must be something biblical, too: the holiness of the number three, the cock crowing three times . . .

— Jesus?

He shakes his head, sniggering.

— Robert De Niro in *Casino*. He says it to his wife, Sharon Stone, who he had picked up from the gutter, making her a queen, when she asked him for 25,000 dollars but wouldn't tell him why. Did you see *Casino*? Do you remember the scene?

He keeps sniggering, pleased with himself. He doesn't even realize he's insulted me.

— Yes, I saw it. But I don't remember that scene.

— Well, it's the most important one. He asks her the question to end all questions, the one on which her life depends. That's why he asks her three times.

— And what does she answer?

— She answers, "Yes."

— And does he believe her?

— He tells her, "So then you could tell me what the money is for."

— And what does she say?

He changes expression again: now he's daydreaming, reminiscing. At this point he's out of control.

— It's strange, — he says, — but I don't remember. What happens next is so tragic that I must have repressed it.

— And the tragedy is caused by the way she answers him?

Bull's-eye. Because in the meantime I've remembered the film; a film about paranoia, by the way: tragic no matter what gets said, no matter who says it, no matter to whom. *Born* tragic.

— Tell me what Steiner told you, — he commands.

Ten-hut! Yes, sir! . . . Go fuck yourself. It's too late to be giving me orders. If you're looking for someone to compare to a two-bit whore, look no further than your wife!

— No.

Boesson wrinkles his brow contemptuously. He's not humble, he's not conciliatory, he's not my equal. He's a paranoid megalomaniac, like Jean-Claude says. He's the guilty conscience of all of us put together. *He's the man who's ruining everything.*

— What a shame, Pietro. — He shakes his head, and smiles,

and hams it up, just like De Niro. — It's a real shame. You said
some brilliant things, and I'd gladly welcome you on board, but if
you're going to act like that . . .

And he looks at me. I know that look; it means "Give in, it'll
be better for you." My father gave me that look when I was a kid
and I wanted to drop out of university to go to America, and I
gave in, and I didn't go to America until after I graduated, and I
always thought that it was actually better for me that way. But
when he tried the same thing on Carlo, and Carlo didn't give in,
and he dropped out of university and went to London, it's not
like he lived to regret it — and today, to put it bluntly, at least as
far as the Internet people are concerned, my brother is eighteen
hundred times more important than me. And he didn't even lose
his soul, on the contrary: he's still grieving for a drug addict who
killed herself twenty years ago, while I can't even grieve for a wife
who died three months ago. But this time I'm not going to give
in. You may think I'm nothing more than the greedy creature
whose eyes you just saw popping out at the loot, but there's a
lot more to me than that. You're sure I said those things to you
for my own benefit, but that was pure chance. I don't think the
way you do. For example, I can still see a ton of good reasons to
exclude me from your delirium. First, I'm not the genius, Enoch
is: a man who spent the past year of his life comforting the people
that had been uprooted by your ambitions and he became so dis-
gusted by you that he is currently living in northern Zimbabwe
loading tanker trucks; he is the Holy Ghost, I'm just a rotten
materialist, an atheist, a subversive, and in my mouth the name
"Holy Ghost" is blasphemy. Second, I don't need to be carrying
around any guilt feelings; and to be rewarded in this way, for a
merit I don't even have and by a boa constrictor that has squeezed
the life out of my friends, and on top of a period when I didn't
grieve even a little over the death of my wife, which happened

while I was saving the life of an unknown woman, with whom I later had a bruising sexual rapport while running the risk of traumatizing my daughter — you do the math, but to me your offer doesn't promise much serenity. Third, this merger is going to fail, like all the others: Jean-Claude knows it, Enoch knows it, and I know it — so what the fuck are we talking about?

— Tough luck, — I tell him. — I'm never going to tell you.

Ask me again now. Go on, ask me. Fourth, I'd promised myself that if little Matteo came out the door I wouldn't tell you anything; he did come out, so I won't tell you anything. End of story. And this is all the reason you deserve, and there's no need to trouble yourself further.

— Okay, — he says. — Do as you wish.

You bet I will. Nod away, wrinkle your brow, keep up the histrionics: whichever way you cut it, I've wiped that smile off your face.

— See you around.

— Bye.

Good boy, shake my hand and be on your way. That's better. Go back to the office — tear up three and a half miles between here and there. And go ahead and fire me if you want. You just told me I'm a genius: fire me. Your fucking megagroup is jam-packed with geniuses anyway, isn't it? And on Monday sign the papers and let the Shark eat you up and spit you out. And tie that fucking shoelace!

There, he's gone. And if everything that's rotten inside of me — because there is a lot of rot, there always has been, and I've always known it — was ever supposed to go away, then it was washed away with you, a second ago. I didn't seize the moment, I'll never ride with the tycoons, but today I've built myself a fantastic memory. Something so great that I'll never be able to talk about it with anybody. I'll remember this moment for years to come — the piles of snow along the sidewalk, the damp smell in the air, the puffs of breath. Then one day, if I do turn into a good man, I'll forget it.

chapter thirty-eight

It's snowing again. The city is paralyzed, we're stuck in traffic. Claudia is sitting next to me, tired, flushed. She's soaking wet, because in the playground after school she and her friends threw snowballs at each other — boys against girls. I let her, even though she's got gymnastics meets tomorrow and the day after tomorrow and she could have gotten hurt; and I also let her sit in the car in her wet clothes: who cares if she messes up the leather upholstery. Everything about this moment seems magical to her, a regression to the depths of the childhood she is about to leave behind: to do things without thinking, feeling joy, emotions, pleasure, without the least concern over what's coming next: it would be a crime to ruin it for her. She'll probably remember it one day when she has become the woman it is still so hard to imagine her becoming: *that day that it was snowing, when I was still in elementary school and we threw snowballs at the boys in the playground*. But more than anything else, I thought that bringing her back down to Earth while she was so intoxicated with the present — to make her start worrying *now* about the meet or even about the upholstery of my car — would be practically the equivalent of reminding her that her mother is dead. So I left her alone, I leave her alone: she's inside a bubble, this little girl, and the best I can do for her is to avoid breaking it. I have to force myself to be as lighthearted as she is. For example: I mustn't think about the crazy day that I've been through, I mustn't think that I've probably lost my job, and on the same day that I could have become — exactly: I mustn't think about it. I have to synchronize myself with the pure frequency of her breathing, of her tiredness with neither past nor future. I have to force myself to stay inside the bubble, too. Snow. Hormones. Emotion. Silence. But for some reason I can't bear the silence. I have to speak.

— That was some snowball fight, — I say.

— Yes, but did you see what that asshole Mirko did?

I mustn't reprimand her for swearing: that's what Lara always did.

— The boy that put snow down Benedetta's neck?

— He made her cry, *meschina* — poor girl.

— *Meschina?* Where did you learn that word?

— Why, is it a bad word?

— Just the opposite. If you're not Sicilian, it's very sophisticated.

— Roxanna always says it. — She turns around, smiling. — Eh, in fact, Roxanna is from Sicily!

Attention: Roxanna is a girl who lives in a foster home. She's not an orphan, but her mother and father are in rehab. Avoid the subject. And Lara's last name was Siciliano. Change direction immediately.

— In Roman dialect we'd say *porella*, — I say.

— *Porella?*

— Yes, like *poverella: porella*.

— And how would you say it in Milanese dialect?

— In Milanese? I don't know: *pora stella*.

She looks at me, thinks.

— Like *povera stellina,* poor little sweetheart.

This is really getting messy. The *povera stellina* must be her . . .

— I don't know. I've never learned Milanese. *Io so' de Romaa!* I'm from Rome! — I say in my best Roman accent.

Shouting *"Io so' de Romaa!"* I raise my voice, honk the horn, wave my arm out the window, make an obscene gesture — which in this traffic jam makes me look like another neurotic losing his cool, while I actually don't mind being stuck in traffic at all: it's just a little show to make Claudia laugh. And she does.

— I've got an idea, — I say. — After the meet, Monday, why don't we go to the Aquarium in Genoa, since we've got the long weekend?

Rather than smile Claudia clouds over.

— What about Uncle Carlo? Isn't he staying until Tuesday?

Shit.

— Uncle's not coming anymore, sweetheart.

— But he said he was coming today and staying for the whole holiday weekend.

— Yes, but he can't. He has to go to London.

— To do what?

— Well, I imagine that he has to go babysit some fussy diva. Elizabeth Hurley. Britney Spears. You know how it is, they're so fragile . . .

— I don't understand, he goes there and what does he do to babysit them?

— I didn't mean anything by it, sweetheart. I don't know what he has to do. Maybe he has to attend a gala. Or present a check to save the lives of two hundred dogs. Or maybe they're supposed to give him an award . . .

She's disappointed, deeply disappointed, but there's no way I could avoid telling her. She's going to have to swallow this one.

— It's definitely for something important, sweetheart. Uncle is a celebrity. He has to pay the price for his success.

An ambulance siren starts up behind us on the completely paralyzed street. I wonder how it'll pass.

— And anyway, — I continue, — for Christmas we're going to the mountains with him. He swore he would, come hell or high water. To Saint Moritz.

She looks at me out of the corner of her eye, suspicious. I smile at her.

— It'll be a nice Christmas, you'll see, — I say. — You and me and Uncle on the slopes.

Sure. As long as the bubble doesn't burst.

— While we're on the subject, why don't you tell me what present you want.

— For Christmas? Now?

— Well, it's not that far away, you know. They've already put up the decorations. What would you like?

Claudia lowers her head, looks down, and starts thinking. She's going to become one of those sensual women who look down when they think.

— A Bratz, — she says.

— A what?

— One of those dolls that instead of changing their shoes you change their feet. Bratz.

— Sweetheart, I meant something more. Something that you really want. Something important.

— An Eastpak backpack?

— No, not that. Those are ordinary presents.

— Maybe you don't know that Eastpak backpacks cost a lot.

— I do know, but everyone has them. I meant something more exclusive. One of your wishes. True. Deep.

Claudia lowers her head again and remains motionless for a little while. I don't know how, but the ambulance is close behind us: the siren has gotten much louder.

— I don't have any.

— Of course you do. Everyone has a wish. I'm sure that if you think hard you'll remember. Come on, think a little . . .

Wouldn't it be better for me to drop the whole thing? Leave her alone? But the fact of the matter is that today I can't bear the silence — it makes me anxious. Now even more than before, with that siren piercing it.

— Oh, — I keep going, — of course I mean even something you can't buy.

Claudia takes a breath as if she wanted to say something, but then she turns to the side, rests her head against the window, and stays quiet. It's as if all at once she needed to look out, to fill her eyes with shop windows, merchandise, people, traffic lights, buildings, and gridlocked cars. It's stopped snowing, and there's a sad light outside — a nonlight is what comes to mind, or maybe a not-yet-dark light.

— Something that you want to happen . . .

Enough already! Why do I keep egging her on? This way I'm steering her toward the only wish that can never be fulfilled. What's wrong with me, am I so inured to seeing people suffer that I want to see her suffer, too?

Shut up. I tell myself to shut up.

The screeching of the siren is starting to get really close, dramatic.

Shut up.

Shut up.

— Well, there is one thing, — says Claudia without lifting her forehead from the window.

— You see. What is it?

— It's a kind of —

All of a sudden the ambulance is right behind us. Claudia interrupts herself because now the screeching of the siren is really loud, earsplitting, unbearable, and it's my turn to let it pass, but how? For a few seconds nothing happens, I don't have an inch to maneuver in either direction; but then the mass of cars in front of me splits like a crust of ice, opening up a long, viable crevasse, and now there is room to pass, but I still can't pull over, the ambulance is right behind me, with its ridiculous backward writing in my rearview mirror, and the screeching of the siren has turned into an act of accusation addressed to me personally, to us, to blame us for what will happen if we don't get out of the way. The only thing I can do is advance through the fjord that has opened up between the cars, and I do, I cross this steel-plated Red Sea, chased by the screaming ambulance, I advance but I still can't find a spot to pull over and let it pass, and so I step on the gas and drag the ambulance along in my wake, I literally blaze the trail, identifying with the emergency and adding my horn to the siren, and this is the worst thing of all, because now it's as if I were one of those desperate cars you sometimes see, hugging an ambulance and racing ahead, horns ablaze — usually behind the ambulance, to tell the truth, and not in front of it — and we all understand why, and their racing is more tragic than even that of the ambu-lance, because there's nothing clever or professional about it, and the only thing it conveys is anxiety. That's what we are right now: a clump of anxiety escorting to the hospital a loved one who may be dying at this very moment . . .

We finally get to a traffic light. It's red but I continue straight into the middle of the intersection, which is pretty clear, so I can pull off to the side and stop. The ambulance races past me like a bullet, barreling down the line of traffic on the other side of the intersection and battering it into bits and pieces with shrieks of the siren. Slowly, forcefully, it advances like an icebreaker and is swallowed up, and the torture that has just ended for us is begin-ning for someone else. I should go straight, but I want to make it obvious that all this drama has nothing to do with us. I want to make it clear to myself and especially to Claudia: this tragedy doesn't concern us. We simply found ourselves on the same route. We were talking about Christmas presents and wishes: we were serene — *we are* serene. Or aren't we?

I look at Claudia. She's calm, impassive: as if she had never been affected by tragedies or ambulances. She makes no comment. She doesn't ask me why I turned rather than go straight. She doesn't say anything. She's seated more comfortably than before, with her back leaning against the seat, and her feet can't quite reach the floor mat. She seems ready to pick up where we left off.

— You were saying, — I start. — A kind of . . . ?

She looks at me, smiles. Then she goes back to staring straight ahead, past the windshield, at this street she's never seen, since it doesn't lead to home, but where at least the traffic's moving. You can still hear the sound of the siren, but it's far away again.

— Dad, — she says. — Do you remember what Miss Gloria talked to us about on the first day of school?

— No, what did she talk to you about?

— About reversibility. Do you remember? *I topi non avevano nipoti?* Able was I ere I saw Elba?

Oh. There's something alarming about these words and the serious tone Claudia has adopted to utter them.

— Yes, I remember.

— Miss Gloria talked to us about it, and right afterward you started waiting in front of the school all day. I thought the two things were connected. Like you wanted to give me an example of something reversible. Something nice that happens for a little while and then doesn't happen anymore. Because it is reversible: no one can stay out there forever, right?

Oh . . .

— Of course not.

— Every day I prepared myself, I told myself: today he's going to tell me he has to go back to the office, and I'll show him that I was expecting it. But then you never said it, you stayed the next day, too, and I was happy, you know, I was really happy. Except that . . .

Oh . . .

— Except what?

Claudia looks down, but she's not thinking. She knows perfectly well what she has to say, she's just gathering her strength to say it.

— Well, in class they've started to tease me about it, that's all. Oh no, dammit, no . . .

— You know how kids are, — she adds. — They're cruel.

She says it as if she weren't a child anymore and she were only trying to understand their cruelty.

— Strange, — I mutter. — I always talk to your teachers, and they never told me anything . . .

— The teachers don't know everything that happens, — she says. — The other kids don't tease me in front of them. They do it more subtly.

— More *subtly* . . . For example?

— For example, they wrote CLAUDIA PALADINI *MESCHINA* on the bathroom door.

— Well, at least you know who did it.

— Yes, but you see, — she replies, — Roxanna says it openly because she's in a foster home and she's always angry, but she's not the only one. When I wave to you from the window and I turn around quickly, I can see the other girls giggling strangely.

Oh, no, dammit, no: *all this time I've been an embarrassment* . . .

— Really? And who are they?

— Nilowfer, Giuditta, Lucilla. All of them, more or less. And even the boys.

— Benedetta, too?

— Once I saw her laughing, too. But not to be mean, you see, or because she's not my friend. It's just because for them it's become a kind of habit: when you and I wave to each other they start laughing, that's all. And since that's the way it is now, I was thinking that . . .

She interrupts herself, a courtesy toward me. I reach my hand over to her mouth and brush it lightly.

— That's all right, sweetheart, — I whisper. — Say no more.

What the fuck. Let her say it — *You gotta go, Dad* — no, not that.

— Say no more, — I repeat. — Say no more.

I'm stung, literally stung with shame. I continue brushing my hand against her mouth, slowly, undeservedly, then I caress her eyes, her forehead, her wet hair. She leans against my side and hugs me.

— Did I hurt your feelings? — she asks.

Hurt is an understatement, sweetheart: you crushed them. *Down for the count* is how I feel, like the wrestling champs you cheer for — the ones who lose, the ones who cry. How could I have been so stupid?

— No, no, you were right to tell me, — I say. — I could hardly stay there all year. I took advantage of the situation, of the chaos generated by that damned merger; but it was a reversible chaos, like you said. On Wednesday the merger will be done and I have to return to work anyway.

— Oh, so maybe I should have kept my mouth shut.

— No, why should you? We have to say things.

Of course we have to say them: if she hadn't said it, I'm so stupid I never would have known. I would never have figured it out by myself. I hid inside the belly of the whale: Who was going to remove me?

— You did the right thing, — I whisper. — That's what you should always do. Always say things.

There, I did it. Look at the mess I managed to make. I'm so ashamed I can't even look at her: it's my fault they teased her . . .

But now that I've felt the hurt, and felt the shame, in what has proven to be the culmination of a long failure — dreaded, perhaps, and maybe also subconsciously sought after, but not addressed openly until now — a sigh of relief starts to thaw. We keep hugging each other silently, and now the silence doesn't frighten me anymore, because it no longer harbors the words she kept inside. What a magnificent child, I think, what a magnificent human being. And what a lesson she's taught me, what a masterly way she found to tell me to back off. Not like that ambulance, a little while ago, with its savage howling, its humiliating accusation — "Get out of the way, asshole, beat it, beat it!" — no: she did it with a dollop of metaphor. *I topi non avevano nipoti.* Hah. *I topi non avevano nipoti.* 348 7667843. 3487667 843. Yolanda's phone number. Hello? Yolanda? Hi, it's me, The Hugging Man. Sorry to bother you, but I saw your number on Nebbia's dog tags and I remembered it — because it's a palindrome, you see, it's the same forward and backward, and once you've seen it you never forget it. I called to say good-bye, Yolanda. We won't be seeing each other anymore. My daughter's right: My place isn't in front of the park, my place is in the office, where probably starting today my place is history. I wanted to say good-bye. Excuse me, would you mind passing the phone to my brother, I have to tell him something. Hello, Carlo? Do you realize you said something really true about Claudia? Do you realize you grasped the secret of her beauty? *She makes you want to be just like her,* you said, and that's exactly it. And you know it's not true that she isn't grieving: her mother is dead, and she has to understand a lot of things by herself, to experience them on her own skin, to tell me what I have to do, and that *is* grieving. And I'm in pretty bad shape, too, you were right. Ever since Lara died I've parked myself in front of that school and I haven't budged, and I let other people do their grieving at me, and my life became a blank — and this is evidently my way of grieving. If I don't grieve

more profoundly, if I'm not destroyed or desperate, it's only because I'm a superficial person, and superficial people can't have
profound experiences. I'm like our father, Carlo. Can't you see
that unlike you I can still love him, I can still manage to forgive
him? It's because I'm like him, that's the honest truth, and in his
place I think I would've done the same thing. Yes, and there's
more, but I want to tell Marta if I may: Can you pass her to me,
please? Hi, Marta. There's more, I was saying. It's that maybe you
were right, I didn't love your sister. Maybe the fortune-teller was
right: she *did not have me*. But — and I'm being sincere, I've never
been more sincere in my life — I don't think that's why she died.
Maybe she was in pain, as you say, maybe I made her suffer, and
maybe you made her suffer, too, as you say, but sadness doesn't
kill you, Marta — not in that way. I'm telling you because I get
the impression you feel more guilty than you should, seriously,
over Lara's death; you also feel guilty on my account, but it's not
our fault, Marta, not yours, not mine. We have our faults, you and
I, but that doesn't mean that *everything* is our fault. Do you understand? Can you pass the phone to Jean-Claude now? Jean-Claude?
What's the weather like in Aspen? Really? Here it's snowing, go
figure. Just one thing: Don't be overly moved by my loyalty. All I
did is the right thing, the one that was most convenient for me; all
I did was avoid a trap. I'm your friend, it's true, I admire you, I'm
on your side and all, but if the opportunities offered to me hadn't
been so lousy, if they hadn't all been destined to fall apart in the
short term, I don't think I would have said no just for the sake of
not betraying you. I think I would have taken your spot, you
know, if it hadn't been so obvious that in a little while it was all
going to fall apart. I would have taken it, and I would have bought
myself a sailboat. That's all. Ah, and another thing: if you want to
know who the really smart one is, the one who is really intelligent
and brilliant, it's not me, it's Enoch. Enoch, the tall, absentminded

one, who looks like an Anglican priest, the head of human resources. He was the best. By a long shot. And would you mind
passing me to the ex-husband of Eleonora Simoncini, please? No,
not her: her ex-husband, the tall guy with the red hair and the
rope in his hand. Yes, him, thank you. Hello? Good evening. I
wanted to tell you something, for what it's worth. I wanted to tell
you that if your ex-wife were to come to me now, with that picture from when you got married, and asked me the same question, I would answer, "I don't remember." Because, you see, the
rope you were holding is still way too short, completely ridiculous for the use you meant to make of it, but the truth is I didn't
get out a ruler and measure it, so I can't say with any degree of
certainty that you were letting your wife die. In other words, seeing as in the end she didn't die, I think that the best thing would
have been not to get involved — at least not to say "yes" so as-
sertively, so arrogantly. But the truth is I was horny, and I wanted
to fuck your ex-wife, so I acted somewhat thoughtlessly. Here we
are, I said. Don't get me wrong, I'm still convinced you're a dirty
bastard and all you wanted was to do her in to get your hands on
all that chocolate money, but I just now got proof that my own
convictions can lead me far from the truth. Imagine, I spent three
months in front of my daughter's school and I was absolutely convinced I was taking care of her, when the truth is I was only taking
care of myself, which is why she, *meschina,* was being teased. Go
figure, I would have kept waiting there, right there in front, calm,
happy, to the bitter end, especially now that I've lost my job, yeah,
since I practically told he-who-walks-on-water to go fuck himself
and he'll make me pay for it, and to make a long story short, in
the end it was my daughter who had to tell me, can you believe it,
a ten-and-a-half-year-old girl who recently lost her mother *had to
ask me to go.* Yes, this paradoxical, unnatural turn became necessary
because, as I told my brother a little while ago — are you still

there, Carlo? Wait, hang on, everyone else, stay on the line, please,
I'm almost done — because, as I was saying, I'm superficial, I have
things right before my eyes and I don't see them — or else, as in
your case, I don't have them there but I think I see them. I needed
someone to open my eyes, do you see? And my daughter is the
one who opened them. She had to, out of desperation, because I
had turned into an embarassment. She had to tell me things I
couldn't understand by myself. Dad, she said, you have to go back
to work; and if you've lost your old job, she said, you'd better find
another one. You have to think of our future, Dad. You have to
deal with Mom's car, you have to report the missing license plate
and recover it. You have to stop being jealous of Uncle. You have
to stop me from sweating and getting soaked when it's cold. You
have to get your life in order, give it a direction, a sense, because
the chaos that governs children's lives is nice, of course, but you're
a grown-up. And you mustn't be afraid of bursting my bubble,
because my bubble has already been burst. That's what she told
me. My daughter, a child. But now I have to tell all of you something important: are you all still there? After that I promise I'll
shut up, because I'm not afraid of silence anymore, but for the
moment I'm going to ask you to pay attention to what I have to
say. It's something decisive that I just understood right now and
that concerns all of you, too. Listen up, Yolanda, because it definitely concerns you. But it also concerns you, Marta, who can't
find peace, and you, too, Carlo, with your fixation on Peter Pan.
And maybe you, too, Jean-Claude. Maybe it really does concern
all of us. Listen to me carefully: the ball we threw while playing in
the park reached the ground a long time ago. We have to stop
waiting for it.

  And now can you please pass the phone to Lara?

acknowledgments

I wish to thank heartily Sergio Perroni for his precious shepherding of the manuscript, chapter by chapter, in the four and a half years that it took to complete; whatever merit it may have would never have been achieved without his help. I wish to thank my father and my mother for the silent faith in the future that they handed down to me. I wish to thank my publishing house, and in particular Elisabetta Sgarbi, for waiting so patiently. I wish to thank Francesca d'Aloja for the support she gave me. And I wish to thank all the people who helped me in various ways, providing me with information, ideas, stories, observations, or even simply listening to me and encouraging me to go on. There are many: Juan Cueto, Edoardo Nesi, Giovanni Martini, Massimiliano Governi, my brother Giovanni, Marco Risi, Nanni Moretti, Bruno Restuccia, Umberto Falaschi, Paolo Carbonati, Leopoldo Fabiani, Elisabetta Arnaboldi, Andrea Garello, Philippine Leroy, Pierluigi Ferrandini, Michel Thoulouze, Ivan Nabokov, Piero Crispino, Nicola Alvau, Carla Cavalluzzi, Simona Cagnasso, Sonia Locatelli, Heidi Kennedy, Laura Paolucci, Luca Buoncristiano, Claudio Scotto, Edoardo Gabbriellini, Michele Forlani, Rosaria Carpinelli, Emmanuel Gout, Chiara Tagliaferri, Stefano Toti, Stefano Ciambellotti, Violante Placido, Lanfranco Marra, Domenico Procacci, Filippo Bologna, Silvia Pacetti, and Manuele Innocenti.

And they say that you're alone when you write.

Sandro Veronesi was born in Prato, Italy, in 1959. A novelist, essayist, and journalist, he also holds a degree in architecture from the University of Florence. His fourth novel, *The Force of the Past,* won the Viareggio-Repaci Prize and the Campiello Prize, and was a Zerilli-Marimó finalist. He lives in Prato and in Rome.

Michael F. Moore is a writer, translator, and interpreter specializing in Italian and the chair of the Translation Committee of the PEN American Center. His most recent translations include the novels *Three Horses* and *God's Mountain* by Erri De Luca, and the memoir *Pushing Past the Night* by Mario Calabresi. He is currently completing a new translation of Primo Levi's *The Drowned and the Saved* and of the nineteenth-century classic *The Betrothed* by Alessandro Manzoni.